BRONX NOIR

BRONX NOIR

EDITED BY S.J. ROZAN

AKASHIC BOOKS
NEW YORK

Published by Akashic Books
©2007 Akashic Books

Series concept by Tim McLoughlin and Johnny Temple
Bronx map by Sohrab Habibion

ISBN-13: 978-1-933354-25-5

Library of Congress Control Number: 2006936535
All rights reserved

First printing

Akashic Books
PO Box 1456
New York, NY 10009
info@akashicbooks.com
www.akashicbooks.com

With great admiration, the editor dedicates this book to Grace Paley, whose childhood in the Bronx was happy.

TABLE OF CONTENTS

PART IV: THE WANDERER

PART V: ALL SHOOK UP

INTRODUCTION
WELCOME TO DA BRONX

The Bronx is a wonderful place.

"Wonderful" in the literal sense: full of wonders. Wonders everyone's heard of, like the Bronx Zoo and Yankee Stadium; wonders that make presidents cry, as Jimmy Carter famously did in 1977, standing in the rubble of the South Bronx; and wonders only we Bronxites seem to know about, like Wave Hill, City Island, and Arthur Avenue.

People are always discovering the Bronx. Native Americans, of course, discovered it first, fishing and hunting in its woods and streams long before Europe discovered the New World. The first European to settle north of the Harlem River was one Jonas Bronck, in 1639. Jonas and his family worked part of his huge swath of land and leased the rest to other farmers. Everyone in the area gave their address as "the Broncks' farm," giving rise to the "the" and eventually the "x." (There—we're giving you not only great stories, but a party trick fact.) And development and industrialization, sparked by the railroad in the early 1840s, probably took care of the "farm."

In 1895, New York City discovered the Bronx, and Westchester discovered it didn't own the place anymore. In 1914, New York State discovered it needed a sixty-second county, and Bronx County was born.

Immigrants discovered the Bronx in waves. Germans, Italians, and Irish came early, and then European Jews. The Grand Concourse, modeled on the Champs-Élysées in Paris, was built to draw them northward. In the 1960s, as the second and third generations of those immigrants moved to the suburbs, Puerto Ricans and blacks took their places. Now they're being joined by Latinos from all over Central and South America, Caribbean islanders, Eastern Europeans, Africans, Asians, and, of course, yuppies. Sooner or later, everyone discovers the Bronx.

Parts of the Bronx suffered badly from the governmental anti-urbanism and heavy-handed "city planning" of the '50s and '60s, and to a lot of people "the Bronx" became another term for "urban decay." 'Twas never true. Though the worst America has to offer its poorer citizens can be found in some areas of the Bronx—this is what brought Jimmy Carter to tears—great stretches are what they've always been: neighborhoods of working-class people, native-born and immigrants, looking for a break. And there were two-family row houses along Sedgwick Avenue, mansions in Riverdale, and fishing boats sailing out from City Island before, during, and after the filming of Fort Apache, The Bronx. (A personal note: In my previous life as an architect, my firm did the new building for the 41st Precinct, which had been Fort Apache until the city clear-cut the blocks around it and the NYPD started calling it Little House on the Prairie.)

If you want to discover the Bronx yourself, you might go up to Van Cortlandt Park to watch white-uniformed West Indians playing cricket on the emerald grass. They're there most summer Sundays, just north of the swimming pool, south of a rowdy soccer game, west of the riding stable, and east of the elevated subway that runs along Broadway. That subway line—the Number 1, by the way, and need I say more?—ends there, at 242nd Street, but the Bronx goes on for another mile. Or you might try the Botanical Garden, the Zoo, the House That Ruth Built—Yankee Stadium, for you tinhorns—or the new Antiques Row just over the Third Avenue Bridge. These are all terrific destinations, but the real discovery will be the size of the place and the diversity of the lives you'll glimpse as you pass through.

And in this wondrous Bronx, the exceptional writers in this collection have found noir corners, dark moments, and rich places of astonishing variety. You can't pack so much yearning, so many people, such a range of everything—income, ethnicity, occupation, land use—into a single borough, even one as big as the Bronx, and not force the kind of friction that slices and sparks. The Bronx has been home to big-time gangsters—from the Jewish organized crime of Murder Inc. and the Italian *Cosa Nostra* to the equally organized drug-dealing gangstas of today. The Third Avenue El was a Hopperesque symbol of urban hopelessness; it's been demolished, but trains on other lines still rumble through the roofscapes of the borough. Prosperity is increasing and drug use is decreasing, but the public housing projects in the Bronx are some of the nation's largest and remain some of its toughest. Many places in the Bronx seem hidden in shadows, just as the Bronx itself is in Manhattan's shadow. And dark stories develop best in shadows.

From Abraham Rodriguez, Jr.'s South Bronx to Robert Hughes's Fordham Road, from Joseph Wallace's Bronx Zoo to Terrence Cheng's Lehman College, from Joanne Dobson's post–WWII Sedgwick Avenue to Lawrence Block's new wave–yuppie Riverdale, it's all here. In this book, we offer a hint of the cultural, social, economic, and geographic range of the only New York City borough on the mainland of North America. Ladies and gentlemen, welcome to Da Bronx.

S.J. Rozan
The Bronx
June 2007

PART I

Bring It on Home

WHITE TRASH

BY JEROME CHARYN

Claremont/Concourse

P rudence had escaped from the women's farm in Milledgeville and gone on a crime spree. She murdered six men and a woman, robbed nine McDonald's and seven Home Depots in different states. She wore a neckerchief gathered under her eyes and carried a silver Colt that was more like an heirloom than a good, reliable gun. The Colt had exploded in her face during one of the robberies at McDonald's, but she still managed to collect the cash, and her own willfulness wouldn't allow her to get a new gun.

She wasn't willful about one thing: she never used a partner, male or female. Women were more reliable than men; they wouldn't steal your money and expect you to perform sexual feats with their friends. But women thieves could be just as annoying. She'd had her fill of them at the farm, where they read her diary and borrowed her books. Pru didn't appreciate big fat fingers touching her personal library. Readers were like pilgrims who had to go on their own pilgrimage. Pru was a pilgrim, or at least that's what she imagined. She read from morning to night whenever she wasn't out foraging for hard cash. One of her foster mothers had been a relentless reader, and Prudence had gone right through her shelves, book after book: biographies, Bibles, novels, a book on building terrariums, a history of photography, a history of dance, and Leonard Maltin's *Movie Guide*, which she liked the best, because she could read the little encapsulated portraits of films without having to bother about the films themselves. But she lost her library when she broke out of jail, and it bothered her to live without books.

The cops had caught on to her tactics, and her picture was nailed to the wall inside post offices, supermarkets, and convenience stores; she might have been trapped in a Home Depot outside Savannah if she hadn't noticed a state trooper fidgeting with his hat while he stared at her face on the wall.

Pru had to disappear or she wouldn't survive her next excursion to Home Depot or McDonald's. And no book could help her now. Travel guides couldn't map out some no-man's-land where she might be safe. But Emma Mae, her cellmate at Milledgeville, had told her about the Bronx, a place where the cops never patrolled McDonald's. Besides, she hadn't murdered a single soul within five hundred miles of Manhattan or the Bronx. Pru wasn't a mad dog, as the bulletins labeled her. She had to shoot the night manager at McDonald's, because that would paralyze the customers and discourage anyone from coming after her.

She got on a Greyhound wearing eyeglasses and a man's lumber jacket after cutting her hair in the mirror of a public toilet. She'd been on the run for two months. Crime wasn't much of a business. Murdering people, and she still had to live from hand to mouth.

She couldn't remember how she landed in the Bronx. She walked up the stairs of a subway station, saw a synagogue that had been transformed into a Pentecostal church, then a building with mural on its back wall picturing a paradise with crocodiles, palm trees, and a little girl. The Bronx was filled with Latinas and burly black men, Emma Mae had told her; the only whites who lived there were "trash"—outcasts and country people who had to relocate. Pru could hide among them, practically invisible in a casbah that no one cared about.

Emma Mae had given her an address, a street called Marcy Place, where the cousin of a cousin lived, a preacher who played the tambourine and bilked white trash, like Prudence and Emma. He was right at the door when Pru arrived, an anemic-looking man dressed in black, with a skunk's white streak in his hair, though he didn't have a skunk's eyes; his were clear as pale green crystals and burned right into Pru. She was hypnotized without his having to say a single syllable. He laughed at her disguise, and that laughter seemed to break the spell.

"Prudence Miller," he said, "are you a man or a girl?"

His voice was reedy, much less potent than his eyes.

Emma Mae must have told him about her pilgrimage to the Bronx. But Pru still didn't understand what it meant to be the cousin of a cousin. His name was Omar Kaplan. It must have been the alias of an alias, since Omar couldn't be a Christian name. She'd heard all about Omar Khayyam, the Persian philosopher and poet who was responsible for the *Rubaiyat*, the longest love poem in history, though she hadn't read a line. And this Omar must have been a philosopher as well as a fraud—his apartment, which faced a brick wall, was lined with books. He had all the old Modern Library classics, like *Anna Karenina* and *The Brothers Karamazov*, books that Pru had discovered in secondhand shops in towns that had a college campus.

"You'll stay away from McDonald's," he said in that reedy voice of his, "and you'd better not have a gun."

"Then how will I earn my keep, Mr. Omar Kaplan? I'm down to my last dollar."

"Consider this a religious retreat, or a rest cure, but no

guns. I'll stake you to whatever you need."

Pru laughed bitterly, but kept that laugh locked inside her throat. Omar Kaplan intended to turn her into a slave, to write his own *Rubaiyat* on the softest parts of her flesh. She waited for him to pounce. He didn't touch her or steal her gun. She slept with the silver Colt under her pillow, on a cot near the kitchen, while Omar had the bedroom all to himself. It was dark as a cave. He'd emerge from the bedroom, dressed in black, like some Satan with piercing green eyes, prepared to soft-soap whatever white trash had wandered into the Bronx. He'd leave the apartment at 7 in the morning and wouldn't return before 9 at night. But there was always food in the fridge, fancier food than she'd ever had: salmon cutlets, Belgian beer, artichokes, strawberries from Israel, a small wheel of Swiss cheese with blue numbers stamped on the rind.

He was much more talkative after he returned from one of his pilferings. He'd switch off all the lamps and light a candle, and they'd have salmon cutlets together, drink Belgian beer. He'd rattle his tambourine from time to time, sing Christian songs. It could have been the dark beer that greased his tongue.

"Prudence, did you ever feel any remorse after killing those night managers?"

"None that I know of," she said.

"Their faces don't come back to haunt you in your dreams?"

"I never dream," she said.

"Do you ever consider all the orphans and widows you made?"

"I'm an orphan," she said, "and maybe I just widened the franchise."

"Pru the orphan-maker."

"Something like that," she said.

"Would you light a candle with me for their lost souls?"

She didn't care. She lit the candle, while Satan crinkled his eyes and mumbled something. Then he marched into his bedroom and closed the door. It galled her. She'd have felt more comfortable if he'd tried to undress her. She might have slept with Satan, left marks on his neck.

She would take long walks in the Bronx, with her silver gun. She sought replicas of herself, wanderers with pink skin. But she found Latinas with baby carriages, old black women outside a beauty parlor, black and Latino men on a basketball court. She wasn't going to wear a neckerchief mask and rob men and boys playing ball.

The corner she liked best was at Sheridan Avenue and East 169th, because it was a valley with hills on three sides, with bodegas and other crumbling little stores, a barbershop without a barber, apartment houses with broken courtyards and rotting steel gates. The Bronx *was* a casbah, like Emma Mae had said, and Pru could explore the hills that rose up around her, that seemed to give her some sort of protective shield. She could forget about Satan and silver guns.

She returned to Marcy Place. It was long after 9, and Omar Kaplan hadn't come home. She decided to set the table, prepare a meal of strawberries, Swiss cheese, and Belgian beer. She lit a candle, waiting for Omar. She grew restless, decided to read a book. She swiped *Sister Carrie* off the shelves—a folded slip of paper fell out, some kind of impromptu bookmark. But this bookmark had her face on it, and a list of her crimes. It had a black banner on top. *WANTED DEAD OR ALIVE*. Like the title of a macabre song. There were words scribbled near the bottom. *Dangerous and demented*. Then scribbles in another hand. *A real prize package. McDonald's ought to give us a thousand free Egg McMuffins for this fucking lady.* Then a signature that could have been a camel's hump. The letters on that hump spelled O-M-A-R.

She shouldn't have stayed another minute. But she had to tease out the logic of it all. Emma Mae had given her a Judas kiss, sold her to some supercop. Why hadn't Satan arrested her the second she'd opened the door? He was toying with her like an animal trainer who would point her toward McDonald's, where other supercops were waiting with closed-circuit television cameras. They meant to film her at the scene of the crime, so she could act out some unholy procession that would reappear on the 6-o'clock news.

A key turned in the lock. Pru clutched her silver Colt. Omar appeared in dark glasses that hid his eyes. He wasn't dressed like a lowlife preacher man. He wore a silk tie and a herringbone suit. He wasn't even startled to see a gun in his face. He smiled and wouldn't beg her not to shoot. It should have been easy. He couldn't put a spell on her without his pale green eyes.

"White trash," she said. "Is Emma Mae your sister?"

"I have a lot of sisters," he said, still smiling.

"And you're a supercop and a smarty-pants."

"Me? I'm the lowest of the low. A freelancer tied to ten different agencies, an undercover kid banished to the Bronx. Why didn't you run? I gave you a chance. I left notes for you in half my books, a hundred fucking clues."

"Yeah, I'm Miss Egg McMuffin. I do McDonald's. And I have no place to run to. Preacher man, play your tambourine and sing your last song."

She caught a glimpse of the snubnosed gun that rose out of a holster she hadn't seen. She didn't even hear the shot. She felt a thump in her chest and she flew against the wall with blood in her eyes. And that's when she had a vision of the night managers behind all the blood. Six men and a woman wearing McDonald's bibs, though she hadn't remembered them wearing those. They had eye sockets without the liquid complication of eyes themselves. Pru was still implacable toward the managers. She would have shot them all over again. But she did sigh once before the night managers disappeared and she fell into Omar Kaplan's arms like a sleepy child.

GOLD MOUNTAIN

BY TERRENCE CHENG
Lehman College

He knocked on the door and waited. A voice called out in English. Usually it was a white man, older, wearing glasses or with a beard or both. Usually the older white man looked into the bag, then at the bill, then went through his wallet for money. Usually the tip was a dollar or two, sometimes more. This did not happen often and he did not expect it.

He heard footsteps and then the door opened.

He stared at the man as he fumbled with his wallet; he was not white and not older, but Chinese—not Japanese or Korean, he could tell right away from the pallor of his skin, the shape of his eyes and nose and mouth. In his mid-thirties, he thought, he wore glasses and a blazer, a pair of dark pressed pants, and shined shoes. A few small moles dotting his right cheek, otherwise his skin was light, his hair longish and wavy, swept back as if blown by wind.

The man gave him a twenty and said, "Keep it"; he could not speak English, but this phrase he had come to understand. He nodded, turned to go. Then he heard the man say in his own dialect, "You are from Fuzhou?"

He stopped, did not turn back right away. When he did he said in his own language, "Yes. Are you?"

"No," the man said, "My family is from the north. But I've traveled." He paused, then said, "Is my pronunciation okay?"

"Yes, very good."

"I'm a professor here. I teach history."

"Right," he said. "Thank you." He turned and went downstairs and out to the fence where he had chained his bicycle. He looked at his watch. He had two more deliveries across campus, had to hurry or else they would call the restaurant and complain.

The orders coming from the college had picked up since the end of August. Now there were people everywhere—the faces black, brown, white, most of them young, some older, even old. Many pensive, serious, many jubilant and smiling. There were Asian faces as well, but only a few, and he did not stare at them too long or try to make eye contact, did not want to seem conspicuous. Most of the buildings were gray and blocky, others weather-blasted with regal columns and stone carved façades. He liked riding by the baseball field, watching people jog along the gravel track or playing ball in the midst of all that green.

The rest of the day he could not stop thinking of the professor who had given him the good tip and the chance to speak in his own dialect, and not Cantonese (to the other delivery men) or Mandarin (to his boss). On sight he had known the professor was Mandarin, northern Chinese, but he was speaking Fukienese and so he had to ask. Maybe his father had been from Fujian province, or his mother. He wondered why and how much traveling the professor had done to acquire a dialect so different from his native one, how he too had wound up in a place like this.

He rode and kept his eyes roving. Too many times during the summer he had almost been clipped by a speeding truck or car while enjoying the warmth of the sun on his back or a cooling breeze in his face. For this he was teased by the other delivery men.

"Pay attention or you'll get run down like a rat," said Fong. He was in his forties but already quite bald, one front tooth capped in gold, a cigarette perpetually dangling from his lips. He had been in the U.S. for over ten years and liked to brag that he could navigate the streets of the neighborhood with his eyes closed. The other delivery man was Wai-Ling, twenty-one or twenty-two, a few years younger than himself, small and quiet with bushy eyebrows and beady eyes. He laughed at whatever Fong said.

Not long after he had arrived, the boss, Mr. Liu, gave him the college campus and neighboring streets as his delivery area. "Can you handle that without getting killed?" Mr. Liu had asked him. He was a wiry old man, originally from Beijing, who ran the restaurant with his small but angry wife. They gave him a map, which he folded and put in his back pocket as Fong and Wai-Ling laughed.

"Like a schoolboy," Fong said. "Don't get lost!"

When a delivery was wrong or late he would be yelled at and sometimes cursed at—he recognized the loud sharp tones, flaring in the eyes. Times like this he was glad he did not know what was said. He would just hand over the delivery and a few times the food was taken with a door slammed in his face, leaving him empty-handed. He thought Mr. Liu would scream at him for this, but he didn't. "It happens sometimes," his boss said. "Better not to make enemies." He thought Mr. Liu was right, but in the end he knew that none of it would matter if no one knew who he was, which was why he had told no one his real name.

After his last delivery of the day he returned the bicycle to the restaurant and counted out with Mrs. Liu. His tips for the day had been poor, except for the professor who had given him almost four dollars. He left Fong and Wai-Ling smoking out in front of the restaurant. As he walked away he heard Fong shout at him, "Don't get lost, eh?" The same joke every day; he heard Wai-Ling snicker and laugh.

He lived close to the restaurant in a stone and brick building, a steel gate in front trimmed with razor wire. His apartment was small: an open kitchen, a living room, and a bathroom. He had found a mattress on the street and scrubbed it clean and now it lay in the corner covered with a blanket. The black-and-white television sat on a plastic crate, and there was one rickety wood chair against the wall that he never sat in but used as a small table instead. He had his dinner in a bag taken from the restaurant—leftover rice and greasy noodles, a slop of chicken, and overcooked vegetables in brown sauce. He set it on the chair and dug in; he didn't like the restaurant's food, but it was easier than cooking and still the closest thing he could get that reminded him of home. Since he had come to this place his pants and shirts now fit more snugly, and there was a thickness growing around his face. Maybe it was the food, or maybe the place itself was changing him. He thought his parents, if they had been alive, would not recognize him. And maybe this was part of the luxury in coming to the Gold Mountain, where food was hearty and plentiful enough to fatten up even a skinny farm boy like himself.

He turned on the television and watched the baseball game. The score was six to two, and only from the body language of the players could he figure out who was winning. When the score became ten to two he turned it off.

He went to the closet and dug out the small suitcase hidden at the bottom beneath empty boxes and rags. He looked out the window, as if someone might be spying on him, then turned back to the suitcase and popped it open. He stared for a moment, then dug his hands down through the four thick layers of wrapped and bundled American bills. He did not know the faces and could not read the words on the bills, but he knew the numbers: 100, 50, 20. When he had first opened the suitcase, months ago, the bills had all been sopping wet, but now they were wrinkled and dry, loose inside their bands. He had never counted it all to the dollar, bill by bill, but he had counted the bundles and estimated: close to a million U.S. More than his entire village back home could have earned in a lifetime.

He closed the suitcase and shoved it back in beneath the junk and waste. Then he flopped down on the mattress with the window open and slept with the sound of the city rumbling in his ear.

A few days later he knocked on the office door again, looked at the order ticket as he waited: beef with eggplant, brown rice, egg drop soup, can of soda. He did not blame the professor for ordering this muck; the restaurant was one of only a few in the neighborhood that made deliveries.

The door opened. The professor smiled at him, was wearing a dark blue suit and pink tie. He handed over the bag and again the professor tipped him more than three dollars. Then the professor asked him, "How long have you been here? In New York."

He said, "One year," even though he had only been in the country since June.

"How is your English?"

He shook his head and said, "Not very good."

The professor nodded, stood in the doorway with his brow furrowed. "Have you thought about taking classes?"

He glanced behind the professor into the office, did not see anyone else in there with him.

"No time for classes. I'm always working."

"If you are interested I can make a few suggestions. I know it can be hard not knowing the language."

"Right," he said. He looked at his watch. "I have to go. Thank you."

The professor nodded again and closed the door.

That night before the dinner rush he sat in front of the restaurant smoking. Fong and Wai-Ling kept to themselves because they were Cantonese and thus did not like him; and because he was originally from Fuzhou, they knew that he did not like them either. He watched cars pass by, admired the curvy women with long braided hair sauntering down the avenue. Eventually, he started thinking about the professor and what he had said. A part of him was offended; they didn't know each other, and yet he had presumed that because he did not speak English and because he was delivering food that . . . that what?

Had he meant to be disrespectful? To speak out of place to a stranger back home might cost you. But this was not home, and maybe he was just trying to offer some advice, one countryman to another. But were they even countrymen? Here, in New York, in the Bronx, it might appear to be so, a bond in the shape of the face and eyes. They were from China, but certainly they both knew that there were different Chinas— like the U.S., there was the top of the Gold Mountain, and then the rest.

He decided to take a quick walk, turned off the main avenue, and passed a small party happening on the street in front of the cluster of brick buildings that lined the road. He had seen these parties all summer: There was music, smoking food on a grill, even dancing. The smells intrigued him. People drank beer from big bottles and laughed. Girls wore short shorts and tiny tops, men in baggy shirts and shorts that came down past their knees, some with bald or close-cropped heads or even big tufts of bushy black hair. Everyone wore pieces of glittering gold—around their necks, in their ears, on their fingers, and around their ankles and wrists—so that with each movement they seemed to glimmer and shine.

All the voices, the bodies, the faces, so new. The skin of one so dark and smooth like a fine leather, and then another so light like rays of melted sun. Men with gold teeth, women with firm bodies, thick in the legs and butt. It was not just a different place, but a different planet, and only by not being there anymore could he sense how thick and smothering his life in Hong Kong had become: the rush and hum of constant millions buzzing his senses, ready to shatter like a crystal cage and crush him. Here he felt free, could move, think, listen. It did not bother him that he did not understand what was being said around him. When he stepped out into the streets there was maybe a woman with a child in a stroller, another in tow; or a small gang of dark-skinned boys cajoling and roughhousing, making their way down the block; or girls walking tall and brazen, whispering to each other and shaking their heads and waving their fingers as they spoke back to the cat-calling boys. On every other corner was an old man or woman with a big umbrella and a two-wheeled cart selling paper cups of crushed flavored ice in the slate of summer heat.

He went back to the restaurant, found Mrs. Liu looking for him. He took the new orders, hung the bags on his handlebars. His first drop was to one of the bigger buildings in the neighborhood, where he buzzed and had to wait for the person to come down. A young woman opened the door. She had dark half-slanted eyes, her skin like a pale chocolate cream. She was his height, but seemed taller because she was so thin, her arms and neck stretched, scrawny. If her face, like her body, had not been so sucked out and sickly he might have thought her beautiful. He took her money and handed over the bag. Her hair was long but stringy and tangled, and the skin on her arms and face and neck was mottled, blotchy. A stained sour smell came from inside the door. He counted the money; she was short more than two dollars, but he looked at the woman and smiled and said, "Okay."

That night in his apartment he kept thinking of her, the woman with the scrawny wrists and neck.

He finished eating, then took a shower, put on a clean shirt and fresh pants, combed his hair, and went out.

He knew his way, though he never made deliveries in this area north and west of the college, which was Fong's area. The roads were mostly quiet and empty, the murmur of traffic on the expressway nearby, the occasional screech and rattle of the train that snaked overhead and through the neighborhood. When he had first arrived he would kill hours on the trains, would pay the fair and ride them end to end. Either the 4 train or the D—he preferred the 4 because it ran above ground in the Bronx, past the enormous stadium with the bright white lights. The trains were much dirtier here than they were in Hong Kong, but this did not bother him. He liked the tossed feeling of motion, liked to think that he was traveling from one end of New York to the other.

When he got to the building he went to the pay phone on the corner. From his wallet he pulled a business card and dialed. Then he stood at the phone booth and waited, knew he was being watched now through an apartment window. It was like this too in Hong Kong, when he went to one of those places, being watched at the front door by a camera or spy making sure he was not a policeman or vagrant or gangster who could not be trusted. He counted to fifty in his head, then he went to the front door and was buzzed in, took the stairs to the fourth floor. He knocked on the door and it opened just a crack. He saw her eyes, the dark painted lashes, then she unlatched the lock.

The place looked exactly as it had the last time he had come. Neat but spare: a flowered curtain, candles on the table, the smell of jasmine and incense. He looked at the woman, short and small, older than he, her breasts squeezed into her low-cut blouse. She had long flowing hair and light gold skin, and from a distance one might think she was ten years younger than she was. He had found her randomly one night. It had been late and he had been wandering, trying to learn this new place so that he did not get lost. She had walked up to him and started talking to him, and by the way she smiled and ran her hand up and down his arm he knew who and what she was.

He gave her sixty dollars as he had that first night. She took him by the hand into the bedroom which smelled thick with perfume. Inside there was only a bed and a chair against the wall and he wondered if she slept on the same bed where she worked. She slid her shirt over her head and he did the same. She smiled and said something to him, but he did not know or care what she was saying. He lay naked on the small soft bed and she on top of him, and for the next thirty minutes he closed his eyes and thought of the women from home he had known and thought he could love.

When they finished he dressed quickly as she smoked a

cigarette. His stomach felt empty, his legs rubbery and weak. She laughed and said something but he already had his shoes on.

Walking home he wondered why he had taken a shower to visit a whore. It didn't make sense, but so many things didn't make sense to him these days. He could have stayed home and watched the game, or he could have taken the subway or bus to a restaurant out of the neighborhood where he could have eaten and drank something other than the slop Mr. Liu and his wife served. But he knew the best food was all the way down in Chinatown, and there he could not go.

He walked and smoked and thought again about the sickly girl who had not had enough money for her food. It was her wrists and her neck that had stayed in his mind, and how her hair was so thin like it might fall out of her head. And he remembered the ship, the woman who had been one of the few wives on board. Three hundred of them packed into the freight, and these two men (one taller, the other very short) started to squawk over a mess made in someone's space. He watched as they argued, did not try to stop it. They had been on the ship for over two months, and below deck, amongst the hundreds of compartments and partitioned areas they had created with cardboard and hanging shirts and towels and clothes, how could anyone tell whose mess was whose? In one corner were big buckets filled with piss and shit that were emptied each day, puddles of waste on the floor where people had spilled. In another corner on a rusted table they tried to cook with two burners and two big propane tanks, the floor littered with empty cans, filthy rags, and ripped empty boxes.

The floor and air stank with their sweat and metal and waste, but still the two men argued and accused. Then they fought.

It was not the first fight that had broken out. People gathered in a circle, some yelling, shouting. Then the tall one had both hands around the short one's throat, choking him down to his knees until his eyes fluttered and a bubbly foam dribbled from his lips. The short one's wife came from behind, hitting the tall man on the back of the head with double-hammer fists until he had no choice but to turn and hit her in the face to make her stop.

The short man lay there gasping, twitching. The tall one turned and looked at the woman lying on the ground. She had bobbed stringy hair, her shirt filthy, too big for her, hanging down off her shoulder. Her neck so thin like a sick bird or child. The tall one reached down and began pulling at the legs of her pants and then she was bare.

He knew he should step in, but he did not. No one did.

When the tall man finished—it did not take long—he stood and pulled his pants up, turned and saw the other man still lying on the ground. He spit on the short man, and then moved through the crowd to the other end of the hold, where he disappeared inside a wall of faces. When the short one came to and saw his wife, he gathered her into a corner where he held her and wept.

A world unto itself: no ruler, no rules.

In the morning they found the woman by the kitchen area. She had used the lid of a rusty can to carve open her wrists. Her bottom still naked, she sat with her eyes open against the wall in a wide dark puddle. The short man was dead too, no signs of trauma beyond what he had suffered during the fight. He had just stopped living. No one knew if he or his wife had died first.

They were still far enough out at sea to dump the bodies, so he was picked to prepare the woman and her husband on the deck to make sure they sank and stayed sunk. He tied them together with rope, stuffed their clothes with any random refuse or wood or metal he could find. Then he rolled them overboard and thought at least they had finished their voyage together.

When he got back to the apartment he found his neighbor knocking on his door, an old woman with white hair and leathery wrinkled skin. A few times she had offered him food—yellow rice with beans and some salty shredded meat—that he gladly accepted.

Now she spoke very fast, kept poking up the corners of her own eyes, then flashing two fingers, then pointing at the floor. She did this over and over again. Finally he took her wrists in his hands and smiled at her and nodded. "Okay," he said. "Sank you." She took a breath and shrugged, then went back to her own apartment.

He could still smell the perfume of the whore on his skin, so he took another shower. Then he turned on the television and sat on the mattress. He knew what the old woman had been trying to tell him: Two men with slanted eyes had come looking for him. This was not a shock or surprise. Since his first steps here, in this new place, this new world, he had known that they would find him, that someone would.

Here the dreams were always the same: the taste of the water, the bubble of salt and surf, smoke and gas and oil in his nose and mouth, leaking down his throat. Knowing that his eyes were open in the water and yet all he could see was black; the floating, the flash and flail of his limbs. Was he watching his own death? He did not know then, but it was what he felt now. He woke in the middle of the night and drank a glass of water. Then he sat in the chair he never sat in, sat by the window smoking and watching the sunrise over the highway.

He thought about home, the person he used to be. How he had grown up in a fishing village in Fujian province, learning to farm as well, to make a living with his hands and back. How his family had no money to send him to school; and how he had come to realize around the age of thirteen that he had no talent for the life that his family and ancestors had paved for him. When his parents died (he was twenty by then), he left.

It took him days to get to Fuzhou, walking and stealing rides with strangers. Finally a truck filled with workers took him into the heat of the big buildings, the lights, the colors, the taste and smell of so many people, so many machines. He was afraid he would be swallowed by it all, that everyone around him would know he was a country boy. He found work in a hotel restaurant cleaning dishes and taking out garbage. He worked as many hours as they would let him, slept little, saved all of his money, but still he did not feel like a rich man.

Then one day in the hotel he was relaxing after his shift. The bar and lounge were half-crowded. A man sat down next to him wearing a dark suit and collared shirt with no tie. The man's watch shined in the lights around the bar. They began talking, and then the man said, "Have you ever thought about going to America?" His face appeared to be young but his eyes made him look old. They stared at each other.

"No," he said, "never thought about it."

The man gave him a card. "Call me if you want to stop wasting your life."

The man paid his bill and walked out. He looked at the man's card and called him two days later. He said he did not want to go to America, but wanted to stop wasting his life.

His job was to recruit, to work the city for potential clients. He was trained to spot who and what they were looking for.

"Dressed shabby, looking a little lost. You know, country folk."

"Is that why you came up to me in the bar?"

The man stared at him and told him to pay attention.

"The police are paid off. So are the officials we need. But don't be cocky. If you show off they will make an example of you."

He learned to spot them in crowds, in markets, on the street. He had his pitch, all the facts that anyone in the beginning would need to know: thirty-thousand U.S. total, at least five to ten up front, the rest when you get there. "How?" they would sometimes ask, and he would tell them by boat or by plane. It cost more if you wanted passports and special work papers.

"We know your relatives, we know where you live. We are watching you on both sides. We are taking big risks to give you the chance of a lifetime. Don't disrespect us. Don't make us or your family lose face."

He knew when clients were satisfied. People would find him to thank him, tell him how well their sons and husbands and fathers were doing over there, the riches they were making, the opulent lives they would all someday lead. "He'll be a citizen in a few years, then he can bring us all over," one wife told him. "He sends me beautiful clothes and jewelry," said another. "We're going to live in a big house with big cars." He would smile and nod and later more people from the same family, the same clan, would come to him to make the journey. They borrowed money from relatives, from friends, from anyone who could afford to give just a little to send them away to find their dreams. No one talked about the ones who did not make it, who were caught and shipped back, held by police and beaten; then sent back to their villages to pay a huge fine, only to begin planning when they would try again.

He worked Fuzhou for two years, then his boss asked him to help with operations in Hong Kong. He practiced his Cantonese, learned the new landscape of police and officials, who knew what, what areas were safe to work. Now he helped to coordinate and find secure holding areas while the boats and ships and passports and payoffs were taken care of. He learned the routes that spanned the world—from Hong Kong or Fuzhou or ports out of Malaysia or Thailand, across the ocean and into South America or Europe. Groups as small as two or three, sometimes as big as twenty, thirty, fifty, more. They might wait in a holding area in a strange country for months, kept by enforcers in a house or warehouse or apartment, until it was safe to move again.

Because they did not want to wind up in the Netherlands or Peru or even Canada. America was where they wanted to go, and even though he was no longer pitching and recruiting the dream, it was still the backdrop of his thoughts—places like New York, San Francisco, cities within cities filled with Chinese; piles of money waiting to be made, the fine clothes and food that would adorn their lives, teachers and schools that would educate their children and make them citizens, so they would never have to suffer.

He had talked so much about it that even he began to believe. But he did not have thirty thousand dollars, and he wondered if he was still wasting his life.

Then he was told about the next big plan: a new shipping route, from Thailand to Kenya, then around the tip of Africa, then on to the U.S. Almost three hundred passengers, they would need extras to work the crew.

"Are you interested?" his boss asked him. "Think of it this way: You get to see the world, spend a few days in New York when it's over."

He did not see any way to disagree.

That afternoon he went to the school to deliver the professor's meal. The professor handed him two brochures, one in Chinese.

"For classes," he said. "The school is close to Penn Station, easy to get to."

He looked at the brochure written in Chinese, on the front a picture of a young Chinese woman, smiling, a book splayed open in front of her. *Learn English—live life!*

The professor said, "It's cheaper than taking classes here, which you might not be ready for anyway. This would prepare you."

He kept staring at the brochures, did not know what to say, what to do.

The professor said, "Let me know if you have any questions, if you need help filling out the forms." The professor reached out his hand. He looked at the gold band around the professor's left ring finger, then shook his hand without thanking him.

The rest of the day, as he made his deliveries he wondered about the professor's life, compared it to his own. On days off he sometimes took the bus to the movie theater in the shopping plaza, and like the baseball games, he could surmise what was happening by the the tone of voice and look on an actor's face. Afterward he would browse through shops in the plaza, sometimes buying socks or undershirts or small things that he did not necessarily need. Other times he went to the open market and bought vegetables and meat and went home and tried to cook, but always seemed to burn his food. Then he would go to a restaurant where he would be surrounded by brown and black people—no whites, definitely no Chinese. He would look at the menu and point, a kind of guessing game, and he knew that no matter what they brought him he would eat it.

No one bothered him in these places, and was this so different from what an American might call life? He did not feel he was much better or worse off than anyone else around him. Except for when he was lonely, when he would argue with himself as to whether or not to go to the whore.

The professor, he thought, did not need to visit a whore. Nor did he wile away his time watching movies or burning food or hording money and constantly looking over his shoulder. The professor had a wife and children, he imagined; a big house somewhere in a neighborhood of identical houses, did not live within the rows of blocky brick buildings with rusted fire escapes draped top to bottom that surrounded the school. He pictured the professor's home decorated with classical Chinese paintings and calligraphy, a shiny new car parked in the driveway, next to a green lawn where his children could safely play. He was sure he had more in that suitcase than the professor had in any bank, but the thought did not make him feel any better. What good was it if he could not spend it?

Maybe that was the problem. He could buy a small restaurant, but he knew nothing about the business except how to bus tables and make deliveries. Or he could open a store here in the Bronx that sold groceries and goods for Chinese people; but that would be silly because there were not enough Chinese. In the end he knew there was no way he could do any of these things without spending money and drawing attention to himself; and this was not like Chinatown where he knew he would feel less lonely, feel as if he were part of something again.

He remembered going just a few days after he had arrived, taking a car from the hotel into the city, all arranged by the desk clerk. (Americans, he thought, were no different than Chinese: You give them enough money and they will do anything for you.) The car dropped him off and the white driver got out and leaned on the hood, smoking and reading the paper, and he began walking toward the crowd of Chinese faces, felt relief hearing his own dialect and Cantonese and Mandarin street to street. The stores selling big crates full of herbs and spices, vegetables, fresh fish, roasted ducks, and barbecued meat hanging in the greasy windows. They sold clothes, shoes, perfume, watches, toys. He had been to a thousand markets like these in Fuzhou and Hong Kong, but here the feel of the air, the smell of the streets, even the ground beneath him felt different.

He walked below an overpass and past plain storefronts with Chinese signs advertising for workers. Here there were no blacks or whites or browns, only others like him. "You want to work? You—you want to work?" They were calling out in Fukienese, Cantonese. He ignored them, kept walking, felt his heart and stomach go slithery inside. He knew this was what everyone on the ship had come for—the chance to work nonstop every day to repay the debt that was their lives.

He went to a small restaurant on a side street and ordered a bowl of beef noodle soup and small dragon buns. When the food came he did his best to eat slowly, the taste of the broth and beef slivers and noodles soaking into his mouth, his first real meal in months.

He picked up a Chinese newspaper from the table next to him and read about the ship, the *Golden Venture*, stranded just off the shore of Long Island, filled with illegal Chinese: two-hundred and eighty-six captured, ten drowned, six escaped. He stared at the pictures of them all on the beach, wrapped in blankets, herded like animals. He tried to recognize the faces but could not.

Six escaped.

He lit a cigarette and the waitress came over and said, "No smoking."

He finished his meal and left. As he walked back to the car he felt the eyes of the city pressing in on him—the people, the buildings, the cars, the birds, the cracks in the concrete walls and streets surrounding. Maybe someone had spotted him and was already following, because this was America, a fast and wild and frightening place. Here, even among his own, he could feel how they were outsiders, transplanted.

On his way back to the hotel he stared out the window, remembered how he had heard the captain and the crew leader talking, how they had not received communication from shore, did not know if and when the boats would meet them out at sea as planned or if they were supposed to press on and dock.

He knew from all the muttering and murmuring that the situation was not good. They had been at sea now for three months. It had been bad from the beginning—those who grew sick and delirious right away, puking and shitting on themselves as if indigent and mad; then the fighting each day, passenger versus passenger, enforcer versus passenger; all of them hungry; breathing the air heavy with the smell of saltwater and sea-soaked metal and piss and shit and bodies festering and congealed. He dreaded his rounds below deck, could not imagine what it was like to be down there every minute of every day, as the passengers were not allowed above deck lest they be spotted from the air.

The things he had done, the horrors he had seen: the short man and the short man's wife, letting them both die, then rolling them into the sea; swinging a club and cracking a man's skull for stealing the crew's water and food; a woman held down and fucked until she bled, and by the time he was inside her, her eyes were still open but she no longer screamed.

He had always thought of himself as a good and simple man, but now he knew this was not true.

He was in one of the sleeping cabins when he felt the crunch of the boat, heard the thunk and grind, thought that they had smashed their way onto shore. He was up on his feet, gliding toward the deck, heard the screaming, the footsteps and pounding, scrambling in the hold below, heard the thwack of the helicopter above, being chased by a swirling beam of light. Then he saw the flood of bodies coming up through the doors and hatches, spewing like a fountain, spreading across the deck like ants. More lights attacking, the helicopter circling, electric voices in English, boats closing in, engines ripping the water.

In the distance he could see the shore, big spotlights and smaller yellow dots maybe three hundred meters away. He looked around for his crewmates, for an escape boat or plan, but the frenzy was too much, people pushing, shoving, the twist and shriek of the fray. He heard the splashing first, then turned and saw them going over one by one near the bow, in groups over the side. He ran for the side and jumped out as far as he could, feet first into the water, flesh locking, the freeze crushing against him. He told himself that he was the son of a fisherman and that he would not die in the water. His arms and legs began to move even though he could not feel them.

Waves crashing over his head, he went under for as long as he could, kept kicking, thrashing, just trying to pull away;

opening his eyes, trying to see, thinking of the boats and the helicopter and what they would do to him if he was caught. He came up for air and went under again, and when he came back up he was further away from the ship and there were more boats now closing in, but he was behind it all, off to the side.

He knew he would not make it like this, his arms and legs like lead, trying to take in as much air as he could, water in his mouth, bloating his stomach, seeping through his lungs. Then he heard a voice, saw his crew leader's head bobbing up and down. He was holding onto something, using it like a flotation device, saw the crew leader paddling in his direction in the hard and heavy surf. They swam toward each other, and when he was close enough he saw his own arm swing up out of the water and then down, his fist landing with a crack against the crew leader's nose, then he was wrestling the small case away into his own arms as the other man's head disappeared. He held onto the case and kicked, kept his head on a swivel as he swam for the dark water and stretch of lights.

When he finally felt the sand in his toes it was so quiet he thought he was dead already. He saw houses with big wooden decks lining the shore. He could not stop his teeth from chattering, could feel all his bones and flesh shaking, his stomach and head filled with fire, and this told him he was not dead. He hugged the suitcase close to his chest even as he crawled onto the beach, spitting and coughing, his innards burning like oil and acid in his blood. When he looked back he saw the lights still shining, the freighter locked down. He had swam more than three hundred meters to get to shore, felt like a kind of superman, alone, freezing, but uncaptured and alive. His father, he thought, would be proud.

The sky was black, but he knew he did not have much

time. He would need a change of clothes, and under the wooden deck of one of the houses he fumbled with the suitcase latch until it opened. He stared in, his blood and brains squeezing. Then he closed the suitcase and walked further down the beach along the row of houses until he had brushed himself off, could still taste the sea and sand in his mouth as he willed his arms and legs to move, his breath thin and wheezing. He made his way in between two houses, and when he came to a main road there was no traffic and no one on the streets. He looked at the signs and recognized only one in glowing neon—*HOTEL*. He had seen it in Fuzhou, and in Hong Kong. He took from the suitcase a handful of wet hundred-dollar bills, walked quickly through the front glass door and up to the counter.

The young man with glasses behind the counter did not look up until he was standing in front of him, waving the money. The young man stared back, wide-eyed, gape-jawed, nodding.

Two hours later he brought him shorts, sandals, a pair of jeans, T-shirts, and underwear. The clothes were big but comfortable. He gave the young man more money, and for the next three days he was brought egg sandwiches and coffee early in the morning, hamburgers and french fries and soda in the evening. All of it was greasy, salty, disgusting, but he ate it. Each time the door knocked he thought it could be the police, but it was always the young man's glasses that shined back in the light.

After his excursion into Chinatown he knew he could not go back. Not now, not like this. In the big yellow phone book in his room he found a map of New York City, and with the desk clerk's help (he must have given him a thousand dollars by now) figured out where Chinatown was. From the young man's finger he then looked north, up the map, pointed at the highest part and nodded.

When he left in a car early the next morning he gave the young man another handful of money. The driver was brown-skinned and wore several gold chains around his neck. The car stereo was loud. An hour later he was dropped off on the main avenue. He gave the driver two hundred dollars without him asking, and the man stared back at him with wide incredulous eyes.

He found the restaurant a half hour later, walked in, and asked for a job.

"You just move here?" asked Mr. Liu.

"Yes," he said. He looked down at the suitcase in his hand.

"You're lucky, I just lost a delivery man. You have any experience?"

"Yes. Back in Hong Kong."

"If you can find your way around Hong Kong you won't have a problem here." Mr. Liu peered at him for a few moments, then said, "You're not a troublemaker, are you? We run a simple family business. We don't need any problems."

"No," he said. "No problems. But I need a place to stay. Do you know where I can look?"

"Sure," said Mr. Liu. "Do you have enough to cover the first month's rent?"

He gripped the handle of the suitcase and said, "Yes, I think I do."

After his final delivery of the day he rode back to the restaurant, the professor's brochures folded and tucked in his pocket. He had never planned on being a deliveryman for the rest of his life, and so maybe it was fate, or a sign from the heavens that now was the time to move on. Wherever he might go, he would take classes. It was a good idea.

As he pulled up to the restaurant he expected to see Fong and Wai-Ling out front smoking, but the sidewalk was empty. The neon sign in the window was off. He looked at this watch—it was only 10, not yet closing time. He tipped his bicycle down to its side and walked up to the open front door. He peeked in, heard nothing. The two front tables were empty with no chairs. The menu signs above the counter were off, leaving only the fluorescent lights from the kitchen aglow. He reached into his pocket and pulled out his keys, clenched them in his fist with the tips like metal spikes jutting between his fingers.

He stepped in slowly, passed the front counter, peeked around the wall, then came to a stop, staring into the kitchen. Pans and bowls still filled with food, cartons half-open, spatulas and tongs left on the counters, as if they had evacuated in an emergency, the restaurant abandoned.

Except for the shoe in the corner by the fryer, Mrs. Liu's shoe; and then he saw the tooth, chipped and glowing like a speck of gold dust on the floor.

He knew that when he died he would meet an army of demons who would make him pay for his sins. He was not afraid, but still he was not ready.

He rode his bicycle back to his apartment, went upstairs, and stood in the hallway outside his door for ten minutes, listening, waiting. When he finally went in everything was as he had left it. He took only the suitcase, and when he got back downstairs his bicycle was gone and so he walked with the suitcase to the whore's apartment. He called from the pay phone and she buzzed him in. When he got upstairs he gave her three hundred dollars and she closed the door behind him.

In the morning he washed himself, wet his hair and combed it back, used her razor to shave his face. He left her naked and curled and sleeping, felt bad for her though he could not say why. He left her an extra hundred dollars, then went to the diner by the college next to the subway station and drank tea and waited.

He still had the professor's brochures in his pocket, along with a map that he had torn from the whore's telephone book. Around noon he walked onto campus, past the security booth and parking gate, through the roaming clusters of students. He headed into the building, up the stairs, knocked on the professor's door.

The professor answered and said, "Hello." An awkward smile. "I didn't order."

"I know." His suitcase in one hand, brochures in the other, he said, "I had some questions about these classes. Could I ask you?"

The professor paused, looked at his watch. "Sure. I have a few minutes. Come in."

The professor was bigger than he had thought. His pants fit him so loosely he needed to pull the belt in as tight as he could. The shoes were at least a size too big, as were his shirt and undershirt. The blazer was big enough to cover him so he did not look saggy and suspicious. All over he could smell the professor's cologne, but there was nothing he could do about that right now.

He had left the empty suitcase in the office, had moved the money into the professor's book bag and another bag he had found in his desk drawer. Close to the train station he found a barbershop where he pointed at a picture on the wall and the barber cut his hair down close, then closer, so when he was finished he looked like a teenager again. Inside the station he looked around and did not know where he would go. He looked at the professor's watch on his wrist, then walked through the massive corridors of the station. With the professor's glasses he saw things with a new clarity. He got his shoes shined, then stopped at a rack with postcards of New York's wondrous sites: the big famous buildings, the pretty parks and rich museums, the baseball stadium with the crossed N and Y emblazoned in white over the field. He took a card out of the rack and gave the man at the counter a dollar.

A young Chinese couple helped him figure out the schedule. He paid for his ticket in cash, pulled the bills from the professor's wallet. He would hold onto the IDs just in case he needed them, until he felt it was safe to be no one again.

On the train he kept both bags at his feet. There were mostly old white people around him, some in suits, some dressed for a day of leisure. No one looked at him or bothered him. The train car was air-conditioned and very cold. The conductor checked his ticket and nodded and then the train was rolling. He pulled the postcard from his blazer pocket and stared at the green field, trying to imagine the next mirage of his life, until they were out of the tunnel and barreling beyond the city.

HEY, GIRLIE

BY JOANNE DOBSON

Sedgwick Avenue

Hey, girlie," the voice rasped down at me from the fourth-floor window. "I want you should get me a coconut cake over by Phillips the baker. Make sure it got a nice red cherry in the middle. And don't smoosh it on the way home like you do the bread."

A coconut cake? Holy crap—Mrs. Blaustein must be in the money. It was usually a nineteen-cent loaf of Wonder Bread with her. The quarter'd come spinning down from the fourth floor, and I'd catch it in my skirt before it hit the sidewalk. Magic: money out of thin air. All I'd have to do was run the bread from the grocer at the corner of Kingsbridge up to 4-C, two blocks round trip and four flights of stairs. I got a nickel, but she always wanted the penny back.

Everyone knew Mrs. Blaustein took care of a crazy lady who never came out of the apartment. Katy-Ann Cooper said she was a maniac killer, the crazy lady, and that's why she wouldn't show her face. But my mother said Katy-Ann was full of shit—excuse her Irish—Miss Cohen was just a poor unfortunate who had gotten in the way of history. My mother said things like that. She liked to read, and not just the racing forms like my father, but books from Kingsbridge library. Me too. The day I bought the coconut cake I'd just come back from the library with a stack of books up to my chin, and I knew I'd finish them all by Sunday night. I flopped right down on the green couch and started *The Yearling*, but my mother said, "Go out and play, for Christ's sake—it's such a nice day. You can read anytime."

So, I was the only one of us kids who ever saw the crazy lady. It happened this way. Mrs. Blaustein made a toss over the window guard, and I made my usual brilliant catch. This time it was a dollar bill wrapped tight around a half-dollar and held together with a big fat paperclip. I bought the best cake at the baker. It cost the whole dollar-fifty. Lemon-filled. Spinkled all over with fluffy coconut. A perfect red circle of a cherry. I carried it careful in its white cardboard box like it was the coronation crown jewels, down Kingsbridge, past the Veteran's Hospital, round the corner onto Sedgwick, my braids for once hanging nice and straight over my shoulders like the good Lord intended instead of slapping my face like when I run with the bread.

I was younger then. Ten. I thought I was tough, but I didn't know nothing. Anything. That was two years ago, there was a new queen in England, Maxie Isaacs next door died of polio, and Mr. and Mrs. Rosenberg went to the electric chair. Julius and Ethel Rosenberg, that is. Not the Rosenbergs from 5-F. My mother said the judge should burn in hell for that verdict. My father said, "Now, Tessie . . ."

We didn't go to church anymore, not since Father O'Mally said little Maxie Isaacs was a baby Christ-killer and that *he* would burn in hell instead of going to heaven like a good little Catholic child. We're big on hell in my neighborhood. So I went to P.S. 86 instead of Our Lady of Angels, and I didn't have to wear a uniform, and Mrs. Marrs didn't yank my braids when she caught me hiding a book on my lap during Math.

I walked that coconut cake into the courtyard, past the stoop, up the three steps. The lobby smelled like apple kugel, the second-floor landing like Mrs. Costigan's cats, the third like sauerkraut with weird Jewish stuff in it, caraway seed, maybe. A radio was playing piano music, but suddenly it stopped with a crash that almost made me drop the cake, then started again from the beginning. Not the radio, then. A real piano. I had just rounded the fourth-floor stairs when Mr. Schmidt came out of 4-C, Mrs. Blaustein's apartment, with his big toolbox. "Vot you doing here, girlie?"

Mr. Schmidt was our new super. German. My daddy said all supers in the Bronx were Krauts. I hoped they weren't all the same kind of Kraut Mr. Schmidt was, with a voice that crunched like broken glass. Mr. Schmidt scared the hell out of me. Maybe it was how big he was, fat, with fists like Sunday hams. Or the way he was always chewing, jaws going from side to side like that hippopotamus at the Bronx Zoo. Or maybe it was his daughter Trudy, the only other not-Jewish kid in my fourth-grade class at P.S. 86. She gave the nastiest Indian burn of any kid on Sedgwick, Trudy did, then batted blue eyes like an angel at the poor kid's parents. Even Lennie Foreman walked the other side of the street when Trudy Schmidt was on the sidewalk. But not me. Not even then. If anyone even tried it I would've bent their little pinkie back till it snapped. Nobody messed with me—not even Trudy Schmidt—not after my daddy taught me the cop moves. Did I say he was a cop? Well he is, and a good one.

"Vot you doing, girlie?" I never knew anyone before who shaved his whole head, but Mr. Schmidt did, and the red stubble made it look like it was coated with corroded rust. *Corroded.* I like that. It's a good word. *Corroded.*

"Just bringing Mrs. Blaustein a coconut cake." The super had his eyes on the cake box, but I slipped past him without another word. My mother said you had to watch out when he came around—things would go missing. Cookies or muffins. The week before, when he was working on the pipes in our kitchen, a pork chop disappeared. *A pork chop! Cooked!* And her with five mouths to feed. So I held the cake box tight to my chest and got past Mr. Schmidt safe, and this was the first time I was ever in 4-C. Mrs. Blaustein came rushing to the door, all out of breath, said to wait a minute and she'd get me a dime for a tip (a whole dime!), but she had to go talk to someone first. Then she went out of the apartment, fast. So I nosed around. It was a big place, two bedrooms. Nothing like our one-bedroom apartment with five people sleeping in shifts night and day. This living room was . . . classy. Pictures on the walls—actual paintings. A piano in one corner. Glass doors with sheer curtains leading into yet another room. Through the half-open door I could see into this second room—shelves and shelves of books, like a library. They were a magnet to me, those books. I couldn't help myself.

At first I thought the gloomy room was empty. The drapes were closed, except for one little slit in the middle, and dust danced in the narrow light. *Narrow light.* Maybe I read that somewhere: *narrow light.* I tiptoed over to the nearest shelf. Mrs. Blaustein wouldn't mind if I looked at just one book . . .

"Iss he gone yet?" It was a woman's quivery voice.

I dropped the book and screamed.

A gasp came from right behind me, and a small woman hunched in a wheelchair spun around. "*Mein Gott.* I thought you vere Hilda." Her accent was sort of like the Jewish mommas who schlepped their folding chairs in front of the building on sunny mornings and talked and talked and talked. Something like the mommas—but different. More like music. "Vere'd *you* come from, child?"

"From the baker." This must be the crazy lady. She was

scary, all right, one eye pulled down, a huge red puckered scar from her forehead to her chin, one shoulder higher than the other. Her eyes were open really, really wide, even the droopy one. Her head was shaking on her neck. I wanted to get out of there—bad. But I wasn't leaving without my money. Where the hell was Mrs. Blaustein? "I'm the cake girl."

"'The *cake* girl'?" She laughed—and for a minute the air in the room got . . . not so heavy. At least I think it was a laugh, a wheeze and a dry chuckle in her throat, and her head stopped shaking. "The cake girl. Oh, it vould be a pity to vaste that." She picked up a little notebook on her lap and scribbled in it with a gold pencil. Her hands were thin and very white. They looked more like they belonged to some younger woman than that horrible scarred face. "Now," she said, "I vill write a poem about the cake girl."

"A poem?"

"Yes. And someday vhen you're in college maybe you vill read it and think of me."

"College?" Me?

"That vas vun thing they couldn't take away from me— my poetry. Do you like them?"

"Like what?"

"Poems?"

"Dunno," I said. "They're okay, I guess. *By the shores of Gitche Gumee, / By the shining Big-Sea-Water, / Stood the wig-wam of—*"

"No. No. No," she said. "Not that drivel. That book you just dropped on the floor? Pick it up, girl, open it and read me a real poem." She had wheeled her chair to the window, and now she pulled the drapery cord. Light came streaming in, and I could see to read.

I could also see Mrs. Blaustein standing in the doorway

with her arms crossed. I cringed, expecting her to yell. But she was looking at the wheelchair lady. "Rachel, I think you might be right." I never heard her sound so quiet.

"Iss he gone?" The wheelchair lady's voice was quivery again.

"For now. Just off the boat last year from Bremerhaven, Esther Meyer says."

The head started shaking again, like this toy I used to have where you turned a key and the tin Chinaman nodded and nodded and nodded. It was like the springs in her neck were broken.

Mrs. Blaustein's lips got white and thin. She turned to me. "Girlie, do like Miss Cohen says. Read a poem from the book."

So I opened the book and read. *"After great pain, a formal feeling comes— / The Nerves sit ceremonious, like Tombs—"* I looked up . . . Pain? . . . Tombs? But the sound of the words seemed to calm her—Miss Cohen—so I kept reading *". . . This is the Hour of Lead— / Remembered, if outlived, / As Freezing persons, recollect the Snow— / First—Chill—then Stupor—then the letting go—"*

I was still there when Miss Cohen's visitor came. The one I got the cake for, I guess. Not many men in suits around our neighborhood. Father O'Mally. Claire Heidenreich's father. Insurance collectors. Fuller Brush men. But none of them wore suits like this one. It fit him like he was born in gray wool. No knee wrinkles or ass sags. Just shoulders and shirt cuffs, pleats at the belt and a sharp crease down the pant legs. I was old enough to know better, but I gaped at this handsome stranger like a two-year-old until Mrs. Blaustein pressed the dime into my hand. "Here's your money, girlie. Go on home now. Miss Cohen has to talk to her publisher."

* * *

"You know the crazy old lady in 4-C?" I said at supper that night. "She's a famous poet. A publisher came to see her today. What's a publisher?"

"She's not crazy and she's not old," my father said. "It's just that they experimented on her in the camps." He took the bowl of boiled potatoes, ladled out three, spread them with margarine.

"They? Experimented?" The meatloaf looked good. Tomato soup on top and slices of bacon.

"What're you now, ten, right?" He took two slices of meatloaf and reached for the ketchup bottle.

"Mike!" my mother said. "She doesn't need to know about such evil—"

"She's a tough kid. She can handle it." He gave me a straight look. "You've heard of the camps, right?" He poured himself more beer from the Pabst Blue Ribbon bottle.

"You mean, like in the Catskills, where Jessica goes?"

"Jeez—what'da they teach you in that school? The concentration camps, I mean. Auschwitz. Dachau."

He told me, but I didn't want to believe it. "They really did those things?" That's how dumb I was.

"Yeah, and worse." He spooned canned peas next to the potatoes. "That's what we fought for in the war, to beat those Nazi bastards. If they won, who'da been next? First the Jews and the Polacks and the qu—"

"Charlie!" My mother clamped a hand over his mouth.

He pushed it away and gave a short laugh. He drinks a lot of beer when he's going on night shift. "Maybe the Irish were next, for all we know. Jews. Micks. This whole neighborhood woulda been wiped out." He laughed again and took another drink.

I put my fork down. I'd lost my appetite.

* * *

That night there were Nazis in the closet by my bed. I didn't know what they looked like, not exactly, but I could *feel* them there. Maybe my father was wrong. Maybe we didn't win the war. Maybe . . .

Mrs. Blaustein called the next day. My mother frowned. "Rachel Cohen must be lonely. She seems to have taken a liking to you. You want to go have cake with her?"

"Okay," I said. I don't know why. I didn't really want to.

Mrs. Blaustein had set the table with a lace cloth and some nice china dishes with gold rims. Very *la-tee-dah*, my father would have said.

"I don't like cake," Miss Cohen said. "But you go right ahead." She drank cup after cup of the blackest coffee I ever saw from what looked like dolls' cups, while I ate two slices of coconut cake. The filling was so sweet I almost couldn't taste the lemon, so sweet it made my teeth ache. I loved it.

Miss Cohen talked almost the whole time. About knives and needles. About acid and electric shocks. About cattle cars full of Jews. About barbed wire. About ovens that weren't for baking cakes in.

"The day they took us away, I put on my white linen dress with the eyelet embroidery. I thought if I looked nice, they'd know I was a nice girl," she said. "Stupid. I was twenty when I went in . . . a pretty girl. When I came out seven years later I was a hundred and twenty. Can you imagine it?"

I could. All too well. It was time for me to go home.

"You come see me again," she said, "and I'll read you some of my poems."

"Okay." But I didn't think I could stand it, to go back again.

There were two more slices of cake left, on a yellow china plate. How could she not like cake? Poor Miss Cohen.

When I got home, I looked all over for my communion dress, white with eyelet embroidery, and then I buried it in the very back of the closet where nobody, not even the Nazis, would ever find it, behind my father's old wedding suit that didn't fit anymore. All night long something tried to drag me through thick, hot air into the dark depths of the closet.

"You been up to 4-C, ain't you?" Katy-Ann Cooper skated around me in circles, her wheels rolling *thumpeta-thumpeta* over the sidewalk cracks.

"What's it to you?"

"My daddy says just because that lady's famous doesn't mean she's not a Jew and a Commie. He knows. He alla time used to listen to Father Coughlin. You should stay out of 4-C—she's nutso."

"Is not."

"Is so."

I wanted to grab that chain around Katy-Ann's neck, the one that held her St. Christopher medal and her skate key. I wanted to grab it and twist. Katy-Ann's big mouth was the one thing that made me decide to go back to 4-C.

Or maybe it was the two leftover pieces of coconut cake. Or maybe it was just because Miss Cohen said I should come, and I was a good girl who did what I was told.

They were horrible, Rachel Cohen's poems, two books of them, and some in magazines. We sat in the library by a table covered with medicine bottles. Tall brown ones with skinny necks. Small fat green jars. But the poems were beautiful/horrible, if you know what I mean. Like—fascinating. That's another good word, *fascinating*. Blood. Bone. Shoes and wedding rings and greasy smoke.

She read them out loud, one first and looked at me, and then another and looked at me, and then just when I wanted her to stop she wouldn't stop. I wanted to put my hands over my ears, but my mother taught me to be polite. I wanted to run out of the apartment. I got up to leave, but she kept me standing by the door while she read one about a red-haired guard named Heinrich.

Helpless. Helpless.
I was his brown-eyed
Dolly. His daily treat.
He gobbled me up in slices,
In blood and bone and ashes.
I was his nobody.
His nothing.
His sweetie, sweetie, sweetie.
Oh, shame. Oh, shame.
No mercy left to me.
No anodyne.

It was the worst of the poems and I had my hand on the knob of the library door, but that last word kept me there. I was . . . *snagged* . . . by it. "What's *an-o-dime* mean?"

"Anodyne. It means *painkiller*. I studied to be a pharmacist before the war. I learned all about the drugs you could take to ease pain. And cause it. Now I'm good for nothing but to sit in this damned chair—" she smacked the armrest. "Sit in this goddamned chair—and remember."

"What happens to people's souls to make them do such

. . . bad . . . things?" I really wanted to know, and I thought if anyone could tell me, she could. In spite of how much her poems terrified me, I kind of admired Miss Cohen. She knew all about words.

"That's the question, isn't it?" she replied.

"But not you and me, right? We could never do anything evil, right?"

"Maybe you'd better go home now, girlie."

I peeked in the kitchen on my way out. One slice of cake left, sitting under a glass dish. The red cherry tempted me, but I got past it okay. The faucet on the sink was dripping bad.

Outside, the sky was as hard and gray as the cracked sidewalk. Someone had drawn a potsy, but I didn't feel like hopping the squares. The red bricks on the walls of our five-story walk-up stared across the street at the yellow bricks of the elevator building. The mommas were talking Yiddish on their folding chairs, Mrs. Yellin rocking the big black carriage back and forth. I looked at them different. The Jewish mommas knew about the camps, for sure. Was that what they talked about in their weird foreign language? *Oy veh. Oy gevalt.*

Oy gevalt—my mother said only the Jews could come up with such a useful cosmic summary. *Cosmic. Summary.*

Oy gevalt.

I said hi to Mrs. Bradford, my father's bookie, and walked past her—right in the middle of the sidewalk as usual. No one could ever get me that way. Terrible things could happen to a little girl on her own. If I walked in the exact center of the sidewalk no one could grab me into a car at the curb or pull me into the cellar of a building. I was religious about it. Mrs. Bradford's peroxide hair was pinned up in curls underneath that ratty green wool scarf of hers, and she was carrying a string shopping bag with a tissue box in it. Everyone knew what the box was for—she hid the betting slips underneath the tissues. Mrs. B. was breaking the law. My father said it was no big deal, but I wondered: *Would Mrs. Bradford burn in hell? Would Adolf Hitler?*

Usually, running to Daitch Dairy for my mother, or to the butcher or the fish store, I stayed on the far side of the street from the huge brick Veterans Hospital with its green lawn and big trees behind the iron-spiked fence. My father said the soldiers in the hospital were ones that got hurt in the war. You saw them sometimes, in wheelchairs or wandering around the paved walks with whacked-out looks in their eyes. Usually I don't pay the place much attention, but that day I couldn't take my eyes off it. I don't remember crossing the street, but next thing I knew I'd grabbed an iron fence spike in each hand and was just standing there, staring in. My father said there was nothing to be scared of—the guys in that place were heroes. Some of them even went into the camps and liberated the Jews. He was in the war too, but I guess he wasn't a hero because he's not in a hospital and the shrapnel in his back only hurts when it's raining out, and he never, ever, talks about it. I watched a dark-haired man on crutches move toward me across the grass. He looked like a tall boy in a robe and striped pajamas. He was walking on one leg—the other one . . . just ended. No knee, no nothing. The man in the pajamas was inside the iron fence, I was outside. I couldn't stop staring at him. I couldn't let go of the bars. "Hey, girlie," he said. "What're you doin' here? God, look at you—aren't you a little sweetie?"

I screamed and ran, and he called after me, "What did I say? What did I say?" I zigzagged across Kingsbridge Road, still screaming and almost getting clobbered by a big cream-and-red bus. The sidewalk swarmed with people. Outside a Kosher bakery I dodged three baby carriages and Julian Levine from school. "Hey, *meshuggeneh*," he yelled, "what's the matter by you?" Sister Mary Michael from Our Lady stuck out her arm to stop me, but I slapped it away and kept going. I'll pay for that, I know, hitting a nun—even a gazillion "Hail Marys" won't atone. So many people on the sidewalk and they were all gonna die. Could it happen again? Like the Jews in the camps? Was Julian Levine gonna burn in an oven? Was Sister Mary Michael? Was I? I whipped past the big stone armory to Jerome Avenue, then up Jerome around the reservoir, past the colleges. It was all I could do to keep from howling the whole time. My legs pumped like those wheel rods on a freight train with cattle cars. What was I running from? From the man with the leg? From Miss Cohen's poems? I didn't know, but I couldn't stop. It was like something was sick in my stomach that I didn't want to vomit into my head. No, that doesn't make any sense. I ran like I had the Gestapo at my heels. I tripped on broken concrete and fell and skinned both knees, and it didn't slow me down one bit. When I turned onto the far end of Sedgwick, I knew I'd never get away from whatever was chasing me so I might as well go home.

In front of our building an ambulance idled, ashy smoke puffing from the tailpipe, revolving lights turning the neighbors' faces red and white. Blood and bone. Blood and bone. Ashes, blood, and bone. Two men in white carried a stretcher out from the courtyard. A sheet strained to cover a huge belly but missed the top of a red-bristled head. A couple of policemen followed the stretcher. One of them was my father.

I grabbed his hand. "Is that Mr. Schmidt?" I heard my voice rise to a screech.

"Yeah, it's Henry, all right—poor son of a bitch." He pulled the sheet from the gray face. "Looks like someone poisoned him. Vomit all down the stairs. Funniest thing—there was a big red maraschino cherry smack in the middle of it."

But I didn't need him to tell me that. Flecks of coconut were stuck to Mr. Schmidt's stubbly chin with lemon goo. It looked like the unbaked scones my mother painted with egg and sprinkles. His chin was like a raw lumpy coconut scone. I never wanted to eat again.

The kids were crowding around now. "That crazy killer lady in 4-C did it," Katy-Ann Cooper said. "Remember, you got her that coconut cake? I just know she did it."

"Shut your mouth, Katy-Ann," I hissed. "You don't know nothing."

That was two years ago. I was a kid. This morning, when I looked for the *Daily Mirror*, my mother lied to me. She said the papers didn't come. Then I saw them at the candy store on the corner. Big headlines—the *Mirror*, the *News*, the *Herald Tribune*.

Concentration Camp Victim's Appeal Fails.
Bronx Killer Gets Chair.
Rachel Cohen, Poet, to Die.

I'm looking for Katy-Ann Cooper right now. When I find her, I'm gonna give her the worst Indian burn of her whole entire life.

I think she'll burn in hell forever.

Somebody ought to.

THE WOMAN WHO HATED THE BRONX

BY RITA LAKIN

Elder Avenue

L inda Blue came from nothing and wanted everything. With the small amount of money she inherited from the last of her soul-numbing foster parents, she was able to go to nursing school. She became a nurse so she could marry a doctor. She would marry a doctor so she could become a doctor's wife. She didn't have the confidence to nab one who was already established, so she played the odds; she picked an easygoing, nice-looking young resident.

Frank Lombardi, who saw himself as just an average guy, thought Linda looked like the movie star Grace Kelly, aloof and unattainable. Grace was soon to become the Princess of Monaco and he felt he'd found a princess too. He was amazed at his good luck.

Linda chose Frank Lombardi as the answer to her prayers. He would save her.

The problem was, Linda picked wrong.

She didn't go to heaven. She went to hell.

He took her to back to the Bronx.

They'd had a whirlwind courtship. During their short engagement, she spelled out her dream, many times, in great detail. She would live in the country, perhaps near Scarsdale, in a pretty house with a little garden, and maybe one child.

He didn't hear her.

Frank shared his goal—giving back to all those who made it possible for a poor kid to get so far. He was talking about his family who supported him through med school and his friends and neighbors who encouraged him. So he intended to heal the sick in his old neighborhood. To take care of those who took care of him.

She was tuned into her own fantasies, and didn't listen.

She talked him into eloping. He wanted a wedding with family and friends. "I want to see my princess in a white gown." She told him she had no one to invite and that he should save his money for setting up his practice.

The first thing brand new Doctor Lombardi did before they left Newark in June was to buy a slightly used '50 Buick LeSabre—he thought the tail fins were nifty, and it was perfect to carry his adored wife to their new home. During the drive up from Jersey, Frank had been secretive about their destination. He couldn't wait to see her response to the place he'd picked out. Linda could hardly wait to see her dream house.

On route, he told her they had to start out modestly until he made some money. She told him she didn't care about money. She thought White Plains would be pretty too. She'd even thought about the new Levittown she'd read about in *Life* magazine. As she told him many times, she just needed peace and quiet.

On the Cross Bronx Expressway, she'd been dozing. When he turned at Bruckner Boulevard, she woke up and found herself looking at ugly brick buildings and vacant lots filled with trash and scruffy children playing in the streets. What shortcut was he taking? Was he lost? But in moments he stopped at a corner and parked. She read the two intersecting street signs, *Elder Avenue* and *Watson Avenue*.

"Where the hell are we?" she asked.

"The Bronx," he said proudly. "The East Bronx, to be exact. On the Pelham Bay elevated line."

She turned her face to the window and pressed her throbbing head against its coolness. *Oh God, no. Not the Bronx again.*

"What's the matter?" he asked.

She wouldn't look at him. "This place will be the death of me."

"Don't be silly. You're gonna love it here."

He helped her out of the car and grandly showed her around like a docent at a fine museum. "Welcome to my neighborhood. Look across the street." He pointed to a brick two-family house directly opposite. "I grew up in that house. Mama and Papa are on the left. My sister Connie and her husband Al and their kids live in the other. You'll meet them tonight."

So close? No, not so soon. I'm not ready for any of this . . .

He fondly recollected for her. "I played stickball in these streets. I rode my sled down that hill. I played *immies* in these gutters. God, it's great to be home." She turned away and he assumed she was ready for the rest of his tour.

"Here's our building. Six stories high."

What she saw were over-filled garbage cans. Dogs running loose. People. So many people. So much noise.

Practically shaking with excitement, Frank turned right and walked her to a door, the only break in the brick structure. "My office! My patients will use this entrance. And . . ." He led her again, this time into the three-sided courtyard. "Look at our great brick courtyard."

What she saw were little boys riding bikes dizzily around small patches of wire-enclosed dirt that looked like scraggly attempts at flower beds. The flowers were all dead. The boys shouted at one another, unmindful of anyone but themselves. Linda looked up. The sun was blocked by crisscrossed clothes lines filled with hanging laundry.

"Come on inside." Now he navigated her through the large lobby, where he hurried her to another door. Tarnished brass letters indicated it was apartment 1A. "Ta da! Our very own private entrance. Isn't it great?"

He took out a set of keys and opened the door. As Frank bent over to lift Linda and carry her over the threshold, they heard clapping.

"Put me down, Frank," she said. He did.

She looked around the lobby. It was very large, and had seen better days.

The floors were black and white tiled squares. With imitation Greek columns and metal ceilings and a long bank of mailboxes against the wall next to the elevator.

There were people in the lobby staring at them. A couple of old guys were playing chess at a card table with a third man watching them. Two women with baby strollers sat on a marble bench. A woman with groceries had just removed mail from her box. They were all grinning as they clapped.

"Hey, Frankie, you're back!" This from one of the chess players. To Linda he said, "I'm Irving Pinsky. 5F. You must be Frankie's new wife."

Frank waved. "Hey, Irv, it's *Doctor* Frankie now. Show some respect."

The lady with groceries said, "Welcome back from the Schwartz family too. Apartment 3D. I'm Helen," she said to Linda. To Frank she said, "So what's the bride's name?"

"This is Linda, my wife, and also gonna be my nurse. Isn't she gorgeous?"

Linda turned sharply at this unexpected piece of news. His nurse?

"Too good for the likes of you, you, *pisher.* Just call me Phil," the other chess player told Linda. A man who introduced himself as Sam teased Frank. "We always had Jewish doctors in this building. When Dr. Mayer retired to Miami, we didn't expect a *goyish kop* like you to show up."

Frank laughed aloud. "I promise I'll be just as good."

Phil shrugged. "Who said he was good?"

"Nice people, your in-laws," said one of the mothers, Alice. "They got great food in their Italian restaurant on Arthur Avenue. That's the Little Italy of the Bronx," she informed Linda.

She shuddered. *Don't tell me about the Bronx. I could tell you horror stories.*

"And speaking of food, don't mind the smell." Mrs. Schwartz pinched her nose with two fingers to make her point. "That's Flanagan in 1G. They always have corned beef and cabbage on Thursdays."

"Phew," agreed Irving. Turning to Mrs. Schwartz, he said, "And your *gribbines* don't smell all that great either. That chicken fat stinks up your floor pretty good."

She made a face and waved a dismissive hand at him.

"Hey, doc." Irving started to take a shoe off. "One of my big toes hurts. Could you take a look at it?"

Again Frank laughed. "Call my nurse for an appointment." He hugged Linda, who stiffened.

"What a blondie, such a cutie," the third man, Sam, commented with a leer. "She can take my temperature any time." There was group laughter at that.

"Frank, get me inside right now!" Linda grabbed his arm, squeezing it hard.

Frank waved again. "Gotta go. Just drove in. The little woman needs her rest."

With that, he lifted her up and carried her into 1A to a chorus of cheers.

When the door closed behind them, Frank faced his wife, beaming with pleasure. He waited for her to say something.

Linda turned away and walked from room to room examining the apartment.

"Swedish modern foam couches," Frank recited, following after her as she looked at the bilious green fabric covering hard-looking flat pillows that sat on wrought-iron frames. "The salesman said it was the latest thing."

He then flung himself into one of the plastic beanie bag "chairs" in the same ugly hue. He bounced around, legs flying upward, to show the fun of them.

She ignored him and continued down the dark hall. Frank dashed after her. The bathroom was small and also dark. She entered the next room and gasped. It was a nursery. Painted in blue. No furniture yet, but toys. Little boy's toys.

He grinned at her and shrugged. "Just thinking ahead."

Not here, never in this place, she thought.

He opened the master bedroom door for her with a flourish. She moved straight to the windows. She was chagrined to see they faced directly onto the courtyard. One of the kids on a bicycle rode by and stuck his tongue out at her. She quickly closed the curtains.

Frank continued his spiel. "And here's our *boudoir*. And there's our honeymoon bed, sweetheart."

Finally she turned to him, red in the face. "Shut up! Shut up!"

That night, with great trepidation, she met Frank's family—

aunts, uncles, cousins, and siblings—as they introduced themselves en masse at the big dinner held in the newlyweds' honor across the street in his parents' side of the two-family building. Too many people pushed in close to meet her. And to offer congratulations to the son who became a doctor. Frank's brother-in-law, Al, laughed. "Yeah, he'd do anything so he wouldn't have to work in the restaurant." Much agreeable laughter at that. She was offered antipasto, which she refused. And she was presented with more names she wouldn't remember.

"Our spaghetti sauce cooks for four hours, our secret recipe," Mama Lombardi told her proudly as she doled her out a huge portion. But Linda merely moved her fork around the plate.

"You marry a girl with no appetite?" Papa Lombardi asked, astonished.

Frank laughed. "Hey, she's gotta get used to you guys. Get your garlic breaths off of her. Let her breathe air."

After a massive dinner of six courses, which Linda only picked at, they finally reached the spumoni and espresso. The men lit up their huge cigars. And Mama asked the inevitable question.

"Linda, where are your folks?"

She spoke in a low, flat voice. "I have no family. I'm an orphan."

There was a silence at that. Mama crossed herself.

Frank put his arm around his wife. "Well, honey bun, you sure have one now."

The tense moment over, Papa grinned and said, "Welcome to *la famiglia*."

Frank turned the key in the lock and made his way back through the foyer into his parents' living room.

Knowing his brother could hear him, Vincent said, "It's what I always said about him. Frankie's such an easygoing guy. Ya have to kick him in the ass three times before he knows you're mad at him."

His sister Connie grinned. "Yeah, what a pushover. Girls always take advantage of him."

Frank addressed his siblings, also grinning. "Thanks for nothing. You're just jealous."

They laughed.

The immediate family was sitting around drinking more espresso "She's all right?" Mama offered him a cup.

"Just tired. Been a long day with a lot of new things to get used to."

Papa said, "I like her. She's quiet."

Mama gave him a gentle hit across his head. "You always were a sucker for the blondes." She patted her pitch-black hair, with the slight gray feathering at her forehead, and winked at him.

They sat quietly digesting.

Mama couldn't resist a shot of guilt. "You had to go and elope? And disappoint the whole family?"

"Mama, what else could I do? I told you, Linda had no one to invite. I didn't want to make her unhappy on her wedding day."

Mama sighed. "I understand. So, all right, she met everyone tonight."

"And we saved a bundle in wedding costs," Papa commented with satisfaction.

"And you lost a bundle in wedding gifts you didn't get, dummy," Connie laughed.

"I'm such a lucky guy." Frank sipped his espresso.

"She's not Catholic." Mama poured Papa his after-dinner *Strega*.

"Well, she ain't Jewish." Al beckoned his mother-in-law for another refill.

Connie put her two cents in. "Not Irish either." She pretended mock horror. "You mean we've got a Protestant in the family?" She laughed. "She will be so alone in this neighborhood."

Linda was alone but not for cultural or religious reasons. Linda belonged only to the darkness within herself. In the numbing blackness of a fog that never lifted. In a mind that shut off unbearable memories. She left the apartment only when she had to. She spent her days reading forgettable books or watching mindless television. She cleaned the house obsessively and cooked simple meals that filled the belly, but not the imagination. She waited for time to pass. She waited for a way to get out of here.

For a month, Frank whizzed about in a whirlwind of happiness, insensitive to his wife's lack of interest. Getting the office fixed up. Getting flyers out into the neighborhood. Though it seemed word of mouth was enough. *Mayer's gone, come see the new young doctor.* They were lining up at his door.

"Sure you don't want to help out?" he asked Linda on the fly. "I could really use my pretty nurse in the office." He intended to give her a peck on the lips, but she turned abruptly and he got her cheek.

"Find somebody else."

A week later, because it was so hot outside, Linda, carrying groceries, decided to take the shortcut through the outside office door to get to their own quarters. As she entered, a set of chimes rang out "O Sole Mio." She thought they were annoying, but Frank liked them because they'd been a house-warming gift from Connie.

Linda was surprised to see someone sitting at the appointment desk. She was somewhat older than Linda. The woman's long, thick black hair was piled haphazardly atop her head. Her blue eyes flashed. She obviously liked bright colors. She wore a dropped-shoulder red drawstring blouse and a multi-colored dirndl. And high heels. This exotic-seeming woman smiled widely at Linda and reached out her hand. She had a husky voice. "I'm Anna Marie. I've known Frankie all his life. I've been looking forward to meeting you."

Linda didn't return the gesture, so Anna Marie lifted an eyebrow and placed her hand back on the desk.

Linda looked closely. A wedding band.

"I'm helping out temporarily until he finds time to get someone else."

Linda glanced at her quickly to see if there was disapproval there. If there was, Anna Marie covered it.

Anna Marie reassured her that she wasn't a threat to the newly wedded Mrs. Lombardi. "I'm married to Frank's old friend Johnny. We all went to P.S. 93 together and then on to James Monroe High. Frank was the only one of us who went off to college."

Linda didn't comment, so Anna Marie had to fill the silence. "He got a scholarship, but you know all that . . ."

Luckily, Frank walked in from his examining room. He grinned. "At last the two loves of my life meet. I was mad about Anna until Johnny stole her from me," he said to Linda with a twinkle. "But all's well. We're happy, aren't we?"

Neither woman spoke. Linda was aware that Anna Marie was attempting to evaluate her.

Let her try, she thought.

The chimes were heard again as an elderly lady walked in the front door.

"Ah," Frank said, "here's Mrs. Green. Please get her chart, Anna." With that he went back to his office.

"Nice talking to you," Anna Marie said sarcastically.

"Yes," Linda replied, and walked past her to get to the inside apartment entrance.

In her fog she learned the streets of the neighborhood. A chubby couple, Betty and Burt, ran the luncheonette, called the *candy store* by one and all. Everyone gathered there. The men came to schmooze and read the sports pages in the *Daily News* or the *New York Post*. The young mothers dropped in for black-and-white sodas or a two-cents plain. The younger kids hung out after school, poking playfully at one another like bear cubs. The teenagers flirted and did their mating dance. At one time or another, just about everyone checked in at the candy store for the local gossip.

Linda knew some of the gossip was about her. She imagined them asking, *What do you make of her?* But she didn't care what they thought.

The grocery was next door. Murray used the stub of a pencil to add up Linda's purchases on the brown paper bag, as other customers sized her up. Were they wondering, *That Linda, who does she think she is—she stuck up or something?* She imagined so.

The butcher was next, and as she waited her turn the women gaped and looked at her brazenly. "Give the pretty doctor's wife a nice cut, Herman." This was from a frumpy-looking housewife trying for sarcasm.

I know what you're thinking. Linda stared back. *She some kinda snob? Right? Well, gossip all you want, you'll get nothing from me. I've got nothing to give.*

Up and down Watson Avenue the neighborhood lived and breathed. And Linda moved like a shadow, speaking only when spoken to. She was meticulous in her dress. She wore calf-length pencil-slim skirts and simple blouses with matching cardigans. Her hair was page-boy length, her outfits in muted colors. Looking as lifeless as she felt.

Nobody knew of the cancer that grew inside her. A cancer called the Bronx.

On an occasional Saturday night, when Frank could make time to go out, they spent it with his best friends. Linda had been introduced to Anna Marie's husband, Johnny. The three buddies were close, sharing childhood memories and private jokes. Frank worried about Linda feeling left out, but she didn't seem to mind. Sometimes they had dinner at Johnny and Anna Marie's apartment in Parkchester, in a fairly new development that was considered very classy for the East Bronx. Linda didn't like to cook so it was their place or eating out.

Tonight they ate at a deli and took in a movie at the Ward Theater. Afterwards, they went for a walk. Anna Marie and Linda lagged behind the men. Typically the guys sauntered ahead to gab about sports and cars and other male subjects and the girls were expected to talk girl stuff.

The guys passed a store that featured sexy underwear. Johnny stopped and whistled at a red bra and matching garter belt. "Whooey. That's my Christmas present for Anna Marie this year. What about something like that for Linda?"

Frank shook his head. "She's not the type."

Johnny finally had to ask. "What type is she—that wife

of yours? What's with her? Can't she help out and sit in your office? What else does she have to do?"

"She's different," Frank told his buddy. "She's shy and fragile."

"Crazy. You have to pay Anna Marie a salary when you're just starting out?"

"I don't mind."

Johnny shrugged "Well, it's your funeral."

Linda walked with Anna Marie who chatted about items in the windows. She laughed when she saw the red lingerie.

Linda gagged at the sight and stopped short. She felt faint and grabbed for a wall.

"I bet I know what Johnny was saying." Anna Marie stopped when she realized Linda was no longer beside her. She turned. "Hey."

"What?" Linda could barely speak. *No . . . no, not those memories . . . go away . . .*

"What? What's with you? I'm trying to be friendly and hold up my end of the conversation and I get nothing back. You don't talk about clothes. Or the movie we just saw, or even Frankie. What goes through that head of yours?"

Linda's voice was so low that Anna Marie could barely hear her. "All I think about is how to get out of the Bronx."

When Linda, to her shock, realized she was pregnant, she didn't tell Frank. She prayed it would go away. But after watching her race to the bathroom to throw up enough times, and realizing her breasts were swollen, the doctor quickly figured it out. He was thrilled. He started calling her his Madonna. Even though she told him not to, Frank immediately announced the good news to his entire family. Of course, they all wanted to be part of it. Connie took her out to buy maternity clothes, not that she really needed them. She couldn't keep much food down and stayed thin. Connie's husband Al worked in a furniture store, so they got baby furniture at a discount.

It didn't take long for the neighbors to find out, and they got into the act as well, bringing her casseroles so she wouldn't have to cook. Frank did the cooking after work or Mama Lombardi had food sent over from the restaurant. Mrs. Schwartz brought down her famous Kosher chicken soup. Mrs. Lee from the Chinese laundry carried over her egg drop soup. Mrs. Flanagan made a huge pot of potato soup. The strength and variety of smells made Linda throw up even more. The entire building was involved in trying to keep the doctor's skinny wife fed.

And the new baby-to-be, clothed. Bassinets were put together. Little blankets were crocheted. And infant sweaters and caps, as well. People were dropping in all the time with their offerings. What little privacy she had was gone.

Frank surprised her one day by bringing home an insurance policy on his life.

"Why did you do that?" she asked. "I would never ask you to do that."

He kissed her gently. "Never say never." As he was about to head to his office, he informed her, "Now that I'll have a son, I want him protected if anything happens to me." Frank was sure it would be a boy.

"Frank."

He turned. "What, my darling little Madonna?"

"I can't take pain. I'm so afraid."

He came back and held her close for a moment. "I'll be nearby, so don't you worry." Then he left.

"I can't stand anymore pain," she said to the closed door.

Linda was aware that all the Lombardis were in the waiting room of Montefiore Hospital the night she gave birth. She knew that Frank was pacing worriedly outside the door, as expectant fathers do. What good did it do her? Let him hear his wife screaming. He knew nothing of her pain. He knew nothing about being torn apart so badly, so many times before, that giving birth was a new pain beyond endurance.

The OR nurses tried to hold her down, but she was too strong for them. Arms flailing, the next scream was blood-curdling. "Damn you, Dyre! Damn you!"

"Push!" urged the doctor.

She pushed, her fingernails digging into the sheet, and shouted, "Prospect!" at the top of her lungs.

And at the final push, the pain more horrific than before, "Damn you to hell, Burnside!"

She fainted. When she came to, her doctor was gone and she listened to the nurses talking about her. The one bending over the bassinet that held her six-pound infant girl said, "Did you ever hear anything like that in your life?"

Her partner agreed. "In all my years they yelled for husbands, for God, or cursing, sobbing, and screaming, but I never heard anyone cry out, *Dyre*."

"Or *Prospect* or *Burnside*. What do you make of it?"

"Who knows? She's peculiar, that one."

You don't want to know, Linda thought. She had dared not call out their names, the ones who murdered her childhood with their foul misuse of her body. Which had they damaged more—her body or her mind? Those foster folks who promised to care for her, who debased her instead. On streets in the Bronx where she had been forced to live. Where her pain had been excruciating and her blood had spilled. She could still see that trembling nine-year-old being forced into sleazy lingerie, her mouth smeared with lipstick, and a monster bearing down on her. But she could shout out those names—that litany of shame—those Bronx street names. Places she thought she had escaped . . . but there was no escape, was there?

Baby Frances (no longer Frank, Jr.) was adored by one and all. Frank was driven to work even harder for his darling little girl. He was taking more and more house calls in addition to his full days at the office.

Frank came home one night, shaken, and told Linda that a doctor on Morris Avenue had been shot by a burglar who climbed in his window to get drugs. He lived on the ground floor too.

He showed her the gun he had bought. Linda was shocked. "I would never want that in our apartment. Not with a child."

He reassured her they'd probably never need it, but for safety's sake it was going to stay in his bedside drawer. He was going to teach her how to use it. "Besides," he said, joking, "the gun probably won't work, knowing Vince's shady friends who got it for him." And he reminded her once again, "Never say never. You never know when you might change your mind about something."

This was her chance and she grabbed at it. "Frank, dear. Now that we have Frances, isn't it time to leave the city? It's getting so dangerous. Can't we move somewhere quiet in the country where Frances will have a better life? . . . Please?"

"Let me think about it."

A few days later he told her he had thought about it. He loved the city. It was a great place to grow up. Didn't he turn out fine? Think of the good schools and the parks. The museums. And all the friendly people. Besides, he didn't want to deprive his family of closeness to their new grandchild. So the answer was no.

Linda lost all hope.

Six unhappy months later, she was awakened from her sleep by a sound. Linda turned to Frank's side of the bed. He wasn't there; he'd gone out on a house call. It was hard for her to pull herself awake because of the sleeping pills she took every night. She squinted at the alarm clock. It was nearly 2 a.m. It took her a few moments to focus. There was a shadow at the window facing the courtyard. She had forgotten to close the curtains. She stiffened. Someone was there. A nosy neighbor? No, it looked like he was dressed in black. With a pasty white face pressed against the glass.

Linda felt her skin crawl. Covering her head with the blanket, she groped for the phone. With shaking hands, she dialed the operator. Her breath raspy from fatigue and terror, she whispered, "Call the police. A prowler, someone's in my courtyard." She gave the operator her address. Moments later, the operator said the police were on their way.

Linda's heart hammered against her chest as she peered over the blanket. The prowler was gone. She bolted out to the baby's room. *Thank God, she's asleep!* She stared at little Frances in her crib. Her throat tightened, on the verge of sobbing. *I'll never let anyone hurt you. Never.*

Why wasn't her husband here to protect her when she needed him?

Linda had no idea how long she had been standing at the crib when the police arrived. They searched the courtyard, and all around the building, found nothing. They were blasé—

routine stuff for them. They told her not to worry—probably some passing neighbor or a Peeping Tom—they're harmless. He was probably miles away by now.

Suddenly she remembered the gun, and suddenly she wanted the police to get out. When they left, she hurried to their bedroom and removed it from Frank's drawer and held it. She thought of the life insurance policy. *Never say never,* he'd said. She giggled. And Frank was always right. *It's now or never.*

Moving as if in a trance, she took a towel and wrapped her iron in it and opened the kitchen window. She reached outside and smashed in the other side of the window, making sure the glass fell inward.

Linda stood in the kitchen for what seemed like hours. When she heard Frank's key in the lock, she dialed the police again. "Hurry," she sobbed, "the prowler's come back!"

Frank was surprised to see her. "What are you doing up so late?" When Frank moved toward her, she raised the gun and fired.

Frank had been right about Vince's contacts. The gun was faulty and it exploded, killing Linda as Frank watched in horror.

The family tearfully buried her in a nearby cemetery. All the neighbors came to pay their respects.

Linda had also been right. She knew the Bronx would never let her go. She would be stuck there for all eternity.

PART II

IN THE STILL OF THE NIGHT

RUDE AWAKENING

BY LAWRENCE BLOCK

Riverdale

She woke up abruptly—*click!* Like that, no warmup, no transition, no ascent into consciousness out of a dream. She was just all at once awake, brain in gear, all of her senses operating but sight. Her eyes were closed, and she let them remain that way for a moment while she picked up what information her other senses could provide.

She felt the cotton sheet under her, smooth. A good hand, a high thread count. Her host, then, wasn't a pauper, and had the good taste to equip himself with decent bed linen. She didn't feel a top sheet, felt only the air on her bare skin. Cool, dry air, air-conditioned air.

Whisper-quiet too. Probably central air-conditioning, because she couldn't hear it. She couldn't hear much, really. A certain amount of city noise, through windows that were no doubt shut to let the central air do its work. But less of it than she'd have heard in her own Manhattan apartment.

And the energy level here was more muted than you would encounter in Manhattan. Hard to say what sense provided this information, and she supposed it was probably some combination of them all, some unconscious synthesis of taste and touch and smell and hearing that let you know you were in one of the outer boroughs.

Memory filled in the rest. She'd taken the 1 train clear to the end of the line, following Broadway up into the Bronx, and she'd gone to a couple of bars in Riverdale, both of them nice preppy places where the bartenders didn't look puzzled when you ordered a Dog's Breakfast or a Sunday Best. And then . . .

Well, that's where it got a little fuzzy.

She still had taste and smell to consult. Taste, well, the taste in her mouth was the taste of morning, and all it did was make her want to brush her teeth. Smell was more complicated. There would have been more to smell without air-conditioning, more to smell if the humidity were higher, but nevertheless there was a good deal of information available. She noted perspiration, male and female, and sex smells.

He was right there, she realized. In the bed beside her. If she reached out a hand she could touch him.

For a moment, though, she let her hand stay where it was, resting on her hip. Eyes still closed, she tried to bring his image into focus, even as she tried to embrace her memory of the later portion of the evening. She didn't know where she was, not really. She managed to figure out that she was in a relatively new apartment building, and she figured it was probably in Riverdale. But she couldn't be sure of that. He might have had a car, and he might have brought her almost anywhere. Westchester County, say.

Bits and pieces of memory hovered at the edge of thought. Shreds of small talk, but how could she know what was from last night and what was bubbling up from past evenings? Sense impressions: a male voice, a male touch on her upper arm.

She'd recognize him if she opened her eyes. She couldn't picture him, not quite, but she'd know him when her eyes had a chance to refresh her memory.

Not yet.

She reached out a hand, touched him.

She had just registered the warmth of his skin when he spoke.

"Sleeping beauty," he said.

Her eyes snapped open, wide open, and her pulse raced.

"Easy," he said. "My God, you're terrified, aren't you? Don't be. Everything's all right."

He was lying on his side facing her. And yes, she recognized him. Dark hair, arresting blue eyes under arched brows, a full-lipped mouth, a strong jawline. His nose had been broken once and imperfectly reset, and that saved him from being male-model handsome.

Late thirties, maybe eight or ten years her senior. A good body. A little chest hair, but not too much. Broad shoulders. A stomach flat enough to show a six-pack of abs.

No wonder she'd left the bar with him.

And she remembered leaving the bar. They'd walked, so she was probably in Riverdale. Unless they'd walked to his car. Could she remember any more?

"You don't remember, do you?"

Reading her mind. And how was she supposed to answer that one?

She tried for an ironic smile. "I'm a little fuzzy," she said.

"I'm not surprised."

"Oh?"

"You were hitting the Cosmos pretty good. I had the feeling, you know, that you might be in a blackout."

"Really? What did I do?"

"Nothing they'd throw you in jail for."

"Well, that's a relief."

"You didn't stagger or slur your words, and you were able to form complete sentences. Grammatical ones too."

"The nuns would be proud of me."

"I'm sure they would. Except . . ."

"Except they wouldn't like to see me waking up in a strange bed."

"I'm not sure how liberal they're getting these days," he said. "That wasn't what I was going to say."

"Oh."

"You didn't know where you were, did you? When you opened your eyes."

"Not right away."

"Do you know now?"

"Well, sure," she said. "I'm here. With you."

"Do you know where *here* is? Or who I am?"

Should she make something up? Or would the truth be easier?

"I don't remember getting in a car," she said, "and I do remember walking, so my guess is we're in Riverdale."

"But it's a guess."

"Well, couldn't we call it an educated guess? Or at least an informed one?"

"Either way," he said, "it's right. We walked here, and we're in Riverdale."

"So I got that one right. But why wouldn't the nuns be proud of me?"

"Forget the nuns, okay?"

"They're forgotten."

"Look, I don't want to get preachy. And it's none of my business. But if you're drinking enough to leave big gaps in your memory, well, how do you know who you're going home with?"

Whom, she thought. *The nuns wouldn't be proud of you, buster.*

She said, "It worked out all right, didn't it? I mean, you're an okay guy. So I guess my judgment was in good enough shape when we hooked up."

"Or you were lucky."

"Nothing wrong with getting lucky." She grinned as she spoke the line, but he remained serious.

"There are a lot of guys out there," he said, "who aren't okay. Predators, nut cases, bad guys. If you'd gone home with one of those—"

"But I didn't."

"How do you know?"

"How do I know? Well, here we are, both of us, and . . . What do you mean, how do I know?"

"Do you remember my name?"

"I'd probably recognize it if I heard it."

"Suppose I say three names, and you pick the one that's mine."

"What do I get if I'm right?"

"What do you want?"

"A shower."

This time he grinned. "It's a deal. Three names? Hmmm. Peter. Harley. Joel."

"Look into my eyes," she said, "and say them again. Slowly."

"What are you, a polygraph? Peter. Harley. Joel."

"You're Joel."

"I'm Peter."

"Hey, I was close."

"Two more tries," he said, "and you'd have had it for sure. You told me your name was Jennifer."

"Well, I got that one right."

"And you told me to call you Jen."

"And did you?"

"Did I what?"

"Call me Jen."

"Of course. I can take direction."

"Are you an actor?"

"As sure as my name is Joel. Why would you . . . Oh, because I said I could take direction? Actually, I had ambitions in that direction, but by the time I got out of college I smartened up. I work on Wall Street."

"All the way downtown. What time is it?"

"A little after 10."

"Don't you have to be at your desk by 9?"

"Not on Saturday."

"Oh, right. Uh, Peter . . . or do I call you Pete?"

"Either one."

"Awkward question coming up. Did we . . ."

"We did," he said, "and it was memorable for one of us."

"Oh."

"I felt a little funny about it, because I had the feeling you weren't entirely present. But your body was really into it, no matter where your mind was, and, well . . ."

"We had a good time?"

"A very good time. And, just so that you don't have to worry, we took precautions."

"That's good to know."

"And then you, uh, passed out."

"I did?"

"It was a little scary. You just went out like a light. For a minute I thought, I don't know . . ."

"That I was dead," she supplied.

"But you were breathing, so I ruled that out."

"That keen analytical mind must serve you well on Wall Street."

"I tried to wake you," he said, "but you were gone. So I let you sleep. And then I fell asleep myself, and, well, here we are."

"Naked and unashamed." She yawned, stretched. "Look," she said, "I'm going to treat myself to a shower, even if I didn't win the right in the *Name That Stud* contest. Don't go away, okay?"

The bathroom had a window, and one look showed that she was on a high floor, with a river view. She showered, and washed her hair with his shampoo. Then she borrowed his toothbrush and brushed her teeth diligently, and gargled with a little mouthwash.

When she emerged from the bathroom, wrapped in the big yellow towel, the aroma of fresh coffee led her into the kitchen, where he'd just finished filling two cups. He was wearing a white terry robe with a nautical motif, dark blue anchors embroidered on the pockets. His soft leather slippers were wine-colored.

Gifts, she thought. Men didn't buy those things for themselves, did they?

"I made coffee," he said.

"So I see."

"There's cream and sugar, if you take it."

"Just black is fine." She picked up her cup, breathed in the steam that rose from it. "I might live," she announced. "Do you sail?"

"Sail?"

"The robe. Anchors aweigh and all that."

"Oh. I suppose I could, because I don't get seasick or anything. But no, I don't sail. I have another robe, if you'd be more comfortable."

"With anchors? Actually, I'm comfortable enough like this."

"Okay."

"But if I wanted to be even more comfortable . . ." She let the towel drop to the floor, noted with satisfaction the way his eyes widened. "How about you? Wouldn't you be more comfortable if you got rid of that sailor suit?"

Afterward she propped herself up on an elbow and looked down at him. "I feel much much better now," she announced.

"The perfect hangover cure?"

"No, the shower and the coffee took care of the hangover. This let me feel better about myself. I mean, the idea of hooking up and not remembering it . . ."

"You'll remember this, you figure?"

"You bet. What about you, Peter? Will you remember?"

"Till my dying day."

"I'd better get dressed and head on home."

"And I can probably use a shower," he said. "Unless you want to . . ."

"You go ahead. I'll have another cup of coffee while you're in there."

Her clothes were on the chair, and she dressed quickly, then picked up her purse and checked its contents. The little glassine envelope was still in there, and unopened.

God, she'd been drunk.

She went into the kitchen, poured herself more coffee, and considered what was left in the pot. *No, leave it,* she thought, and turned her attention to the bottle of vodka on the sinkboard.

Had they had drinks when they got to his place? Probably. There were two glasses next to the bottle, and he hadn't gotten around to washing them.

What a shock he'd given her! The touch, the unexpected warmth of his skin. And then his voice.

She hadn't expected that.

She uncapped the bottle, opened the glassine envelope, poured its contents in with the vodka. The crystals dissolved immediately. She replaced the cap on the bottle, returned the empty envelope to her purse.

She made her cup of coffee last until he was out of the shower and dressed in khakis and a polo shirt, which was evidently what a Wall Street guy wore on the weekend. "I'll get out of your hair now," she told him. "And I'm sorry about last night. I'm going to make it a point not to get quite that drunk again."

"You've got nothing to apologize for, Jen. You were running a risk, that's all. For your own sake—"

"I know."

"Hang on and I'll walk you to the subway."

She shook her head. "Really, there's no need. I can find it."

"You're sure?"

"Positive."

"If you say so. Uh, can I have your number?"

"You really want it?"

"I wouldn't ask if I didn't."

"Next time I won't pass out. I promise."

He handed her a pen and a notepad, and she wrote down her area code, *212*, and picked seven digits at random to keep it company. And then they kissed, and he said something sweet, and she said something clever in response, and she was out the door.

The streets were twisty and weird in that part of Riverdale, but she asked directions and somebody pointed her toward the subway. She waited on the elevated platform and thought about how shocked she'd been when she opened her eyes.

Because he was supposed to be dead. That was how it worked—she put something in the guy's drink and it took effect one or two hours later. After they'd had sex, after he'd dozed off or not. His heart stopped, and that was that.

Usually she'd stay awake herself, and a couple of times she'd been able to watch it happen. Then, when he was gone, she'd go through the apartment at leisure and take what was worth taking.

It worked like a charm. But it only worked if you put the crystals in the guy's drink, and if you were too drunk to manage that, well, you woke up and there he was.

Bummer.

Sooner or later, she thought, he'd take the cap off the vodka bottle. Today or tomorrow or next week, whenever he got around to it. And he'd take a drink, and one or two hours later he'd be cooling down to room temperature. She wouldn't be there to scoop up his cash or go through his dresser drawers, but that was all right. The money wasn't really the point.

Maybe he'd have some other girl with him. Maybe they'd both have a drink before hitting the mattress, and they could die in each other's arms. Like Romeo and Juliet, sort of.

Or maybe she'd have a drink and he wouldn't. That would be kind of interesting, when he tried to explain it all to the cops.

A pity she couldn't be a fly on the wall. But she'd find out what happened. Sooner or later, there'd be something in the papers. All she had to do was wait for it.

BURNOUT

BY SUZANNE CHAZIN

Jerome Avenue

When does something happen for the last time? Do you get a sign that Mike Boyle missed somewheres? For sure, it was that way with Gina. One minute, they were doing the usual dance—fighting and screaming and her throwing the lasagna pan at him and then making up and making out and all the sweet heat in between. And then *bam*, it's all different. Like a Yankee's pitching streak gone south. Instead of throwing the pan, she throws his duffel bag. "Go live with your other family!" she yells. "You like them better anyways." She means the guys down at the firehouse on Jerome Avenue. That was six weeks ago. Forty-three days. More than a thousand hours and counting. And sex wasn't the only thing that died for Mike Boyle that night. Something else died too—something even more important, if there was such a thing.

Mike Boyle forgot how to sleep.

Oh, he could lie down on his bunk. He could slip blinders over his eyes to shut out the fluorescents that automatically flick on when there's a run. He could stuff foam plugs in his ears to mute the peal of sirens and the deep throttle of the diesel engines. But the plugs were about as useful as a Band-Aid on a bullet wound. Who could stop noise that reverberated through every pore of your body? If it wasn't the static-charged dispatch reports over the department airwaves, then it was the gut-wrenching roar of the roof saws the fire-fighters started every morning. Or the air horn jackhammer-ing the nerves as the truck or engine (this was a double house) barreled out of quarters. Slamming lockers. Ringing phones. Guys snoring. Guys farting. Rufus, the firehouse dog, barking. All of it twenty-four-seven in the tiled echo chamber of an FDNY firehouse.

"You look like hell," Captain Russo had told Mike just before he started his shift the other evening. Mike was at the kitchen table, slumped over a chipped mug of coffee, stirring in spoonfuls of Cremora. Whole worlds of thought went into each swirl so that when he finally looked up at the captain, it seemed he was being lip-synced in a foreign film.

"I'm good," said Mike, already unsure what remarks he was addressing. He noticed he had difficulty following con-versations these days. Time seemed to compress and expand randomly, like pulled taffy. Espresso—that's what he'd ask the guys to buy next time they shopped on Arthur Avenue. Maybe a dark roast that he could drink with a little lemon peel the way some of the old Italians who still live over in Belmont do. He pulled out a pack of cigarettes from his pants pocket and lit one, watching the smoke curl upwards, a gray plume to go with the white one in his coffee. Smoking was banned in city firehouses. It said so right on the bulletin board behind him—the one with all the burn marks in it. There are city laws. And then there are firehouse laws.

"Don't you have some place besides the firehouse to stay?" the captain pressed. "I mean, look at you. This is no life."

Even in the best of times, Mike Boyle never looked robust. He was Irish pale—with skin like gauze that showed every blotch, from the flush of a single beer to the shadows of a little missed sleep. His fine hair—maybe blond, maybe brown, depending on the light—tended to take the shape of any pillow or fire helmet that laid claim to it. He'd taken to wearing his navy-blue uniform pants and T-shirts around the clock, even sleeping in them.

"I'd rather stay here," said Mike. Moving someplace—in with his brother Patrick's family in Yonkers, or his sister Mary and her tight-ass lawyer of a husband over in Riverdale—that would mean this thing with Gina was real. If he stayed in the firehouse, time would stand still. A watch just waiting for a new battery. All he had to do was stick it out a little longer.

Captain Russo started to say something, then seemed to think better of it. He was a dinosaur in the department—one of the last around to recall the Bronx of the 1970s and early '80s, when whole blocks blazed like Roman candles, and firefighters sucked down equal parts black smoke and Budweiser on every tour. Whether it was smoking or leaving your wife, he wasn't inclined to argue the particulars of how any man lived his life.

And besides, on shifts at least, Mike was still pulling his weight. He pumped himself full of nicotine and caffeine and kept busy—making beds, fixing meals, washing the rig. When the alarm sounded, the adrenaline kicked in. Break a window, cut a hole in a roof, climb a ladder, take a door. As anyone who's seen combat will tell you, you can pretty much keep going when the shit hits the fan. It was the empty, off-duty hours that were killing him. Even the simplest tasks seemed monumental. He started to toast a bagel one day, then watched with no particular interest as black ribbons of smoke emanated from the toaster. It was Tig—firefighter Jimmy Francesco—who unplugged the toaster and fished the cremated bagel out. All the while Mike just watched, not even sure if he'd really been hungry in the first place. When a firefighter in the engine company mentioned that he was going in the hospital for stomach surgery, Mike found himself daydreaming about the man's anesthesia. Right now, he'd gladly trade a gut full of staples for a few hours of blankness.

When the insomnia first hit, Mike fought it by driving his car up to his former house—a semi-attached stucco in Woodlawn across from the cemetery. He parked across the street and imagined Gina inside sleeping, wrapped up in one of his old FDNY T-shirts. Except she wasn't—not one night anyway. She never came home. Then his car got stolen—he'd parked it too far from the firehouse doors. (The guys on duty got first dibs on the "safe" spots.) That ended his evening excursions.

"If my wife kicked me out, I'd go home and beat the crap out of her." Marital advice from Chuck of all people, the senior man in Ladder 123. Twenty-two years in the same firehouse and he still insisted on driving the rig all the way over to Arthur Avenue to buy groceries from the Italians. "I don't buy from these," he'd say, bringing the flat of his hand in front of his face: firehouse code for blacks. Chuck's real name wasn't Charles. It was Harry. Harry McGreevy. Chuck was short for "chuckles," firehouse black humor. No one ever accused Harry McGreevy of being lighthearted. To Chuck, women were whores or lesbians, kids were parasites (he should know, he had five, all grown with two still living at home in Throgs Neck), and the city was personally out to screw him. His hobby was writing up parking tickets (a power no other firefighter in Mike's memory had ever invoked). And he spent much of every tour talking about his theory that intelligence was inversely related to how close your ancestors lived to the equator. Mike wondered whether that meant people in the Bronx had a leg up over the other boroughs, but he wasn't taking bets on it.

"My church runs a prayer group for couples." More advice. This time from Frankie Bones—a.k.a., Frank Bonaventura—the biggest guy in the firehouse. Six-foot-four, three hundred and fifty pounds, he looked like a Mafia enforcer out of central casting and used to have a reputation to match. But about ten years ago, Bones and his wife found Jesus and it had transformed him entirely. Of course, the joke around the firehouse was that if Frankie Bones went looking for you, you'd better damn well be found.

"I'm not religious," Mike reminded him.

"The Lord works in mysterious ways."

"None more mysterious than you," Chuck told Bones. Being senior, Chuck could say anything he wanted, even to Bones.

"Hey, man," Jimmy Francesco piped up, "you can stay at my place."

It figured that Tig, of all the firefighters, would make the offer. Francesco was everyone's favorite firefighter, nicknamed after the Disney character Tigger because he was always bouncing around, ready for action. Too much action, as Mike saw it now. If his hands weren't slapping his thighs, then he was doing a drumroll on the table. Or stroking the ever-needy Rufus. Tig had been a cop briefly before joining the FDNY, but no one could picture him arresting people. If he ever managed to collar some gangbanger, he'd have probably let him off with some cheery Disney advice like, *Don't do that again, buddy boy, okaly-dokely?*

"We've got the spare bedroom," said Tig. "At least until the baby comes."

Mike watched Tig doing a drumroll on the table and wondered what twenty-four hours of that would feel like. Wondered how his wife stood it. A baby thumping at her insides, a husband doing the same from without.

"Naw. Thanks anyway. I'm good."

Well, maybe not good. But insomnia did have its up side, even if it seemed to take longer and longer for Mike to tie his shoes or fit together two lengths of hose. The less sleep he got, the more he noticed he could manage without it. Had he really been spending a third of his life in willing oblivion? Death before death, as he saw it now. He watched firefighters napping in their bunks, people dozing on the subways, and he studied them with almost scientific detachment. They were dying every day and they didn't even know it, slipping into their own private heaven and hell. Maybe that's all heaven and hell was anyway, a longer bit of sleep.

"I'm filing for separation," Gina told him over the pay phone at the firehouse one day. "I think we should call your folks."

The morning crew was testing the saws and two other guys were arguing the Yankees batting lineup, so it took him a minute to process the news.

"Was it the uniform?" he asked finally.

"What?"

"The uniform. My coat. My helmet. The big red truck that went *ding ding* through your neighborhood?"

"You're not making any sense, Mike."

"You get turned on by a little Nomex cloth and plastic?"

She said something after that, but Mike couldn't hear. The guys on duty had a run. Curses. Shouts. Feet slapping the rubber mat as they slid down the pole. The diesel throttling. The gears in the apparatus door cranking away as they rolled up to reveal the hot, steamy August morning heat and the vague smell of urine on the pavement.

"You even know who I am?" He wasn't sure if he'd said those words or just thought them before hanging up. It was hard to tell over the noise.

For a blessed moment after the truck pulled away, it seemed to suck all the noise with it. He didn't feel the rumble of the Jerome Avenue elevated overhead or the honk and grind of buses and gypsy cabs on the blistering street. Then the great doors closed again and he felt for one panicked moment like he was drowning.

He needed a cup of coffee. (*Gotta get that espresso with the lemon peel.*) And a couple of smokes too. And then what? The rush would last twenty minutes tops, then he'd forget how to connect a hose, or which way the walkie-talkie batteries went in. He'd write the wrong month in the housewatch book. He'd dial the wrong combination to his locker.

What he needed was to get out. But without wheels, his options were limited. This was Tremont, after all. What wasn't paved over in housing projects and six-story crackerbox apartments was covered with storefront strips of check cashing joints, bodegas, liquor stores, and Pentecostal churches. The heat made the days untenable. And at night, what pale-faced Irishman was likely to feel at home here?

It was Rufus who finally drove him out. Rufus, that rangy, bowlegged mutt who suffered the animal equivalent of a panic attack every time the firefighters left on a run. Mike couldn't sleep when the firefighters were in quarters and Rufus couldn't sleep when they were out. A walk would do them both good.

So he tied a length of rope around Rufus's collar late that night and off they went, the dog—part retriever, part Sherman tank—gleeful at their escape. Rufus plowed along the boulevard with the determined gusto of an evangelist. He liked everyone—toddlers in soggy underwear dancing under the sprays of uncapped fire hydrants; fat old women in housedresses drinking beer on tenement stoops; drunks slugging it out for the right to bed down under an overpass. None of it tired him out. Or Mike, for that matter. But it did give him an odd feeling of liberation to be crisscrossing housing projects at 2 a.m., sidestepping the hulking young men with looks as sharp as razor wire.

He called Gina when he got back. Woke her up. At least she was there. He felt giddy and a little breathless from his walk.

"You had no idea who I was, did you?"

"Who else would call me at this hour?"

"I mean when I first asked you out."

"I don't remember."

"You'd met me twice. Through your cousin Maria. And you still didn't know who I was when I asked you out."

"That was a long time ago."

"Four and a half years is not a long time ago." He found himself gulping for air. He hadn't walked that hard. Maybe it was panic. He had the same sensation when he crawled down a smoke-charged hallway. He was heading into something he couldn't see that would only do him harm. "You know when you remembered me? When I told you I was Mike the firefighter."

"So?"

"Like I said, it was about the coat. It was always about the coat."

"Mike?" Her voice was hoarse and tentative. "I've met someone."

He hung up. He'd bailed out of enough windows to know something about outrunning flames. No point in standing there, letting yourself get burned. Maybe she would call back and tell him it was all a mistake. Maybe she would be tearful and apologetic. For the first time in nearly seven weeks he longed for noise, and that damn phone never made a sound. He was shadow-boxing with himself.

* * *

"Hey, Mikey," Chuck growled the next morning, "you want to be target practice for the natives, go ahead. But Rufus doesn't need any shell-casings as souvenirs."

"I thought a walk would help me sleep."

"They put a bullet through you, brother, you'll sleep. Trust me."

Tig got him alone in the locker room the next day—they were on the same shift—and handed him a gym bag. "If you're gonna walk around this neighborhood all hours, least you should do is take this." Inside was Tig's old NYPD windbreaker and an authentic-looking replica of his badge. All the guys had replicas made so they could keep the real ones at home. That way, if you lost it, you wouldn't face departmental charges.

"Thanks," said Mike, stuffing the bag in his locker. He felt guilty he wasn't more appreciative of Tig's generosity, then angry that Tig never seemed to notice. The man was awash in admiration, the sun in all its glory. What difference was the light of one more star?

"I figured most people will think twice before messing with a cop," said Tig. "Just don't let it get out that I did this, okay? I shouldn't have a copy of my badge when I don't have the real one anymore. The PD might get sore at me."

"I'm good," said Mike. Whatever that meant. It was all he could manage of conversation these days. Lately, he'd begun to confuse words, calling Bones's decision to become a Jesus groupie his "salivation," and Chuck's worldviews, somewhere to the right of the Michigan Militia, his "egotistical theory." Not that those interpretations were entirely incorrect. Still, it irked him the way his thoughts seemed to fly around like mosquitoes these days, tormenting and annoying him, without the sweet reprieve of sleep.

Mike continued his walks alone at night. Of course, in Tremont *alone* was a relative term. Even at 3 a.m., salsa and rap blared from open windows along with the smell of fried porkchops, rice and beans. Beer bottles shattered on concrete. Dirty diapers dropped off the edges of fire escapes. Car alarms whooped. Trains rumbled overhead. Babies wailed. Fights spilled out of doorways like liquid mercury, carried along on whatever current picked them up.

No one bothered Mike. The NYPD jacket and badge probably helped. But he suspected he inhabited the jacket the same way he inhabited his turnout coat. He wasn't a cop any more than he was a firefighter. Not in his marrow—not like some of the guys. Not like Tig. He knew this when he saw Tig lower himself unflinchingly into a fire-charged room or push forward when his alarm told him he had just minutes of air left in his tank. Never a minute of self-doubt or hesitation. Three fucking years in the FDNY and the guy was more of a firefighter than Mike, with his ten, would ever be. And the goddamn prick slept well too.

Was there a connection here? Mike wondered. Lose the fear of death and you lose the fear of sleep? For what was death, really, but a longer, richer cousin?

He needed a place to test his hypothesis. He didn't have to look far: Jerome Avenue, a test of nerves if ever there was one. One wide lane of traffic in each direction. Double-parked cars that made pedestrians nearly impossible to notice. Badly timed lights. Third World gypsy cab drivers who thought stopping on red was merely a suggestion. Four people had died in the past six months crossing near his firehouse. The guys had taken to tying Rufus up on nice nights so he wouldn't decide to follow the rigs and end up as roadkill.

* * *

Two nights later, at dusk, when traffic was at its peak, Mike crossed against the light. His heart thumped, his bowels turned to jelly, but it did not help him sleep. The next night he was off, he hopped onto the Jerome Avenue elevated tracks, just to see how long he could stand there before he lost his nerve. Again, his limbs quivered when he heard the approaching train and felt the vibrations along the tracks. Again, he shivered and sweated, felt his bowels go weak and a giddiness overtake him as he scrambled up the filthy concrete wall that separated the tracks from the platform. But sleep did not overtake him. Both the engine and truck went out all night for small fires, false alarms, and medical emergencies. Short of being in a coma, there was no way to sleep through an air horn.

Still, Mike felt convinced there was something to his hypothesis. If only he could find the right test of nerves. The third night he was off, he set a fire in a trash can at the back of a five-story tenement under demolition. The lot was rimmed in razor wire, but a set of bolt cutters, borrowed from the firehouse, cut through the chain-link cleanly.

The tenement, still imposing from the street, was a shell at the back. No windows or doors. Just a warren of crumbling plaster rooms held up, it seemed, by iron scaffolding and plank walkways. A brace on a withering limb.

The plan had been to set the fire, see how long he could take the heat, then extinguish the flames. But it didn't work out that way. The flames burned hotter and higher than Mike had intended. They latched onto one of the overhead planks on the scaffolding, then curled around it like an old woman's fingers. Gray-black smoke snuffed out the reflected glow of streetlamps, leaving Mike confused and disoriented as he stumbled backwards over mattress springs and old tires. When he regained his bearings, he became aware of a new light. It was pale and flickering at first, but it was growing inside one of the second-story windows.

He had become so used to the sirens, it took him a full minute to understand that the rigs he was used to seeing from the back were now barreling toward him, lights ricocheting like gunfire off the surrounding low-level buildings. Smoke was churning out of the second-story window now. There was nothing Mike could do but run. He tossed the bolt cutters in some weeds and scrambled over to the hole in the fence. His foot caught the remains of a shopping cart and he stumbled, bruising an elbow and knee in the fall. He didn't even feel the pain as he climbed through the fence, then ran down a narrow gap between a bodega and a liquor store. He felt certain that at any moment he'd feel the thud of a fist on his back— Chuck's probably. Somebody from the firehouse had to have seen him. What could he say? What had he done?

It took less than five minutes to reach the firehouse, but it seemed like an eternity. Both rigs were out. A firefighter on housewatch had recorded a 10-75, FDNY code for a working fire. Mike could hear the dispatch reports across the department radio. Box 4311—he'd remember that number for the rest of his life. It was a second alarm now. Fifteen companies. A hundred and twenty men and a deputy chief to boot. Jeez, he was up to his eyeballs in this one.

He couldn't just be here waiting when the guys returned. Should he call a lawyer? The union rep? He walked into the locker room and stared into his hands. Did they smell of smoke? He couldn't be sure given the pervasive odor of mildew and chlorine disinfectant. Were there telltale burns? He looked at himself in the mirror. His eyes were bloodshot. He needed a shave. His left elbow and knee had begun to swell slightly but the discomfort was nothing compared to the dizziness and nausea that had overtaken his body. He stumbled to the bunk room and collapsed on his bunk. No rigs. No fire-fighters. Even Rufus, for once, stayed away.

It was five hours before he awoke—the longest sleep he'd had since he left Gina. He couldn't recall where he was. A shaft of morning sunlight shot across the bunk room, illuminating dust motes in the air. Tig was drinking a cup of coffee and checking his work calendar in his locker.

"Hey, Mikey, ten minutes more and I was gonna check you for a pulse. We're on duty at oh-nine-hundred, you know."

Mike tried to speak, but his throat felt as scratchy as the city-issued wool blanket across his bed. His elbow and knee were tender to the touch.

"I hear we both missed a good fire last night. At that va-cant on Tremont Avenue. It went to three alarms."

"Shit." Mike closed his eyes. He'd been hoping he'd dreamed that. "Anyone hurt?"

"I think a couple of the usuals tapped out. Back injuries. But you know a lot of that stuff is bullshit."

"Ummm." Mike studied Tig tapping a pencil on his work calendar. Tig wasn't the subtle type. If he suspected anything, he could never have hidden it this well. Then again, he wasn't on duty last night. They were both working the exact same schedule.

"Are the fire marshals investigating it?"

"Probably. We just put the suckers out. The rest is some-body else's problem, right?" Tig frowned at him. Mike's hands were shaking. "You gotta get out of this firehouse, my friend."

"I get out."

"I mean for real. They ever find your car?"

Mike shook his head no.

"I got a friend at the police impound lot. Sometimes stolen cars end up there and it takes awhile before anyone gets around to letting the owner know. I'll give him a call, see if he can find out anything."

Downstairs, Mike's presence was regarded with the usual mix of blank stares and indifference. No fire marshals came to the firehouse. No one asked where Mike had been last night or what he'd been doing. No one seemed to miss the bolt cutters. Only Mike felt strange. Clenched and claustrophobic—like he was breathing through a straw. But as the day wore on, as he went into his next tour and the next night with no sleep, only the dull ache of his elbow and knee for company, he began to look back longingly on those few hours when he made the trucks and firefighters and noise go away. He—Mike Boyle, a ghost in his own firehouse—he controlled the shots. Not Tig or Chuck or Captain Russo or some staff chief downtown. They only reacted.

Oh that sweet, sweet sleep. Why couldn't he get it back? There were other runs that kept the men out, but some of them were during the day when it was too hot to sleep, even with the ancient air conditioners running full blast. Others came during maintenance checks or bouts of Rufus's barking or times when the guys left food on the stove and told Mike to keep an eye on it. What he needed was a working fire he could count on. A good three-alarmer after midnight. No casualties. Just fire and plenty of it.

So he set one. At E-Z Discount Furniture on Fordham Road. Ten years of fighting fires had given Mike Boyle a pretty good idea how to start them. Ventilation systems were good. Just pry off a cover, stick a road flare and a little kerosene down a shaft, and let it simmer for ten minutes. E-Z was just that. It yielded six hours of uninterrupted sleep. Belmont Air-Conditioning and Appliances was good for another four. They'd ripped Tig off on a busted air conditioner he'd bought a few weeks ago, so Mike felt especially good about gutting their store. A track fire in the subway netted another three and a half.

"Hey Mikey, my friend found your car." Tig waved a piece of paper in his face. Typical Tig, he couldn't just write down the information, he had to doodle all over the page and get his smudge prints on everything. "It's down at the impound lot like I figured. It got stripped for parts, but it wasn't totaled, at least. Your insurance will probably pay for the damage. Just tell them your friend Jimmy Francesco sent you and there won't be any hassles." Tig handed Mike the slip of paper with a phone number and his friend's name down at the impound lot. "Now that you'll have your wheels back, you'll be able to find a place to settle down."

"I don't want the car."

"You're buying a new car?"

"I'm not buying any car. Gina holds the insurance. Let her get it towed to Woodlawn. I don't need it."

"You can't live here forever."

"So now you're going to tell me where I can live?"

Tig's face tightened, like he'd just taken a punch. "Take it easy, Mikey. Everybody's just worried about you."

"Maybe you're the one they should be worried about."

Captain Russo tried talking to Mike later. So did Chuck. And Frankie Bones. But no one wanted to be the one to force a brother out of the firehouse.

Except Rufus. He was the one thing—the one hairy, smelly thing—that still stood between Mike Boyle and a perfect night's sleep. Mike tried tying Rufus up, but that made him whine. He tried locking him in the basement weight room, but that made him bark. The stupid dog ruined a perfectly good 10-75 Mike had set at a laundromat. The fire would've given him a good five or six hours if Rufus hadn't loused it up.

It was the dog or him.

So one hot night in late August when the guys were on a run, Mike took Rufus on one last walk. Along Jerome Avenue. Without a leash.

"How did this happen?" Chuck's voice actually cracked when he asked the question. Mike had to admit he was a little surprised to see the inventor of the equatorial theory, a man who considered Hitler one of the world's greatest leaders, broken up about a stray mutt.

The guys avoided Mike after that. Even Tig kept his distance. Mike didn't care. He wasn't leaving, and that was all there was to it. He wasn't scared of anything anymore. Not Gina leaving him. Not fighting fires. Not charges from Captain Russo or pressure from Bones. He wasn't even scared the day two fire marshals came around the firehouse asking to speak to him.

"You know why we're here, don't you?"

"I believe I do," said Mike evenly. They had called him up to Captain Russo's office, a boxy little room with one grimy window overlooking the street. They had asked the captain to leave.

"We found an NYPD jacket and badge and a scrap of paper with the number of a police impound lot. It was all there, stuffed into a trash can near the ruins of Belmont Air-Conditioning and Appliances."

"Really?"

"You know who it might belong to?"

"Should I?"

The two marshals looked at each other. "We'd like to talk to you—privately—at headquarters, if you don't mind."

Mike walked over to the window. A black sedan was parked below with the motor running. "Is it air-conditioned?"

"Headquarters?"

"Your car?"

"Of course. The trip to Metrotech in Brooklyn is likely to take at least an hour and a half in this traffic."

"And dark?"

"The car? We have tinted windows, if that's what you mean."

"And quiet?"

"See for yourself," suggested one of the marshals.

Mike Boyle followed the men downstairs to the backseat of the car and stepped inside. The vinyl was deliciously cold. A gentle purring of frosty air hummed out of the vents. The department radio had been thoughtfully turned down. One of the marshals stepped in beside him and closed the door. A tiny puff of air escaped, giving Mike the impression that the whole compartment was hermetically sealed. The outside noise—the subway, the car alarms, the sirens—all ceased.

"Do you know any reason why James Francesco would want to set all those fires?" asked the marshal who'd stepped in beside him.

"Tig? Oh, I have my theories," said Mike, settling into the seat. He tilted his head back so his neck rested on the icy vinyl. His sweat condensed instantly and a chill rolled down his spine. "People who sleep well don't fear death, you know. They're always the ones to watch." Then he closed his eyes and gave into the sensation of falling from a great height and landing onto something so soft, he could stay like this forever.

THE CHEERS LIKE WAVES

BY KEVIN BAKER

Yankee Stadium

When he got off the train he could already hear the stadium, the noise of the big crowd breaking like the waves out on Jones Beach, from when he was a kid. First there was the low preliminary hiss of anticipation, then letting out with a long, full-throated rush. The wave breaking over him, knocking him off his feet in the water. He put the cheap suitcase down on the platform and stood there with his eyes closed, remembering. Remembering how they had waited for that second rush, down in the basement of Mercedes's husband—waiting to kill a man.

He opened his eyes and wiped a sleeve across his forehead, the seams of the ancient suit he wore nearly tearing out at the shoulder. The jacket was too small for him now, stretched nearly to the breaking point where his torso bulged from so many years of prison iron and prison food. He worried about the suit. The last thing he wanted was to look ridiculous in front of her, but he couldn't wait. He had come up as soon as he got off the prison bus, after the endless jolting ride from upstate; making only a quick stop to pick up something he needed, in the back of a bodega that his last cellmate had told him about. Taking the 4 train from there, until it poured up out of the tunnel to the 161st Street stop, past the vast blue-and-white monolith that was the stadium.

Now he was finally here, after so many years of thinking

about it, and everything was . . . off-balance, as if he were a little dizzy. All the same, but different. From the train platform, he could look into the open half-shell of the stadium's upper deck and see the big crowd there, the people laughing and enjoying themselves, drinking their beers. *That was us.* That whole *loco* summer, when everything had seemed unreal then too. *Thirty years ago.* The two of them sitting night after night up in the last rows of the upper deck, sipping slowly at the stale stadium beer, trying to make it last—trying to make the whole night last. Hoping for one more rally by the Yankees, anybody, so he could stay a little while longer with Mercedes, touching her smooth brown knee beside him, kissing her mouth.

He had heard the games all his life, growing up in one of the pale-brick apartment buildings along Gerard Avenue. He could follow them by the ebb and swell of the crowd noise alone; the collective, disappointed sighs; the cheers, the boos—the vast, hissing intake of breath when something good was in the offing. The wave roaring in after that, a feral, vicious noise, fifty thousand voices sensing the kill. Everyone in the building would lean out their windows on a sweltering summer's night and listen to it. The old folks smoking and chatting quietly with each other in Spanish; the younger people bored and silent, staring down into the concrete courtyard.

That was where Luis had first seen her, walking her path through the courtyard to the basement. Making her way like a nun across all the trash that *he* didn't bother to clean up even for his woman. Head down, arms crossed over her chest, moving quickly through the smashed brown beer bottles, and the cans, and all the other junk in her open shoes. That was where he had seen her, and decided he had to talk to her, even though she kept her head down all the time, never looking up at the men who laughed and called to her from their windows.

Now he was finally back, and about to see her again. He headed on down through the cage of iron bars that encased the 161st Street station. Latecomers scurried down the steps in front of him, kids skipping and prancing about in shirts bearing the names of players he had never heard of. He kept his distance from them, still walking in the careful prison shuffle that was second nature to him now, carrying the cheap suitcase easily in one hand. All it held were his remaining clothes from the old days, a few mottled snapshots, the Bible he had been given on his confirmation, and a deportment medal from grammar school. Everything that his mama had left for him near the end, when she knew that she was dying. They were all that remained of his previous life, the only possessions he had in the world—save for the item he had just acquired in the back of that bodega down on East 124th Street, wrapped carefully in a paper bag and secured in his inside jacket pocket. Any con would see it coming a mile away, he knew, but he didn't expect that to matter.

He made his way down to the street, and it all came back to him in a rush. He missed his step and staggered off the curb, stunned momentarily by the sheer, overwhelming familiarity of it all. His eyes blinking rapidly, trying to accustom themselves to the dappled, pigeon-streaked world beneath the elevated that he had run through so many times as a boy. There was the same newsstand on the corner; the same seedy row of souvenir booths; a bowling alley. The smell of pretzels and hot dogs cooking over charcoal in the vendors' carts. All the same, somehow. Back when he was still her Luis, her *amado*, and his hair was still thick and black, his stomach flat and hard as an ironing board from packing meat on the trucks all day.

She had loved him then. He knew it. *Why else would she have been there, up on his floor that day? Why would she be there now?*

Despite his vow to meet her, to talk to her, he hadn't had any idea how to do it. She belonged to Roberto, the super, walking every evening like a novitiate to his fiery kingdom in the basement.

Roberto was not a man to go up against—everybody in the building said that. He was short but built like a bull, with a mat of hair on his chest. Stripped to the waist, summer and winter, always strutting about, flinging open the furnace door and digging vigorously at the grate ash with a fire iron. People in the neighborhood whispered that it was there he burned the bodies of all the men he had killed. He kept a .38 jammed into the front of his jeans, where everyone could see the handle. He wore a pair of wraparound aviator glasses, so that with his pointed beard and his perpetual leer, Luis thought he looked like some kind of demonic insect down in the fiery half-light of the basement.

When Luis came down to pay the rent for Mama, Roberto would bully him. Forcing Luis to wait while he told him his stories about all the things he had done, the women he had taken, the men he had killed. He bullied everyone who came down to plead in vain for him to fix something, or to give them a couple extra days on the rent. Sure that he could keep them all in line.

"I don' even need the gun. I give them a taste of this, and that's all!" he would laugh, waving the iron poker just underneath Luis's chin, and Luis would have to stand there, not

daring to leave; trying desperately not to flinch, though the
iron was so close he could smell the heat coming off it. Keeping that beautiful, beautiful girl, with those beautiful, large
brown eyes, all to himself. But Luis had seen a dozen other
beautiful girls who belonged to men cruising down the Grand
Concourse in big cars. Laughing loudly, showing off the gold
around their necks and on their fingers, always ready to reach
for the piece under their shirts and show that off too. Men like
Luis looked at her beautiful eyes and looked away, going about
their business.

Then one day she was there, in his hallway. Appearing like
a vision amidst all the trash there, like the faces of the saints
people were always seeing in a pizza somewhere out in New
Jersey. Where they lived used to be a nice building, for nice
people, with marble floors and mosaics, and art deco metal-
work on the doors. Now the people were not so nice, they
left their garbage out in the hall, where the paint peeled off
the walls in long strips, and the roaches and the waterbugs
swarmed around rotting paper bags full of old fish, rotted fruit,
and discarded coffee grounds. The most beautiful woman he
had ever seen, suddenly appearing there before him, just as
he got home from work in the early summer evening, with his
muscles aching from loading the trucks all day, and the climb
past five flights of busted elevator.

Yet he hadn't even thought about what she was doing
there—at least not until much, much later, after it was too
late to do any good. He hadn't thought about anything much
at all, he had simply reached out and touched her hip—the
boldest thing he had ever done in his life—as she tried to
move past him in the hall.

And to his surprise she didn't try to pull away but stayed

there, stopped by his hand, those great brown eyes looking right back at him. The first thought that occurred to him was how tall she was with those long legs, her gaze nearly level to his. The second was how bad he knew he must smell, his shirt and jeans soaked through with sweat, and smeared with blood, the way they always were after another day filling the bellies of the trucks.

Yet he could not let go of her, could not stop looking at her there. He moved his other hand to her hip and pulled her slowly to him. Then he touched her all over, petting her long, pitch-black hair; caressing her smooth brown flesh through the open back of her blouse. Still resting his other hand on her hip, as if she might try to move away. But she didn't.

The hard part was finding a place to be together. They would have gone to the movies, but there were no more movie houses in the neighborhood, they had all closed up years ago. Sometimes they went up to the roof and made love under the water tower, where they could hear the nighttime rustle of the pigeons in their nests. But you never knew who might be up on the roof—kids fooling around or firing guns; junkies shooting up. They couldn't even go up at the same time, there was too much of a chance they might be seen.

Instead they went to the games. It was cheap enough to get in, only two-fifty to sit up high in the upper deck. They would climb up to the last row, where they were cloaked in the shadows and the eaves of the big park. From the leftfield line, Luis could just make out where they lived—staring out now from inside the gleaming white, electrified stadium that looked like a fallen moon from the roof of their building. From where they sat too, they could see the fires out beyond the stadium walls, more and more of them every night, until it looked as if the whole Bronx was burning down that summer.

"It's all goin'," Mercedes said one night, while he watched in amazement as apartment buildings he had passed his whole life—buildings that had seemed as large and eternal as mountain ranges—went up in flames. "We should go with it."

"What about Roberto?" he had asked, but she just made a disdainful shrug, and turned back to her beer.

Roberto didn't care where she went in the early evening. That was when he did his other business—dealing horse, coke, bennies, guns; whatever he could get his hands on, out of his basement kingdom. Even so, they always made sure to sit up in the last row, and they would touch each other only when something big was going on and the rest of the stadium had turned its full attention to the field. He would lose track of the game, but he was always attuned to the rise and fall of the cheers, breaking like the waves on Jones Beach.

"He's a pig," she told him. "He hurts me, you know. When I say somethin' he don' like, or just when he's drunk." She had leaned her back toward him, lifting her soft pink shirt to show him the bruises Roberto put on that exquisite skin. Luis felt as if he were on fire when he saw those marks on her, he wanted to go out of the stadium right then and there and find Roberto in his basement.

"Every night, I wanna die before I go back to that *bruto*," she told him.

But she did go back. They both did. Nights when the Yankees were out of town were the worst. Then all he could do was stand by the kitchen window, looking to catch some glimpse of her going by on her walk through the courtyard, while his mama cooked dinner and asked him what was so fascinating down there. He would watch her moving through the trash to Roberto, the same as always—arms folded over her breasts, head down. Only now she would look up at Luis where he stood in the window, even though anyone might see her.

He walked slowly up the hill of 158th Street with his cheap suit and his cheap suitcase and his little package in the brown paper bag. He turned onto Gerard Avenue and then he was there, in front of the old building. Like everything else, it was disconcerting in its familiarity. It seemed so much the same, only cleaner, the bricks scrubbed, most of the graffiti gone. Even the high red, locked iron gate that had surrounded the front entrance was gone, completely vanished. *Easier and easier.*

He lowered the suitcase to the ground and stood there for a moment. Feeling the package in his inside suit pocket. Looking up at the floor he knew she was on—his old floor. *Mercedes*—this close now. He picked up the suitcase and went up the front walk, grabbing the door as a pair of laughing kids came dashing out. He stepped in, marveling at how clean and new everything looked here too. The walls were painted a bright new color, the layers of grime scrubbed off the floor so that he could make out the original mosaic work in the marble again; the outlines of a big fish about to eat a little fish, who was about to eat a fish that was littler still.

He almost walked past the elevator, from the force of a habit suspended thirty years ago. But then he noticed how the door gleamed, all the original silver-and-gold art deco work shining brightly. He pulled tentatively on the door, got inside, and pushed a button. To his astonishment, the elevator started to rise.

He couldn't stand to see her walking through the trash in the courtyard, a woman like that. Not that the stadium was much better. They had just spent two years rebuilding it, but it was an ugly place; the grime already ingrained in the rough concrete floors, old hot dog wrappers and mustard packets and peanut shells blowing up around their ankles, and spilled coke sticking to their sneakers. He wished he could take her someplace better, someplace worthy of her.

"It's no better anyplace aroun' *here*," she told him. "No wonder they want to burn it down."

As the season went on, he was more and more preoccupied with thinking about what she wanted, what they could do. He didn't follow the games much, though the Yankees were supposed to have a great team. Instead, they behaved like a bunch of soap opera queens. The players fought with the manager, the manager fought with the owner. Everybody fought with everybody, it was in all the papers. A crazy season.

Then, as if they had finally decided to get serious, the team came back to the stadium in August and began to win game after game. The crowds grew bigger, the games quicker and more intense. Suddenly, it seemed as if everything had become much more urgent. Mercedes had started to talk about going away somewhere. She told him that she thought she could become an actress on television down in Mexico, even if she was Puerto Rican; maybe even go to Los Angeles and get on American TV.

She had never talked like this before, and Luis had the uneasy feeling that there might be layers of her that he had never previously suspected—that she might be much smarter than he would ever be, able to effortlessly conceal certain desires from him. But he didn't really care. Sitting next to her there in the upper deck, just looking at her beautiful face, the gentle slope of her breasts, her bare legs. Touching her, absorbing her scent, sitting next to him game after game, he felt as if he were falling again, enveloped by the wave. There was nothing about her that didn't surprise him, didn't excite him down the whole length of his body.

"But how do we do that?" He had bit. "How do we go away?"

"We need money."

"*Sí.*"

"*He* has money. We could take it."

"He'd come after us for sure then."

"Yes, he would," she said, then looked him in the eye, her gaze as level and meaningful as that first evening he had touched her in the hall. "If he could."

All that August, he pretended he didn't get her meaning. The Yankees kept winning and the fires kept burning, more and more of them. But he knew she was right, that it was all going. Every week, he walked past another store closed on the Grand Concourse, even the bodegas boarded up. The streets were filling with broken glass and old tire treads that nobody bothered to clean up; the fire engines screaming past him, night and day. In the evening, after his job, he would climb the five flights of stairs past the same broken elevator. Making his way down the hallway with its same bags of garbage and its roaches; the dingy hospital-green paint peeling off the walls, a single bare lightbulb dangling from the ceiling. There was nothing more for them there.

But to kill him—

"You really wanna leave him alive, be lookin' over our shoulders for him the rest of our life?" she asked him, straight out, in the last week of August, during a game where the Yankees were battering Minnesota.

"No."

"All right then."

"All right," he said slowly, and when he said it he had that marvelous falling sensation again.

Yet he still agonized over how to do it. Sometimes late at night he could hear Roberto working down there, even up on the fifth floor. When he wasn't dealing, he was always doing something vaguely sinister with his saws in a corner of the basement—cutting up something, making something; the shrill sound of metal cutting into metal echoing all the way up to Luis's sweltering bedroom when he was trying to sleep. It kept the whole building up, but nobody dared to complain.

He knew it wasn't just talk what they said about Roberto. Luis had seen him chase some junkie who had cheated him clear across the courtyard, tackling him and pummeling his face with his .38 until it was a bloody mess. The junkie had laid down there for half a day, before he was finally able to drag himself away, with nobody so much as daring to call the police.

"Mercedes, I don' know if this is such a good idea—"

"You *said* you would do it," she replied before he could back out any further, a mocking, angry look across her face. Then she held his hand. "Let me take care of everything. All you have to do is be a man."

He agreed to let her make the plan, thinking just maybe she *was* smarter than he was. She told him it would have to be done before the end of the season. He didn't understand why, but she assured him they needed the big crowds.

"We need the noise," she explained. "To get away. Leave the rest to me. I know where his guns are. I know where his money is."

She set it for the last weekday afternoon game of the season—so they would do it before his *compañeros* came around, before all the junkies were up and looking for their next fix. The weather had finally broken, and there was the first taste of fall in the air. The day was cool and overcast and he remembered that she looked more beautiful than ever, wearing a short baby-blue rain slicker over her shirt and shorts. It was also the first time that he could remember seeing her nervous—looking up repeatedly at the gray, swirling skies, wondering if the game was going to be called.

They had gone to the upper deck as always, and there, to his amazement, she handed him one of Roberto's .38s, wrapped in a brown paper bag—the weight of the gun surprisingly, thrillingly heavy in his hand.

"You got this from *him?*"

"Tha's right. You know how to use it?" she asked him, her face more serious than he had ever seen it.

"*Course* I know how to use it!" But he was still worried. "Don' he got more?"

"Not anymore," she told him, pulling back the edge of the baby-blue rain slicker, showing him the handle of another pistol shoved into the belt of her shorts there. His stomach nearly convulsed, but the sight of it there both excited and comforted him, knowing that they would be doing this together.

She waited until the Yankees began a rally, got a couple men on. Then she stood up abruptly, motioning for him to hurry.

"C'mon. We don' know how much time we got."

He saw that she had already plotted the best, quickest route out of the stadium, past the perpetually broken escalators. They were back on the street within seconds, legging their way rapidly up the hill on 158th. Luis had felt his knees shaking under him, hoping it wasn't visible to her—consumed by that falling sensation again.

They reached the building and ducked down the metal steps at the side, walking under a brick archway to the court-yard. She had gone first along the littered path, telling him to wait in case Roberto was watching. But they could already hear the whine of his saw, knew that he was preoccupied with his mysterious work. They could hear another sound as well. The noise of the crowd from the stadium beginning to rise—a short, tense, staccato cry, signaling something good; a hit, a walk, a rally in the offing. She looked back at him and bit her lip, touching the handle of the gun at her side.

"Hurry," she ordered.

They went in the basement door, Mercedes first, Luis fol-lowing. The whine of the saws stopped, and now Luis could only hear the noise from the stadium, gathering, growing. He could see Roberto in the far corner of the basement working on some-thing over a pair of sawhorses. He slowly unbent and turned to face them as they came in, scratching at his hairy stomach. He looked as if he had just gotten up, Luis thought, his eyes squint-ing dully at them through his hideous insect glasses.

"Wait for it," Mercedes told Luis.

"What? Wait for what? What he want?" Roberto asked, looking back and forth, from one to the other.

Mercedes didn't answer him, only wandered casually off to one side, pretending to look at something, so that they formed a triangle with Roberto at the top. She put her hand on her hip—and then Luis could hear it. The cheers like waves, louder even than the blood pounding in his head. That low prolonged hiss, like the first lap of the waves coming in—

He thrust his hand inside the paper bag, felt the handle of his .38.

"Wha's that? Money?" Roberto's eyes gleamed with a sud-den interest.

Luis said nothing, using the growing noise to slip the safety off. Feeling her eyes on him from the shadows across the room.

"What *you* doin' here anyway?" Roberto turned his gaze on her, his brow creasing with suspicion. "You supposed to be at the game."

Luis let the paper bag float to the floor, raised his arm. Roberto waved a hand at him dismissively, his eyes still on her.

"You go away, come back later. I don' do business in the day," he said.

That's when the wave crashed over them all, the noise from the stadium suddenly one long, atavistic roar. He aimed the .38 at Roberto's chest and fired, then he walked forward, firing again as fast as he could, making sure to steady the gun with both hands. The first shot tore through Roberto's hairy bull chest and spun him around. The second one ripped into his back just under the shoulder blade, the third going through his neck and spraying a geyser of blood against the wall as Roberto fell forward over the sawhorses and Luis realized that he was almost on top of him, where his body was jackknifed like the butchered hogs that Luis loaded onto the trucks all day.

That was when he felt the blow in his side, just below the rib cage. The next thing he knew he was on the basement floor. Surprised by it at first, the gun skidding away from his hand and his head bouncing off the concrete. He was certain Roberto hadn't had time to reach for a weapon, he hadn't even had time to put his hands up, and Luis laughed to himself, thinking that he must have slipped on something. He struggled to raise his head from the floor, and he wanted to make a joke to Mercedes, but he realized he had been almost deafened from the sound of so many gunshots in so close a space, the cheers from the stadium still sweeping over him, even through the ringing in his ears.

He saw that Mercedes had her gun out too, and that she was approaching Roberto, her wonderful legs moving across the room in long strides. She took one look at him splayed over the sawhorses, then thrust the gun into the dying man's hand; wrapping his fingers around it and making them fire another shot into the dark recesses of the basement. After that she went over to the wall, removed three bricks, and took a couple of packages out, pushing them up under her windbreaker before she replaced the bricks. Only then did she come over to Luis where he lay on the concrete, staring down at him, her big brown eyes thoughtful and almost sad.

"What?" Luis shouted into his deafness, still unable to understand that she had shot him. "Was this part of the plan?"

"Oh, yes it was, *cara mia*."

She knelt on the floor beside him. Her cheek against his cheek, the exquisite smell of her flesh still redolent even through the metallic odor of the guns and the blood.

"You did just fine, *amado!*" she shouted into his ear, and smiled down at him more affectionately than she ever had before.

Then she ran out the basement door, screaming bloody murder.

Luis got off the elevator at his old floor—*her* floor now. He shuffled down the hallway, one hand still carrying his suitcase, the other one clutching the paper bag inside his jacket. He was not really surprised to see that the hall too was now immaculately clean and bright, and freshly painted; all the bags of garbage and the roaches were gone.

He walked down to the end of the hall, to his door—*her*

door. There he stopped, frowning, surprised to see that it was slightly ajar. Suspicious, he gave it a soft push with one hand, just enough to let the door swing open another couple of feet, and dodged back to one side as he did so. But nothing happened. There was no noise, no reaction. Only a wave of heat emanating from within, something else he remembered well enough. That, and something else. There was a terrible smell of decay, something putrid, coming from deep within the apartment. He sniffed at it curiously for a moment, and silently lowered the suitcase to the hallway floor. Then he pulled the gun he had picked up at 124th Street out of its paper bag and went inside.

At the trial she was all tears and rages. Refusing to be consoled, pushing away the aunts who came to court with her, then folding into their arms. Proclaiming how much she loved Roberto from the stand, to the news crews outside. Dressed all in black, but with her hair uncovered and freshly cut, her picture on one tabloid or another for almost a week. Through it all, Luis had to admit that she was a fine actress, even if it was his life at stake.

And he had done fine, just as she had predicted. When the trial began, he was still weak from his long stay in the hospital, groggy from the painkillers. Learning to live with one kidney, with the knowledge that she could have done such a thing to him. All he had been able to do was make weak protests against the questions when it was his turn on the stand—admitting to the assistant district attorney that he loved her, claiming that he had never had anything against Roberto, claiming it was all in self-defense. Afraid to confess that they had planned anything together, knowing that it wouldn't help him—knowing that they wouldn't believe him anyway.

She had been all fire and ice on the stand, talking about how she had spurned his come-ons in the courtyard. A dozen other men from the building confirmed it, their pride unable to let them admit that anyone had succeeded where they had failed. She told the jury that she had never believed he would do such a thing, not a man like *that*—and they had believed her.

It hadn't surprised him in the least when the thirty-year sentence came down, and he was transported on the prison bus for the long ride upstate. He had worried only about explaining it all to Mama, though he had no words for that, no words even to explain it to himself. What he regretted most of all was that he would never see Mercedes again.

Now he was moving steadily through the rooms of her apartment—*his* old apartment—everything both stranger and more familiar than ever. To his surprise, it all looked much as he remembered it, as if this were the only part of the building that hadn't been refurbished. There was still the chipped, dingy, inch-thick paint on the doors, and the woodwork. The windows more streaked and dirty than ever, as if they had barely been cleaned at all in the whole time he had been away.

But stranger than any of that was how the rooms had been stripped bare. No clothes, no furniture, no TV in the living room, no curtains on the windows. Almost nothing at all, as if the apartment were still empty and no one lived here. He began to feel more and more apprehensive as he walked through the rooms of his former life—almost as shaky as he had been that day, going into the basement. He held the gun out in front of him, wondering when he was going to touch off the trap. Wondering—much worse—if she could have just moved. Then he turned into the kitchen, where the smell of corruption was worst, and there she was.

"Luis. You're back."

"Mercedes."

She was sitting at the table where he and Mama used to eat their meals, a shriveled, white-haired woman behind a sea of pill bottles. Wrapped up tightly in an ugly pink robe that was much too large for her. Propping herself up at the table by her elbows, her head balanced on both hands.

"Mercedes."

He said her name again, more as a question than anything else. At first he could not believe it was her, this husk of a woman. Her cheeks sallow and caved in on themselves, the rest of her a pile of bones and papery flesh. But her eyes, her eyes were just the same as ever, large and dark and fierce.

"Yes, Luis, it's me," she said calmly, her voice hoarse but threaded with sarcasm. "How ever did you find me?"

He brought up the gun in his hand and moved across the kitchen toward her, shouting, "Never you mind!"

She had left the neighborhood right after the trial. Nobody from the building, nobody at all knew where she had gone, or what had happened to her. Prison had been just as bad as he thought it would be. Years had gone by in a fog, while he just tried to survive.

Then the computers had come in. He had signed up to learn them, volunteered for a job in online marketing. He had used his access to search for her everywhere, even in Mexico, but there was still nothing—*less* than nothing—as if she had never existed in the first place.

It was only a couple years before, long after he knew he should have stopped looking, that he had come up with his first trace of her. A credit card number in her real name. He could scarcely believe that it had been there all along and he had missed it. Soon after that, her whole history had opened up to him—everywhere she had been, the different names she had used; all the jobs she'd had over the past thirty years. He had read it like a paperback novel from the prison library. Following the jobs she had taken—waitressing, running a cash register, answering phones—but never once anything that he could find that included acting. Tracing the places she had lived, weaving across the country to Los Angeles, then down to Mexico City, Miami, the Island—then back home. To the very same address, the very same building where *they* had lived. Beyond that, even. To his own apartment.

He had thought that over for days, after he discovered it. Lying in his cell at night, thinking about her living there, wondering what it meant. He sat up and stared at the picture of her from her driver's license, the one he had printed out surreptitiously when the supervisor had gone to take a leak. The color was blurry, but from what he could see she looked remarkably similar, as if she had barely aged at all. Her hair the same pitch-black color, her face grave and beautiful and nearly unlined, staring back out at the camera. *So much as it was—*

Yet when he got to look at the mirror in the Port Authority bathroom, he saw an old man before him. His hair not even gray but white, an old man's mustache doing nothing to rejuvenate his face, his slouching jowls, and his unmistakable prison pallor. He had seen it on old men before, back in the neighborhood, wondering how long they had been away. Now he was one of them, his life gone. But he could at least do *this*.

He had picked up the .38 in the back of the bodega his

cellmate had told him about. Strangely pleased when the man handed it to him wrapped in a paper bag, just as she had given him Roberto's gun thirty years ago. He had rolled out the bullets, checked the firing mechanism in the back lot behind the store, then, satisfied, had paid the man and taken the 4 train on up to 161st Street. Where he had stood again on the platform, listening to the crowd in the stadium.

"Don' be angry," she said, unfazed by his charge across the room. Her voice a long wheeze that broke down into a cough.

"You're sick," he said, lowering the gun again and staring at the array of pills.

"Ah, *amado*, you always were obvious," she sighed, and he straightened.

"You know what I came back for," he said coldly, though even now he had to fight back the urge to help her somehow.

"I imagined you would," she said, and he thought he heard a hint of triumph within that dim voice, something that infuriated him all over again.

"So that's why you moved in here. Hoping to surprise me."

She said nothing, but made a small, neutral gesture with one hand.

"Why did you do it?" he asked despite himself, hating the pleading sound in his voice. "Why did you do it? I thought you loved me."

"I needed the money," she wheezed. "And I didn't need you."

"What about all your big plans?" The anger growing in him again, baffled and enraged that she had so little to say for herself. When he had first glimpsed her, in her decrepit state, he had expected her to do the pleading. Now he was con-

scious that he could hear the sound of the ballgame through
the windows, much louder than he remembered it—the rising beat of the organ, the noise of the crowd building in that
steady, dangerous way.

"What about being an actress?" he tried to taunt her.

"*Mierda*. Well, I wasn't an actress after all," she told him,
and gave a little cackle that trailed off into a cough. "I couldn't
do anything. But I tried. I left this place."

"So—maybe you needed me after all," he said, lowering
the gun and trying to smirk at her. Desperately wanting to
hear her say it, to hear her admit it, even this sick, dying rem-
nant of the woman he had loved. "Maybe you wish you had
stayed with me now."

She fixed him with another look, a glint in her eye.

"Why would I ever need you? A man who is too afraid
to take what he wants? A man who lets a woman plan for
him—who is too afraid to stand up to another man on his
own?" She gave a short, scornful laugh, and drew herself up
as straight as she could at the table. "Why would I ever want
such a man? What could he ever do for me?"

Luis walked forward again, knowing then that he was going to do what he came to do. Through the windows he could
hear the sharp intake of the crowd's breath, like that hiss of
the waves out at Jones Beach. He took another step toward
her, but at that moment she held up a hand, her tired, pain-
filled eyes staring into his, stopping him for a moment.

"Luis!" she said. "Don't you remember? Wait for it . . .
That's it. Ah, *cara mia*, I *knew* you would do fine!"

The crowd noise came up then, the full-throated roar, just
like the wave enveloping him along the beach, and he took
one more step and pulled the trigger, just as he had done it—
done it so well—that afternoon thirty years before. But only

as he fired, in that very instant, with the noise rising within and around him, and the feeling that he was falling, falling into the wave, only then did he finally put it all together—how she looked, and all the pills on the table; how easy it had been to find her after so many years without a trace, the way his cellmate had suddenly remembered someone who could sell him a gun, the triumphant, knowing way she looked at him even as he took that last step and pulled the trigger; how she had made him wait until the crowd noise rose up from the stadium, and what she really meant when she said those words, now and thirty years before, down in the super's basement kingdom, *I knew you would do fine!*—and confirm, once and for all, that she always had been too smart for him.

JAGUAR

BY ABRAHAM RODRIGUEZ, JR.

South Bronx

To Scott, with love

I ris operated right from the stoop. She lived upstairs with her mother. It was the kind of building where she didn't have to be too obvious about it, because of the crack traffic. Sometimes fishnets on her long curvies, but for her it was enough to just sit there in jeans and tank top and that smile, the eyes dizzy like she's seen it all and just had another hit. She might wave to passing cars, plant the lingering stare on the shy ones. Her brown eyes were deep murkies and made people look away. There was just something about her, as if something was about to happen. Her olive skin tanned easy dark. If her hair was up, so much curvy smooth neck, if not, it fell in curly clumps onto her shoulders. A different girl everytime. Some days makeup, some days no. Some days she was a loud brash sound. Other times quiet meek and she could only sit there on the stoop like a lost girl staring back.

Her pimp was Pacheco. He was very nice and didn't beat her. He was like family because he used to be her mother's pimp. He sometimes watched out for her on the street but usually just went up to be with her mother, something Iris resented because he was supposed to protect her. There was this guy running around right now, gutting hookers like fish. Three already on the slab and the cops didn't seem to be doing anything about it. The papers hardly cared. On South Bronx streets life is worth maybe a subway token. Cops don't take subways. If the hookers were white maybe it would be more of a story, more tragic TV reports. But South Bronx killing zone is an everyday thing, and so one more hooker body appearing near Hunts Point market is not really a crime, just seen like waste disposal. Like a man dumping his trash.

Her mother had the same brown eyes planted deep in a wider face, hair longer but crunchier and usually up out of the way. Body sagging some now, which was why she didn't do tricks anymore. "My time came and went," she said, always laughing, lying in bed where she always could be found, mumbling vague words about finding some kind of real work. (She would have to get out of the apartment for that, though.) Iris, junior high dropout, did everything in that steamy three-room. She cooked, she cleaned, payed the bills, did the shopping. Her mother went out sometimes, disappearing up Westchester Avenue to come back late, empty bottle in her hand. Eyes swimming like she was trying to knock the feeling out of them. Iris would put her to bed.

"I feel bad," her mother would say a lot, especially on Sundays when the big church on Wales Avenue would toll its bell. "I'm *nada*, you hear? A waste. I shitted up my life. Shitted up your life. Gaw, I wanna die."

"Shh." Iris would massage her head softly until her eyes closed.

"Iris. Do you love me?"

Her mother seemed to be talking through a dream.

"Yeah. I love you, Ma."

"Don't call me *Ma*. Call me Angie. We partners, okay?"

Iris called her Angie all the time. The two of them would dress up in spandex, high heels, and big shirts. Pacheco would drive them around. Angie would always remember the days when she was a hooker, and men would stare breathlessly.

"Ahh, don't cry, baby," Pacheco would say, his wide sturdy face creased up as he drove. "Iris. Stop her from cryin'."

Iris would pull her close.

"You don't understand, Pacheco. You don't, 'cause she's not your daughter. I just wasn't a good sample for her."

Pacheco lost his cool pretty fast, times like that.

"Look, you took care of her. Everything you did in life was for her. She know that. We talked about it, right, *muñeca?* All she wants now is to pay you back an' help you. Right?"

"Right." Iris nodding to reassure. "Don't worry about it, Angie. I'll be fine. You an' Pacheco take good care of me."

And she would kiss and hug her like she was at an airport, then go off to meet her date for the night, Angie slithering up into the front seat as Iris went into the hotel. Iris was used to Angie coming all apart when she drank. It was a good thing she didn't drink anymore. Now all she did was crack. She smoked in the morning and in the afternoon and at night. Pacheco would bring the stuff and Iris would help her prepare the pipe. Angie would light up and then her eyes would glass up.

"You really love me, *muñequita?*" Always asking in the whirl of crack steam.

"Yeah, I really love you," Iris always replied with an involuntary flinch.

Iris had seen her mother fucking for money for as long as she could remember. Used to operate from a tiny apartment on Avenue St. John. Would bring the men in there while Iris sat on the living room watching Pooh videos and playing with blocks or Holly Hobbies. "It's the way I make my money, honey," Angie would singsong with so much color and life and maybe a little too much lipstick. To Iris it was just normal life. If she opened the bedroom door and caught her mother in action it didn't mean anything because there was food on the table, money for clothes and toys, plus enough time to go shopping and jump all over the sofa and love seat chasing each other. There was time between assignments for Angie to do Iris's nails and Iris's hair, to buy her skirts and pantyhose and to play with her face in front of the bedroom mirror where there was always a liquor smell like medicine. "My baby is beautiful," Angie would say after applying all the makeup to miniature carbon-copy Angie. Iris remembered being in the stroller, crowded Third Avenue, outside Alexander's in the rush of Christmas shoppers, and Angie blocking traffic there by the entrance so she could stoop down on one knee and re-apply the mascara to Iris's little face. Iris soaked it up. It was attention, it was love. They were girlfriends. They fought over lipstick and pantyhose, and once when Iris swiped her red minidress to wear to school Angie beat the fuck out of her.

It was in school that things turned sour. The kids there knew about her mother. They made jokes. Sometimes guys would come over and say, *Hey, yesterday night I had your mother.* Made her get all butch—lots of fistfights. Cut her hair short, perfected the crotch-kick, three fights a week and lots of notes home until Angie put a stop to it. In junior high she was a girl again, long hair, but the talk went on. The South Bronx was still a small town, no matter how many tenements went how deep. The only kids she could hang out with were crackheads and other street creeps who couldn't figure out why she even came to school. She started to cut classes and smoke reefer.

One day she was made to stay after school by a teacher.

His name was Mr. Berlin, so white he pink, spit when he talked and had curly blond hair. She sat at her desk and he sat at his.

"I've heard talk about your mother," he said slowly. "Is it true, Iris? Is it true what the other students are saying?"

Iris nodded, her face bloodless burning.

Mr. Berlin got up from his desk and walked over to hers.

"And you. What they say about you. Is that true?"

Iris nodded again, her face a mask. She felt like she knew what was coming. She had seen that face on men who honked their horns at her mother as they walked home some nights from tricks. He took his wallet out and laid a twenty-dollar bill on the table. "Is that enough?" he asked. Iris shook her head. He peeled off another twenty. "How about now?" His face looked moist. When there were sixty dollars on there, then she nodded, though she had been a little curious as to how much she would be worth. That girl who sat in the third desk first row now stood up, lowering shades, pulling down drawstrings. Her voice was now gravel, her eyes like she had won. Mr. Berlin watched the professional take over.

"Okay," she said like she was in charge now. "What do you want? Blowjob? Handjob? Sixty-nine? Doggie-style? Ride 'um cowgirl? Missionary?" A grin so twisted menace.

"I don't know if I can," Mr. Berlin said, looking a little pale like he had lost control.

"Take the pants down," she said.

After she went down on Mr. Berlin she could have her way with him, could walk in and out during class, he wouldn't even raise a mumble. She never abused it—she liked his regular sixty dollars, and Mr. Berlin was her first regular. He was a married-with-three-kids kind of guy. Pulling money off him was easy. It was so easy, it made her want to get into the business. There was a sense of power that went with it that left her feeling almost high.

One night she was sitting with Pacheco and Angie on the bed. A trick had just left and they had changed the sheets, then lay there with their legs intertwined, eating chicken from a bucket. Pacheco had just started with a tale from his army days when Iris came right out with the story about Mr. Berlin.

"Are you serious?" Angie jumped off the bed, giving Pacheco a punch. "Did'ju hear that shit? I'll kill that bastid!" She paced, arms windmilling. "I'll take the bastids to court, the whole fucken school! That dirty fuck!! Pacheco!! Why the fuck you just sittin' there? She's only fourteen!"

Pacheco and Iris exchanged glances. Iris went into her room and came back with a cigar box. She emptied it on the bed. Three hundred and ten dollars.

"I'll sue the city!! Just look at that!! All that talk about morality!! Like I'm garbage, right? And lookit what they do!! All of them fulla shit, alla them!"

"You don't have a case," Pacheco said, riffling through the bills. "The daughter of a local hooker? Gimme a break. They'd laugh you outta court. All the nice decent hard-working white guy has to say is that she propositioned him. Who ain't gonna believe him?"

Angie glared, eyes teeming wet. "But we gotta do something!"

Iris said, "Fuck school. I wanna go to work."

Angie stood there staring at the two of them. Trembling a little, looking as if they had just presented her with the terms of surrender.

"I don't know," she said. Her lips quivered. She passed a

hand through her hair, sat on the bed, reached for her crack pipe. She took it into the bathroom and shut the door.

"Did he sex you?" Pacheco asked while lighting a cigarette.

"Yeah."

"You want I should set you up?"

Iris didn't even hesitate. "Yeah," she said.

She turned tricks every day, every night, even on weekends. She still managed to cook for her mother, who wasn't doing much of anything, and paid for her crack habit. The career started like a party, and turned into chain gang.

She used to feel in control. She'd get into a car with some guy and feel like she was holding the cards. She had what she wanted, and when it was over she still had it, while the guy was fifty bucks poorer. (Or forty or thirty or whatever it was that night that moment.) She liked seeing some guys over and over, a stable of "steadies" like her mom had, young dudes who cruised with booming hip-hop cars. They had flashy gold rings, gold chains, big gold watches with diamonds glittery, big belt buckles, and she so sparkling pantyhose girl, so high-heels clingy skirts, she looked so young, she looked so edible, and the business did not show on her. They'd take her to parties in the early days before gangs became posses. She would give them group rates so they wouldn't have to fight over her. She liked them. In their arms she imagined being with a lover, and sometimes she might cum.

A few months later, and things started to change. Posses became strict; she couldn't go from this boy to that without some other boy getting mad. You can't go from posse to posse and do business; a girl that fucked someone in TTG would not be touched by someone in FNB. Iris found she couldn't stay with a posse either, as all of a sudden posse boys weren't so interested in hookers. There was plenty of fresh girl meat out there eager to get "tagged" by a posse, to be owned and belong, and they refused to have Iris anywhere near them. Iris couldn't be tagged; not only was it bad for business to confine herself to a select group, but no one would tag a *puta* anyway, so she had to hit the streets again and kiss the pretty boys with the fine rides goodbye.

After six months she was tired. Sleepless eyes. The young guys who would fuck her were abusive, pounding into her like hammer-thrust speed is of the essence, the great twitching shudder coming so fast. She'd sit on the stoop and not even look at their cars anymore. There were fat old greasy types waving bills, men who stank of cologne and cigarettes. She'd give them hand jobs while they talked about their wives, slipping their palms up her thighs in the *cuchifriteria* where she went to get lunch. She'd overcharge them in hopes of discouraging them.

"I have this weird dream," she told Pacheco one night on the stoop. "I'm with this older trick, and we fuck an' all. I'm sleepin' with him in Ma's bed, when she comes in an' starts screamin'. 'My Gaw, whachu doin' in bed wit'cha father?'"

Pacheco started sending her out on cushy assignments, dates where she'd end up at some hotel like The Penta, all spruced up like an office lady, to meet some flaky spick borough president or some shit like that. Those kind of people pay a lot for a fifteen-year-old. It meant not working so many tricks but the bastids did wear her out, all those pretzel shapes and that stripping shit they love. After one of those, she'd take the day off, sit around and watch TV. Row after row of soap operas, her mother lying on the bed behind her. Pizza delivery, and Pacheco's visit to bring the crack. The hurried breath of Angie's torch, the suck of cold white flame. A curl of freeze and then the glassy fishtank haze.

The soap operas put a lot of stupid ideas into Iris. She thought about the rest of her life, and how much she didn't want to end up like her mother. It was starting to hit her, those nights when Angie sat there blind-eyed in float-daze, drool hanging drip—she was the only support her mother had. She was trapped. It was going to be tricks and tricks and tricks. The wear-and-tear was starting to show, those circles under her eyes, for starters, that rough feel to her skin that face creams and makeup would not hide.

"And in my old age," she whispered to Pacheco while her mother slept, "I'll have to have a daughter just to take care of me." Tears tracked mascara down her cheeks. Pacheco could only add that he had no more cushy jobs for her. Those "*jaitones*" only want girls who look like virgins.

The week she went back to street duty, the first hooker body appeared strewn over empty fish crates behind the Hunts Point market.

"I want a boyfriend," she told a Jose, a young trick she shared a joint with, after she heard about the second body, found seven blocks from her stoop. "Someone to take care of me." She looked at Jose, but he wasn't buying, just renting. There seemed nothing to hold her in her world, no handles no grips and no brakes to slow the speed.

"I'm saying I want all of you to keep your eyes peeled," Pacheco told all the girls one Friday night, after the third hooker turned up barely three blocks away. "The guy is close. You stick together, an' if you see anybody actin' weird, you get me. Okay?"

The first time Iris saw the Jaguar, she told Pacheco, but

he didn't seem too interested. She noticed the Jaguar coming by at least two or three times a week. It would usually crawl over quietly, not far from her stoop. The windshield was tinted slightly. Iris could make out a young face behind the wheel, maybe a mustache. Not too sure if it was real or just soap opera. He would puff on a cigarette sitting like a sphinx behind the smoke. She could imagine those eyes, deep-set and pinned to her. The Jag was red slick and so heavy with mystical that she never dared go over to it.

"Maybe he's that nut runnin' around," Pacheco told her when she spotted it again one night.

The Jaguar hummed just down the block, headlights off. Iris was glad he saw it too now, so maybe he wouldn't think she was imagining it.

Pacheco grinned. "He's lookin at'chu an' thinkin how good you'll look as pork chops!"

"Thass not funny," Iris said, miffed at thinking of her mystery man as a murderer. Pacheco wasn't the least bit entranced.

"He's a cop or a nut," he said on his way upstairs to dose her mother. "Stay away from him."

Iris did. She was content to leave the dream alone. She loved the sensation of being watched. Many times she was the only thing on the stoop, only her, nobody else. One night she was hanging there with Yolanda, who had just dyed her hair red. Yolanda had no imagination, no sense of mystery. When Iris told her about the car as it sat up the block breathing soft, Yolanda walked right over to it, swinging her hips like a dare. Iris froze to the spot. She watched Yolanda lean down to the window, her yellowed birdlike face steaming as she turned and walked back to the stoop. The Jaguar growled and roared past.

"What did you do?" Iris asked, pissed off and worried that maybe the car would never return.

"I axed him if he wanted some company," Yolanda said, shaking crunchy red from her face. "An' you know what he say? He say, 'Get away from my car.' The bastid."

For the next couple of days all Iris could do was worry about the Jaguar not coming back. If she heard a certain car roar she would run to check, sometimes doing rush jobs for fear of missing the car while she was with some trick. It was a relief when she spotted the Jaguar again, resting behind a group of parked cars. There was that mysterious dark shadow, the swirl of cigarette, or maybe she was imagining him behind dark glass. She would become aware of her every pore, every movement of her body like she was an actress on a stage working to always present her best side. There might be a radio playing—she would dance voluptuous teasing like a stripper in a cage. Whenever she heard that Jaguar growl its goodbye, something inside her would sink, as if her ride was leaving without her.

She could see his sharply featured face, the deep-set eyes, sweet long lips pursed around the cigarette. A trace of mustache, but baby face, never shaved. He was young, an ex–drug dealer tired of the daily kill. He had his money now. He didn't need all this. He wanted to take just one thing with him on his ride out.

"I tell you, he's a nut. Don't think about it," Pacheco scolded when he heard her wonder why the Jaguar hadn't turned up for three days. "He gonna carve you up."

Yolanda, sitting beside Iris, made an ugly grimace. "You such a fuckhead, Pacheco, man. You a pimp or what? Do ya job! Go out there an' scare the fuck off."

"Yeah, right," Pacheco laughed. Iris puffed on her cigarette so shaky. "Like I'm gonna walk up to a Jaguar and scare the guy off. Like, that bastid could own this block an' shit."

"Drug dealer?" Iris pulled the pinky out of her mouth.

"Damn straight drug dealer. Or a psycho cop. An' they both carry guns, right?" He laughed as he went upstairs.

"Jaguar" by Iris Robles

He made like he was a trick, when finally she went over to him. She liked his smell, something all spice and tree bark. She didn't kiss tricks but she tasted his long smooth lips to kiss forever. Stayed in the motel for three days. "I don't have to be anyplace," he said, biting the crotch off her pantyhose. After that, she moved into his duplex on Long Island, where her mother would join them after she got through the detox program.

"Ma, you think tricks fall in love sometimes?"

They were watching *Lifestyles of the Rich and Famous.* Angie was in bed, pipe slipping from her hand. A misty white vapor floated.

"Uhhh," she said, her eyes round as saucers.

"I mean, say a john you did was really rich and you did him so good. You think he might fall in love and keep you?"

Angie's round blank eyes flowed into the distance.

Iris closed her own eyes. Iris by candlelight, by midnight, in the mirror staring so. Waiting for the ugliness to come to her too. Bruises, welts, lines, sallow hollow-eyed street-sucked. Like so many of her friends. Like her mother. Like the street with its cracks and tears and chunks of gravel where the trucks hit. She couldn't just sit and wait anymore.

She suited up. The minidress with the glittery pantyhose and high heels was just too *putona.* She wanted classier, something subtle gray, ladylike. She let her hair tumble loose. Not too much makeup, a more professional corporate look torn from a magazine ad. The buzz on the street all of a sudden was that Iris Robles was making her move. Mr. Romero at the meat market brought her the side of ham personally and walked her to the door, purely taken by how she looked this day.

"Now this," he said, "is what I call a change for the better. You look so responsible, reliable, efficient, with just the right touch of feminine to keep you looking sexy but not slutty. A real fine lady is what I see. Yessir, a fine young lady. You tell your mother I threw in a little more ham for her. Will you be gone long into the real world?"

"I'll be gone for a lifetime," she said.

Her mother just thought she had a special date. Pacheco thought she was applying for a job, and gnawed a toothpick nervously. He was relieved when she sat on the stoop and thought he could maybe make a few calls, now that she was somehow looking so good. The way she pulled out a long thin cigarette and lit it reminded him of some '40s movie, some Rita Hayworth, some Lauren Bacall. And he ran to get to his phone.

She had finished two cigarettes and just lit the third when she felt that vibrating rumble in the pit of her tummy. She could sense him already by instinct. The Jaguar crouched at the end of the block, headlights off. Iris stood up, walked to the curb. She stepped out onto the cobblestone street, face-to-face and staring back. The two of them not moving, the two of them still.

The first step was the deepest, with a crack of shard re-sounding forever slow-motion hip-move whirls of smoke on the outer edges of the frame and all that blue lighting. Every step closer took too long. At any moment she thought the roar would come, those headlights snapping on, all pounce. She spotted the flash of a match, the orange tip of his cigarette glow. The outline of those young, stern features. Closer, now closer, she standing golden in the glare of a parked UPS truck's lights.

His eyes were not on her. They stared ahead, squinting through cigarette smoke, thin lips moving as if he were memorizing some poem. She put her hands on the door as if needing a handrail, felt the Jaguar throb tremor her insides. She leaned in to look. His cigarette hand was trembling something fierce. Her voice failed right then. She cleared her throat of cigarette, of car freshener, of some stale rubber smell.

"Hey, honey," she said, troubled. "You need some company?" Her head tilted to one side, hair cascading down, her smile a little scared like a plea. He turned to look at her slow, machine-like, the muzzle mounted on a swiveling turret. Now she could finally see the eyes, how blank dark nothing they were.

"Get away from my car," he snarled. The next instant his hand hit the stick shift. The car thundered and buckled. Iris had barely gotten her hands off the door before it lurched with tire shriek, racing off down the street without her.

PART III

ANOTHER SATURDAY NIGHT

EARLY FALL

BY STEVEN TORRES

Hunts Point

Yolanda Morales was on her knees on Farragut Street. There was the distant sound of strays. There was a cricket. There was no life on the street. Whoever worked in the area was long gone. The ladies of the night never worked so far from the main flow of traffic on Bruckner or Hunts Point Avenue. To her left was the fencing that kept people out of the transfer station where the borough of the Bronx separated out household garbage from recyclables. To her right was a warehouse loading area. In front of her stood a man with a gun. The muzzle was pressed to her forehead.

She smiled. It was a bloody-tooth-missing smile. One of her eyes had a cut running deep through the eyebrow above it. If she lived, it would swell shut.

If.

She raised her right hand—not to grab the gun, just to add emphasis to what she had to say if she could say it. The hand was ugly, but she didn't feel the pain of it anymore—could not have told anyone without looking which fingers were broken, or that a splinter of bone from her ring finger had erupted through the skin. Those weren't her only broken bones and that wasn't her only broken skin.

"Listen, Mister Man. You do what you gotta do. I done my duty, and I'm ready to meet the Lord."

The man she spoke to pressed the barrel of the gun harder

against her forehead. She pressed back. If this were a battle of wills only, it would be a dead draw.

Tucked between a Spanish food joint and what is sometimes a Spanish Pentecostal storefront church and sometimes just a storefront, boarded over, just off the Bruckner Expressway, there's a nudie bar. Girls dance topless, bottomless too if you ask right, and all kinds of deals get made in back rooms or even in the front rooms. Once in a great while they're raided. More often they're ticketed, but the place is never shut down. Possibly some of the police in the area are on the take. Possibly no one cares enough to do anything permanent—arresting a couple dozen people just to hear "*No hablo Ingles*" all night is never high on any agenda. Besides, no one cares if the Puerto Ricans or the Dominicans or the Guatemalans or whatever the flavor this month, no one cares if they all open each others' throats with razor blades. Half of them are here illegally. For the other half, their citizenship is the only legal thing about them.

For a set of the regulars, one the favorite dancers in the summer of '91 was a small girl named Jasmine. She had cinnamon skin and dark brown eyes, and a crooked smile that people thought she must have practiced to make her more seductive. Her breasts were tiny compared to all of the other girls, her hips and ass unpronounced, and when she was asked to show it all, she was hairless like a girl who hadn't fully entered puberty yet. She hadn't. There was no fake ID involved until the guy who owned the placed made one up for her. In real life, she was just thirteen. The look in her eyes, the drugs in her veins, the dying ember of her heart made her soul far older. She was paid in smack, a place to stay, and all she could eat and drink. Small as she was, drugged as she was, the food bill was negligible. The drugs were cheap; the managers even shot her up. The place to stay was a mattress, and when she was high, high as a kite or higher, men paid well to have her any way they wanted as long as there were no marks.

That was July. By August she was wasted, fresh girls came in, even a blond one, and Jasmine was out on the street.

The streets in the Hunts Point area were tough. The strip club was like a high school where they prepare you for the rigors of real life. The streets were the real life. Jasmine wandered over toward Spofford. Toward the juvie correctional facility, toward the water of the East River, and toward the transfer station. Hunts Point was famous for its meat market—truckloads of beef and pork were sold wholesale in the early morning hours to supermarkets and grocery stores and delis. The neighborhood was also famous for its other meat market, where girls showed themselves and sold themselves, little by little, until nothing was left and they died. A baseball jacket and G-string was the normal uniform here, with a pair of stilettos and a Yankees cap as accessories.

Jasmine wore sneakers, same ones she had left home in a half-dozen weeks earlier. She had on a Mets jacket and cut-off shorts, cut off so high there was really hardly any point to them at all. Her hair was in a ponytail, held by a rubberband. In one pocket she had a cigarette lighter for whatever she could get that needed lighting up, melting down, or smoking. In the other pocket she had a butterfly knife. Young but not entirely stupid.

One night, so late it was almost morning, Jasmine was negotiating with a gypsy cab driver. He was Indian or Pakistani or Arab or . . . well, she didn't care what. He mentioned having drugs, and Jasmine was listening. Then the smile on his face dropped off like a rock sinks in water and he grabbed for her. He tried to pull her into the cab through the driver's side window. He had her by the head and she had both hands on the door frame to keep from being pulled in. If she could reach for her knife, she'd stab him, she thought fleetingly. But if she let go for a second, he'd win. She'd be in the car with him, and she knew as a fact heartless and cold as a stone that she would never get out of that car alive. Suddenly, the man let go. He was shouting something. There was a funny sound and someone else was shouting too as Jasmine fell sitting onto the asphalt. It took her a minute to focus.

"You all right?"

There was a woman standing over her. Jasmine nodded. She couldn't speak.

"Here. Have some." The woman offered Jasmine a bottle and she grabbed it greedily. It was three gulps before Jasmine figured out the bottle had only water in it. She handed it back. They were silent together for a moment.

"What was that sound?" Jasmine asked. She was holding her head with both hands as though making sure it was still on.

"What sound?" Yolanda Morales asked back.

Jasmine shrugged.

"Oh, maybe it was the glass. I popped that dude's back window with a rock." More silence.

"Thank you," Jasmine said. She said this quietly and it hurt her. If it hurt her any more, she'd shed a tear. The last thing she'd told her parents was that she was thirteen and didn't need anyone's help. This went through her mind, she wasn't sure why.

"Maybe you should call it a night," Yolanda said.

Jasmine looked up at the woman. The adrenaline had

cleared her vision, but it was wearing off and she was return-ing to her normal stupor.

"I gotta work."

"Come home with me. Get some food, some sleep . . ."

"I don't do women," Jasmine said as she got back on her feet and started to walk away.

Yolanda snorted out a laugh.

The girl turned back to her. "What you laughing at?"

"Baby girl, I was out on these streets way before you was born. Believe me, if you ain't done a woman yet, you will. They'll come a time when you'll do anything that walks. That's when you hit rock bottom. Call me then."

Yolanda moved off and so did Jasmine, in a different direc-tion, but then she stopped.

"How am I supposed to call you?"

Yolanda gave the girl a business card. She worked in one of the offices of St. Athanaisus over by Tiffany Avenue. "We give out food to the hungry."

"I ain't hungry."

"Not yet, baby girl. Give it time. It'll come. In the daytime, you got my office address. Anytime you want, you call that number. That's my home number."

"I don't do women," Jasmine said again, this time a little louder. Maybe this old lady didn't hear too well.

"Quit it," Yolanda said. "I ain't axed you to do me. I don't do women either. Hell, it's been a long while since I done a man. I'm just offering you a hand up—a place to stay a few days, get a little food in you, a little rest."

Jasmine thought this over a moment. She sized up Yolanda and took a chance. "How about a little money now? A little something so I can get what I need and get off the streets."

Yolanda smiled. "Nice try, baby girl, but I ain't got no money."

"I got a knife," Jasmine said. She pulled it out of her jacket pocket and tried to open it, but she didn't quite have the hang of it. The move was clumsy.

Yolanda laughed. "Maybe so, but I see that taxi man drove away with all his blood still inside of him. Put that thing away fo' you hurt yourself. Even if you kill me, I still ain't carrying no money."

Jasmine did what she was told and felt a little foolish, but only a little.

Yolanda walked away calculating how long it would take before she got a phone call in the middle of the night asking for a place to stay. She gave Jasmine a week.

The next night, 3 a.m., the phone in Yolanda's one-bedroom apartment rang. Jasmine was sobbing and couldn't get the words out.

"Baby girl, I can't understand you. I'll come pick you up. Where you at?" She really didn't even have to ask. The spot Jasmine had worked the night before was the worst territory—secluded, dangerous, and low in traffic. Most johns wouldn't drive that far from civilization and the ones who did probably wanted to get away with something they couldn't do where screams might be heard. That was the only spot a small girl like Jasmine could work, especially if she couldn't flick a butterfly knife open. The older, bigger prostitutes wouldn't let her near their territory.

Hard to imagine what rape is to a prostitute. The two young men Jasmine told Yolanda about had done all they wanted with her and some of it involved pain—deliberate, not incidental. It wasn't until the men were zipping up that it became a rape.

"Which one of y'all got my money?" Jasmine had said. Her voice was quiet. Shaky. Maybe that's what gave them the confidence they needed to just laugh at her.

"What money, bitch?" one asked. He was tall, blond, muscular. Maybe he played football. He smelled good. His hair was short. That was the description Jasmine gave Yolanda.

The other one, a bit shorter, heavier, sweaty, dark-haired, glasses. He didn't laugh. He had been the more painful, the more degrading one—this man reached into the car, found an empty forty-ounce beer bottle, and walked up to her. He smashed her in the face twice. She fell to her knees and he slammed the back of her head twice more. She was on hands and knees and would have fallen flat on her chest if she had thought of it, but she wasn't good at playing the whipped dog yet. She wanted to stay as close to on her feet as she could get. This dark-haired one kicked down on her back several times until she collapsed. He continued to kick until his friend dragged him away, pulled him off her. Then he launched the beer bottle into the night, over a fence.

"Shit!" The dark-haired guy yelled at her. "Shit! Shit! Shit!" His last kick was aimed at her ear, but he missed her altogether and stumbled back to the car. The car, she remembered in full detail. Porsche, black, New York license plate—YODADY.

All of this took until sunrise for Jasmine to explain. The story went through her mind so often, starting and stopping at different humiliations. By the time she got to the details of the descriptions, she was broken again, crying herself dry.

"There, there," Yolanda said, patting her back. "Let it all out. It'll make you feel better."

"I'll feel better when we put these guys in jail."

For what? were the words Yolanda wanted to say. She wanted to explain that no one was going to care if two white boys beat up a Puerto Rican prostitute. Hell, they wouldn't care if the prostitute was killed. You could see from the news that you had to murder a whole string of prostitutes before anyone started searching. Instead, she said nothing.

Jasmine fell asleep on the sofa. Yolanda brought a chair over from the dining room and sat watching her.

The next day she asked for leave from her job. It was a mission from God she was on, and the priest she ultimately reported to was a man who respected missions from God.

At the start of September, three weeks of vomit and chills later, Jasmine was mostly clear-eyed. Yolanda's eyes, however, were bleared from lack of sleep. It was hard work making sure a young drug addict didn't just escape and get what she wanted by trading herself.

Yolanda had asked over the last weeks where Jasmine ran off from, who her parents were, what her real name was, but she hadn't gotten anything more than, "My name is Flor," which sounded like a lie. She preached at the girl about the value of one's own name.

"My father was a very proud man. No money, no education, no fancy nothing, but he had his name and no one could take that away from him. He could give it, but it couldn't be taken away. You understand?"

"My father is an asshole," Jasmine said.

Yolanda didn't have an answer for that and gave up on the subject.

"School's started already, baby girl," she announced a few days later.

"I can't go to school," Jasmine answered. Of course, she was right. What were her experiences compared to those of her potential classmates? How could she make a friend? How could she answer, *What did you do last summer?*

Yolanda dropped the subject. She wouldn't know how to enroll the child in a school without being the legal guardian anyway, though she figured that couldn't be too hard.

The next day, Yolanda went out for groceries. When she came back, there was no Jasmine.

"Shit," she said. It was afternoon. She wouldn't know where to find the girl until night had fallen.

Yolanda sat for a moment. She was tired. She tried to calculate the chances that Jasmine had already scored and was shooting up or snorting or smoking something. Chances were good.

It was near midnight before Yolanda found Jasmine coming out of a parked car right where Farragut Street met Hunts Point Avenue. She was high and giggling, and she didn't know how many men she'd been with.

Back in Yolanda's place, Jasmine fell asleep, and Yolanda made a phone call. When Jasmine woke the next morning, Yolanda was out, and Ray Morales was sitting in an armchair, smoking a cigarette, and reading the *Daily News* comics. She was frightened and it took a few moments for her to figure out where she was.

"Who you?" she asked without getting up from the sofa.

"Ray," the man said. He flicked his cigarette into an ashtray and turned the page on the comics. Ray was a small man—five-foot-two and maybe 110 pounds. Wiry. He wore shades though there wasn't much sunlight coming in through any of the windows. His hair was dark and wavy, slicked back. He might have been forty years old like Yolanda, but if he was they had been forty hard years.

"You know Yolanda?"

The man looked up and smiled. "No, I just broke in for a cigarette and the comics" He laughed at his own joke. Jasmine wasn't sure she got it, but she laughed too.

Ray just sat and read while Jasmine went about her morning business. She took a piece of toast for her breakfast—her hunger was for other things—then headed for the door.

"Nope," Ray said.

"What do you mean?"

"I mean no. You're not going out. Yolanda wants you here when she gets back."

"I'm just going to the store to get something."

"No."

"I really need to go."

"No."

"But—"

"No infinity. Sit your ass down."

Ray looked mad when he said this. He hadn't taken off the shades and he held his cigarette between index and middle fingers jabbing at Jasmine as he said his *nos*.

Jasmine did as she was told, but thought of some ways around this man. Her best option, she thought as she chewed her nails, was to make a dash past him to the door. If he caught up with her, she'd start kicking and screaming rape. With all her bruises, it didn't seem like it would be that hard to get people to believe her. She was making up her mind to try this, trying to avoid Ray's shaded eyes, when Yolanda returned.

"Who's that?" Jasmine jumped to shout, a finger pointed at Ray.

"That's Ray," Yolanda said. "He's my husband."

Ray smiled again and went back to his comics.

Ray and Yolanda had married when they were teenagers and divorced a couple of years later when Ray was sentenced to eighteen years in a federal penitentiary for his part in a liquor store robbery that went really, really bad. He hadn't pulled the trigger, but that didn't matter as much as he thought it should have. He did every bit of his time and collected bottles and cans and did odd jobs for his living now. He lived in an SRO on Bruckner, paying his room rent weekly. Yolanda explained all of this while making sandwiches for the three of them. Jasmine listened, wiping sweat from her brow and scratching at her arms and face.

"Where's he going to sleep?" she asked.

"In my bed," Yolanda said.

"I don't like this. I don't want him here. No offense," Jasmine said, turning to Ray. He shrugged and moved on to the sports pages.

Jasmine's reaction to coming down off whatever she had taken the night before was mild, but she was twitchy and everyone including her knew that if she had the chance, she'd go out and get high again.

That night in bed, Ray and Yolanda talked in voices low enough to hear the creaking of the floorboards if Jasmine got any bright ideas.

"She's not Rosita," Ray said.

"I know that."

"And she never will be."

"I know that too."

"And no matter what you do for this girl, you'll never get Rosita back."

"Shut up and go to sleep," Yolanda said. When he had done as she told him, she got out of bed, put on a robe, and went out to the living room to watch Jasmine sleep.

Twice more that same week, Jasmine slipped out of the apartment. Both times Ray and Yolanda found her before she could do herself any harm.

"You can't do that, baby girl," Yolanda said both times. "These streets are bad. This is New York. They'll eat you up and they won't even spit out the bones."

Each time, Jasmine cried and complained, cursed and argued, but she said she understood and promised never to hit the streets again.

The third time, Ray and Yolanda were too late. They walked along Tiffany all the way down to the docks near Viele Avenue. Homeless people sometimes hung out there since you could fish, but there were none that night. Just a vehicle with its lights on.

"What kind of car is that?" Yolanda asked. She had stopped in her tracks a hundred feet away and grabbed Ray's elbow.

"That? That's a Porsche."

"Oh no." Yolanda went off at a sprint toward the car. The driver noticed her and pulled out fast.

"License plate, license plate!" Yolanda yelled out.

Ray ran into the street and squatted to get a better look at the rear of the car as it pulled away. When it had turned a corner and disappeared, he jogged over to Yolanda's side.

Yolanda sat amongst the weeds on the crumbled concrete of what had once been a sidewalk and cradled Jasmine's head on her lap and soothed her brow. She wept. The small girl's body was naked and broken. The beating had been more vicious than before, and by the time Ray and Yolanda had arrived, the life had been shaken and battered out of her.

Ray didn't know what to say. He told her he had gotten the first three letters of the plate: *YOD*. Yolanda began to wail, and the sound grew.

"Yoli. Yoli, that's not Rosita, Yoli," Ray tried. He thought this might at least be some tiny consolation. He should have kept his silence.

"I know that!" Yolanda roared at him. "I know who she is . . . Just call 911." She used a hand with blood on it to point out a pay phone across the street.

Ray jogged across and did as he was told, then jogged back.

"Yoli, let's get out of here. I called the police, they're coming."

"Go," she told him.

"Yoli, I can't get mixed up in something like this. You know I can't. Let's get out of here."

"I'll stay by myself."

"Yoli . . ." He wanted to remind her that her past wasn't spotless either and that she couldn't afford a dead girl's blood on her hands when the police came by, but he couldn't bring himself to say any of it. "Yoli," he said again, but she wasn't listening anymore, just looking into the face of the girl she had known as Jasmine, and when he heard the sirens in the distance, he jogged away. "Yoli!" he called out over his shoulder, but she didn't move.

The officers who arrived first on the scene put Yolanda in handcuffs. They asked a few questions, and when she told them she'd prefer to talk to the detectives, they shrugged. Yolanda had put her light jacket on the girl, covering most of her body. She knew that the first officers on the scene probably wouldn't move it, and if they got a look of the girl's nudity, there might be jokes and talk that she wouldn't be able to stand to hear.

The officers called in a second time for the detectives and crime scene people and quieted down for the wait. After what seemed like an hour, Yolanda heard more sirens approaching. Crime scene technicians set up lights and took pictures and searched halfheartedly through the underbrush.

Later still, two detectives arrived on the scene. Both men were white and middle-aged. Both wore light trench coats and dark ties. One, "DiRaimo," he identified himself, was heavy and the other detective called him "Fats." The other, "Hamilton," was thin by comparison, but his face was lined with deeper grooves and wrinkles and his teeth hadn't recovered from smoking days.

"So what happened here?" Hamilton started. He seemed impatient, like he just wanted to take Yolanda in as a suspect.

Yolanda told the whole story, starting with the first time she met Jasmine, and Hamilton wrote some of it down. DiRaimo interjected a couple of times to ask for clarification—for instance, how did Yolanda know the girl's name? After a short conference between themselves and a consultation with some of the crime scene technicians and a talk over the radio, the detectives came back with one last question.

"The dispatcher says this was called in by a man. Any idea who?" Hamilton asked.

Yolanda shook her head. "But if a man called it in, then he's a hero. Now go and get those rich white boys I told you about."

The detectives kept her a while longer and got all her information before letting her go. DiRaimo walked her a few yards away from the scene.

"You'll be around?" he asked, even though she had already been told it would be better for her if she stayed easy to find.

"I'll be around. You gonna catch those guys?"

DiRaimo wanted to say yes. With a license plate, it should be easy to find the owner of the car, but there was a long distance between finding the owner and finding whoever was in it the moment Jasmine died. And even if they found that out, the young men could just as easily say that they saw Yolanda at the scene. There were clear footprints on the body and they didn't match Yolanda, but that wasn't the greatest evidence. Since the dead girl had been a pro, even the blood and semen on her was going to be useless. He believed everything Yolanda had said, but the most he was hoping for was to scare the young men. A stern talking-to from an assistant district attorney. Who knew? Maybe they could be tricked into saying something stupid. Of course, with wealth came lawyers, so this was unlikely, but anything was possible.

"We're going to try," he told Yolanda. She rolled her eyes, and he didn't blame her. She went her way home and DiRaimo headed back to his partner.

"The McElhones of Westchester," Hamilton said. "Tim McElhone, Jr. He's the registered driver. Dispatch just got back with the info."

"Are we going to talk to the McElhones?" DiRaimo aked.

"What the hell for? Look at the address." Hamilton passed his partner a scrap of paper. "One of the swankiest addresses in the state. I've been up there. You need to get through security gates. That's going to take a warrant right there. Can't even ring the doorbell without getting a judge out of bed."

"So let's get one out of bed. It's a murder case." DiRaimo didn't like dragging feet.

"Oh, and I forgot the best bit of news. Here, take a look at this." Hamilton passed another slip of paper.

DiRaimo read it and felt a headache creeping up his spine.

"Yep, you read that right. Our good Samaritan here did seven for *accidentally* killing her own daughter, two-year-old Rosaura Morales, way back when. Accidentally with a knife, you see. Drug-induced blah blah blah. Got off light, I'd say.

Oh, and here's the best bit." He passed DiRaimo another slip of paper. "Yep. Known associates include Raymondo Morales, a.k.a, Ray, a.k.a, Rosaura's father and this Yolanda's ex, a.k.a, guy who did eighteen long in a federal pen for his part in a murder. Probably our mystery caller. So tell me, you feel like waking up a judge for this? Say the word, I'll let you make the call yourself."

The headache took a firm grip on DiRaimo. He looked at the pieces of paper in his hand and then at the body of Jasmine Doe. Hamilton cut into his thoughts.

"Look, I'm thinking this Yolanda lady and her ex are back together and they were probably pimping this poor girl out. Maybe little Timmy McElhone got a bit carried away, but there isn't going to be any way to prove that unless we can find witnesses . . . witnesses that haven't done time for serious crimes. Hell, I'd take a homeless guy. And this isn't exactly Grand Central here."

"So you're saying just forget about it?" DiRaimo asked.

"I'm saying we probably have a much better chance of getting a conviction against the people who called it in than getting to even talk with McElhone. Look, it's a shame what happened to this girl, but there are better ways of spending our time. We could be tracking people who kill real citizens."

"Well, we got a job to do here anyways."

"Sure, sure, but we're not going to get anywhere with this. Guaranteed."

"Well, let's make sure that if the case doesn't go forward, it's not because of anything we failed to do."

"Whatever you say, chief."

The two men drove back to their precinct to start the reporting on the case. Before dawn, both had made phone calls. DiRaimo called for the warrant to speak to the McElhones and search the car, the garage, and anywhere else Tim McElhone might have disposed of the clothes and shoes he had worn that night. Hamilton had gone out of the precinct for some fresh air and during his walk had used a pay phone to make calls too private for the precinct.

A few hours later, the detectives rolled up in their unmarked car behind Ray as he was walking down the street. He had been on his way to see Yolanda, but then thought it would be better to just walk past her building. Couldn't think of a good reason to be on that block, but then he tried to remind himself that he didn't need a reason to be anywhere in the entire world. He was a free man.

"Raymundo," Detective Hamilton called out, "what brings you to this neck of the woods?"

"Woods?" Ray asked. Playing dumb was a strategy that often worked with detectives.

"Here to see your wife?"

"I don't know what you're talking about."

"We're talking about a murder charge, you idiot. You should know all about that kind of stuff. Had plenty of time to think about it."

"That's right, and I did my time. All of it."

"That's right, you did. But I'm thinking you might have a fresh murder charge. Yolanda told us everything," Hamilton said.

Ray looked at both detectives up and down, then pursed his lips. "You guys ain't said nothing to her."

"Well, if you're so sure of that, why don't you come down and tell us everything you know?"

"About what?"

"About this little girl your wife says was called Jasmine."

"Don't know anything about it."

"So you're cutting your wife off? Not very heroic of you. How are you ever going to win her back?"

Ray didn't have an answer for that.

"Uh-huh. I thought so," Hamilton said. "We'll be talking to you again. Don't disappear."

After letting Ray go on his way, the detectives went to Yolanda's place, but she wasn't in. They decided to execute the McElhone warrant.

Everything Detective Hamilton had imagined about the McElhone home was true. There was a gate where they had to be buzzed in, and a long drive up to the front door. The house was huge and could have been featured in an architecture magazine. Tim McElhone, his parents, and his lawyers were waiting for the officers in the formal garden in the back. A servant offered them tea off a silver tray. As Hamilton had predicted, nothing came from the search of the house and garage. The car, the detectives were told, was on loan to a friend for the day. The interview with Tim was almost as fruitless. DiRaimo asked about the person who was supposed to have been with Tim when he allegedly encountered Jasmine the first time.

"Detective," one of the lawyers jumped in, "as we've said before, Tim has never driven into that part of the Bronx and we certainly don't admit that he even met this . . . this girl. Your witness is mistaken or lying. There is no reason for Tim to supply you with the names of random friends just in case one might fit the vague description you have. 'Husky, sweaty, short dark hair.' Talk about fishing. You found nothing in your search and you've had ample time to interview my client. This farce is over. If you have any other questions, please direct them to me or one of my colleagues."

The detectives were escorted out by the same servant who had shown them in.

"Did you see Timmy sweat?" DiRaimo asked.

"So what?" Hamilton answered. "You're sweating too."

"Yeah, but I'm twenty-five years older and a hundred pounds heavier."

The banter was interrupted by the servant. "Sirs, I hope I am not out of place in saying this, but I think I know the man you were describing." He went on to give them a name and address just a quarter of a mile down the road. The detectives decided to knock on that door.

This house was smaller and had seen better days. There were no servants answering the door, but the lady of the house was so meek that she could have easily been mistaken for one. The father of Tim's friend was a lawyer and let the detectives know it. The friend, David Franklin, was also a lawyer, newly minted.

"Don't know what you're talking about . . . Never been in that part of the Bronx . . . Never been in Tim's car . . . Yes, we're friends . . . Don't know any Jasmine or any other prostitutes," were the highlights of this conversation.

Back in their car and headed for the house of the friend who had borrowed Tim's vehicle, DiRaimo made another observation.

"Did you see that boy's hands shaking?"

"Yeah, that was a little strange," Hamilton agreed.

"You like him for this?"

"I'd like anyone if we could find the smallest piece of evidence," Hamilton answered.

Tim's car proved elusive. The girl it had been loaned to had gathered a couple of friends and taken it to an upstate lake for the day. It was nearing night when the detectives and the local police were able to find the car and lift fingerprints from both the outside and inside.

"But you see how useless this is," Hamilton pointed out. "Even if we find the girl's prints on this car, all that tells us is that she touched it. Hell, we'd basically have to find her body in here for anything to stick on anybody, and then this car's been through a lot of hands."

Nearly a hundred prints were lifted from the car, but Jasmine's hands were very small and many of the prints could be discounted without even a close examination. The rest would be left for technicians to sort out.

"Progress?" the squad captain asked when the detectives finally returned.

"Started out cold and is getting colder by the minute," Hamilton answered. "Right now we're thinking it was either the lady who says she found the body and who happens to have spent time in the pokey for killing her own daughter *and* who was married to a guy who did serious time for a robbery that wound up with three bodies in the ground. Or maybe we're looking at a squeaky clean millionaire's son and his lawyer friend who also has no record. Who, by the way, are placed at the scene only by the aforementioned daughter-killer."

"Physical evidence?"

"Sure," DiRaimo said. "We have a body with a bunch of indistinct stomp and fist marks all over. Other than that, we're waiting for forensics or the prints. Maybe some miracle . . ." He left it at that.

There was no miracle. No prints from Jasmine showed up on the car, forensics found nothing at the scene that might tie Tim or David or anybody else to the murder. What did show up, after announcements in the news, were distraught parents of Antonia Flores. She had run away from a loving home, they said. Just two miles from where she died.

They were saddened by the death of their daughter, but then it was explained to them that she had been drug-addicted and a prostitute.

"Can the city bury her?" the father asked. "It's such a waste of money . . . she had become such a terrible person."

"But she was only *thirteen*," they were told.

"Yeah, but imagine if she had lived longer," her father said. "She could have been a murderer."

Almost a week later, Detective DiRaimo took a couple of hours of leave to place a bouquet of flowers on the newly carved grave in St. Raymond's Cemetery. There was a potted Jasmine plant sitting there already. He had a good idea who it was from. He called on Yolanda.

"You put the flowers?" he asked from the doorway of her apartment.

"Wait," Yolanda said. "Let me see. You find the killers?"

"For all I know, I could be looking at the killer right now."

"Then you don't know jack. But I know you playing me, because if you thought I could be a killer, I don't think you'd be standing outside my doorway without backup. Listen, I like you . . . Can't stand your partner, but I like you. Let me tell you something: I'm getting witnesses, I'm getting information. I know about your two Westchester County boys, Tim and Dave. I know where they live, I know what they do. I know how they like their sex, and I know where and when they get their action."

"And why are you collecting all this information?" DiRaimo asked. He didn't like the sound of an amateur sleuth working his case. Good way for people to get hurt.

"Don't you worry. I'm not going to kill anyone or do anything like that. But y'all will know the next time these boys take their pants down. I'll get you pictures, I'll get you tape recordings, I'll get the ho's who work them. You want proof they lying? I'll get you all the proof you want. These boys been to the Bronx, they been in that neighborhood, they been with the working girls there, and they like it rough. I already got a couple of girls who'll swear on a stack of Bibles that these guys been beating on them."

"Why don't you let me talk to these women?" DiRaimo asked.

"Nah-ah. Wait. In fact, tomorrow morning I will bring you all the evidence. If they stick to their routine, I know exactly where they gonna be tonight, and I'll be waiting."

"But if they're killers—"

"Don't you worry about me, Mister Man. I been taking care of myself for plenty long time. And you know what? I don't even care. I'm on a mission from God. I been waiting almost twenty years to pay Him back for what I done to my baby girl. Now I finally get to square that up . . . Do me some good in this world."

Back at the precinct, DiRaimo sat quietly at his desk. He was weighing up what Yolanda had told him about getting tapes and photos and testimony from a flock of prostitutes. He wondered if all of it stacked high could amount to a murder charge. He didn't see how it could.

"What you thinking about, partner?" Hamilton asked him.

"Oh, I just talked with that Yolanda Morales lady. You know, from the Antonia Flores case."

"And what? Did she confess?"

"Nope. She says she's going out tonight to get some evidence on Tim McElhone and David Franklin. Pictures, recordings, testimony . . ."

"You told her about them?"

"Of course not. She's been snooping on her own."

"That's dangerous," Hamilton said.

"Yeah."

Hours later that night—too late—Yolanda Morales found out that while she had been hunting the two young men, they, in turn, had been stalking her. And they had a guide. As she opened her apartment door, a badge was put before her eyes. She took a stutter-step back to get the badge in focus—the badge and the gun that was aimed at her. She went quietly out to the unmarked car. Behind them was a Porsche, black.

When they got to deserted Farragut Street, Yolanda was praying for strength for the test to come. Detective Hamilton ordered her out of the car.

"You see these two nice gentlemen here?" he asked. He pointed to Tim and David getting out of the Porsche.

"You've been very naughty. You've been harassing these men, and it is time for you to learn a lesson. These men are going to teach it to you."

Hamilton stepped back and let the two do their worst. There were parts that Detective Hamilton did not have the stomach to watch. He sat in his car until the men got tired of their frenzy. Then he got out with a throwaway handgun. He raised it and aimed at Yolanda.

"Let me," David Franklin said. He reached out for the weapon.

"But you paid me to—"

"I want to."

Hamilton handed over the gun, and Franklin pressed the barrel up to Yolanda's forehead.

"What you got to say now, bitch?" There was blood dripping from his chin. Her blood.

"My name," she rasped out. "My name is Yolanda Rivera Morales." She almost laughed at what she had thought of to say after all this time, as her life was ebbing out, pooling inside of her.

"I'm going to kill you," Franklin said. He tried to put some special emphasis into the words, but there is no emphasis to be put on those words. He pressed the gun to her head with more force.

"Listen, Mister Man. You do what you gotta do. I done my duty, and I'm ready to meet the Lord."

She pressed back against the gun.

Franklin pulled the trigger and put a hole in her head. She flopped onto the sidewalk, and he put another two bullets into her chest as though she needed them. Then he stepped back and turned to Hamilton. He was breathing hard.

"If we pay the same amount next week," he asked, "can we get this same service?"

Hamilton widened his eyes, then shook his head. "You guys want to do this again, you find another way. I'm a cop. I can't do this every week."

"Every month?"

Hamilton shrugged. He took the gun back from the young lawyer.

"Maybe," he said.

HOTHOUSE

BY S.J. ROZAN

Botanical Garden

A week on the lam.

The beginning, not so bad. In the first day's chilly dusk, a mark handed up his wallet at the flash of cold steel. Blubbering, "Please don't hurt me," he tried to pull off his wedding ring too; for that Kelly punched him, broke his nose. But didn't knife him. Kelly didn't need it, a body. He'd jumped the prisoner transport at the courthouse. A perforated citizen a mile away might announce he hadn't left the Bronx.

Which he'd have done, heading south, heading home, risking the *Wanted* flyers passed to every cop, taped to every cop house in every borough, if he hadn't found the woods.

Blubber's overcoat hid his upstate greens until Blubber's cash bought him coveralls and a puffy jacket at a shabby Goodwill. Coffee and a Big Mac were on Blubber too, as Kelly kept moving, just another zombie shuffling through the winter twilight. *Don't look at me, I won't look at you.* His random shamble brought him up short at a wrought-iron fence. Behind him, on Webster, a wall of brick buildings massed, keeping an eye on the trees jailed inside, in case one tried to bolt. *You and me, guys.* Winter's early dark screened Kelly's vault over. Traffic's roar veiled the scrunch of his steps through leaves, the crack of broken branches.

Five nights he slept bivouacked into the roots of a monster oak, blanketed with leaves, mummied in a sleeping bag and arp from that sorry Goodwill. Five mornings he buried the bag and tarp, left each day through a different gate after the park opened. One guard gave him a squint, peered after with narrowed eyes; he kept away from that gate after that. None of the others even looked up at him, just some fellow who liked a winter morning stroll through the Botanical Garden.

The grubby Bronx streets and the dirty January days hid him in plain sight, his plan until the heat was off. He thought of it that way on purpose, trying to use the cliché to keep warm. Because it was cold here. Damn cold, bone-cold, eye-watering cold. Colder than in years, the papers said. Front-page cold. Popeye's, KFC, a *cuchifritos* place, they sold him chicken and *café con leche*, kept his blood barely moving. Under the pitiless fluorescents and the stares of people with nothing else to do, he didn't stay. The tips of his ears felt scalded; he got used to his toes being numb.

The first day, late afternoon, he came to a library, was desperate enough to enter. A scruffy old branch, but he wasn't the only human tumbleweed in it; the librarians, warm-hearted dreamers, didn't read *Wanted* posters and were accustomed to men like him. They let him thaw turning the pages of a Florida guidebook. The pictures made him ache. Last thing he needed, a guidebook: pelicans, palmettos, Spanish moss, longleaf pines, oh he could rattle it off. But he couldn't risk the trip until he wasn't news anymore, until they were sure he was already long gone.

Then, last night, a new scent in the air, a crisp cold, a rising wind. Bundled in his bag, his tarp, and leaves, Kelly heard a hush, everything waiting, a little afraid. He slept uneasily, knowing. When he woke, he felt new weight, heard a roar like far-off surf. He climbed from his root den to see more shades of white than he'd ever known. Ivory hillocks, eggshell swells, chalky mounds burdening branches. And huge silver flakes still cascading from a low-bottomed sky. The surf-roaring wind whirlpooled it all around. Ice stinging his face, Kelly was in trouble.

Snow as insulation can work, you in the bag in the leaves in the tarp in the snow. But you can't climb back in; you'll bring it with you, and melt it, and lie in a freezing sodden puddle. Once out, in trouble.

A sudden howl of wind, a crash of snow off the crown of a tree. He tugged his hat low, wrapped his arms around his chest. The wind pulled the breath from him. He wasn't dressed for this, coveralls over his greens, puffy jacket, boots—but he wasn't dressed. Who ever was? Why had anyone ever come to live here, where casualties piled up every year? All the green leaves, the red, yellow, purple, solid or striped, small or gigantic, lacy or fat flowers all dead, the birds gone, the ones who stayed, starving. Every year you had to wait and pray, even if you weren't a praying man, every year, that life would come back.

At home the air was soft, the struggle not to make things grow but to clear yourself a corner in the extravagance, then keep it from getting overrun by the tangle that sprang up the minute you turned your back.

Up here everything ended and you shivered, as he did now. From cold, from anger, from fear. Eight years he'd shivered, the last four in lockup. It had been a month like this, cold like this—but heavy and totally still—when he'd killed her. Would he have, back home?

No. Why? In the warmth and openness, her taunts and her cheating would have been jokes. Back home, he'd have laughed and walked out, leaving her steaming that she hadn't gotten to him. She'd have screamed and thrown things. He'd have found another beach, another jungle, lushness of another kind.

Here, there'd been nothing in the cold, nowhere in the gray, only her.

He shut his eyes, buried the memory. His face was stiff, his fingers burning. He had to move.

Astounding stuff, snow this dense, this heavy. Your feet stuck and slipped at the same time. It was day but you wouldn't know it, trapped in this thick, swirling twilight. Fighting through drifts already to his knees, it took him forever to get near the gate. And the gate was locked. Beyond it, no traffic moved, no train on the tracks. A blizzard so bad the Botanical Garden was closed. It wasn't clear to Kelly he could climb the fence in this icy wind, not with gloves and not without, and not clear there was any reason. No one was making Big Macs or *cuchifritos* out there, no sweet-faced spinsters in the reading room.

Two choices, then. Lie down and die here, and honestly, a fair idea. They said it was comfortable, in the end warm, freezing to death. Maybe keep it as an option. Meanwhile, try for a shelter at one of the buildings. He'd stayed away from them, not to be seen, not to be recognized, but who'd see him now?

One foot planting, the other pushing off, leaning on the wind as though it were solid, he made for the rounded mounds of the big conservatory. A city block long, two wings, central dome half-lost in the twisting white. Iron and glass, locked for sure, but buildings like that had garages, garbage pens, repair shops, storage sheds. Some place with a roof, maybe even some heat, there might be that.

The conservatory was uphill from here, and for a while it seemed to not get any closer. He almost gave up, but then he got angry. It had been her idea to come north. That she'd wanted to was why he was here, and that he'd killed her was why he was *here*, struggling up this icy hillside, muscles burning, feet freezing. Maybe he'd kill himself when he got back home. Then he'd never have to be afraid he'd end up here again. But damn her, damn her to hell, not before.

Snow boiled off the arched glass roof. One foot, the other. He fell; he got up. One foot. The other. A glow stabbed through the blinding white, made his watering eyes look up. Lights. A vehicle. He was insane, the cold and wind had driven him mad. A vehicle? It came closer without vanishing. No mirage, then. Some caterpillar-tread ATV whining across the tundra. Didn't see him or didn't care. Lumbered to the conservatory, growled to a stop at the end of the wing. A figure, dark parka, dark boots, blond hair swirling like the snow itself, jumped down, pushed through the storm. To the door? She was going to open the door?

She did. He followed. When he got to the ATV it was there and real, so he eased around it, inching to where the storm-haired woman had disappeared. He stopped, startled, when through its thick quilt of snow the glass suddenly glowed, first close, then along the wing, then the high dome. She was turning the lights on. And moving toward the conservatory's center, away from the door.

He wrapped numb fingers around the handle. He pulled, and the door came toward him. Slipping inside, he closed it after, shutting the violence out.

First was the silence: no howling storm, no ripping-cloth sound of pelting snow. Then the calm: no wind ramming him, the ground motionless. Slowly, with nothing to fight against, his muscles relaxed. He pulled off his soaked gloves, his crusted hat, felt pain as his ears and fingers came back to life. His eyes watered; he scrambled in his pocket for an aged napkin and blew his nose. Looking down, he watched a puddle spread as melting snow dripped from his clothes.

The smell hit him out of nowhere. Oh God, the smell. Sweet and spicy, damp and rich and full of life. Warm, wet earth. Complicated fragrance thrown into the air by sunset-colored blossoms hoping to attract help to make more like them. *I swear, I'd help if I could. There* should *be more*, Kelly thought. They should be everywhere, covering everything, they should race north and smother this dead frigid pallor with color, with scent, with lavishness.

Amazed, gulping moist vanilla air, he stood amid long rows of orchids, gardenias, who knew what else. He was no gardener. Back home you didn't need to be. Back home these plants didn't need you. Here, they had to have pots, drips, lights, towering glass walls to save them from vindictive cold, from early dark, from wind that would turn their liquid hearts to solid, choking crystals. Here, soft generosity had to be guarded.

He started to walk, farther in. He wanted to walk to the tropical core of the place. He wanted to walk home.

Each step was warmer, lovelier, more dreamlike. But when he got to the giant central room, something was wrong.

Plants with man-sized, fan-shaped leaves roosted on swelling hillsides at the feet of colossal palms. They were colored infinite greens, as they should be, and moving gently, as they would be, under the humid breezes of home. But this was not that breeze. A waterfall of icy air rolled into the glasshouse, vagrant snow flying with it but melting, spotting the high fronds the same way rain would have, but not the same. Outraged, Kelly bent his neck, leaned back, trying to find the offense, the breach. Near the top of the dome, he saw greenery bowing under the cold blast. Trying to shrink away.

And some other kind of movement. The woman with the

wild hair. High up, near the gaping hole, pacing a catwalk. He watched her stretch, then jump back as jagged glass she'd loosened tumbled past, crashed and shattered on the stone floor not far from him. The echo took time to die.

She hurried along the catwalk, climbed over something. Machinery whined and a mechanical hoist lowered. A square-cornered spaceship, it drifted straight down past curves, bends, wavering leaves. Kelly flattened into the shadows of a palm's rough trunk.

The woman jumped from the basket. She swept her wild hair from her face, whipped off her gloves, pulled out a cell phone. She spoke into it like a two-way radio. "Leo?"

"I'm here," it crackled. "How bad?"

"Two panes gone. Some others cracked, four at least. A branch from the oak."

"All the way there? Jesus, that's some wind."

"This weren't a blizzard, it'd be a hurricane." She had a breathless way of speaking, as though caught in the storm herself.

"If it were a hurricane," the distant voice came, "we wouldn't have a problem."

"Agreed. Leo, the cracked panes could go. Weight of the snow."

"It's not melting?"

"Too cold, falling too fast."

"Shit. You have to get something up there. You called security?"

On icy air, snow tumbled in, unreasonable, antagonistic. The temperature had dropped already, Kelly felt it.

"Only one guy made it in," the woman was saying. "Wilson."

"Oh, mother of God, that Nazi?"

"On his way. But he won't climb. He already said. Union contract, I can't make him."

An unintelligble, crackling curse.

"I called Susan," the woman said. "She's phoning around, in case any of the volunteers live close."

"And you can't do it alone?"

"No." She didn't justify, explain, excuse. She was gazing up as she spoke, so Kelly looked that way too, watched the palms huddle away from the cold. Stuck here, up north where they didn't belong, rooted and unable to flee. They should never have come. If that hole stayed open they'd die.

"I'm going to make more calls, Leo. See if I can find someone. I'll keep you updated."

"Do. Jesus, good luck. If they clear the roads—"

"Right, talk soon," she cut him off, started punching buttons. A massive wind-shift shook the walls, shoveled snow through the hole. She looked up at the palms. Kelly read fear in her eyes. Fear and love.

He stepped forward. "John Kelly."

She whirled around.

"Volunteer," he said. "Got a call."

Suspicion furrowed her face. "How did you get here so fast?"

"I live on Webster."

"How—"

"Door was unlocked." His thumb jerked over his shoulder, toward the wing. Silent, she eyed his inadequate jacket, his bad boots. His five-day growth. "You've got trouble," he said, pointing up. "We'd better seal that." And added, "That's what Susan told me. On the phone."

It was the best he could do. She'd believe him or not. Or decide she didn't care, needing his help.

She looked him up and down, then: "You good with heights?"

From a supply room they gathered tarps, ropes, the one-by-fours they used here for crowd-control barriers. They dumped them into the hoist, climbed in.

"We'll have to improvise." She flicked a switch and the lift rose, quivering. "The crossbars have bolts and hooks. For emergency repairs. A hundred years, never anything like this." Snow whipped and pounded on the roof, cascaded through the approaching void. "We'll string the tarps where we can. Brace them with boards. I turned the heat up. If this doesn't go on too long, we'll be okay." She turned worried eyes to the trees they were rising through, then swung to him, suddenly smiling. "Jan Morse. Horticulturalist." She offered her hand.

"John Kelly," he said, because what the hell, he'd said it already. Should have lied, he supposed, but he'd been disarmed by the heat. The softness. Her eyes. "You must live close too."

"The opposite. Too far to go home, once the storm started. Stayed in my office."

"And you were worried," he said, knowing it.

"And I was worried. And I was right."

"You couldn't have heard it. The break." He had to raise his voice now, close as they were to the hole, the storm.

"No. Temperature alarm. Rings in my office." She turned her face to the intruding snow, blinking flakes off her lashes. Hands on the controls, she edged the hoist higher. It shuddered, crept up, stopped. "Wait," she told him. She climbed from the basket, prowled the catwalk, inspecting the hole, the glass, the steel. The wind, rushing in, lashed her hair. She shouted back to him, "If we start here . . ."

He'd never worked harder. She was strong as he was, his

muscles prison-cut, hers maybe from weights, or determination. Snow melted down his neck, ice stung his eyes. Wind gusted, shifting speed and bearing, trembling the dome. The catwalk slicked up with melted snow. With her pocketknife they slashed expedient holes in the tarps, ran rope through them, raised them like sails in a nor'easter. He wrenched, she tied, he tugged, she held. He wrestled boards between tarp and rope. Like seamen in a gale they communicated with shouts, pointed fingers. Straining to hold a board for her, his feet lost purchase. He skidded, slammed the rail, felt her clutch his jacket and refuse to let go. He'd have gone over, but for that. "Thanks," he said. The wind stole his voice away, but she understood. They worked on, lunging for rope ends, taming flapping tarps, tying knots with bruised fingers. She bled from a forehead cut, seemed not to notice.

Sweat-soaked and aching, it dawned on him that the chaos had slowed. A few more tugs, another pull, and suddenly, quiet on their side of the improvised dam. They stood side by side on the glistening catwalk, breathing hard. Overhead, the overlapped, battened tarps quivered, shivered, but didn't give, not where the hole was or where they'd covered and buttressed the panes in danger. They stood and watched for a long time. Kelly felt the temperature rise.

A pretty sound: He looked up. She was pointing at their handiwork and laughing. "That's really ugly." She shook her wild head.

"You mean we were going for art?" He folded his arms. "Damn!"

She smiled, right at him, right into his eyes. "Really," she said, "thank you."

"Hey. It was fun."

"*Fun?*"

"Okay, it was terrible. But," he shrugged, looked around, "I'm from the South."

Her gaze followed his. "I've been looking after them for eight years. Some are rare, very valuable."

"But that's not the point, is it?"

Again, a direct look. Her eyes were an impossible blue, a lazy afternoon on a windless sea. "No."

He smiled too, lifted a hand, stopped just before he touched her. "We'd better take care of that."

"What?"

"You're hurt."

"Me?" In true surprise she put fingertips to her brow. She found blood. That made her laugh too. "Okay," she said, taking a last survey, "I guess we can go down."

They climbed into the basket, leaving the catwalk littered with fabric, with rope.

As the hoist inched down, she asked, "What do you do here?"

"I . . ."

She waited, still smiling. A volunteer, he'd said he was a volunteer. He'd gotten a phone call. How could he answer her? What do volunteers do at a place like this?

"Lots of things," he settled on. "Variety, you know." The start of doubt shaded her eyes. He didn't want that, so he said, "I build things. Temporary barriers, that kind of thing." Every place needed those. No matter how carefully you planned, there were always changes in what was allowed, where you could go, how close.

She nodded. Maybe she was going to speak, but a shout blasted up from below. "Doctor Morse! Is that you in that thing?"

They both peered over the basket rail, found a uniformed

man craning his neck below, obscured by foliage. "Of course it's me!" she shouted back, her voice full of disgust. "Wilson," she said quietly to Kelly. "An asshole."

Takes care of Wilson. And when they reached the glass-house floor, it got worse.

"Who's that with you? Dr. Morse, you know you can't take people up without a signed waiver! You—"

"Shut up, Wilson. This is John Kelly." *Don't tell him my name!* "A volunteer. He almost got killed helping me plug the break. Which you weren't about to do, so shut up." She jumped from the hoist's basket, gave the guard a hard stare. He flushed. Once that happened she turned her back, clambered onto a bark-mulched mound to inspect a broken frond, a casualty.

The red-faced guard regrouped. His glare bounced off her back, her riotous hair, so he turned to Kelly. "John Kelly?" He said it slowly and squinted, and shit, it was *that* guard.

Kelly climbed from the basket too, spoke to the horticulturalist worrying over her plants. "Listen, I better go, see if—"

"Kelly! I thought so!" Wilson's bark was full of nasty triumph. "They gave us your photo. They want you back, boy. Big reward. Saw you the other day, didn't I? At the gate." He came closer, still talking. "This guy's dangerous, doctor." He said *doctor* like an insult.

"No," Kelly said, backing. "Keep away."

"You're busted."

"No."

"What's going on?" She jumped down, between them.

"He's a killer. Escaped con."

"I don't think so."

"You're wrong," Wilson sneered. "Cops passed out his picture. He sliced his wife up."

She turned to Kelly.

"That was someone else," he said, and he also said, "I'm leaving."

"No!" the guard yelled, and drew a gun.

"Wilson, are you *crazy*?" Her shout was furious.

"Doctor, how about *you* shut up? Kelly! Down on the floor!"

"No." *Walk past him, right out the door. He won't shoot.*

"*On the floor!*" Wilson unclipped his radio, spoke into it, gun still trained on Kelly. "Emergency," he said. "Dispatch, I need cops. In the conservatory—"

That couldn't happen. Kelly lunged, not for the gun, for the radio. Pulled it from Wilson's grip, punched his face, ran.

And almost made the door.

Two shots, hot steel slicing through soft, spiced air. The first caught Kelly between the shoulder blades. To the right, so it missed his heart, but all it meant was that he was still alive and awake when the second bullet, flying wild after a ricochet, shattered a pane in the arching dome. Glass glittered as it burst, showered down like snow, with snow, on waves of icy air Kelly could see. The wind, sensing its chance, shifted, pulled, and tugged, poured in, changed positive pressure to negative and ripped through an edge of the tarp patch. Collected snow slid off the tarp onto a broad-leafed palm. Kelly saw all this, heard a repeated wail: "No! No! No!" He tried to rise but couldn't draw breath.

Looking around he saw blood, his blood, pooling. She knelt beside him, wild blond hair sweeping around her face, and he heard her knotted voice, choked with sorrow not for him. "All right, it's all right. An ambulance is coming."

In this storm? And he didn't want an ambulance, he just wanted to go home. *The trees,* he tried to say to her, watching the palms cringe away from the cataract of frigid air. But he couldn't speak, and what could she do for them? *I'm sorry*, he told the trees. *I'm sorry none of us ever got home.* Sprinkled with glass shards and snow, losing blood fast, Kelly started to shiver. As darkness took the edges of his sight, he stared up into the recoiling leaves. At least it wouldn't be as bad for them as for him. Freezing, they say, is a warm death.

LOST AND FOUND

by Thomas Bentil

Rikers Island

I've been running for six months now. *What from?* you ask. The answer isn't that simple. To find the right answer, you have to ask the right question. So let's try that again. The question is, *What am I chasing and who's chasing me?*

In certain circles, they call me Ice T, but my name, date of birth, and Social Security number change more often than songs on Hot 97. I'm a fugitive. I'm a tweaker. Today I'm lost, just holding on for dear life. My minutes are running low. Any day now the heat will come knocking with an all-expense-paid ticket to the not so far off Island—the carcarel hell that will soon be my home. Face it; there are only so many places the Bronx will let you hide. Nothing changes, the streets are still watching.

Here I am, spun out on crystal meth once more. I stink and I'm weak. I'm penniless and friendless. No more credit cards to squeeze dry, no more checks to wash. The spreads are all used up. *What's a spread?* you ask. It's basically everything you need to know about a person to rob them of everything they have. Cough up 250 bucks and I'll get you everything you need to be John Smith today and Michael Phillips tomorrow.

I might look and feel like shit right now, but after taking a shower and putting on an Armani suit, I could talk a pretty bank teller into doing just about anything. Granted, of course, the vic's got decent credit and hasn't notified the bank. I sometimes wonder why they call my racket "victimless" crime. I've left hundreds of victims in my wake. But let me tell you, it takes balls to walk into a bank and cash a check that's hotter than the surface of the sun. You gotta have heart, but you also need brains, wit, and charm. You have to know how to talk to people. Those stick-up kids I met the last time I was on Rikers Island would put a cap in your ass in a heartbeat, but they wouldn't touch my racket if their lives depended on it.

It takes a good measure of intestinal fortitude to hustle banks, but I'm a bona fide addict. From the high-end hookers to the high-priced hotels, from the grams of ice to the pure ounces of MDMA, somehow I had to support this lifestyle. Ice, my drug of choice, is driving this bus. Hence the street moniker Ice T, bestowed upon me by my dealer.

Those days have lost their luster. Every bank and plush hotel in and around the five boroughs is on alert for this "multi-state offender" known to defraud innkeepers and bankers alike.

Life has taken that proverbial turn for the worse. I need a place to stay and a chance to stave off the creepy meth paranoia that's quickly approaching. That's what six straight sleepless nights will do to you.

The streets of the Bronx at 3, from Gun Hill Road to 161st Street, have morphed into a bizarre netherworld of voracious fiends, dealers, hookers, and the hungry. Tonight, I'm one of them.

Broke and scared, I call Heidi's pad looking for Billy. He's my "business partner." Heidi is his girl and she's a sweetheart. She spends her days smoking shards and her nights turning tricks. Sometimes I wonder if Billy is her man or her pimp. He's my partner in crime, but hardly a friend. I'm always welcome in their home, but that comes with a cost. Any devious heist Billy has planned will now include me. Nothing in this life is free. They're never without crystal meth, which they always share, without question. Once I hit that pipe, I will agree to whatever scam he has in mind, usually cashing some dirty check. At times like this I'll pounce on any opportunity to line my pockets. Billy's generous with his drugs and the loot we make. I usually get half. He's also smart, never taking the chance of cashing checks himself.

I failed to mention that Billy is also my dealer. Whatever money I make with the check and credit card cons ends up going right into his pocket for a few grams of ice, and again I find myself at square one.

"I'm spun out and the warrant squad is on my ass," I say with a shaky tone. Billy senses the desperation in my voice when I call him from Jerome Avenue. Visions of dollar signs dance in his head. The last thing I want is to be part of another heist. I soon would have no choice. He's a viper with a clean face and he's turning me into a monster like him. There's some devil in me—he didn't craft it, but he promised life to it if I would just *ride* with him.

Heidi's apartment is in Hunts Point, smack dab in the middle of a thriving crack scene. Billy is the only apparent source of crystal meth in the neighborhood. As I ramble on from block to block, on my way to their building, I can't help noticing how much this part of the Boogie Down feels like a ghost town. Warehouses and abandoned tenements line these dark avenues. On every shadowy street, thugs wearing black hoodies loiter, whistling at cars as they cruise past, running up to the few vehicles which pull up, and making sales. In murky corners, pressed against walls like statues, ebony figures appraise foot traffic. Some young bloods use laser pointers in what seems to be a code to warn of approaching cops, while shabbily dressed baseheads try to hawk everything from boom boxes to jewelry in exchange for a taste of poison. These same apparitions I will soon rendezvous with in the sullen halls of C-76, Rikers Island.

I'm looking at these streets through the eyes of a fugitive and a tweaker. The Bronx has become a carnival of flesh and bone. I step over an older white guy who's obviously been jacked for money, drugs, or both. He's lying facedown on the street, the back of his head smashed open and raw. It's the best Hunts Point has to offer, a street dealing scene that would make any hustler proud. Offers of every kind fill my ears as I make my way to Heidi's apartment. To some, these streets are neon dreams come true, but to me, a speed freak at the end of his rope, it's a ghost town.

Billy and Heidi live the typical tweaker life in the ever-so-typical tweaker pad. Billy is a complete and brilliant idiot. When I step inside their small, musty studio apartment, Billy is scrunched over his computer like something kept in the closet. The front room is damp. Torn wallpaper covers large holes through which the scuttle of crablike creatures can be heard. Postmodern artwork embellishes the back walls.

Heidi steps from the dimly lit recesses of her closet completely naked except for a pair of electric-blue lace panties. She's a beautiful blond nymphomaniac whose appetite for spiking speed is insatiable. At times her eyes reveal a glimpse of the lost innocent nineteen-year-old from Petaluma, California.

It's late, almost 3 a.m., and she's getting ready for work. Ice, she always tells me, is essential for turning tricks—all the girls she works with do it. I can't help feeling sorry for her, but at the same time, all I want her to do is shut up and offer me a hit. She approaches me wearing a dirty-blond wig and I assume this is a request from one of her regulars. As she gets closer, I notice she's holding something against her small chest. Curling it outward with the needle-tracked arm of a nightmarish ghoul, she reveals a glass pipe packed with crystal meth. Heidi hands me the instrument of my demise. Before she disappears into the bathroom and just as I'm about to get a taste of the sweet poison, she flashes in front of me a New York State Driver License bearing the picture of one of the most beautiful women I have ever seen.

"I need to look like her by tomorrow, think I can pull it off?" she asks.

Never, I think to myself, but appease her by agreeing. At that moment I know Billy is working on something big, something with many zeros attached to it, the ultimate grift. I will be getting my assignment soon.

The first hit I take fills my lungs and makes the synapses in my brain fire off like the Fourth of July. Dopamine overflows. At the edge of my hazy percept, I can barely make out something Billy's saying about how "hot" their apartment has become. He's convinced a guy we work with is a snitch. This is the last thing I want to hear.

The sky in my mind suddenly grows darker. Visions of decay and violence fill me with a sense of doom. Is my paranoia rooting deeper or is it a premonition of events yet to come?

A month on Rikers Island, then I was bailed out. Like a fool, I ran. I became totally aware of my situation, of the utter hopelessness of where I was and where I would end up. All of my demons came to the surface. I got two grams of speed, then what? I pull off another one with Billy, make $2,000, then what? Now I'm back where I started.

A black chasm of despair opens inside of me. Here I am, six months later, strung out worse than ever, out of money, trying to rest my beaten body in some sketchy tweaker pad. I am miserable and want this to end. I don't just want a break from the drugs and crime, I want to go back to before I snorted that first line of crystal, before I knew how fuckin' amazing that feeling was, before I experienced the rush from a successful heist and tasted the pleasures of other people's money.

Five days of being awake begin to take their toll. I feel myself getting drowsy, slipping into darkness. It's that half-drugged sleep that comes at the end of every run, coupled with the handful of Valiums Heidi gave me earlier. Everything fades to black.

It's late in the morning when I'm violently awoken by a cacophony of sound: deep guttural voices, the distinct clinking of metal cuffs, and an orchestra of bleeps, blips, and chirps from a police radio.

"Wake up, ya piece a shit, and let me see your hands," orders a red-haired freckle-faced detective with an uncanny resemblance to Richie Cunningham from *Happy Days*.

I get up slowly in a half-asleep, half-dazed stupor, wearing only jeans and a T-shirt. I'm still having trouble making sense of this scene when from the corner of my eye I see Billy being dragged out of the apartment by two uniformed officers. Here I am, smack in the middle of a raid. The bench warrant I have is hanging over my head like some dark and dreary cloud ready to release torrents of rain.

"Get on some shoes, pal. Had a nice run, but it's over now," another cop says. He reminds me of this thugged-out Puerto Rican brother I knew the last time I was on Rikers, covered with jailhouse tats. I have an eerie premonition of where I'm going and the company I will soon keep. I feel a dampness permeating my palms and can hear my heart palpitating loud enough, I think, for everyone else to hear too.

Anxiety is rearing its ugly head. Rikers Island will be my new home.

Central Booking is the first stop. "Inside" again. I'm thrust into the wheels of justice and the long, drawn-out grind of due process. All of it leads up to the Day of Judgment when I will hear the inevitable: One year on Rikers.

Though I've taken this trip several times before, I'd usually be out within a week. But a year? A year without ice? A year without women, decent food, privacy, freedom? Despair overwhelms me. Something about this bus ride out to the Island seems different, darker. The level of hopelessness I have reached, somewhere between wanting an eternal slumber and desperately needing to see the faces of my family, is at a depth I never knew existed. An image of my mother bidding me farewell leaves a smoky crater in my mind.

I glance across the aisle and notice a heavyset Latino brother with a tear drop appropriately tattooed on his face. With a look of utter anguish, he gazes out the caged bus window.

From the shores of Queens, a mile-long bridge rises over the East River toward an island officially located in the Bronx. This sprawling city of jails waits with open arms to welcome the pariahs of the five boroughs.

As we approach C-73, the reception jail, the mood is a blend of somberness and tension so thick you could cut it with some crudely fashioned prison dagger. It takes four hours to get through the intake process; forms to fill in: name, age, height, eye color, identifying scars, religion. By the time it's over, the Department of Corrections knows more about me than my mother does.

I strip down to my boxers. Each item of clothing examined, then packed away in a yellow canvas bag. I'm assured everything will be returned upon release. *Yeah, right*, I think. I'm handed a "full set-up"—towel, soap, bedding, and the green jumpsuit that will mark me a bona fide criminal for the next twelve months. Finally, I'm escorted to a housing area. Through several sets of doors, each one unlocked, opened, closed, and locked again, before going on to the next, down dimly lit, cold hallways rich with that institutional stench.

The weight of a six-day speed binge, a day in court, and another day of "bullpen therapy," as cons call the endless hours in holding cells, have taken a toll. All I want is to pass out. Through my exhaustion I gladly accept the metal cot, thin and tattered mattress, and the wool blanket that looks and smells like it hasn't been washed in months.

I'm assigned to housing area: 9 Main. It's a barrack dorm with beds lined up next to each other, separated by three-foot lockers. This is how I will spend the next 365 days—stripped of everything but a locker and a cot.

It's close to 12 a.m. when I enter the dorm. Most of the residents are wide awake, even with the facility lights out. This is the typical after-hours scene in most housing units on Rikers. It's called "breakin' night," staying up after the lights are out to hustle tobacco, do push-ups, or simply pass the time by reminiscing about the street life. It's a picture alarmingly similar to the scene on the blocks so many come from. These ghetto celebrities and 'hood movie stars are energized by the cover of darkness.

Despite the ruckus, I settle into my space and drift into a catatonic state. For a moment, I linger in that zombie-like state between wakefulness and deep sleep and think the last forty-eight hours were a surreal dream. That first morning in 9 Main is the darkest dawn I've ever known.

The entire dorm is roused for chow at 4:45 a.m. It feels

like the coldest winter ever as I lurch toward the mess hall. The echoes of large steel prison doors slamming wake up each and every prisoner confined within this penal colony's unforgiving walls.

Just a harmless speed addict, I think to myself, *I never intended to hurt a soul.* Especially not the retired couple whose pension checks I pilfered or the single mom whose life savings account I drained. What a time to be thinking about my vics. How will I stay afloat with the weight of my conscience suddenly acting like a ball and chain? I will surely drown in the insanity of this institution, and I realize how urgently I need a life preserver.

Down the concrete and steel hallways of the jail, I walk alongside misfits of the morning. Entering the large steel dining area, still half-asleep, I'm assaulted by the echo of clanging, banging, and hammering steel. The noise, the noise! Steel walls, steel doors, steel pots, steel pans, steel benches, steel tables—all of which underscore the hell society has banished me to.

As I drag my tray down the stainless steel line, kitchen workers throw and splatter food on my plate. I don't make eye contact, just try to put one foot in front of the other.

I sit next to an older, bespectacled junky who obviously doesn't know the meaning of water or soap. I eat cold cereal. With my face down, I think about how I can't wait to get out, get out and . . . then suddenly it hits me—I have nothing to get out for. I have no life on the outside worth returning to. The girl I loved, an addict like me, was lost to the streets last I heard. I'm a college drop-out with only lies to put on a resume. When I get out, the only choice I have is to return to the mix, the only thing I know, which will land me right back in this hellhole. For the first time, I consider hanging up, end-ing it all. Believe it or not, it's hard to pull off in a place like this. I go back to my cot and sleep another eight hours.

"On the chow!" the CO barks, alerting inmates it's feeding time again. I drag myself out of bed and kick on some slippers. I have no idea what day or time it is. I try not to think. My thoughts lead only to one place.

On the way to the mess hall I notice a door with the words, *New Beginnings . . . Create a new life and a new future today.* Why does the name resonate so much? I repeat it to myself over and over—*New Beginnings, New Beginnings.* Then, like some prizefighter's left hook, it hits me. It is one in a long line of stories Billy's told me. Last time he was locked down on the Island he managed to weasel his way into being a trustee. He was assigned to sweep and mop some program office. Bits and pieces of his tale are coming back to me. All he kept telling me is that he was so smooth he could find a vic anywhere, even on the inside. "Simple, old-fashioned justice," he called it. It was his way, he thought, of sticking to the system that stuck it to him so many times. The last thing I want to think about is that world.

God works in mysterious ways, I think, but did he really expect me to join a stupid jailhouse program? Been there, done that. I shuffle along to the mess hall.

I get my food, some kind of slop meant to be meatloaf, and walk to a gray steel table that's probably been painted for the twentieth time. I sit down and bury my face in my hands. I consider throwing the tray against the wall. I'm filled with rage and desperately need a hit. I haven't felt my emotions in years and the pain is unbearable.

"Hey." The guy sitting next to me tries to start a conversation, but I wave him away.

"Don't wanna talk, man," I tell him.

"Listen, I know where you're at," he says. "I've been there. I can see it. New Beginnings is what you need, brotha." As he goes on about the program, how cool the counselors are, how they help you find a job and get clean once you're released, I just want him to shut up. I don't have the energy for hope.

To get him off my back, I grab an application for the program from a table and fill it out. He tells me he'll give it to the director. The next chapter of my life suddenly has promise, however slight.

I pick up my spoon and take a portion of the meatloaf and place it in my mouth. I chew once or twice, then slowly open my mouth, letting the disgusting fodder fall back onto the tray. This isn't the first jailhouse meal that has repulsed me, but it's the first time the pain has run so deep. I push the tray aside and sit there staring at the New Beginnings mural and wondering what that phrase means to me.

I return to my housing unit and wait for the count to be cleared. The jangle of keys attached to the belt on the spreading waist of a CO signifies the change in shifts.

Clank! The crash of metal against metal, bouncing apart, then meeting again with another steely thump tells me that the day is beginning. Soon it will be business as usual in the facility.

By 7:30 a.m., the facility count of inmates will be complete. As I lie on my bunk, I look toward the east and catch a glimpse of the rising sun. I think to myself that no matter what, the sun will always rise and the world is given a chance at a new beginning. What we do with it is up to us.

"Laundry crew!" a CO blares as inmates move toward the front gate. I'm yet to be assigned a work detail, but maybe I'll get into that program, I think, and I won't have to do some grimy jail job.

As soon as the dorm CO appears to have nothing to do, I'll approach him and ask for a pass to the New Beginnings office. Getting the officer on duty to assist you in any way requires a skill all its own. Timing is everything. Miss that opportunity and you'll be forced to sit in the house all day, wasting away. I'm not one to let that happen. Like I made things happen on the street, I'll make things happen here.

I'm given an "OK" and a pass to the New Beginnings office, where I hope to be screened for admittance into the program. This is my chance to make good. Redemption, they say, only comes once in a lifetime.

I enter the office and the first thing I notice is how down-to-earth the counselors seem. They're like everyday people, hardworking and dedicated to what they do, probably like my victims, I think. That's one thing about jail, your conscience works overtime. The guilt and shame you've suppressed for so long come bubbling to the surface. As I wait for the screening process to begin, I'm overcome with these thoughts. What does this all mean?

Unlike the rest of the jail, with its dreary gray walls, the director's office is painted a calming beige. Fresh flowers sit in a vase on her desk. The sign on the door tells me her name is Ms. Frey.

"Nice to meet you, Tron," she says, extending her hand. The office is snowed under with books. Books on the wall, books on the floor, books to the right, and books to the left. Framed photos and artwork line the walls. A picture of a smiling little girl on a swing with Ms. Frey catches my attention. The warmth of the photo has a disarming affect on me, and anyone else who enters here, I think. The picture defines the bond between mother and child. No matter how "hard" you think you are, the image softens you.

She gestures for me to have a seat and instantly I'm attracted to her. If for no other reason, please let me be accepted into this program because the director is fuckin' fine. I pray to whoever's listening.

She looks at me with emerald-green eyes that make me think how easily I could fall for this woman. As she tells me about the program, I fixate on her face. Oddly, a fleeting thought tells me I've met her before.

The interview goes well and I'm told I'm accepted into the program. I never share my deep thoughts with anyone, but somehow she got me open. I've seen the inside of jails and rehabs from here to Los Angeles, and bullshit-talking counselors are a dime a dozen, but I may have found the one therapist who truly cares. My life is a mess and I desperately need the help of this program.

Days go by in this jungle, and as in any jungle made of concrete and steel or gnarled green vegetation, only the strong survive. By no means am I the super thug type; my IQ earns me respect and is regarded in much the same way as a seventeen-inch bicep. Behind these walls that's all you've got, and both will earn you props.

I find solace in the New Beginnings office, exchanging feedback with others in the program and building on ideas with positive people. One-on-one sessions with Ms. Frey keep me afloat and I have found an oasis. She will rescue me from the sea of toxicity I'm floating in.

I tell her about the dark places my drug addiction brought me, about the hookers and the drugs, but I don't tell her about the scams, spreads, and the dirty checks—I'm too embarrassed and don't want to scare her off. Her office is where I dump my guilt and shame, and she willingly carts it away.

"You don't have to live that way anymore," she tells me. *What other way is there to live?* I wonder. This is all I know.

About a month into the program, I'm sitting in her office talking about the future. She's telling me about a job she thinks I'd be good at—working with a team of researchers studying patterns of drug use in the city.

"They're looking for people who have firsthand knowledge of crystal meth," she says. "You'd be doing ethnography—studying a subculture . . ." She pauses to take a phone call. "It might be my daughter's school," she says.

I sit there thinking about the job. From what it sounds like, I'll be great at it. I laugh to myself and think, *I study patterns of drug use every day anyway—who's got what, where, and for how much.*

Suddenly I notice her usually unflappable demeanor shift. She looks like she's been slapped and says only a few words during the ten-minute phone call. "Never, not at all, what should I do?" she finally exclaims.

She hangs up, looking stunned, and apologizes for the disruption. She tries hard to regain her composure.

"Is everything all right?" I ask.

She doesn't answer at first, she just picks up the picture of her daughter. She stares into it as if trying to draw strength from its aura.

"I apologize, but I just received some devastating news," she finally says. What she tells me next tears through me like a bullet. It was a credit bureau calling her, investigating "an unusual number of revolving credit accounts being opened and now in arrears." Her savings account has nearly been drained—the account she built for her daughter's education. Only pennies are left. Now the arduous process of repairing her credit and proving to the banks that it wasn't her will begin. Sadness envelops me.

Images of Heidi's apartment suddenly play like a slide-show in my mind. She had flashed that picture in my face that twisted night I found myself in her apartment. It was the ID with the pretty face Heidi was determined to duplicate. Billy's tentacle prints are all over this scheme. Was this the "justice" he was talking about? The woman who now sits before me was our prey: chewed up and spit out like countless others. I was a part of a wicked machine that ruined lives and now I'm face-to-face with my evil. The problem is, without the drugs I have a conscience, and I'm devastated.

I sit there listening to her tell me the story I played an integral part in. I can actually feel her confusion, disenchant-ment, and anger, coupled with the urge to exact some sort of revenge or instant justice. If she only knew. Now here's the question. Would she be more at ease if I were to disclose my connection to this wicked scheme? If anyone would under-stand, it would be Ms. Frey. She makes a living out of caring and being sympathetic, right?

Well, I never come clean with Ms. Frey. I quit the program after that day. I had a chance to make good and it disappeared as quickly as it revealed itself to me. I can't bear to be around Ms. Frey at all. It's true what they say: *Secrets keep us sick.* I'm still as sick and twisted as ever.

Months pass and I've got two days before I'm released. Soon I'll be back in the abyss, and I'm sure this time it'll be deeper and darker than ever. The game is funny that way—just when you think you're on your way out, it pulls you back in. Rikers Island can't change years of what life in the Bronx has bred. Who the fuck was I kidding?

LOOK WHAT LOVE
IS DOING TO ME

BY MARLON JAMES
Williamsbridge

T his is the year of the monkey. A Chinese john told me this after coming back from downtown to celebrate Chinese New Year. I was just shocked to see somebody Oriental cruising ass anywhere past Grand Concourse. I think he was rich too. But then they're all rich, these johns who have wives and kids back home but then whisper to me that after feeling how tight an asshole is, could never truly love pussy. They tell me all sorts of stuff. Mostly they tell me to act like a girl, so I call them *honeychile* and flick my wrist like a faggot and that makes it easier, I guess.

Hey, white boy, watchu doin uptown? Lou Reed, the original signifying monkey. I'm older than I seem and younger than I look. Clever. Brains couldn't save me last year when my dad kicked me out because I didn't dig girls. I was like, *Yo, Pops, I don't eat pussy but I suck a mean dick.* Not really. Not at all. After he got through with me, after my mom was more sick at the beating than what I was getting beat up for, she screamed and he stopped. Now I walk like Ratso and one day I'll fuck him back up.

Right now it's 11 in the night and I'm by Hammersley and Ely, right outside Haffen Park, watching cars go by. Cruising of a different flavor. Yeah, boyee, clever. I'm at Hammersley and Ely and I'm waiting for Gary to come shuff me off this mortal coil. Gary likes a good old mess so he'll probably use that sawed-off of his. Or maybe his bowie knife. It's weird waiting for somebody to kill you. Knowing that you're going to die, knowing the end of the movie before the middle makes you do all kinds of shit. Wicked fly shit. It's like knowing you have cancer so you can do that live-every-minute thing. So I went to McDonald's and bought *two* fries. I shoplifted some Garnier Fructis from Rite Aid on Eastchester because I should at least smell good when they find me off Gun Hill Road somewhere.

A snapshot. We're in the living room of my parents' house on Gunther. We're Jews, baby, the last of a dying breed in the Bronx. Gary is sprawled on the love seat, legs spread wide with boots on the chair arm. His vest is dirty as fuck and he's wearing no shirt underneath. Baggy jeans, the brown ones I don't like with speckles that look like dried blood. He really looks like shit, but it works. As I said, we're in my parents' house.

My mother is dead now. So too is my father. Both died this year. My sister Diane died several years before but just a few years after Dad stopped fucking her. Andre, he's in jail with nothing but a conviction and no remorse. Ten months before they found him at the gate, trembling like they had dunked him in ice. Dude was still clutching the bloody hatchet and shaking like he got fits or something. The *Post* said they charged him for double murder and resisting arrest. My father had three hatchet wounds in his forehead, fingers chopped off, probably from trying to block the blows. My mom had to be buried with a closed casket. But enough about them. Gary is going to kill me.

Like just about everybody in the Bronx now, Gary is from Jamaica. I don't know if he was doing guys given how Jamaicans, like, kill homos and shit, but I know he used to kill back there. Back in the ghetto and shit. See, I know, I represent. I miss him. I hate that. I sound like somebody old, and I have to be tough like him. I want to say I miss him, but I can't. Maybe I'm just relieved. I don't know. Some things you can't unsay and some things you can't undo. I'm at Hammersley and Ely and a car just slowed down. They used to kill people in this park almost every night before Rudy cleaned things up.

Another snapshot. When I met Gary I was already turning tricks, like four months after Daddy kicked me out of the house and I went downtown just to see the river. Nothing but boys in the street. I was so fucking hungry, yo. One of the boys was eating fried chicken. He handed me a piece and I ate the bone. Mad hungry. *Chill, bitch,* he said. I asked where he got the chicken, and he said I should let an uncle pay for it. One of them will be driving up in his Chrysler minivan soon enough. I'd only have to do two things. One was wait. He didn't tell me what the other one was.

A car pulled up. He got in and waved at me. Darkness was hiding everything. I turned to go back to, I don't know, uptown, I guess, even though that would take forever. Then this car pulled up and stopped beside me. "You're new," the man said. I didn't know what he meant. I asked if he could get me some KFC and he said, "Get in." I'm not stupid. I was sixteen and I knew a lot of shit and it's not like I was going to vomit. Part of me wanted to be in the car. He got me some chicken and when I started to eat he unzipped his pants and took it out. I thought jacking off a dude was the same as jacking myself off and I was hungry. I grabbed his cock and he said, "No, baby," and pointed at my mouth.

Gary's coming for me. So stupid, all the shit that lead to this.

Third snapshot. So one day, or night, rather, I'm walking

down Baychester, looking for a better highway to sleep under, I guess. First mistake, nobody looks for cock on Baychester. One person in the car says, "Yo, you one of them good-time boys?" and me, I'm thinking that I'm a pro so I can show some sass, so I say, "What kind of time you think is good?" And I'm riding this moment because I get to be all witty and shit, clever, and the car stops and he tells me to get in. And I'm looking around because this is the Bronx yo, not Chelsea, and I don't want any trouble. But the man shows me some cash and I get in. Second mistake: Don't jump in a car with a john without checking the backseat first. And the man, another Jamaican, says him don't buy puss in a bag so open the bag and make me see the goodies, and I zip down my pants and take it out, and then he asks me to jack off and I'm feeling weird, like this is one of those real freaks who just wants to watch me cum, so I start to rub my cock even though it feels really, really weird, and suddenly the car stops and three guys jump out from the backseat. "Fuckin' batty boy," one of them says, and they open my door and pull me out. I didn't even notice that we had turned down some lane and the only witnesses would be rats. So they form this circle and one by one they grab me by the shirt, spin their arms like a whirlwind, and punch me in the face or the stomach, and every time I get hit it's like another explosion, and I vomit and that just makes it worse. And if I fall they pull me up and punch and kick me over to the next one, who punches and kicks me in the balls and I fall to the ground again and taste the garbage on the asphalt, and my eyes are so blurry that I can't see nothing. All I see is four blurs bent over me, then all of a sudden there are three blurs, then two. Two blurs jump up and try to fight a new blur. The new blur is black and white at the same time. The new blur flashes something shiny and plunges into one of the two. The last blur runs to the car and drives off. The new blur smells like sulphur. I see a hand coming toward me and I try to push it off, but this last blur is too strong. Then I realize that I was in the air. Gary picks me up and carries me back to this place.

I'm in this shack for I don't know how long. Back then I thought he was a miracle, but not long after that I realized that the only reason he was on that street was that he was cruising for ass too. I would have laughed if it wasn't so hard. A gunman on the road, Jamaican at that, looking to pick up a male whore. That said, I barely saw him. His room stunk. It was a hotel room—no, it wasn't, it was some Christian-home thingy. I soon realized that it was not his house that stunk, but outside. One of those places where garbage is never picked up on time. I didn't care, I would have followed him anywhere. I was there weeks or months, I don't know. He was barely there though. Sometimes I would wake up in the night only to hear heavy breathing beside me. He would smell like sulphur and he would be fast asleep. I'm wondering if people have asthma attacks in their sleep.

For a good while I couldn't see very good so I thought what I was seeing was not really real. I thought I was making it up, but when my eye swelling went down and I woke up and saw who was in bed beside me, I had to slap my mouth shut to stop the scream. In the bed was the whitest man I'd ever seen in my life. I wish I could say how it shocked me, I wish I could. At first I thought he was white. I couldn't form a word or a fucking thought. He was in the bed, sorta curled up in a red brief. His hair was light yellow, lighter than any blond I know, and his eyebrows were white and his skin was just covered in white hair. I stooped down beside his face and saw that his lips were thick and his nose kinda flat. I'd never seen an albino before. He was the most beautiful thing I'd ever seen in my life. I touched his hair, which was really coarse, and when I moved my hand he was looking at me. We just stood there. I was looking at him and he was looking at me.

Every now and then—shit, who am I fooling, every goddamn day Gary will just disappear like that and don't come back for hours, sometimes days. And he'll either be in a really good mood or a really fucked-up one and ask me for coke. I will tell him that I never do that shit and I can feel his punch coming before he even clenches his fist. This is so damn pathetic. I feel like the woman who loved too much. Then again, *love* is way too strong a word. And sometimes you blur the line between love and gratitude so much that you don't know if you showing affection or repaying a debt.

Fourth snapshot. We're in KFC on Gun Hill because the lighting sucks, and we're eating and fooling around. When he isn't pissed, or scared, or just in a mood to fuck things up, Gary is the funniest person to be around. And that place, especially in the darker corners round back, is one of those places where he can be himself. He lets out this nervous little laugh and says, "Boy, if some people ever find out, especially me girlfriend them, I don't know if they'd kill themselves or me first. Then again, they wouldn't believe it even if they heard it from my own mouth."

"That you are a faggot?"

"I not no bombo raas claat faggot!" This he says to me even though, for the entire time we have been here, his hand hasn't left my balls. This is not the kind of situation to get him mad.

"You can call a hardcore gangster *faggot?*"

"Well, you're not feeling up a pussy."

I shouldn't have said that. He grabs hard, and pain, fucking splitting pain that feels as if something is clawing its way through my stomach, causes me to double over on the table.

"Sorry, sorry . . ." he says, and he sounds as surprised at what he did as I am. I stomp his foot hard.

"No, you not, you son of a bitch."

He looks at me long and hard, then lets out a loud laugh. "Well, you certainly go on like a pussy sometimes. Look, how much time you want me to say sorry? Shit, you can gwaan like girl eeh, man? All this intense fuckery. Me can't deal with that. Look, I have to go do some business, me'll see you when me see you."

Three weeks later he shows up at the room we're staying, almost unconscious, trembling and bleeding. I will never forget the look he had on his face as long as he lets me live. Almost as if he saw God or something much worse. And he'll never forgive me for seeing him that way. I knew that he barely got away from something. I put him to bed and have to hush him three times when he wakes screaming that they're out fi get him wid forty-four bullets. You'd think he was reduced to nothing but a little flower in the palm of my hand and all that was left for me to do was to make a fist.

My name is Rockford Goodman. My mother thought she was being cute naming me after *The Rockford Files*. Even at her most depressed she was superficial that way. Gary calls me Rock and I'm not sure why either. Rockford sounds like shit, I know, so either he can't be bothered with saying the whole name or maybe he thinks I have some inner strength or something. Right. He's probably calling me Rock Hudson. I go back home. He's either waiting for me or coming for me. One or the other.

Fifth Snapshot. I'm alone in this house and can still see the bloodstains. On the living room wall where Andre took the house rifle and shot Daddy in the shoulder. Andre didn't know all that much about guns so he threw it away and went for a hatchet in the kitchen. By the time he found it, Daddy had already made the mistake to run upstairs. I can bet he was screaming. He must have grabbed the wall to support himself, because it had frantic bloodstains, which have fear written deep in them. Fear written deep. Clever. Man, I should be a writer. A blood trail leads halfway to the bathroom at the top of the stairs. It begins again and continues to Diane's room. There's blood in the closet. This strikes me as so damn ironic that he would run for safety into a closet that couldn't save any of us.

I imagine it happened the same way. He'd be crouched under the musty clothes, so shit-scared that he wouldn't even realize that his own blood was ratting him. Andre would open the door, and Daddy would see him, and that would be the last thing he saw before his eyes went red. I can imagine the hatchet becoming a part of him with a life of it's own; taking control of his actions and plunging into flesh like a jackhammer. It feels as if it commands you and there is nothing you can do to stop it.

Actually, I didn't say any of that shit, but the criminal psychologist did, at his trial. Personally, I think that is all bullshit. I don't think he lost it when he killed my parents. I don't think he was possessed by some temporary insanity or some *Night Stalker* bullshit. I think he just had enough. He told the court that he knew how Jane Fonda felt in *They Shoot Horses, Don't They?* My brother was tried as an adult and is serving two life sentences.

I wonder where Gary is. I wonder why this kinda exhilarates me, and I don't use that word every day. Maybe he's doing something that he always wanted, some kinky shit that he'll take too far. Maybe he'll enjoy it. He always talks about taking some asshole out in Kingston and how he'll let him bargain for his life by sucking him off, then kill the guy anyway.

Final snapshot. Yesterday I was sitting on this bed that I'm sitting on now and I hear the door crack. It fucks me up how these things just happen. I know it's the front door. Living here all these years, I remember the whole house coming to attention when one heard the click and clang of the front door being opened. Gary's at the door and he's laughing loud. This is strange. I lived here most of my life and never felt like I belonged, but this man who has never been here already sounds like his name is in the will. He laughs out loud again and I'm thinking he's either mad or with somebody.

I'm forcing myself not to give a shit. Sitting on the bed, staring into space as if downstairs is some new dimension entirely. Fuck it. I have to see who . . . No, I hate how this bothers me and I wish it didn't.

Damnit.

Damn him.

I get up and move to the door. Then turn back. It's none of my damn business. He laughs again. She laughs with him. Louder, longer. I'm out the door before it can even swing back, feeling the cold concrete and hearing my own feet. The bedroom door bangs shut and rats me. Downstairs nobody seems to notice. Damn that son of a bitch. I don't want to look, but I deserve to see who's having so much fun in this miserable house.

She's already on the floor smiling broad, with white teeth. Her hair is a big red Afro. I hate her already. She's got these huge breasts with big black circles on each nipple. He grabs one of her legs and slaps her pussy a couple times with his cock. Then he pushes it in and begins to fuck her. She screams immediately. Of course she's faking it, she could never know what true pain from being fucked feels like. He lies down on top and I see muscles in his back and buttocks flex and release as he moves in and out of her. She looks as if she's being battered to death. They don't say a word, only grunt like dogs or something. How does he do it? How does he fuck both ass and pussy but can't stand either? He rolls over and sees me.

"Ohhhh, Rock. Big, bad Rocky."

He's looking at me with a big grin and humming the tune to that fucking Sylvester Stallone movie.

"Baby, look up, some people watching the show. Ooooh, slow down, baby, this train soon reach the station. Rock is one bad girl this you know. You know how bad? She talking 'bout how when pussy getting fucked, ass must get fucked too!"

I hate him.

"Hers or yours?" I say.

I watch the albino man go red. The woman laughs out loud. He jumps up and starts to kick her in the belly. She's screaming, but he grabs her by the hair.

"You know say me a bad man, bitch? You know say me a bad man?"

He pulls her up and tells her to get the fuck out. She runs, pulling down her dress and forgetting her shoes. I run to my parents' room, but before I can close the door he kicks himself in. He grabs me and I'm kicking and fighting and trying to hit his balls, but he's not feeling anything.

"What the fuck wrong with you, eh? What the fuckin' fuck!"

He pulls me on the bed and straddles me and starts to punch me in the face and slap me and cuss me. And I can't do anything but fumble around the night table beside the bed, reaching for something, anything, to hit this son of bitch. He's still slapping me and cussing about me fucking up his business and how it's my fault that people looking for him and white people just love to fuck up ghetto man life, and he's still hitting me. I grab around the table and knock the lamp off and pull the crochet off and finally grab onto Mom's letter opener. Then he swings his hand back to give it to me this time, his final superfuckin' colossal shot, and as he swings his hand to my face I swing the letter opener to his palm and crucify the motherfucker.

He's looking at me all shocked and shit, and I'm shocked too. And I think about saying something, and he's pulling this puppy dog thing that disappears as soon as he notices that I notice. He climbs off me and leaves and I'm watching the door.

That's why he's coming back for me.

I'm beginning to think that there's some deep shit to loneliness. People think loneliness is the absence of people, but I'm starting to think that it's the opposite of people. And if that's the case, then loneliness is just as real as having a warm john next to you. Think about it. If you look at loneliness as this perfect state, like this universe of just yourself, then it's like perfect. I'm impressed with myself, this is some deep thinking. Clever, clever shit. Gary said I think too much.

Gary's coming. I'm in my father's deathbed waiting for my blood to join his. I took off all my clothes. You ever notice that most suicides took off their clothes before? Call me suicide by murder. The room's all dark now. I'm a big boy. I don't think I'll cry. But then I do, thinking about my pops and my bro and my sis and wanting to make a bath red from my wrists so that I can be with her. She was always my girl and I still think that by giving in to my pops she was taking the hit for me. Jesus, Jesus, I miss her so much. I just want to tell her I'm sorry and I understand if she doesn't want me in heaven with her.

I wish this darkness would just take me, then out of the dark he appears, and by the time his eyes and teeth match a description I recognize, I'm already screaming. He slaps me.

"What the fuck wrong with you?"

"Nothing. Why the fuck you hitting me?"

"You in the dark talking to yourself like you brain gone pan screw."

"I wasn't talking to myself."

"Then you thinking out loud?"

"Just forget it."

"Forgot it already. Move over."

He throws his shoes off and then 200 pounds of sweat and cigarette smoke land beside me. His hand is all bandaged up and his gun is missing. He does not look at me. Just climbs in the bed. Even when he is not snoring he breathes heavily, it sounds like sinus but to me it's like he's cursed to a lifetime of adrenalin overdose. I don't know how I feel. Kinda I want to, I think, but that's just a stupid song from Nine Inch Nails and proof to him that a faggot with white skin is the worst kind of faggot. I feel like Jane Fonda in *They Shoot Horses, Don't They?* Clever, I know.

PART IV

The Wanderer

HOME SWEET HOME

BY SANDRA KITT

City Island

I t had been years since I was last on City Island. That's the official name of the community that's a little spit of land connected to the Bronx by a bridge, one lane in each direction, not far from Pelham Bay Park. The bridge is the only way on or off the island.

I came back for only one reason, and it wasn't to order a plate of fried clams or shrimp bisque. I wanted to find out what really happened to Brody Miller. The two people in the entire world who would know still lived there on City Island.

I remember it was an adventure to go to City Island with my family and have dinner. Seafood and pizza predominated the businesses that ran the full length of the main street, City Island Avenue, from the bridge at one end down to Belden Street and the pier with its unobstructed view of Long Island Sound at the other. There were two other smaller islands as well, accessible by ferry. As far as I knew no one lived on either. (I now know, however, that short-term jail inmates from Rikers Island are transported there almost daily, for the grisly job of digging holes.) My family had its favorite places to eat, but since then most of those restaurants have been taken over by new owners and new names. Same food.

I never used to believe that anyone actually lived on City Island, as if the stores and restaurants along the main street were a back-lot façade. The restaurants located on the water were the real reason to go. Because of the view of the marina, and the bay beyond the small harbor, and to watch the occasional slow-moving pleasure boats on a nice day. There was something maybe a little exotic about this other world, because it was just barely connected to the rest of the city.

It was only after I met and started hanging out with Jenna Harding in high school, and she met and fell in love with Brody Miller, that I found some of the real charm of the place. Brody had fallen hard, granting City Island the status of Eden. Yeah, Jenna was our official safe passage into the tight-knit community of people who'd lived there for generations. But it was Brody who embraced the island with fervor and devotion as if it was also his own. I could never see City Island through either of their eyes, but I went along because Jenna and Brody somehow brought both worlds together, his and hers. But in the end the island showed them both that, either oil and water don't mix, or never the twain shall meet.

When I heard that Jenna still lived on City Island I knew I had to return. But it wasn't about her. She was always going to be welcome there; she was one of the island's own. I always felt more protective of Brody because, as everyone else and everything proved, he had no one but himself. I thought he was still there somewhere. I imagined I even knew where.

When I met Jenna in high school it was the first time she'd been off the island without her family or friends. But she had no choice. City Island schools only went through ninth grade and then all students had to go somewhere else to graduate high school. She said her parents wanted to send her to private school but couldn't afford it. They were afraid that urban life, and all those ethnic types, would open its great jaws and swallow their redhaired, green-eyed baby whole. I was one of "those people," but I'd add a little spice to my family by mentioning my American Indian background, effectively demonstrating that, in one way, I was here way before anyone else, like the Indians who originally inhabited City Island.

I started going over there to see Jenna and that's when my tunnel vision began to broaden peripherally. There were real homes and families. The side streets were small, the blocks short, the homes very close together, barely a human width apart. The island was Old World, like parts of Queens and Brooklyn, with a touch of New England coastal towns before redevelopment. It was sweet. It looked kind of rundown, but interesting. I hardly ever saw other people who looked like me.

When I met Jenna's parents they seemed, at first, suspicious. Years later I realized that their reception was probably no different from what my parents might have shown had Jenna ever met them and visited where I lived in Washington Heights. My mother worked. Hers didn't. My father owned a business that had him traveling through three nearby states several times a month. Jenna's father managed a business on City Island that his family used to own. My mother was the strong family matriarch. Jenna's father ruled because he was a chauvinist.

Tommy Harding liked to boast that his father was once the unofficial mayor of City Island. The Harding family had been there almost five generations. Tommy took over the title by default after his father died, and was inordinately proud of it. He wasn't a very big man; slender, a chain smoker, and a big storyteller. Not a lot of formal education, but by no means a stupid man. Mrs. Harding was almost invisible the few times I visited. She kept a clean if unimaginative house. There was a lot of crochet and quilted accents. One was a framed *Home Sweet Home* sign that greeted visitors just inside the front door.

As much as I was a little bit afraid of Tommy Harding and his big ego, I was more fascinated by his stories of life on the island, what it used to be like. Jenna once confessed, embarrassed but honest, that she thought her father was probably prejudiced. He'd told me that his best friend in the navy was black. But I wondered what he said about me behind my back after leaving his house.

I came to believe that Jenna's father treated me with the generosity of someone who felt perfectly safe in his universe, and was assured he was far better than I was. Jenna had two brothers. One who'd left right after high school to join the marines. The other had simply moved to a different boating town in Maryland. I wondered if in either case it was to get out of the shadow of their father. Jenna was the baby of the family, a distinction that held pros and cons, and that would ultimately decide her future.

And then Brody entered the picture.

Jenna and I met him at the start of our junior year when he'd transferred in to finish his senior year. He was tall, athletic, good-looking in a bad-boy, smartass way, even though he was neither. He was also an unknown. Neither white nor black, nor Latino, Brody was classic Heinz variety. That meant, whatever racial mixture went into his makeup, the end result was a guy who stood out, drew attention, seemed bigger than life. He had the open personality and charm of someone who went by his own rules but tried hard to get along.

Brody became my friend, the kind of male friend that is only possible when you're sixteen, and when you have something in common. In our case it was ambiguous background and heritage. Like me he had a curiosity about people, places, and things that made us fearless. But Jenna fell for Brody in the way of a young girl whose heart can be captured, true and fast, just once in her life.

Their romance became public domain, and everyone in school followed its development with personal interest. The other boys wanted to know how long it would take Brody to score. The other girls upped the ante and did what they could to get Brody's attention for themselves. I was witness to all of it, awed and deeply jealous that no one ever looked at me or sought me out the way Brody and Jenna did for each other.

Yet he wasn't a player. There was, however, something a bit dangerous and tense about him, like a predatory animal who had very tightly drawn parameters around his space and himself. Even Jenna hadn't picked that up about Brody, her eyes glazed over with infatuation, and defiance.

Once, Brody and I got to talking outside of school. We'd been let out early because of teacher meetings. Jenna hadn't bothered coming at all. I felt aimless and not ready to head back home to take up my role as babysitter to my younger siblings.

"So, Jenna didn't come in today," he said. He rolled the one spiral bound notebook he ever used, and forced it into the back pocket of his jeans.

"She said it was a waste of time just for a few hours. Anyway, it's a long bus ride from City Island," I said.

"Yeah, I know. If I'd known I would have skipped to be with her."

I looked at his profile. "You've been over there? To City Island?"

"Sure. Lots of times."

"With Jenna?" I thought of her father and the boundaries he'd laid down.

He laughed. "Before I ever met her. I use to fish off the

pier near the bridge. I once tried to get a summer job at the marina. Jen and me, we get together and walk around Orchard Beach Park. I have to do the right thing. I want to meet her folks, see where she lives. Let them know straight out Jen and me are together. I love City Island. I could live there."

"How come?"

"'Cause it's small. It's surrounded by water. It feels like home. Kind of cozy and safe and cut off, know what I mean?"

"Like your home?"

"Not where I live now. Where I'd like to live one day."

"But there's nothing there. There's nothing to do but eat. Jenna even says so and she liked growing up there. It's so different from the rest of New York."

"Maybe that's why I like it."

"Maybe your family could move there."

"I don't have a family. I live in a group home. My last foster parents moved before the school year started. I didn't want to go with them to Norfolk. I was old enough. I could decide to stay on my own."

I looked at Brody more closely. I was afraid to be too nosy and ask the questions that would give him a history and fill in the blanks.

"Aren't you afraid to be by yourself?"

"I've always been by myself. It could have been worse, I guess. I always knew I was really on my own. I don't know why my real mother gave me up. I don't know who my father is. Bottom line, I have to take care of myself."

"Doesn't that make you mad?"

"I used to be, but now all I want is my own life, my own place, and to do what I want. I've been working part-time near boats and water since I was fifteen. South Street Seaport promised me something full-time when I graduate, but I'm thinking how cool it would be to find a job on City Island. Then I could really stay."

Brody had always struck me as a guy who said what he meant, and knew what he wanted and pretty much how to get it. But what I wasn't hearing was where did Jenna fit in? Was she just a stepping-stone to his need to belong somewhere?

His self-confidence was amazing, and it made me wonder if there was some great advantage to having to build your own life, create your own family from the ground up. To not be afraid of the world, not be afraid of being told no. City Island must have seemed like a cosseted haven to him, the safe harbor at the end of the crazy world he came from, where kids were discarded like garbage.

Brody was already eighteen by the time we started our senior year. He looked and behaved older than most of us, which was part of his attraction. We still didn't know yet how combustible those kinds of traits could be. Awesome to us, threatening to others.

We all had to plot and plan how to get together on Friday nights and weekends for parties and occasional trips into the city to a club. Elaborate lies were created that tested the boundaries of our lives, our families, our communities. Brody had no such concerns and became our de facto leader. I know for me it changed the idea of how big and complicated the world was beyond my own neighborhood. For Jenna I think it was more confusing. How far was she willing to go before she had to turn back home?

"My father is going to kill me," she inevitably moaned on each new adventure. Like the one that took us to Staten Island, another remote outcast of a place.

In the spring before graduation, Jenna's parents insisted on hosting a birthday party for their daughter in the tiny backyard of their home. The idea both embarrassed and frightened Jenna, but everyone looked forward to the evening, hoping that the Hardings were cool enough to just disappear so that the real party could go down.

I got there too early, and sat on Jenna's bed and watched as she finished dressing and did makeup and decided on a pair of cute but treacherous high heels. Her friends started arriving in earnest around 8:30, quickly spilling into the front yard, and the street to the side of the house. Some boy who'd once dated Jenna, before she'd left the island and met Brody, actually showed up, his presence blessed by her father. Good-looking but, to my way of thinking, too much like a Tommy-in-the-making.

By 10 the party was on, but Jenna was nervous and excited waiting for Brody to appear. Me too. It was such a mixed party that everyone thought Jenna's folks surely knew about Brody by now. Her father especially was jovial and in good spirits, joking with the boys and drawing lots of raucous laughter. Gracious and flirtatious with the girls, drawing whispered comments like, "He's kind of cool." Music and voices and laughter floated like a breeze and wafted over the neighborhood.

Brody arrived a little before midnight, making an entrance that was not soon forgotten because of its simplicity and class. Those are my words. There are some who might give a slightly different spin. In any case, some kind of energy shifted in the yard. With it came anticipation.

Jenna, who had been giggly all evening, ran to greet Brody in a way that left no doubt they were an item. Before greeting anyone else, Brody presented Jenna's mother with flowers. She was so startled that she barely managed a thank you before escaping into the house with the bouquet. For Tommy

Harding, Brody had a bottle of Johnny Walker Red. Brody shook Tommy Harding's hand and thanked him for inviting him to the party, and into his home.

The ice had been broken.

The critical initiation had been passed. Brody was in. All of us closed around him and Jenna like the good buds, comrades, classmates that we were. It totally excluded her parents.

From his pocket Brody took out a delicate chain necklace with a sparkling gem pendant dangling from the center. Jenna turned so that he could fasten it around her neck. We *woo-wooed* like a team cheer while Jenna kissed Brody her thanks, and her love.

Given a real choice, I'm not sure that Jenna's father would have included Brody Miller, and it seemed to me Brody was an unwelcome surprise. Brody wasn't just another high school friend, he was a young man. He was not just another guest, he was seeing Tommy's daughter.

The music and laughter continued, and so did the drinking. At one point I noticed that the cake had been brought out and placed on a sawed-down tree stump that served perfectly as a small table. On previous visits to Jenna's house her father had always complained about the stump, promising to dig it out and get rid of it one of these days, while admitting that it had its uses, like now. The appearance of the cake was a good sign. By 1:30, 2 at the latest, the party would be over and we'd all leave. I wouldn't have to bare witness to whatever humiliation Jenna's father was making a case for, as he watched his little girl enjoying herself.

Jenna and Brody held hands, or put their arms around each other. Sometimes they danced, swaying together, hip to hip. Facing each other, the intimacy in their gaze naked and exposed. They looked great together. Years later I'd recognize that Jenna and Brody were setting an example and a standard for our own possibilities in love.

Tommy Harding drank too much. Mrs. Harding tried to draw him aside, away from the party that was not meant for him. Too late, Tommy's insecurities surfaced and he set out on a course aimed directly at Brody Miller. He suddenly stumbled across the yard, grabbed Brody's arm, and jerked him around, squaring off.

"I don't appreciate you comin' in here and taking over my daughter's party. Who the fuck are you anyway? Don't touch her."

"Daddy!" Jenna gasped in genuine shock.

The crowded yard grew silent so quickly it was as if we were all holding our breath, waiting for this moment.

Jenna's father and Brody were chest to chest. Brody had the advantage by about three inches. Standing with yet another beer and a cigarette in one hand, Tommy used the other to jab a finger in Brody's face. Brody took a step back. Jenna was holding his arm. That only infuriated her father more.

I closed my eyes before the first punch could be thrown. All around me people were on the move; standing way back, or pushing through the side gate onto the street. I heard a lawn chair scrape against the flagstone ground and then fall over, as did a bottle that broke. I heard Jenna screaming at her father to stop, her mother wailing like a Greek chorus. I heard Brody quietly telling Tommy Harding to calm down, but I was waiting breathlessly for the tipping point. Brody's next suggestion that maybe he should leave was overridden by Jenna's declaration that she was going with him. That sealed it. Both were cut off by a sudden crunch and a thud, a grunt. A high-pitched scream rose over the music.

Jenna got between her father and Brody. Her red hair was

like a flag, and the only color to be distinguished in the yard lit by lanterns. She was not trying to stop her father but trying to protect Brody. Her choice spurred Tommy Harding into a fury. And it was as if some silent call had gone out. Suddenly, nearly half a dozen men, including Jenna's former boyfriend, were rushing Brody. They surrounded him, tackling him to the ground.

I heard them calling Brody every dirty word and name they could utter.

"Call the cops. Call the *cops!*"

It was my own voice I heard, disembodied and shrill. I wanted to make them stop, but I was terrified of the men turning on me as well. No one went to Brody's aid, and Jenna was wrenched from his side. Once again, he was on his own. He didn't belong on City Island, and he sure as hell wasn't going to get a chance to be with Jenna Harding.

I don't remember hearing police sirens. But the fight had lost its momentum and the men were weary. I couldn't see Brody, but I knew I had to get out of there. Fear took over. I stepped over the debris that was now the backyard. The birthday cake had been smashed and destroyed, the colorful frosting a globby mess on the ground.

Jenna was crying hysterically and being comforted by her mother, but she kept calling out Brody's name. Her father was slouched on a step at the back of the house. Another man sat bent over on the tree stump that minutes ago held the birthday cake. Brody was on his knees, silently hunched over and motionless. Two men stood over him, as if daring him to get up. Finally, I took a hesitant step toward Brody, but someone stood in my way to prevent my passage.

"It's all over. Go home. There's nothing to see. Just go home."

"Brody? Come on. Get up. Let's get out of here," I heard my own trembling voice.

"Don't worry about him. We'll see that he gets home. It was a fight and now it's over."

"But he didn't start it," I said.

The man got right in my face. "Go . . . *home*."

I hung around outside, shivering not from the night air but from having watched Brody outnumbered by five or six able-bodied men. There were still a couple dozen partygoers hanging around. I waited for Brody to come out so we could head back into the city together.

Maybe twenty minutes later a police car ambled its way up the street. The two officers got out and approached the house as if they were just stopping by for a friendly cup of coffee. No rush to see if a teen named Brody Miller was hurt and maybe needed an ambulance.

I decided that Brody would probably be okay.

I went home.

Jenna was not in school the entire next week. Neither was Brody. The talk was not about the ruined birthday party but about the fight, and Brody getting his ass kicked. There was also talk that Brody and Jenna had run off together. I preferred that story to the one that kept playing in my mind.

Jen returned, sullen and standoffish, for the last three weeks of school, and finally graduation. She had nothing to say about anything, except that she and Brody had broken up.

Okay, I could see that happening. She wasn't going to defy her own father. She wasn't going to take a risk, or stand up for what she believed or what she wanted. I can't say if that was a mistake, but it was certainly her loss.

I, for one, never saw Brody again.

* * *

It was years before I thought I'd figured out what happened to Brody Miller. I couldn't tell Jenna. Anyway, I kind of lost touch with her a few years after we graduated. Once I did ask her, flat out, if she ever heard from Brody. She said, simply, no. End of conversation. I heard that someone contacted his group home supervisor only to be told that Brody was no longer there. He was past being a minor, a ward of the state, and if he chose to take off without telling anyone, he had the right.

Jenna and I drifted further apart. What used to hold us together no longer existed. I guess that was as much by choice as it was by circumstance. I know now that you have to work at the things you want, like friendship or love. She landed a job at a law firm in New York. I finished college and returned home. Then one day I realized that I had never returned to the island since the night of Jenna's birthday party. But that was also the start of some not-so-far-fetched thoughts that wouldn't go away.

Like believing that Tommy Harding and his friends had killed Brody Miller that night and buried him in the Harding's backyard.

After a while it didn't even seem so crazy an idea. I'd already witnessed some of the terrible things people were capable of doing to each other, all to protect themselves, their families, their homes . . . or in the name of God.

Then, one day, I took a bus back to City Island, getting off the first stop outside a restaurant called the Sea Shore. That was as far as I got. I made myself sick wondering, *What if I'm right? What if Jenna's father goes to jail? What if her family is forced to sell their home, and they leave the island in disgrace? What if Jenna hates me?* If Brody was really dead, could I be forgiven for catching and turning in his killer, the father of a friend?

But I wasn't prepared for a full-fledged flashback of the night of the fight, chilling me to the bone on an eighty-degree day. I turned around and caught the next bus off the island. I was shaking like crazy.

It was a year later when I came up with a real plan. I first went to the police precinct that covered City Island and asked about an incident one spring night nearly seven years earlier at the home of one of the residents. The cops made a show of checking old ledgers and computer databases, and said they could find nothing out of the ordinary. The only thing recorded for that Saturday night was an incident involving a small boat that had been stolen by teens and later run aground.

I did a search of newspapers articles and reports for that entire week. Nothing. I kept thinking, *Cover-up*. Or, had the police arrived to drive Brody off the island, maybe all the way home? But that was part of the problem again. Brody had no home. He'd wanted City Island to be his home. Maybe he'd gotten his wish.

I Googled his name and the date and still got nowhere. But it was more likely that without anyone to champion him, Brody could have met with foul play. Another thing . . . people vanish all the time. Sometimes, right under our noses.

There was no help for it. I knew I was going to have to go back and see Tommy Harding.

I don't think I was prepared to learn that Jenna was back, although I'd heard rumors over the years. She was no longer with her parents but in her own place. I couldn't find her listed in the local directory, so I called the City Island Historical Society, located in a converted school. An elderly voice answered. Of course he knew the Hardings. He also knew nothing of the night that stayed in my memory.

It was a weather perfect day when I next returned. I got off the bus several blocks from the corner where I'd turn to approach the Harding house. I used the walk to look around and found, eerily, that everything seemed pretty much the same as the last time I'd been this far. There was a craft fair in full swing, and the sidewalks were crowded with tables and makeshift booths of local folks selling their stuff. I bypassed it all.

I turned the corner and approached the Harding house. I was caught off guard when I realized that someone was sitting on the tiny porch. It was Tommy Harding in the flesh, alive and well. I stood on the curb and silently stared at him, too struck by warp time to be able to say anything. He leaned forward in his decaying wicker chair.

"Can I help you? You lost or something?"

"Mr. Harding?"

"Yeah. Who's asking?"

"I went to school with Jenna. Maybe you remember me?"

He silently regarded me, so still and so coldly that I expected him to yell, *Get the hell out of here!*

"Sure. I remember you now. How've you been? Jenna hasn't mentioned you in years. Well, come on in."

I walked through the open gate and up to the steps.

"I know you weren't expecting me. I'm meeting some friends for lunch in a while," I improvised smoothly. "I thought that since I was here . . ."

"You want to know how Jenna's doing?"

"How are you and Mrs. Harding?" I stalled, minding my manners.

"Fine, fine. Grandparents now, thanks to my son living in San Diego. Wife's out at that street fair. Come on up and have a seat."

"Thanks, but I can't stay long," I said. "I did want to ask about Jenna. How's she doing, and everything. I lost touch with her a few years ago."

He didn't say anything for a minute. I wondered if he was putting together Jenna leaving City Island to go to high school and meeting me. And Brody.

"Well . . . you know Jenna. She became Miss Independent after she finished high school. Moved into the city, got a job . . ."

"Did she ever get married?"

"Two years ago. A young guy she grew up with from around here. He's a cop in the city. Ran into Jenna when he gave her a speeding ticket, and *boom*. Before you could say City Island they're planning a wedding." He cackled gleefully at his own joke. "Sorry you weren't invited."

He wasn't sorry at all, and neither was I. Things change. "I hope she's happy."

"She sure did make a beautiful bride. Come inside. I have an album with all the pictures."

He got up and headed into the house. I hadn't expected Tommy Harding to make it so easy for me. The inside of the house had not changed either. The first thing I still saw was that *Home Sweet Home* sign on the wall. It suddenly bothered me a lot to see it. While he was trying to find the right album, I walked toward the window that faced out on the backyard.

"Here it is. Let me turn on the light. See, wasn't she something? Her husband is a great guy. Known him all his life. They live on the other side of the avenue."

"So, it's true. She moved back to City Island?"

His smile was knowing and amused. "She never really left. City Island is a great place to raise a family. The fruit don't fall all that far from the tree, you know."

I knew. But I'd hoped that the story would have turned out differently. I bent over the album opened to Jenna's wedding ceremony. She made a stunning bride, the smiling man standing just behind her a handsome groom. I stared at the images wondering if there'd ever been a chance that Jenna's future husband might have been Brody? I leafed through the pages but quickly lost interest.

"Why don't you stop over and say hello? I'm sure Jenna would like that."

I wonder.

The phone rang and Tommy Harding excused himself to take the call.

That was the moment I needed. I hurried to the window, my heart racing, knowing that this was the moment of truth. Out the window the yard had changed, but not in the way I expected. A small deck had been built, squeezed into one corner. But I also saw that the tree stump was still there. It had not been dug up to provide a convenient hole. The only thing likely to be found beneath it were very dead roots.

"How do you like the deck?"

I grabbed at the opening. "The last time I was here was for Jenna's birthday our senior year. It ended in a fight with one of our friends, Brody. I don't know what happened to him after that night. Do you?"

"Well, I sure don't. Don't remember the guy very well. Lot of drinkin' went on that night. Wife told me the next day I made a fool of myself, embarrassed Jen. Too much beer," he chuckled, unrepentant.

He walked back to the door. I knew that was my invitation to leave. He'd been gracious and let me in. But I wasn't going away till I got what I wanted. Information. The truth. The whereabouts of Brody.

Halfway across the small living room I happened to spot a bottle of Johnny Walker Red on a bookcase. It was still sealed. It could have been a different bottle than the one given to Jenna's father that night. It could have been the same. It was something else I'd never know for sure.

I said goodbye to Mr. Harding and walked off his property. Behind me I heard him whistling, comfortable and safe in his kingdom on the bay. He'd given me Jenna's address, but in that moment I don't know how much I really wanted to see her again. Too much distance had formed between us, and I was really pissed off with her. She got to come home again, get married to someone else, and settle down like Brody never existed. How could she forget what they'd been like together?

Nevertheless . . . I crossed City Island Avenue to the quiet streets on the other side, looking for her address. When I found it and saw the life she was living I knew for sure the past was over. Dead and buried.

I was startled when a door slammed on the side of the house and a tall man walked around the car parked in the narrow driveway and prepared to get into the driver's seat. He stood poised with one foot on the doorframe.

"Come on, Jen. Move it. We're late."

A second later the door opened again and the former Jenna Harding rushed out. She hadn't changed either.

Her flaming hair was still the same length and style as in high school, as in her wedding photos. And she was still answering the call of men like her father who had never ventured very far from this place. Brody might have made a difference. But I forget. He wanted to live here too.

I was going to leave without making my presence known, but Jenna saw me and stopped dead in her tracks. Over the top of her white picket fence, and about seven years, we stared at each other. In her eyes, for a split second, I saw someone I used to know.

"Hey," she smiled brightly. "What are you doing here?"

Over the fence we air-kissed. The man in the car gently tapped the horn.

"Wait a minute!" she yelled, irritated, turning once more to me. The smile reappeared. "Wow. It's been so many years."

"Congratulations," I said.

"So you heard I got married," she shrugged.

Just then something sharp and bright sparkled at her throat. It was the pendant that Brody had given her on her birthday years before. I couldn't believe it.

"Let me introduce you to . . ."

"You're in a hurry. I just saw your father. I . . . stopped by to say hello."

"You did?"

"Well, I actually came for the street fair," I fabricated again. "He told me you live here."

"You should have let me know you were coming. I would have invited you to visit, but we're heading out to his folks for dinner."

"Go ahead. I won't hold you up," I said, stepping back.

She suddenly reached out to me. "Wait. Did you ever hear from Brody?"

Her question was so unexpected that I looked at her hopefully. "I was going to ask you the same thing."

She silently shook her head. "I don't know anything. Daddy kept telling me everything was going to be all right."

"What did he mean by that?"

"I don't know."

"Jen, come on, already!"

"Stop yelling. I'm coming," she pouted.

We stared once more at each other.

"I never saw him again after that night," she said.

"Maybe he never left the island, Jenna."

"He did talk about signing up for military duty, and then coming back here."

She didn't get it.

The car sounded again.

"I really gotta go. Call me sometime, okay? We'll get together." She hurried to the car and got in.

I knew I never would. I stood and watched as the car backed out of the driveway and the former Jenna Harding proceeded with her life as a newly minted matron of City Island, having given up all opportunities to become someone else.

I was overwhelmed with disappointment. I'd held out hope of solving the mystery, positive that something terrible had been done to Brody after the party and he'd never left the island. The body buried in the backyard turned out not to be true. Worse, Jenna appeared as much in the dark as I was.

So, what had happened to Brody Miller?

Had he crept away alone to lick his wounds? Been threatened to stay away from Jenna and City Island? Had he given up on his dream and moved somewhere to create a new one? Was he hiding in the military, always looking for a few good men, and the only place that would give him a home, no questions asked?

The fair was still in high gear, the beautiful weather bringing out more people than the sidewalk space could actually support. Many had given up and drifted into nearby cafés and restaurants to get out of the heat. I stopped in my tracks and was grabbed by another thought.

What if, as I'd believed for so long, Brody was still here. Just not *here*.

I turned around and began walking again. This time I was looking for a sign that would point the way to one of the other small islands just off the north shore of City Island.

It was called Hart Island. Well-known, but not often discussed. There was a ferry that went over, but no one ever went there just to visit.

I found Fordham Street, which cut through the middle of City Island at its widest point and extended to the ferry stand. I walked there and then stood on the dock staring out at Hart Island. I really don't understand why I continued to believe, deep in my soul, that Brody's final resting place was over there. In any case, this is where it ends.

With no family or real address, with only a name known in a very small circle, it would be so easy for him to disappear. With no record of his existence, there would certainly be none of his passing. Like so many others who never fit in anywhere, a final home may have been made for someone once known as Brody Miller in Potter's Field.

A VISIT TO ST. NICK'S

by Robert J. Hughes
Fordham Road

I could have found it in my sleep, I could have made my way by touch, or even sense, through the turnstiles, to the trains, to the seat, my seat, the one at the middle, the one that let me out closest to the Fordham Road exit, the one I'd considered my stop, my station, my neighborhood, for too long. But I kept my eyes open. I wanted to see how it had changed, I guess, I wanted to see how it had not, and how twenty years had wasted away—twenty years of my life, my half-life.

It was all so new to me. Again. This life, this freedom, this air. Even the fetid smell of the sweating subway station, even the feral rats that nibbled on the black and glistening garbage bags, even the putrefying corpse of a drunk wheezing on the end of the oily platform, they all meant freedom to me. In the car, they all meant the world had gone on. The big-busted Latinas in their halters with their hoop earrings and stilettos, perched on the benches giggling, half women, all girl. The attitudinous black boys, boastful and wary, manful and scared, sitting with hooded eyes in the corners. The plaid school kids in clutches, the Laotians, the Vietnamese, the Cambodians, whose features I couldn't figure, whose Asian geographies had populated the place when some more of the Irish had seeped out in the recent past. But not all of them had gone. Not my mom. Not my sister. Me, yes. My brother, of course, gone. This had been mine once, this neighborhood where all I saw was squalor, all I savored was stench, and all I felt was opportunity slipping away. This was now mine again, at least in time, for an hour, for two, for today. For more, though. For more. Always, for more.

My neighborhood. My home, once. My home never again. My home was far away, had been, for too long, for too needlessly long. And all because I'd been afflicted with stupidity, and never thought about repercussions. I'd never figured that a victimless crime would eventually have one. We are all victims, somehow, sometime, somewhere. No matter. But though I would never live here again, I had to come back just for now.

The train pulled out into the air and became an el, and the light made me feel, as always, as if I had just discovered grace. The sun blossomed over the rooftops. A few people on the car took out cell phones, and began to shout over the din, din themselves. At Fordham Road, I stepped down again onto the street. I cupped my hand over my brow and got my bearings. Not that I needed to. But I wanted to survey the shifting landscape. The stores were different, but the sidewalk held the same hubbub, now less Irish, now more other, less pink, more beige. The views I had thought vivid faded as my memories met new banks, aging bodegas. There was that White Castle, still going, still open twenty-four hours. Mike's Papaya, too, dusty and yellow. There the 99-cent store. And there the Mega 99. There the pawnbroker, now with debt solutions in seven languages. And new nail and hair palaces. China Nail. Beauty J. Fordham Nails Ltd., tatty and limited indeed. And the restaurants: Centenario V, Comidas Latinas y Mariscos, Excellents II. English must have been new for them once, but twice? I'd taught ESL upstate, part of my good works there, my rehabilitation. If good had meant anything. It got me here, then, partly, it helped my release. But here, I still didn't know. I gazed again. There, on the corner, the little bakery, and across from Devoe Park a white van, El Rancho, selling *frituras* and *chimichurri*. There, tucked away just off Father Zeiser Place, Patsy's Bar, the old reliable, and, oh, up ahead, my undoing.

Across University Avenue at the Fordham Road intersection stood those stately gray twin bell towers. Positioned between them above a stained-glass window, a cross, small and unnecessary, punctuated the hot blue sky, as if anyone needed reminding that this was a church. St. Nicholas of Tolentine. Unwelcoming below were the same wooden doors still blistering paint a shade of iron-rich dried blood. My church. My parish. My grammar school. My baptism, my communion, my confirmation. My *bête noir*. My childhood in a granite sanctuary. Here was my soul anointed in the baptismal, my brow moistened by the holy-water font, my fingers sulfured by matches snuffed at the foot of the saint, my conscience soothed by muttered pleadings at the altar rail, cosseted by lies in the confessional. Shadowed by scuffling in the sanctuary. Haunted by the shouting. Sickened by the blood. Hounded in the darkness. I shouldn't be here.

I noticed on the sign outside that mass was beginning in ten minutes. I looked over to my right at Devoe Park, where a listless player was shooting hoops, his ball hitting the court in lazy thuds. I ascended the seven heavy marble steps. A Latino man was more sure than I and, coming up behind me quickly, held open the creaking door. I nodded *gracias* and followed him in, staying a moment in the dank narthex. The stone fonts were empty. Had they been filled, would I have dipped my finger in and touched the water to my blasphemous temple? Attempted my own atavistic ritual of ungranted forgiveness? I would have. I would have relished the blessed water fizzling to steam on my iniquitous fingers as I dared dishonor God. But I was spared that visible damnation for now. I ignored the dusty fonts and went in, standing at the back under the choir loft, letting my eyes adjust.

It was sticky here in the muffled light. A fan at the back whirred, faint against the humid afternoon. Two stained-glass windows on the right side near the choir loft were cracked open at the bottom, under a scene of Jesus speaking to the elders. His early years. When he was filled with promise. Millennia until they'd discovered speed and crack and all of that delightful nastiness.

About twenty-five people were here in church, dropped like random seeds along the hard furrows of the pews. Most of them were at the front, sprouting near the apse. A few knelt to the right side, under the white figure of St. Nicholas floating on a high shelf by the transverse door, a rare papal touch of statue in a church austere enough to have been Episcopalian. But no, here was more sign of a particular denominational kitsch, a chapel at the left transverse, a shrine to the Virgin, *Nuestra Señora de Providencia*, for the defiantly devout and luckless. I walked that way, barely genuflecting in front of the altar, just another worshiper. The church was empty on the far side but for one man wearing in this heat a camouflage jacket, perhaps from the Army-Navy store on Davis around the corner. Perhaps a veteran. Perhaps a murderer. Perhaps a brother in carnage. And still touched by his religion. Or his disgrace. Or his memories. He could have been Puerto Rican. He could have been Irish. His white hair glowed as if dappled by some interior star, and he held his head down, in sleepy prayer, a cane propped against the pew before him. I walked past him into that side chapel. The front of the church had begun to rustle with the movement of the priest; he checked the sound system, a few taps on a mike, followed by a rumple of fabric as his surplice sleeve scraped across it. Testing.

The chapel was dark too, with but a few candles glowing electric in their enclosed ruby glass biers. I put in a quarter, and another light sprang to feeble life. Before, in my distant youth, this place had been a vague chapel for the Virgin of the Whatever. She wasn't particularly providential for me, whoever she'd been. I couldn't recall her mission, or mine, for that matter—beyond offering her candles, real ones then with flickering flames unlike the repellant little flashlights now. The battered kneeler, imprinted with the depression of countless others, was still there, askew, pushed away from the array of fake votives; someone had risen awkwardly and shifted it. Perhaps the camouflaged veteran Garcia-Gerrigan out there finding way to his unsteady feet and lamentable cane. On the wall was a plaque in Spanish and several overemotional icons of the Virgin's face. A painted statue of that fortunate Mary guarded one corner, and a small onyx one kept sentry at another. Here was a shrine of true belief, simpleminded, strong, primal.

I left and moved softly back to the rear, to another corner, where a statue of St. Nicholas, this one brown instead of white, more earthbound, rested at the wall. This was one I had hoped to find; I hadn't seen it at first, its own beige camouflage hiding it from my greedy eyes. Its feet were polished from countless eager peasant fingers. I ran my hand along its pedestal myself, feeling as obvious as if I were a surplice brushing an open mike. I looked around me, a furtive supplicant. I felt around the back of St. Nicholas, searching for an indentation underneath. I stepped back, to bow in specious prayer, to scrape my mind for where it might have been placed. It had to be there. They never moved these plinths, they were bolted to the floor and their false idols to them, secured against the marauding horde, the petty us, the larcenous me. I felt again, pious and plaintive, my fingers touching the worn marble feet. There. Yes. A nib of something metal by the back right side, wedged tightly in. Just as Jimmy had said there'd be. I would return.

I dropped another quarter into a candle slot, saw that it lighted, picked up the parish bulletin from a wall holder, and found an empty pew. The bulletin was in Vietnamese. I didn't try to read it, but turned it over, as I had always done in church, to examine the advertisements on the back, for funeral homes and auto repair shops, for abortion counseling and broker-free apartments, all in English. The list of priests was there on the second page. One Irish. Two Latino. One Vietnamese. The church hours. In English. Evening vigils. What was today? Yes. Tonight.

I looked up along the long, high-ceilinged nave from where I sat. I had remembered clerestory windows above the aisle roofs and the vaulting, but that must have been in a dream, or I'd imagined someplace grander than this. A conflation of conscience and hope, perhaps. The light softened toward the altar, where the apse lay in a wooden shadow.

The priest, russet-faced, bearded, sixtyish, Irish, walked out again. He wasn't wearing a chasuble, a nod to the warmth that permeated even the usual coolness of a stone church. Just an alb, and his surplice, the barest vestments of office, the merest priestliness. He had an open, kind face. He began the service, hands apart in a limp crucifix, saying, "We open up to a God who loves us." I bowed my head as if in prayer. But no. No. No love here. I wondered how much he believed himself, and how much was a scam. I'd wondered that aloud to the prison chaplain, and toyed with the idea of vicardom or something like it myself—it could beat the library. But that was then.

I looked back at the statue. A leaning parishioner with a boozy paunch and droopy neck met my eye from the row behind me. I tilted my head down a fraction. Just another believer biding time.

A church can breed its own defiance and devotion, personal and fierce. I looked up and considered what the window to my left might mean to me, in my own dim trepidation, had I considered a metaphor of suffering for myself. *In Memory of the Schmitt Family*, with its scene of the Sermon on the Mount, maybe? They died too long ago for me to care, for either the paltriness of their demise or the hubris of their son remembering them in glass. What about the Doyle Family, by their brother? The incorrigible Prodigal Son. No. He would never return, at least not repentant. Or, on the right side, the window depicting Jesus' mother at the foot of the cross? No remembrance from a guilty son or battered brother marked it. Just a generalized suffering. Mary's face here cowed by grief, her followers propping her up, others holding Jesus' body limp with temporary death. The words *Mary Sodality* were painted at the bottom. Mom's group of rosary-wielding hysterics. She now, I thought, would be waiting sullen at the Oxford apartments just there in screaming distance on Webb Avenue. Not waiting for me. But maybe waiting for news of me. And perhaps, too, like Mary, for release. Mine, perhaps. Hers, maybe. And she too had her own ministry. Of shame. I'd be there later to serve under it. It was important. Not the service. The being there.

One of the parishioners announced a reading from the book of Hosea. I heard just a few sentences, as my thoughts wandered outside, into the glare oozing through the windows.

"I will lead her into the desert, and speak to her heart . . . the days of her youth . . . The Lord is gracious and merciful . . . I will espouse you the right of justice."

The gospel just after that went by quickly. It must have been a paragraph, a weekday snippet of good news. I'd missed it, turning around again, as if to look at the choir loft, as if to fool my friendly parishioner there behind me. The priest spoke. I turned to face him, settled myself, head slightly bent. His sermon. He said, "How do you see God?" He paused; not too oratorical. He meant it. "Do you remember your youth?" Do I. It's all I ever had and squandered. "Can you awaken in yourself the love you had?" No. Because I didn't. So many questions. Like the thoughtful believer he obviously was, the priest tried to connect the readings, to make quotidian sense of them for us in our tawdry lives, here amid the perspiration and second thoughts of Christ's distant followers.

My mind meandered through the consecration. The key. The sanctuary. I'm sure the stash hadn't been found. It must still be there. Had to be. We stood. The Lord's Prayer. We all murmured it, even me, finding the words again easily enough. The people at the front were holding hands. When had this touching begun? I hadn't been in a church since that night, ten years ago. I hadn't attended mass for ten years before that. When had we all become so, I don't know, Pentecostal? They'd be speaking in tongues next.

"Let us offer each other the sign of God's peace," the priest suggested, and the hand-holders held on and looked at each other with shy disbelief in actual forgiveness, while those of us until then blessedly free of contact turned and made nice to strangers. I reached back and grasped the fleshy hand of the man behind me, who gave me a weird little smile. *No, you don't*, I thought, widening my gaze. *You don't know.*

I shuffled out of the aisle, and slowly went up to take communion, along with the redeemed brethren beside me. It meant nothing to me, I convinced myself, this ritual, but still my heart began to thump with the inchoate tremor of the damned. I did not believe in this tasteless wafer, but I feared somehow the wrath. I had always believed I'd be found out further, even after being discovered back then, limp and bloody, curled fetal in the chancel where I'd collapsed after the beating, after hiding, hoping to remain hidden. Then, it was fear of my punishment. Now, it was dread of another crime. Now. But then. Not back then. Not when I had not killed my brother. It hadn't been me. Despite what my mother believed. Now, I wanted to see the sanctuary door again. To remind myself of where I'd been, or broken in. I thought it looked the same, but couldn't be sure. Even the church changes—witness the newfangled grasping. I took the host in my hands, muttered my false thanks, and gave a little glance to the right of the altar. Later.

I shuffled back in holy ignominy to my pew, and leaned forward against the row before me, aping prayer, as we all do no matter what we think we believe. I prayed to Our Lady of Providence. I prayed to the sad spirit of my brother, wherever he ended up. Wherever my mother's useless prayers might have positioned him in the afterlife.

The priest sat after the communion rite, to read announcements and utter remembrances. "Let us pray for those who are isolated in institutions, prisons, nursing homes, hungering for the warmth of home." How many of this sparse little congregation knew prisons? How many of them knew what the warmth of home was, or did they just pretend to carry with them a phony memory of affection to get themselves through their leaden days? I had cut off my family. I had turned back all letters. I knew they would be filled with the screeches of my mother's despair, my sister's keening anger. I kept aside only that one of Bella's, thicker than most, the guard signaling it contained cash for when I got out. But I could barely read even that except to take her offering and deny her the satisfaction of forcing me to hear of her generosity and deluded, misguided, untoward hope. Her stultifying superiority in matters moral.

"Let us pray for Father Tran, who is visiting family in Vietnam," the priest said. "For Father Guzman, in Argentina, working with the missions there. And Father Terranova, in Costa Rica this July." No one was at home. These roaming Augustinian mendicants spent their summers proselytizing among the heathens of the world. And tonight—I looked over the pastoral staff list on the bulletin—only white-haired Father Farrell would likely be on hand. "Let us go in peace. The mass is ended," he told us. I waited as the church emptied, to walk about. But a clutch of Latinas were nattering on with the reverend Farrell there by the altar rail, his own trio of "excellent women," Excellents III, perhaps. I left, after having walked once more toward the apse, to glimpse the chancel door.

Before heading to what my ma considered home, I decided to stop at Patsy's again. Temptation, no. Just, I don't know—people, places, things, all of which I'd been warned against. As if it mattered, when there were fewer people I knew. The places I'd remembered were few too, and the thing I wanted, well, it was the only reason to be here. But it wouldn't be at Patsy's. Where I shouldn't be either. I was supposedly clean. At least I was no longer using, had broken that habit fairly early on, managed to get through the years unimpeded, but for one lapse. I could handle the bar now, I thought. Just not yet my mother.

It was just after 1, and the westerly sun had begun to shaft along the bar just as it had back in the day, turning the sudsy beer golden, the shots of rye amber, swathing the nursing codger briefly in light before a sepulchral pallor reclaimed him. Danny—God, it was he, still here, lanky as a Joad—leaned against the till, a towel draped over his shoulder, his attention taken upward by a blaring documentary. A standard-issue sot leaned over the bar, his elbow nestling his grizzly chin, his face turned downward but biased in the direction of the television. In a booth among those that lined the back a couple cooed inebriated nothings at each other; on their table were a tall-neck Miller and a highball, half finished, plus a few empties. The lovebirds' heads turned briefly toward the door as I came in, and Danny glanced my way, but only to sigh slightly. This was his afternoon quiet, so to speak, and a trio of tipplers was enough for him. Reluctantly, he turned away from the television.

"Can I get ya something?"

He didn't recognize me, haloed as I was by the sun.

"Coffee."

"There's a bakery round the corner." Not unfriendly, not inviting. His voice carried a trace still of his mother's Ireland. He had spent summers there, I recalled, his ma's folks' Donegal place. This bar was his now, I took it, had been his father's, but he must be dead, ancient as he'd been back then. They all must be gone.

"I see a pot there."

"That's tar."

"Ah. Club soda, then. With cranberry."

He gave me a wary nod, assessing me for hipsterdom or worse, sobriety. But my clothes, though clean, were down-market and decades-old, my demeanor humble. *Please, war-*

den. He scooped some ice into a glass, squirted soda onto it, and added a pink splash from a plastic jug. He tossed a cardboard coaster before me, nestled the glass on the word *Patsy's* swashed across its center, plunked a swizzle stick between the cubes, and tapped the bar with his knuckles. On him.

"Thanks." I gently lay a couple of surviving bucks down. I had nothing, really. My sister's regretful wad, folded into that recrimination I didn't read when I'd reclaimed my belongings, had disappeared quickly. Train fare, subway fare, fare. I was down to tips. And maybe that key.

He turned again to the TV. "The church?" He spoke over his shoulder, but shifted his position so his back wasn't to me. I remembered. People did come to see it, St. Nick's. The local landmark. Basilica of the Bronx, sans basilica, sans historical interest, really, but passing tragic for me.

"My mother."

"The Oxford, then?" Where most of the remaining Irish lived, the well-tended, tired apartments in the shadow of the church, in the clutches of it, off Devoe Park.

"I've been away."

"You do look sorta familiar." My hair was thinner, my sallow face held penitential hollows. I had the bearing of forbearance, which is to say I looked beaten down. He eyed me, his brow furrowing. "What's her name? Your ma?"

"Doyle. Agnes Doyle. My sister Bella lives with her."

"And you're Davey. You must be. I remember Bella. I still see her at church every now and again." Danny had folded his arms across his chest, the bar rag draping over his left shoulder. I couldn't read his expression. It was, if anything, neutral. "You must be out."

"Must be. Yesterday."

"So. A new life then."

"I hope so."

"At mass, were you?"

"Yeah. Don't believe much, now, but it couldn't hurt."

"No. But."

He meant the memories. Even in a changing neighborhood, some things are remembered. The scene of the crime. It had actually been part of a long scene, that had begun at the check-cashing place where my sister once worked.

The lump of a drunk down the bar turned from his drink and looked over at me, sensing something. I assumed my prison face, and he shifted his glassy eyes down again. I'd spent several unremembered years here, in various stages of blackout and fury, seething over something petty, something my brother said, something my mother did, something my sister wanted.

"So you're off the sauce."

"Yeah. Best thing for me. Ruined my life."

"It can."

"You must see a lot of that."

"Sometimes. But it's an old crowd here."

"So . . . how's business?"

"We manage."

"And your ma?"

"Back over. For a while now, with her sister, near Ards. Rural ass of backwards. It'd drive me batty. We manage here."

"We."

"My wife's a lawyer now. You remember Sheila. Sheila Corrigan, from seventh grade?"

"Of course." Bouncy and becurled and just a little shifty-eyed. I was surprised she'd made it through the LSATs, let alone passed the bar. "That's great. Good for you."

"We live over in Riverdale, near her mom now, but we own this building, so it's an investment. I'm a landlord now too."

"And it's all starting to come back."

"We were lucky."

"Location."

"It's coming back. Near the church is good. And the church isn't going anywhere. So then. So."

His unasked question: my plans. Practice for me for Ma, perhaps, and for Danny something to tell later to wee Sheila, as we used to call her, the cute curly-haired little minx. Jimmy had a thing for her back then. Before we were old enough to fail, which wasn't too old at all.

"Weighing options. Such as they are. Open to suggestions."

Danny nodded.

"I taught a bit up there, English to some of the cons, reading too, and the library. I worked there. Maybe, I don't know. Something. I don't know." They don't hire cons in the school system. And I'd never seriously considered it anyway. "Social work, maybe." A lot of us end up there, facing what we laughingly called our demons. "I see White Castle is hiring."

"You'll find something. You always were the smart one," Danny said. "Good you're on track again." Such forgiveness. Well, we hadn't hurt him. At least, not that time, not directly. God knows I'd been thrown out of Patsy's enough before that night.

The tough little man from the back booth came up for a refill. He looked at me. I looked at him, the rough-hewn snake tattoo on his wiry forearm. We knew where we'd been. We were marked, tattooed or not. We nodded barely, and he turned back to his girlfriend, or moll. Nah. That would be me. Top o' the world, Ma.

"Say hi to Sheila for me. Thanks." I headed out, and over to the Oxford.

I ambled along University Avenue, and turned left at

Webb. They didn't know I was out, let alone in the neighborhood. I was taking a chance here—they could be away themselves. But Ma never went anywhere, or at least she hadn't when I'd roamed the neighborhood spreading unhappiness, and Bella wouldn't be far from her. Apart from a Catskills hiking trip or some such with one of her other chubby spinster girlfriends, she didn't do much except judge harshly. I had no idea how she spent her time. I did know she was a nurse, and probably had become one so she could talk back to our mother with the impunity of the health care industry and treat her patients with the contempt she always showed me, seeing as I had been unavailable for quite some time.

The building looked the same, a little older, but cared for. Pachysandra thrived on the ground behind the iron fence, and window boxes flourished above. I pushed open the fingerprinted glass door to our old lobby and saw her name there on the buzzer in the vestibule. I hesitated a second, then put my finger on the button and buzzed. There was a crackle on the other end. I buzzed again.

"Who is it?" Creaky and old.

"Davey."

Crackle again.

"It's Davey, Ma. I'm home." I hated using that term, but I had to. The door didn't click. Was she considering? I pressed the buzzer. "It's Davey, Ma!" I shouted into the crackling once more. The door clicked, reluctantly it seemed, and I scooted in before she changed her mind.

I pulled open the elevator door and stepped in. This old elevator, from the 1950s, struggling under the weight of years, musty with the aromas of pot roast and futility. I hadn't been in an elevator since I could remember, since that night, perhaps. I got out on the fourth floor, made the right to our old apartment, and rang the bell there. I heard a fumbling with locks following a long pause, as she probably checked me out in the security peephole. She opened the door.

"Ma. It's me," I said, bending to embrace her.

"Oh, Davey, you're killing me." She pushed me away. "Why didn't you let us know?"

"I wanted to surprise you."

"Well, you have. I never knew what to expect. You didn't write."

"I couldn't, Ma. I was too ashamed." I was lying immediately, back to myself of old. I'd be high as a kite next.

"Come in, come in, let me look at you then." She took my hand in a Pentecostal grasp of her own and drew me toward our living room. She had withered a bit, and her hair, like mine, had thinned, though hers nestled in soft cirrus clouds above her head. What was left of mine was shaved close.

"Ma, I'm so sorry," I lied again.

"I can't get over it," she said, sitting down in a recliner that still had the same crocheted throw I'd last seen who knows when. She stared at me, as if I were an apparition of the sort she prayed against. "What are you doing here?" Her tone had shifted quickly, as if she realized it was me, and not my brother come back from the dead.

"I'm from here."

"Not for ages. Not since you left. The only time you came back, there was trouble."

"I've been through a lot. I've changed."

"So have we all."

"I wanted to see you."

"What is it you need?" Sharper now, again. I could never fool her. "Is it money? What are you doing? When did you get out?"

"Ma, it's not money." Though it was, it always was, in the end. And at the beginning. I noticed on the little table next to her recliner a photograph of Jimmy and me, from our reckless teens—when weren't we reckless though?—taken at our cousin Patty's wedding. I had hair, Jimmy life. My mother saw me eyeing it. Tears had begun to shine in her eyes. "Last night. I came right here."

"We never knew anything about you."

"I was safe there. As safe as you can be. In there."

"That's not what I meant." She paused. "You were never safe."

"I was though, on my own."

"I'd already lost one son."

"There's no excuse. I know."

"And after that night, after you come back for one day, you and Jimmy—"

The phone rang. Mom stopped sniveling and picked up the receiver. "Of course I'm crying. Yes. Yes. No. Not that. Davey's here. Yes. No, don't come. I don't know if he wants to—no. He didn't. I'm fine. Yes. No. Alone. I will. But . . . no. I'll try." She put the receiver down and kept her eye on it for a second, as if expecting it to spring to life again.

"How's Bella?"

"Oh, she's angry she isn't here." She turned her face to me.

"That's nothing new."

"Don't start."

"I haven't. I just came to see you." Bella was a necessary by-product of the visit, like gas.

"Do you expect to stay here?" Not unkindly. Not motherly.

"No. Don't worry. I thought I'd spend a little time with you—"

"Before moving off again."

"You don't want me here."

"You don't want to be here. You never did. Ever since your father died."

"That wasn't it."

"And what have you found on your travels, your wandering? What great insights have you uncovered? We've been in the dark for, what, twenty years? You've been here and there and shut up without a word. Except for that one time, that one night, that one day when everyone knew. But since. It's like we've been dead."

"You could've considered me in some friary somewhere if that would've helped put your mind at rest. You always wanted me to be a priest. And I didn't want to bother you."

"Bother? Bother us? That's like a suicide thinking he's helping others by shooting his face off. That's a lie. You know it. It's cowardice. And it's wrong. It's wrong. Oh, Davey." And she began to weep, her head falling onto her arms, her bony back contorted with her sobbing.

I watched her cry. I couldn't ask her to stop. I couldn't comfort her, certainly. I couldn't demand anything of her. I just needed to wait there until dark, so I could leave, retrieve the stash from the church, and be on my way wherever. I looked around at the room, different from what I'd remembered, but when you remember only in decades, some things lose focus. The sofa was new. To me. And the big television. But the picture of Jesus, that famous painting that graced every Irish household in the Bronx and Queens and every damn borough, the Lord looking nothing so much as a film star, like a schoolmarm's dream of the savior, that was there, in laminated eternity on its own little easel on the buffet table. There were palm fronds from Easter, dry behind the painting of a thatched house in County Cork, a generalized scene of whimsical poverty. Those hadn't changed. The furniture was new, from what I remembered, but then, that was not to be relied upon.

My mother calmed down after a few minutes, and we sat there in relative silence for fifteen minutes or so. I was reluctant to speak further, and I thought Ma was too rundown by her outburst. But I was wrong. She'd been waiting.

The latch turned in the door. My mother and I looked toward it. Bella bustled in, older, wider, white-clad, wrathful.

"What have you done to her?"

"Bella." I stood. She pushed past me, in her best busy-nurse mode.

"Ma, is everything okay?"

"We were just sitting here."

"Has he done anything?"

"I'm fine."

"What are you doing here?"

"Hello, Bella."

"Never the courtesy of a reply in ten years and you show up unannounced. You. You never changed." She glowered at me. "Sit, Ma. And you—sit where I can see you. And don't move. I hope you hid your purse, Ma." She went into the kitchen, returning with a glass of water and a pill, giving them both to our mother. "Drink." She sat on the sofa facing me.

"So. You must have used up all the money I sent you."

"Thank you. I never thanked you."

"You didn't. But I didn't expect you to. When did you get out?"

"Yesterday," Ma said.

"And you're here now. For how long?"

"Not long. Just a visit."

"So you must have something planned."

I didn't answer that, but assumed an expression of surprise.

"You might fool Ma, but you can't fool me. You may think we're dummies here in the old neighborhood, those of us who never left, too stupid to get out, but then, you thought everyone was stupid except you, didn't you?"

"All I'm here for is a visit, Bella," I said. "I know I was wrong."

"You have never been right. Ever. And you and Jimmy together, I don't know which one was worse."

"Bella," said Ma.

"Oh, Ma, cut it out. He was no saint. He's dead and buried, and it's been ten long years, but for heaven's sake—"

"I didn't kill him."

"I have never believed that."

"What? That I didn't kill him, or don't you believe me?"

"I have never believed you."

"Bella, I'm not here to explain myself—"

"Then why are you here, Davey?"

"—but to try to make things right. I even went to mass, for God's sake."

"They'll never be right while you're roaming the streets. And you've never believed anything long enough to make a go of it. Mass. Hah."

"It was all Jimmy's idea."

"So you said. So we heard."

"That was the truth!"

"So you say."

"I didn't kill him. He told me to get away. He didn't expect we'd run up against anyone else."

"You left him there, bleeding."

"It was an accident."

That was the thing: It had simply happened. We had not counted on evening services, the sodality of tiresome bleating women leaving just as we'd arrived, the priest closing up, finding us at the statue, panicking at the sight of us at a time when the neighborhood had transitioned downward and dangerous, shouting, hitting me with the bronze candlestick he'd grabbed from the nave. Jimmy had hit him in turn after grabbing the candlestick from him, and being stronger, had brained him. I could see the screaming, leaching gash on the priest's bald skull, and Jimmy, not realizing I was dazed, had thrown me the gun, which slipped and revenged the priest right there, the shot resounding like a chorus through the church. "Run," he had said, always my protector and often my temptation, pushing it amid his shock and gasping, hot and smoking to me, and I did run, hoping to hide it, and myself, and had stumbled back bruised and bloody up the aisle toward the chancel where we'd just broken in and hidden the stolen cash. I'd tripped at the altar rail, like Cagney stumbling through the bleeding snow in *The Roaring Twenties*, and fallen finally in the sanctuary, victim at last to the ferocious bashing the priest had inflicted upon me. The adrenaline had kept me aloft until then, but at last I had collapsed, unconscious, while Jimmy lay dying and the priest lay dead. I was supposed to have kept watch while Jimmy hid the key under the statue for us to find later, I was supposed to have prevented the priest from finding him, I was supposed to have made sure the church had been quiet. No one was supposed to die.

"You two together were an accident."

"You were always led astray," Ma said.

"As if Davey needed coaxing. Always the easy way, always too smart to work."

"I told you. I've changed."

"If you'd changed, you'd have stayed away. You want something."

"I had to make amends to you."

"Don't, Davey. Just don't. Spare us having to believe you and regretting it later. I'll fix you something and you can be on your way. I'll give you some money to tide you over, how's that? I'm sure you've got some chippie stashed away somewhere, or some prison pal's pad you can crash at, right?"

"I don't want your money, Bella. You've been too generous already."

"I know. I shouldn't have sent you a thing. You might have never come back. How stupid I was to soften even for a moment."

"I've never had a chance to tell you how sorry I truly am. About Jimmy. About what happened."

"Apology accepted." Which meant it wasn't.

"It's been a long time," Ma said.

"We've gotten used to the peace, Ma and me, haven't we, Ma? We've gotten used to knowing where you were, and not being a danger to us."

"So then. I see. Look, I never hurt you, or never meant to. And you've never left."

"You don't just leave, Davey. Oh, *you* do, but I like it here, all of the mix."

"It was getting rough."

"*We* lasted though, didn't we, Ma, didn't we? The Bronx is in our blood, just as it's in yours, along with something else."

"Jimmy hated it."

"Jimmy was a fool. A criminal like his father."

"Bella!"

"Ma, enough. A criminal like you. I expected more from

you, after the scholarship to Prep. But a little learning is a dangerous thing. It gives you ideas."

"I always had ideas, Bell."

"You had a fool for a counselor, Davey, and that was your brother, and when it wasn't him it was yourself. Things came too easily. You never had to work for them."

"You think prison was easy."

"Maybe you learned a little about yourself."

I had. That didn't mean I'd actually changed.

"You can sit there proud, Bella, and look down on me from your moral mountain, but I don't hear you. I served my time. I did my obligation to society. I regret what happened, but we all make mistakes, some of them larger than others. You're no one to talk about Jimmy. He can't defend himself against your slander. He had more life than you'll ever have, dead though he's been these ten years. So we took a few easy steps. It wasn't as if you hadn't left hints about all the security problems at that cheesy job of yours. Jimmy told me you were going on so about the idiotic systems there—you were practically begging us to rob it, you might as well have given us the key to the front door and the combination to the safe, which both were easy enough to find, and you think you'd be more trusting, wouldn't you? But you've got more there going on underneath your stuffed shirt than you let on, don't you? You're your father's daughter too, you know. So don't act all high and mighty with me."

"Unlike you, I worked for every penny I've ever got."

"And resented every minute of it too. So I'm a dreamer." She snorted.

"So sue me. I'm sure Jimmy did his magic on you too. Don't say he didn't. You look for someone to blame, and never look inside."

"Oh, please, you with your holier-than-thou act—you're a con, and you always will be."

"Ex. And at least I owned up to my part in things."

"Don't fight, Davey," Ma said. "Don't. Don't come home after all this time and start fighting. But stay for dinner. Bella, let him be. For me, now. It's been too long." She hauled herself up and headed to the kitchen.

As soon as she was out of earshot, Bella leaned toward me. "I don't trust you, Davey. I don't believe you're here to make amends, as you call it. In twenty years, you've shown up exactly twice, and the second time was a total disaster. So forgive me if I think there's a fifty-fifty chance of things not working out so great now that you're back."

"I can't control what you think, Bella. I'm not here to hurt you, or Ma, or take anything from you or expect anything of you. I don't know what I'm doing, where I'm going, but it won't be here. I've always hated here. I don't want a home. I don't want a home here."

"And yet, you are here."

"Not for long. Listen—I know I hurt Ma, but it was killing me here. It was better that I disappeared. It was better. Jimmy stayed, and look what happened to him. He went job to job, hating every single minute. Only he told me he had a way out."

"He did. Thanks to you."

"And so I was the sucker. I showed up for him. He asked me to. He said he needed me. He was my brother. He said he was breaking out of here. He wanted my help. He needed money. He knew where to get it. So I came."

"And saw, and conquered. I got it. Davey, I'm not going to argue with you. I want you out of here, because you'll drive Ma crazy like Jimmy did, with his drinking and drugs and thievery and scheming. You're the same, with your lying and acting as if you know everything that's going on, acting like because you read a few books you know more than anyone. What did you think would happen after you helped Jimmy? That he would reform? That you would become upstanding? You always spoke like someone who knew something about the world, but you never got beyond the sound of your own words, you never really made sense. I don't think you believed yourself even, what you said. And like I said, I can't argue anymore. I want to make sure Ma is all right—and let her have a memory of you where you're not getting someone killed."

"And what did you think you'd do, once they found out we'd used your key?"

"I knew nothing about that, and that was proved in court. The money was never found."

"Sometimes the dice falls the right way."

"And don't start with your accusations. I was never in on your scheme, and I won't have you saying that." Her voice had been rising. She turned toward the kitchen and back to me. "And I don't want you hanging around anymore. Giving Ma ideas that you're going to change. It's been hard enough, goddamnit, getting her stabilized all these years without you giving her false hope again about whatever. I don't know what you're planning, but you wouldn't be here if you weren't after something."

"I promise. I'll be out of here tonight."

"And going to mass. As if you believe in anything. Stay away from church."

That wasn't going to happen. But the rest of the afternoon and early evening passed without too much palpable rancor on Bella's part or too much uncertain regret on Ma's. I told them in so many words about prison life, about tutoring cons, about escaping the drudgery by reading, about keeping my head low. I didn't tell them about the money, or the plan, or why Jimmy and I had thought that we'd escape the police by running into the church after we'd tripped the alarm like the rank amateurs we really were. Churches don't offer sanctuary to petty thieves. But we'd managed to stay ahead, and since both Jimmy and I had been altar boys, we knew the layout of St. Nick's, the stashing places in the chancel, and one particular cabinet behind the vestment closet that had a trick bottom, which one of the older boys had told us about in secret years before. It had been a hiding place during Prohibition, where a generation of miscreant boozy clerics concealed their illicit hooch and extra altar wine. We'd stored comics there and, in our gormless Catholic way, porn of the lamest kind, succulent pouts and ballooning breasts, along with the odd pint of Night Train to glaze the eyes and heighten the erotic possibilities of marginally naked half-beauties. But the priests had long since cottoned on to our feeble depravities, and had nailed the compartment shut so that it could no longer be a repository of half-baked filth and vice. Yet both Jimmy and I had remembered the drawer down the years, and he'd told me to come back and retrieve our stuff when things had cooled down, in case he couldn't get to it first. I'd opened that false bottom that night, and then replaced the nails carefully, so it would remain closed and not tempt a new breed of clerics, altar boys, or minor thieves. We'd planned to break through at a later date, weeks perhaps. That date had dawned ten years on.

I left my mother and Bella's apartment with no promise of anything other than an effort to let them know where I might be, how I might be reached, what I might do. In the end, I almost regretted—almost—my leaving, as Bella had lost some of her hostility and Ma had become less alternately weepy and accusatory and more resigned and benign, like the flock of women in the window captioned *Mary Sodality*.

Dusk had crept in and settled over Devoe Park when I left the Oxford. The white El Rancho van had moved on for the evening, and the ball courts were quiet. The church shadowed the trees below it there, and I walked around the building in shadows myself. Someone was exiting the side door. Good. It was still open. I dashed up just as the door swung closed behind her.

"It's over," she said to me. "The service just ended. You missed it."

"Just a quick candle," I said. "My Ma's sick."

She nodded, as if it were the most reasonable thing in the world for a far-too-skinny middle-aged bald man wearing shabby clothes to pop into church and say a prayer for his mother. The baleful predator's ex post facto atonement. But the door had shut behind her, and it locked with a thunk. I pulled on the handle, but it stayed. No way in here. But no mighty fortress was our Lord: I'd remembered that the windows of the vestibule were sometimes kept ajar on hot nights, like this one, and the priest might not yet have gotten around to locking them. I hurried around toward the front in the growing gloom and spied a window cracked open to let in the city air. This side of the church was quiet, abutting the rectory. The tined fence was designed to keep thieves from getting over, but nothing prevented me from leaning against it to get my balance. I managed to shimmy myself up a bit, gripping the granite ridges with my fingers as my feet perched on a small crossbar between the rails. Leaning over with one hand on the outside wall of the church, I pushed the window further open with the other, but it stuck just six inches above the sill. I took a breath and, more forceful—and desperate—I pushed again. This time it unstuck and shot up with a rumbling clack. I heard it echo inside, but I pulled myself over the sill, and squeezed in before I was noticed. I stood in the vestibule, calming myself, wiping a trace of sweat from my forehead, and pushed open the door to the main part of the church, as quietly as possible, its hushed creak sounding like a screech to my ears. But I was in.

The priest had his back to me. The services were indeed over. He was near the altar, actually toward that providential chapel, and didn't see the new arrival trying to make his own luck. I slipped down the far aisle, and snuck over to the statue of St. Nicholas at the back. That key to the sanctuary, to the vestment drawers, was my chance. That drawer was hiding close to $25,000.

In the dark at the rear of the church, I was invisible. I felt quickly around the statue's base, and located the nib of the key. It barely protruded; Jimmy had done a good quick job of shoving it under there. I needed to tilt the statue to get to it, but it was a little too highly placed for me to do it with ease from where I stood. But I had little time, and couldn't draw attention to myself by searching for a bench. Ah, but there, by the vestibule door, a little table with the parish bulletins. I was able to lift it, and position it near St. Nicholas. I didn't see the priest, that Father Farrell, who must still be getting ready to close for the night. I managed to get myself atop the table, though I scattered a couple of bulletins, which floated down to the aisle. They sounded like a rush of leaves to me, but they were, I hoped, still too faint to be heard up by that chapel.

Standing on the table top, I pushed the head of the statue toward the wall. It was heavy, heavier than I had thought. I didn't know how I'd get that key from the bottom without making noise. Jimmy and I hadn't thought of that back then on that fatal night. We hadn't fully thought things through, as usual with the two of us, especially when we were in our cups, as we had been since I'd returned the day before to see him. But now I was sober. Or at least not drinking or using. And I needed that key. And that money. And to leave.

I tested the statue's angle of repose, and it stayed leaning against the wall. I hopped off the table, exhaling an unfortunate *oomph* as I hit the hard floor. I was no longer young. But I heard no sounds of alarm. The light was almost nothing here, though my eyes had adjusted. I reached under the tilt of the statue's base and found the key, scooping it back and pocketing it. I wanted to leave the statue where it was and get out fast, but that would be foolhardy in the extreme, as I'd forgotten gloves and my prints were all over the patron saint of this benighted parish. I crept back up onto the table, repositioned the statue, and rubbed it over with my shirt sleeve, hoping I'd erased everything I touched. I was careful descending from the table this time, managed to move it back to its place by the door and retrieve the fallen bulletins. I placed them back on top, in no particular order of language, the Babel of parish news.

I still saw no one, and apparently no one had seen me. I'd been planning this moment for so long—pictured myself à la Shawshank on a Mexican beach whiling away my twilight years.

I crept toward the chancel. I hadn't heard the door shut, but the priest must have gone home, perhaps through the sanctuary door that connected to the rectory. I hoped the lock hadn't been changed—another point we'd never considered—and then that purloined key fit easily in the slot. As I turned it, the door swung open and the lights went on ablaze.

I squinted. Before me was Father Farrell. And Bella, a look of menacing satisfaction on her face.

In my shock, all I could utter was a stupefied, "What are you doing here?"

"We could ask the same of you," Bella said. "Father Farrell, this is my brother Davey, long lost and now returned. Father Farrell's fairly new here, Davey, and probably would have noticed you at mass earlier. Luckily, I gave him a call as to what you were probably up to, and my hunch proved, as you can see, correct."

I started to turn.

"And don't try leaving. The police are on the way."

"My money."

"Oh, I know why you're here. But even if you'd managed to get in, you wouldn't have found it. Do you think you were the only one who knew about that trick drawer, you and Jimmy? You think you were the only altar boys, and only altar boys knew about that hiding spot that the priests had nailed shut? You think altar boys are sworn to a vow of silence? You think we schoolgirls knew nothing about your filthy ways? Hah. You didn't live in a vacuum, Davey, though for all you noticed about what was going on around you, you could have. Just because you didn't talk to anyone didn't mean people didn't talk about you, or about the church, or about anything that went on there. Your secrets. Brother. You thought you'd had it over everyone, didn't you?"

"You said the money hadn't been found."

"So I did. So I lied. So, in your words, 'sue me.' We found it soon after you were sent away. I told the cops where they might look, and your little stash was history."

"So you planned it. All afternoon. Pretending to be nice to me."

"You never did see the obvious, Davey. Always too smart for everyone. You think Danny wouldn't talk? You think Ma was feebleminded by your Prodigal Son returns act? You think no one but you knew the score? Too many books and not enough sense. You thought you kept things close to you, but you were like a bad movie. You always wanted the easy way out."

"That was my money."

"Never. Father, do you hear this?" The priest was silent, uncomfortable, a bit ashamed, I felt, to be witness to a sister selling out her brother, her only surviving brother just returned from years away, unseen, unloved. Father Farrell's head tilted; the sound of sirens grew closer.

"In my own home. You betrayed me."

"It was never your home, Davey. You said that yourself. You couldn't wait to leave. Your home is far away now, and has been for a long while. You took us for fools. Now you can go and stew on it once again, and figure out where you went wrong."

I shook my head at her. I would not let her win. The police arrived and I submitted to the handcuffs as if I were a Pentecostal penitent in the arms of rebirth. I looked away from Bella, and at the priest. Maybe I'd seen the light, or at least I could make do with what I had. "I will espouse you the right of justice," I told him, keeping my eyes on his horrified face as the cops led me out to the car. "I open myself to a God who loves me."

NUMBERS UP

BY MILES MARSHALL LEWIS

Baychester

Kingston believed he wasn't a regular at Golden Lady, seated at the bar sipping a plastic cup of whiskey. Silky served his Scotch and amaretto without asking only because she had a great memory like most bartenders, he thought. Kingston considered the cup in his hand and reminisced over the club serving bottles of beer and glasses of mixed drinks years back, before some brawls with smashed Coronas forced a policy change. He also recalled gonzo tricks Silky used to perform with Heinekens in her dancing days, way before her transition to barkeep. Kingston raised his Godfather to Lacey, onstage sliding down a silver pole at the center of her baby-oiled, spread-eagle legs, eyeing him from upside down. Lacey was just the thing to take Kingston's mind off the hundreds he'd lost earlier at Yonkers Raceway, the robbery of his house days ago, and other recent troubles.

Disorienting strobes bathed Lacey and two other bodacious young women pacing the stage, gyrating hips and stripping under the synthesized pulse of Ciara's "Oh." Kingston didn't consider himself a regular but Lacey's partners knew from experience not to bother trying to entice money out of the black guy in the stingy-brim fedora. Lacey sauntered over to the head of the crowded bar, bent down, and flashed her fleshy ass just for Kingston, flexing the muscles of each cheek to the beat. Kingston shifted her garish yellow lace garter belt with a finger to place one, two, three paper-cut-crisp twenty-dollar bills between her thigh and the elastic band. Lacey undulated her thick behind in ecstatic waves of motion.

Come 2 o'clock, Golden Lady's neon sign—a naked blonde lounging in a martini glass—quickly faded into the distance. Kingston and Lacey sat in his onyx Buick zooming up the Bruckner Expressway and out of Hunts Point. Full-blast cool air circulated new-car smell throughout the ride. Kingston's radio, per usual, tuned in to CD101.9: "I'm in the Mood for Love," King Pleasure. Plastic jewel cases of smooth jazz CDs cluttered the floor and butter-leather backseats. En route to Baychester Diner, Lacey peered into the illuminated sun visor applying foundation, lipstick, and eyeliner, bitching about the shady tactics Butterfly and Sunflower used to dominate lap dances all summer long. Kingston's characteristic silence was so typical that Lacey never considered that her sugar daddy might be disturbed.

The all-night Baychester Diner harbored the same two wisecracking women in kempt hairweaves found at the counter every weekend past midnight. Each sported something slightly outré signaling her street profession. One wore a bright Wonder Woman bodice with deep cleavage on display, the other scarlet fishnets with a spiked leather dominatrix collar. Both brandished five-inch stilettos. At the far corner banquette a young couple argued in Creole patois.

"*Si ou pa vlé bébé-an, ale vous an,*" hissed the pregnant teen in the pink Von Dutch cap.

Kingston and Lacey found an isolated booth and ordered breakfast from a homely waitress. Rain broke the August humidity, slicking the asphalt of Boston Road, while Kingston explained all about the Hernández brothers pushing their numbers turf further down Washington Heights into Harlem, their violent efforts to force him out, and his contingency flight plan to New Orleans.

"King. You gonna up and leave just like that?" Lacey asked. She craved a Newport.

"They ain't runnin' me out," he bluffed. "I done made plenty these past fifteen years. I don't mind it. Business ain't like it used to be nohow. Playin' the numbers is old school, kiddo. More white folks is movin' into Harlem now and they don't know nothin' about me. They play Lotto."

Lacey laughed.

"You never talked about retiring to New Orleans before." *Not to me*, she thought.

"I done told you 'bout the house. We ain't never been to-gether, but it's down there. Since 2000. My cousin look after it, she over in Baton Rouge."

"When are you talking about going?"

"I ain't right decided yet. Could be two weeks."

"Two weeks? That's enough time for you to wrap up ev-erything?"

"We gon' see."

Kingston held the door for Lacey and a trucker hand-in-hand with the collared mistress from the counter. Outside all four smelled a faint aroma of barbecue sauce wafting from the local KFC. The illicit couple commiserated on the corner and crossed Baychester Avenue, stilettos clicking on concrete, to a motel with three-hour rates.

Kingston pulled his sedan out of the lot and down Bos-ton Road blaring "This Masquerade." By the song's end he'd parked again, less than a mile away at Boston Secor Houses. Lacey grabbed his humidor from the glove compartment.

On the red leather sofa Kingston silently flipped stations searching for baseball scores and fiddled with his cigar while

Lacey showered. His sky-blue fedora rested on the adjacent pillow, revealing the receding hairline of his freshly cut Caesar specked with gray. He clicked off her TV and leaned over to untie his Stacy Adams, tightening abdominal muscles buried underneath a stout stomach. His growing belly caused him to chuckle at his own jealousy, wondering what sort of younger man her own age a sexy girl like Lacey would attract once he was gone. Lacey would adapt easily, Kingston imagined. She was all of twenty-two. Life adjustments would come harder to Kingston. Comfortably set in his ways, he never vacationed away from his St. Martin time-share, never ate anything outside of the standard ten dishes he either bought from takeout restaurants or Gussy cooked for him, never deviated from his usual Yankees game, jazz concert, or horse race for recreation. Deciding to uproot his life from 1839 Bruner Avenue to the bayou sprang as much from Kingston's recent unidentified angst as the threats from Héctor and Eddie Hernández. Kingston finally took a lighter to his cigar.

"One of us has too much clothes on," Lacey said.

She left her cream silk robe untied at the waist, smoking her own tobacco of choice. Tracey Lott bore only fraternal-twin resemblance to her onstage character, always fragrantly oiled, primped, oversexed. Nearly naked again for the second time tonight—clean, shea-butter-exfoliate scrubbed, and nail-polished in her own apartment now—Tracey looked softer, younger.

Kingston called her Tracey at times, Lacey most often, but it didn't bother her. The last time they saw one another Lacey had dropped X before his unexpected arrival at Golden Lady and rambled all sorts of private personal information afterwards, about her Jehovah's Witness upbringing, her strict mother (the neighborhood crossing guard), her young cousin's molestation, her absent dad, and her first fuck at fourteen. Maybe too much for Kingston, she thought.

Lacey flicked cigarette ash into a seashell and sat in Kingston's lap. The leather sofa farted. As she unbuttoned his shirt both their thoughts clouded with notions of tonight maybe being their last tête-à-tête.

Kingston and Lacey were both more passive than active participants in their own lives, mirrors of each other in that sense. Kingston had inherited the mantle of running numbers from his late father, working under his wing after a brief enlistment in the Gulf War. His life's work was more due to his own passivity than the passion for the numbers game that his father had held close. Kingston loved Gussy in his way but their union was mainly convenient. She was his Girl Friday on the job. Their relationship saved Kingston the trouble of seeking a woman attracted to his limited social graces who could also be trusted and accepting of his illegal trade. Money only goes so far. Despite over half a million squared away from almost two decades of business, Lacey, an exotic dancer from the projects, was the most ideal mistress he found himself able to draw.

Lacey, too, let her life dictate its own direction, leading from a bust-up with her mother at seventeen to accepting dubious advice from her stalker ex-bf Tré-Sean to sell nude photos to websites and dance at Hunts Point holes like Al's Mr. Wedge and Golden Lady. The night a zooted pair of homeboys roughly snatched off her thong and dashed out the club with their booty nine months ago, she was comforted by Kingston, a familiar, benevolent customer, and their affair began.

Stripping his shirt, standing and leading him to her bedroom, she felt powerless to trip up the chain of events sweeping Kingston out of her life. Lacey thought sex might solve the problem, her familiar recourse. Their cigarette and cigar sat burning away in an Orchard Beach conch, plumes of smoke dancing an acrobatic tango.

Kingston returned to 1839 Bruner Avenue in the early morning to discover the SUV stolen.

Gussy would find the charred BMW of their steady bettor Wallace parked outside Fordham Hill Apartments on her nighttime jog to the Harlem River, stripped and torched to black cinders save for the pristine license plate: *CRM-114.*

Like aging hippies cooking organic groceries in a kitchen full of all-Hendrix-all-the-time, Gussy and Kingston were throwback '70s soul babies. This wasn't immediately obvious but there were telltale signs: Gussy's leonine Afro and multitudinous silver bracelets, Kingston's allegiance to jazz musicians like George Benson and Grover Washington, Jr., who were on the rise when he first started buying vinyl.

The couple met in Kuwait and were instantly simpatico. For Kingston the army was brief, another way to synchronize his life with that of his father, who served in WWII. Buckshot shrapnel lodged near his heart resulted in a quick honorable discharge. For Gussy the army was a career move lasting five years longer than the Persian Gulf strike. With her discharge nine years behind her, former Private Augusta Wilson still hit the shooting range a few times a year and took weekly power runs through Fordham with Parliament on her headphones.

On Monday, Kingston and Gussy put in a normal day at the spot. The sparse bodega Kingston rented on Amsterdam was locally understood as a storefront for his operation. Starting shortly after 12 o'clock, Harlemites stopped by with their three-digit numbers on betting slips, handing them off (with their cash) to Hillside at the front counter. Some old-timers sat for a spell with the *Daily News,* picking out items to talk shit about: the Maori-inspired tattoo covering Mike Tyson's face; Michael Jackson's expatriation to Bahrain. Both Kingston and Gussy fielded calls in the large back office, jotting down more phoned-in numbers. (Lacey played Kingston's DAV-485 license plate in a box combination: 485, 548, 854, etc.) All day Kingston's two runners—Pookie and Elliott—returned from the backs of bars, bodegas, barbershops, beauty parlors, billiard halls, and street corners throughout the Bronx and Harlem, dropping off their books of bets. Gussy tallied the incoming cash on an old adding machine till her index finger was sore, at which point she'd use the end of her pencil. From noon to 6 each of the three numbers would post based on the last dollar digits of the total handle from Yonkers Raceway's daily win, place, and show bets.

By 5 o'clock, Monday's number was four-two. Hillside left for the Bronx, picking up Chinese takeout from the Orient. Kingston and Gussy, alone, still spoke in code, agreeing to hold off talk of the Hernándezes until after work: City Island, Sammy's Fish Box. Finally a zero came in. Not one person had hit the number. The three totaled all the final slips, over five hundred dollars gross profit.

Hillside walked to nearby Hamilton Terrace to score from his coke dealer. Kingston and Gussy drove onto the Macombs Dam Bridge out of Manhattan just after 7 o'clock. CD101.9 started a David Sanborn marathon as they sped up the Major Deegan Expressway.

Kingston felt like a ghost, but in a good way. Ever since deciding to give up his patch of Harlem to the Dominicans, Kingston was more conscious of his interactions with the people he'd leave behind, more aware of places he probably wouldn't see for a long time. He thought of getting skied with Hillside for old times' sake, or fucking Joie, the former girl-on-the-side stripper over at Sin City who preceded Lacey in his life. Stress was at the root of his recent ulcers and so this new feeling of liberation was welcome. Kingston felt relieved, like knowing the exact date of his approaching death (and rebirth) and appreciating his last moments on earth.

"I know you been scheming. Them motherfuckers got it coming. What's the plan?"

Kingston was getting distracted by the general lilt of a nearby conversation, two overweight brothers seated behind Gussy eating whole Maine lobsters and linguini. The larger man continually mispronounced Nikes to rhyme with Mikes. They waited on their own platter to arrive.

"Gus . . ." Kingston laughed. "You sound like Foxy Brown. Ease up, Sheba baby." He took hold of the thick white napkin underneath his flatware, spreading it in his lap over navy velour sweatpants.

Gussy smiled, holding her head in her hands. Bangles slid to her elbows, jangling. "Héctor and Eddie were safer than they knew till they burnt up Wallace's Beemer. They gotta pay for that shit if anything." The BMW was in Kingston's possession as a marker, till one of his regulars finished paying off a big debt. Now Wallace's X5 was ashes. "Who the fuck are they threatening?" she asked heatedly. "They think they're just gonna keep upping the ante until we get the fuck outta Dodge? Is a goddamn car bomb next?" Gussy lowered her voice. "I was thinking, maybe we could pay off somebody over at the racetrack to report what we tell 'em, like a fixed hit. If we had one of our own hit the number with Héctor and Eddie for some gigantic amount, then we could bankrupt the sons of bitches. Or . . . I don't know who they pay off at the NYPD but we could find out, make a deal, and get 'em locked up for a while."

"That's good thinkin'. But really, kiddo, the way to do this is to leave in peace," Kingston replied wearily. "We'll send word back by their baby sister. Elizabeth was the one rollin' up on Hillside last month from the get. She doin' her brothers' biddin', we'll let it ride like that. Once they know we fixin' to leave, that's the end a that."

Gussy sighed, just as their bald, husky waiter returned delivering shellfish on a Formica tray. (Kingston, as always, ordered the lobster, king crab legs, and Spanish yellow rice for two.) She tied the plastic bib around her neck thinking back to when she first suggested Kingston invest in property. The Creole cottage he bought five years ago in the French Quarter had become the getaway home he'd never have brainstormed on his own. Though Kingston wasn't much for vacations, running numbers six days a week, Gussy planned ahead for whatever retirement might come with forethought he consistently lacked. A condo in North Carolina, near an old childhood friend of Kingston's, was Gussy's first choice. But Kingston overruled, choosing New Orleans instead, for its jazz history.

Gussy reconnected with Kingston after leaving the service as a tie to the civilian world and to continue what they had started during their twenties in the Middle Eastern desert. She considered love to be an active decision, a conscious choice. She gave her heart to Kingston because, from her viewpoint, he needed the direction it was her nature to provide, and becoming the main woman in his life gave her access to his ample savings. Marriage might never be on the horizon but Gussy always appreciated the cushy situation she long ago stepped into as his assistant and lover.

The attached row house at 1839 Bruner—passed down from Kingston's parents—must be put on the market, Gussy thought, cracking a lobster leg. She'd be breaching her own lease at Fordham Hill. Their collective furniture would need to be packed and shipped south, sold, or given away. (The cottage was sparsely furnished and completely undecorated.) They'd require two tickets to Louisiana sooner than later. Hillside, Pookie, and Elliott would have to be informed fast— Gussy was sure they wouldn't have seen this coming—and the Amsterdam lease would also be broken. This was all irreversible stuff. She hoped Kingston had measured everything carefully.

"Is it worth it?" she asked softly.

"It's time for a change," Kingston replied, his mouth full. He finished chewing, measuring his words. "Seem like ain't nobody wanna end up like they parents nowadays, and I gotta count myself in that too. Daddy always promised my mother he'd give all this up and retire down to Florida someplace and never got the chance to do it before she passed. I worked right up beside him till the end and it was clear to me . . ." He paused. "I just know he'd a done things different if he coulda. Fuck Héctor and Eddie, it ain't about them. The house been robbed before. I just don't wanna do this no more."

Kingston's initiative took Gussy a bit by surprise. "Well, I'll handle the details, just let me know what you intend on doing yourself and I can take care of everything else. I can leave enough for Hillside and the fellas to take care of themselves till next year." She smiled. "I can't believe we're really going! I do love it down there."

"It's a new day, Gus. I done made ample money off a this, God bless Daddy. There got to be more to life than Baychester and Amsterdam Avenue. Y'know, New Orleans is a big jazz town."

"Really?" Gussy knew this already.

"Hell yeah, the Marsalis family hails from down there and . . ."

Kingston Lee never wore an earring. Back when he was a teenager at Evander Childs High, putting a hole through your right ear branded you a fag. But the year his boys all pierced their lefties together at a jewelry store on White Plains Road, Kingston just couldn't do it. He failed to understand why everybody now seemed to get tattooed at the drop of a hat. He'd always had an aversion to anything that could make him substantially different than he was when his personality gelled as a youngster. Gussy learned this about him early on, deciding it was how Kingston had reached forty-two without any children. Moving from New York City, leaving the only real profession he'd ever known, felt to Kingston like bungee jumping with a sometimey cord.

His father had started the business in the '60s, from a nearly bare stationery store on 233rd Street. Waiting for Jiffy Lube to service his ride that humid, overcast Sunday—he intended to leave it to Wallace and call things even—Kingston walked from Boston Road and up Baychester to 233rd, taking rolls of mental photographs. Passing Spellman High's football field he remembered fingering a cheerleader before a game underneath the bleachers; he was a mean running back, she favored actress Jayne Kennedy and knew it. Up the hill he passed the Carvel stand his mother crashed into when he was ten. ("Fasten your seat belt," she had said dead calmly, realizing the Oldsmobile's brakes were failing.) Comics & Comics was long gone, another memory now. And the Big Three Barbershop.

Zack Abel, Jr. cut hair at the Big Three Barbershop with his father Big Zack from the time he and Kingston attended

Evander together. Big Zack and his wife were staunchly religious; the Big Three of the shop's namesake were naturally the Son, the Father, and the Holy Spirit, though the secular folks coming in for their fades had no clue. Muhammad Ali had his Afro trimmed there once sometime after the Thrilla in Manila, and a yellowed photo of Ali sitting in Big Zack's highchair stayed taped to a mirror till the shop closed. Kingston and Zack's fathers both died in 2000. Big Zack's death seemed to mature his son. He summarily sold his father's shop, moved to North Carolina for a Cablevision job, fell in love, and had a son two years ago. Kingston missed Zack, the only friend he felt he really had outside of Gussy. Zack's move left Kingston a bit ill at ease ever since, as if his life was a jumped-the-shark TV show the network refused to cancel.

Kingston reached the address where his father's operation first started, now an insurance office. He stood there and removed his Kangol as if out of respect, wiping sweat from his brow with the white cap. He recollected his aunts, uncles, and his own mother dreaming up the number when he was a child, searching through slim stapled pamphlets by Madame Zora and Rajah Rabo listing corresponding numbers for different dream themes: love, sex, death. He got spanked for losing his great-grandmother's tattered *Aunt Sally's Policy Players Dream Book* once. His parents let him play occasionally; he recalled hitting for the first time at nine: a whole twenty dollars, all spent at the Good Humor ice cream truck that crept down Bruner playing Sammy Davis, Jr.'s "The Candy Man." His neighbor Miss Lois once scored a combination hit on the very day she needed to pay her back rent to avoid eviction; she threw a lavish block party and bought herself Jordache jeans for every day of the week. And how many misadventures had young Kingston heard about Chink Low, one of his dad's first runners, the brother with folded eyelids who never wrote down a number that police could confiscate, memorizing them all without fault? Or Chink's running partner Clarence, who ended up as a regular on *The Mod Squad?*

The memories were cathartic. Just one month away, September 2005, Kingston would turn forty-three—with not much more to show for his life than what was left him by his father. He tried to pinpoint the source of his recent melancholy attitude; he knew it had started before the Hernándezes. Was it the birthday of little Zack the third, Gussy pressuring him for a baby? Kingston refused to believe his near depression had anything to do with a midlife crisis; he had a curvaceous kept woman on the side and hundreds of thousands of out-of-circulation Ben Franklins hidden in a safe at the spot on Amsterdam. He tried to envision what he wanted that he didn't yet have, and it came down to this: He wanted to be his own man.

All his life, Kingston had been following his father's path to uphold a perceived legacy, yet he couldn't feel the same obligation on his shoulders anymore. Time and circumstance had moved on, and now, so would Kingston. His father had migrated from Georgia to lay his own path to personal freedom on the streets of the Bronx. Now Kingston would reverse-migrate back, attempting to find his very own life purpose in Louisiana. This one-sided turf war was the perfect excuse. *Let 'em play Lotto*, he thought, liberated.

The phone in his pants vibrated.

It was a message. His battery must have been low, he imagined, having missed the call. Lacey's voice. They hadn't spoken since she rang in her number a week ago. She'd reconciled things with Tré-Sean. She wished him well in New

Orleans. She asked him to not drop by Golden Lady or the Secor projects before leaving. She hung up the phone.

How intriguing, Lacey thought, that she found herself magnetized by two of the older black community's archetypes, the numbers man and the pimp.

Tré-Sean Niles ostensibly sold crack from his apartment on Webster Avenue, but persuasive game was his true métier, and Lacey knew it. Never mind how he convinced her to try their relationship again after scary antics like sitting in his beat-up Benz near Boston Secor obsessively monitoring her subsequent men and one-night stands or surreptitiously checking her answering machine until getting caught. Forget how he convinced Lacey to work out her exhibitionist tendencies by posing naked and selling the images to the likes of PlumpRumps.com (splitting the profits) or sharing her shake-dancing take. Days ago, Lacey dog-eared *Confessions of a Video Vixen* on a night of weakness brought on by Kingston's leaving, called Tré-Sean, and navigated the following conversation.

Isn't it fascinating how certain women create whole careers from men wanting to have sex with them? Tré-Sean asked. As a kid he had questioned his horny older brother on why he was so transfixed by *Elvira's Movie Macabre* when he knew the pasty, buxom Goth girl would never actually show her breasts. For Tré-Sean this was the same disappointing tease performed at stripclubs with all the incredible-looking naked women (like Lacey) who one could never really fuck. Madonna in *Penthouse* made an impression on his young mind, but when he saw Pamela Anderson blowing her husband on a homemade tape, his philosophy all came together.

Tré-Sean told Lacey that Paris Hilton giving head, having sex for all the world to see on the web, and then becoming even more popular, made perfect sense. The only reason Paris and Pam Anderson had celebrity in the first place was because men fantasized about how they'd be sexually. Tré-Sean recently met a friend of a friend of a friend in the adult film industry who rationalized that the relation between seductive music videos and hardcore pornography was identical to the relation between a funny joke and an explanation of what's funny about the joke. Lacey thought she understood.

Tré-Sean finally laid out his scheme. He was given tickets to the Adult Video News Film Awards from this same new acquaintance. He proposed they go to Las Vegas for the ceremony and network. So much more money could be made in porn for so much less work than dancing, Tré-Sean reasoned, and they'd already made some private sex tapes of their own. Celebrity in this field might lead to celebrity in another, he said. (And if not, it's the same thing underneath it all anyway, he thought privately). His contact guaranteed him a meeting with a producer, Max Hardcore.

Lacey held the line silently. Kingston's decision bothered Lacey up until the point she accepted that she didn't mean enough to him for an extended invitation to the bayou. That Monday Lacey lost the number, but the numbers man lost Lacey; she had called her ex the same night.

"So whassup?" Tré-Sean asked.

In the service, another grunt who'd been a bartender in New Orleans taught Kingston and Gussy how to mix a Tom Collins: gin, tonic, lemon juice, sugar, and a maraschino cherry. In his friend's honor, Kingston entered their spacious backyard carrying glasses of the poison from the cottage's indoor bar. Sweltering Southern sunrays beamed through his loose T-shirt and bright Bermuda shorts. Gussy reclined on the powder-blue deck chair by their concrete pool dressed in a gold one-piece swimsuit and Onassis-style shades, rubbing sunblock over her toned legs. Kingston seated himself and passed her the drink; he sipped his own and fired up a cigar.

The two celebrated the impulse purchase of a quicksilver Cadillac that morning, Gussy's choice. Kingston drove it straight out of the dealership. Like the sensation of a phantom limb, they both considered playing the new GNU-556 license plate for that Friday and had to stop themselves from phoning it in to Hillside. BellSouth had just connected their phone service the day before. Cousin Dot left a message from Baton Rouge about an issued hurricane watch for a nearby tropical storm, Katrina. The tempest had just touched Florida, with a seventeen-percent possibility of hitting New Orleans. Kingston, puffing a Havana, couldn't imagine it being worse than the storm he'd just weathered.

THE BIG FIVE

by Joseph Wallace

Bronx Zoo

It was like the punch line to a stupid joke.

Q: How cold is it?

A: So cold that the dogs are sticking to the fire hydrants.

Only, in this case:

Q: How cold is it?

A: So cold that even the polar bears are shivering.

And it *was* that cold, eight degrees above zero and headed down. So frigid that clots of ice bobbed and clattered down the stripped-bare Bronx River, that the bison he'd passed on the way in, their shaggy humps edged with frost, breathed out huge gouts of steam like irritable snow-capped volcanoes.

But Akeley didn't mind. In fact, the plummeting temperatures made what he'd come here to do easier.

Though not too easy. No point if it was too easy.

He stood beside the ice-skimmed pool, between the concrete wall and the jumble of manmade rocks that were supposed to remind visitors of the Arctic. If there was anyone there to be reminded on this gray, deep-winter day, when the zoo was open but no one came, when this patch of the Bronx was the least populated two hundred-plus acres in the city.

The only place, the only time of year, when you didn't feel like an ant, one among eight million scurrying along predetermined pathways, carrying food back to the giant rectangular mound you called home.

And the zoo was even emptier than usual today. Akeley had known it would be. Known that even the keepers would be hidden safely inside, except when the feeding or cleaning schedule forced them to venture out into the deep freeze.

Almost as empty as the Arctic itself, where great white bears might live out their entire lives without seeing a human being. Carnivores so wild, so untamed, that they didn't recognize the danger in a rifle, didn't understand what a large-bore cartridge could do, didn't realize they were supposed to go down, and so instead kept on coming at you, as if they were above death.

But you had nothing to fear from these zoo bears. They had lost their freedom, their wildness, their *purpose*. You could see it in the way they got fat, the way they smelled, rank, like something inside them was rotting away. You could see it by the toys the zookeepers had given them. A pink ball, a split plastic barrel, a metal garbage can.

Akeley had often seen them tossing their toys into the pond, then belly-flopping after them, making enormous splashes as the spectators laughed and cheered. It was like watching a kitten cuffing a catnip-stuffed toy mouse, safe and easy and cute, and these defiled bears seemed to respond to human approval just the way kittens did.

Only . . . not today.

The big one, the sow, lay at his feet. She had sunk down onto her belly and laid her head on her paws. Her eyes were on his, eyes normally sharp as obsidian, but growing rapidly duller, more distant, as the seconds passed. Akeley watched until the last glimmer of light drained out of them.

A small trickle of blood ran from the hole where the bullet had entered, but most was trapped beneath her layers of blubber. To anyone outside the fence looking in, she would seem merely asleep.

The cub stood just a few feet away. Perhaps three years old, but already weighing six hundred pounds or more. Big enough to fight, to attack, to kill, but in its defiled state able only to stare down at its mother, then up at Akeley. Its body was shaking so hard that he could hear its teeth chattering.

So cold that even the polar bears are shivering.

But this one, of course, was shivering in fear.

The hunter hoisted his heavy duffel bag over his shoulder and turned away.

It was a good-sized show at the Holiday Inn Aurora, one of many hotels carved out of wrecked farmland on the outskirts of Denver International Airport. Something like two thousand tables spread across the floor of the convention center, holding endless rows of double-action safari rifles, police revolvers, shotguns, military hardware. Cartridges lined up like rows of gravestones. Knives and nunchaku and pepper spray. Signs saying things like, Laser scopes must be operated only by exhibitors.

Antiques too. A twenty-one-inch-barrel Volcanic rifle in .41 caliber, a circa-1650 Spanish epee, bear traps from the Colonial days, even a 1940s Jeep that had crossed the Sahara which the kids could climb on.

In other words, the usual. The same stuff you'd find at a hundred other gun shows on a hundred other exhibit floors in a hundred other cities.

One thing was different this time, though.

Up on the eighth floor, in the Executive Suite.

It had been a poor shot.

He could see the animal near the rear of the enclosure, leaping again and again off the floor, landing sometimes on its belly, sometimes on its back. Then getting onto its feet and flipping upwards once more, like a marionette dancing from the ends of a callous puppeteer's strings.

A golden lion tamarin, one of the world's smallest, rarest, and most beautiful monkeys, its spun-gold fur stained with black blood.

Akeley studied the hole in the glass front of the enclosure and saw what had happened. The glass had deflected the .22 round, just a little, but enough to prevent a clean kill.

He shifted his gaze to the wounded monkey. The others clustered above it on the vines strung across the enclosure, wide dark eyes showing the human emotions of fear and pity, the twittering of their birdlike voices coming through the glass to his ears.

The hunter sighed. He couldn't leave it like this. Someone might notice, figure out what had happened, and stop him before he was done.

A door leading behind the scenes was located just inside the Monkey House's entrance. Before he tested the handle, he looked around, seeing only a small group of teenagers over near the Zoo Center and a pair of nannies wheeling strollers toward the tropical warmth of the World of Birds.

No one paid him any attention. If they had, they'd likely have mistaken him for a keeper anyway. He'd dressed in khaki for this day.

He had his tools ready, but the door was unlocked, the passageway inside deserted. It smelled of rotten fruit and old urine, and the calls of captive animals came to him through the small hatches that led into each enclosure.

He found the entrance to the tamarin exhibit without trouble—he knew the layout of every building—and ducked inside. The little golden monkeys flowed away from him in alarm. They knew he was no zookeeper.

The wounded one, still leaping and falling, fully occupied with trying to escape its agony, didn't notice him. Droplets of blood from its gut wound lay scattered across the floor.

The hunter reached for his duffel, then paused. Decided there was a better way to end this.

He squatted down and lifted the tiny monkey, insubstantial as a flake of ash in his hands. As he brought it close to his face, it stopped struggling and lay there looking at him, its gaze full of unwarranted trust. So used to humans, so tame, that it expected him to take away its pain.

So he did.

He laid the corpse behind a thick growth of plastic ferns, then straightened and looked into the eyes of the little blond-haired girl who was watching him with rapt attention through the glass.

There were five of them in the hotel room, sipping single malt and telling stories. Taking their time before getting to the matter at hand.

The Big Five, they called themselves. A joke, kind of, but also a boast. The Big Five: The most dangerous mammals in Africa. Lion, leopard, elephant, rhino, Cape buffalo. The ones you stalked if you were a real hunter.

Among the Masai, you weren't a man until you'd killed a lion. For European and American hunters a century and more ago, just a lion wasn't enough. You needed all five.

And you knew where to get them. The Serengeti. The Mara and the Selous. Amboseli, under the shadow of Kilimanjaro. You could shoot till the barrels of your bolt-action repeater melted, or till a rhino got his horn into your gut. Either way, no one cared.

Today, though? Today, all those places were preserves, and you were supposed to head to game ranches in South Africa or Zimba-

bwe instead. Places where all you had to do was hand over your plastic and choose from a price list of what you wanted to shoot. As if you were sitting in a restaurant and ordering off a menu.

A baboon, your basic appetizer, cost seventy-five dollars. Two hundred for a warthog, two-fifty for an impala, nine hundred for a wildebeest, all the way up to two thousand for a waterbuck and twenty-five hundred for a giraffe. Most of them so slow and stupid that you might as well have been some Texas bigwig blasting away at farm-raised quail.

The original Big Five were on the menu too, though their prices were never listed. You had to ask. But if your pockets were deep enough, you could still follow a guide out and knock down a semi-tame lion or sluggish buffalo on a groomed veldt that looked like something you'd see on a golf course. And then go home and brag on it to your friends.

The state of big-game hunting in the twenty-first century.

Unless you wanted more, and knew how to get it.

Standing close to the glass, the girl peered up at him. She looked to be about seven, with fair skin, a scattering of freckles across the bridge of her nose, curly blond hair emerging from a green knit hat, and eyes so large and pale blue that he thought he might be able to see through to her brain if he looked right into them.

How much had she seen? She was old enough to understand, to tell her mother, to scream. She could ruin everything.

He leaned forward, looked past her, seeing only a young woman in a black parka glancing at the squirrel monkeys across the way. No one else was in the Monkey House.

He had choices, then. There were a couple of different ways this could go.

He tried the easiest first, and smiled at her.

She smiled back.

Okay. Good. Tilting his head, he gestured at the golden lion tamarins on the branches around him. Alarmed, they leaped away toward the farthest corners of the enclosure. But the girl saw only adorable little monkeys doing tricks, and laughed. Then she pointed to her mouth and made chewing motions. *Feeding time?*

He gave an apologetic shake of the head and showed her his watch. *Later.*

Her lips turned downward in disappointment, and she shrugged. Then she glanced over her shoulder. He heard her voice dimly through the glass: "Hey, Mom—there's a man in there!"

But by the time the woman turned to look, he was gone.

Wilson and Crede, the lawyers, had bagged a bull elephant whose crossed tusks, as pitted and yellow as mammoth ivory, weighed a combined 407 pounds. Smithfield, the bluff and hearty CEO of a company with offices in Hong Kong, Singapore, London, and New York, had shot a black-maned lion in Namibia that measured eleven feet from head to tail. Clark, the lobbyist, tall and skinny, had faced down a charging three-thousand-pound black rhino, standing his ground and firing his Brno ZKK-602 until the great beast came crashing to the ground not five feet from where he stood. And Kushner, the tanned, nasal-voiced neurosurgeon, had discovered that the leopard he'd shot was still alive, and had finished the job by jamming his fist down its throat until it died of asphyxiation.

Or so the stories went. Who knew what the truth was? And who cared? They were good yarns, and to the Big Five the telling was almost as important as the feat itself.

Taking their time, they opened a new bottle. Soon the room was filled with a familiar camaraderie.

The only thing slightly off was the presence of the sixth man in the room, the one sitting a little back from the circle. A decade older than the others, tall and rangy, he had sun-creased skin, a mustache that had once been blond but was now white, and deep-set eyes the faded blue of sea glass. He sat slouched comfortably in one of the teak-and-gold chairs, his long, tapering fingers occasionally drumming an odd rhythm on his thighs. His piercing gaze moved from one to another, and though he smiled at their loud jokes, he spoke only rarely himself. His drink sat untouched on the table beside his chair.

The others would have liked it if he'd joined in, maybe shared some of his own stories. But no one even considered asking.

They all knew his reputation. He was the one who sometimes disappeared for months at a time, going where no satellite could find him, living off the game instead of just bringing it home to show off. The one who people said could read a landscape with cheetah's skill, follow the herds as relentlessly as a hunting dog, stalk his prey as silently as a leopard. The one whose obsession for the kill had once made his guns seem like extensions of his body. The one who had seen everything, shot everything, lived a life the rest of them could only dream of.

He was the one they all wanted to be.

Which was why they'd come to the Executive Suite.

A red-tailed hawk was circling over the thatched roofs of the zoo's fake African village, peering down from the steel-gray sky at the shaggy baboons milling about on their pitiful, barren hillside.

Akeley had seen ospreys here, peregrines, once even an eagle that had wandered over from the Hudson. Predators all, their brains always processing the information their eyes transmitted. He wondered what they thought when they looked down on the apes, tigers, and wolves below.

Probably something like: *Man, if I could kill that, I wouldn't have to hunt again for weeks.*

"Sir?"

Shit. He'd been drifting, something he did a lot more frequently these days than he once had.

Drifting could get you killed.

"Sir, I need to talk to you."

A deep voice, Spanish accent. Slowly the hunter swung his gaze down from the sky and focused on the man dressed in white shirt and blue slacks, an inadequate navy-blue jacket zipped up in a hopeless attempt to block out the icy wind. A walkie-talkie swinging from his belt. The name on his white laminated badge read, *F. Cabrera.*

A zoo security guard, with chapped cheeks and watering eyes. Unhappy to be outside in this weather, but staying polite for now, probably because of Akeley's age.

Still, the hunter could see that F. Cabrera was young and self-confident. A smile and a few conciliatory words wouldn't stop him. And his politeness wouldn't last long if he didn't get the answers he was looking for.

Too bad.

"Sir, I had a report of a man fitting your description exiting an authorized-personnel door of the Monkey House."

Akeley didn't reply, just turned away and started walking, heading south and east, his strides eating up ground.

"Hey!" Cabrera sounded shocked by this display of insubordination. "Hey, I'm talking to you."

Akeley kept going.

The guard got in front of him again. Now his face was

stony, and he showed some teeth when he talked. His hand hovered over the walkie-talkie.

"Papi, you really think it's a good idea to make trouble?" he said.

Akeley took stock. Down the path toward the African Plains he saw a family—Mom, Dad, ten-year-old, toddler, swaddled baby in a stroller. They were out of earshot, and even if they hadn't been, they would merely have seen two zoo employees talking. Nothing worth giving a second thought to.

Cabrera cut a glance at Akeley's duffel. "What you got in there?"

"Books."

"Huh." Imbuing the single word with scornful disbelief. "Why don't you open it and show me?"

The hunter shook his head and started off again, moving faster this time. He felt a hand on his arm, shrugged it off, then felt it grab him again, hard, and half-spin him around.

"You come with me." Cabrera spat out each word. "*Now.*"

"Okay," Akeley said, "I won't fight you."

"Good." But Akeley thought that the guard looked a little disappointed.

They walked together, Cabrera still holding his arm. Up ahead loomed the dark, squat stone walls of the World of Darkness. Akeley waited until they'd gone ten more steps, fifteen, and then broke free and headed up the path toward the building's front doors.

"Oh, for fuck's sake," Cabrera said, and came after him.

They went through the turnstile, the door slamming open once, and then again, and into the permanent near-blackness designed to encourage nocturnal animals—bats, skunks, snakes, wildcats—to put on a better show. The hunter could see perfectly in the darkness, an ability he'd possessed for as long as he could remember. But the people inside, hearing the sound of the slamming door, turned dim, clouded eyes in his direction.

Behind him Cabrera, blind, fumbling, tried to put him in a bearhug. Akeley turned and hit him three times, hard, twice in the gut and once in the jaw.

The guard made a small, despairing sound in his throat and slid to the floor. The hunter spoke into his ear, a whisper that no one else could hear over the squeaking of bats and the rustle of porcupine quills.

"You don't stop me," he said, "before I'm done."

One corner of the exhibit was roped off for construction. Quickly Akeley carried the unconscious man past the barricade and dropped him against the wall. No one would see him there, and he would stay quiet for a while. For long enough.

Akeley headed back toward the door, past a pair of teenagers staring at the fruit bats and a small figure bent over the glass scorpion case: the little blond girl from the Monkey House, turning to look at him as he went by. Her eyes had adjusted to the darkness by now, and she recognized him as well.

"It's you," she said in a half-whisper.

"Yes."

"Look at this." She pressed a button, and instantly a black light came on. Under the glass, a pair of large scorpions fluoresced, a brilliant glowing blue. "Aren't they cool?"

"They sure are."

As he went out the door he heard her say, "Hey, Mom, look—"

He stood for a moment outside, the north wind in his face. The sun, heading for the horizon, had at last pulled free of the low clouds, and cast weak shadows behind the spindly trees and litter-snagged bushes.

The hunter drew the cold air deep into his lungs and started heading west, toward the setting sun.

Wondering if he'd already lost too much time.

Was "Akeley" even his real name?

No one asked. Even where he came from, where he'd been born, was a mystery. Some said Germany, others England, still others swore he was the son of a ranching family that had lived in Rhodesia for generations. His quiet voice, with its gruff edge, seemed to carry a slight accent, but gave no firm clue to its origins. Nor did anyone know how he had gotten the scar that began beneath his jawline and ran along the side of his neck before disappearing under the collar of the long-sleeved safari shirts he always wore.

A man out of time, people said. Stories told at gun shows, in gentlemen's club lounges, and in the field, creating only this blurry portrait, all the more compelling for being so incomplete. If he chose to call himself Akeley, that had to be good enough for them.

Even Smithfield, the CEO, had seemed awed when they first met. "Were you the one—" he had started to say, before something in Akeley's expression made it clear that he shouldn't finish. Smithfield didn't usually care what other people wanted—why bother when you could fire anyone who disagreed with you?—but he'd stopped short, cleared his throat, and finished, lamely, by saying, "Glad to know you," in an unexpectedly hoarse voice.

But he'd recovered by the time they got down to business. "Fifty thousand each?" he said. "Why not make it a hundred?"

Getting some pleasure watching the others wriggle a bit. Then seeing Kushner, the guy who drilled into your skull and fucked with your brain, frowning as he put an end to that. "Fifty," he said. "As we discussed."

Everyone else nodding.

But Kushner's eyes were on Akeley. "And you'll match it."

"That's what I said."

"Make it five hundred thousand?"

"What it adds up to," Akeley agreed.

That had been the deal from the start, but still, there was something about hearing it out loud. Smithfield laughed, a sound like a zebra's bray.

But Kushner wasn't smiling. "Why?" he asked. "Why are you raising the stakes?"

The hunter stretched like a cat in his chair. "Added incentive," he said.

Though, really, this group hardly needed any.

The zoo would be closing soon.

Not that it mattered much, not usually. In preparation, the hunter had spent a week living here, on the grounds, and no one had ever gotten a hint of his presence. You couldn't "close" something so big and sprawling and overgrown, you could just tell people it was time to leave and assume they'd listen.

And because people were sheep, they usually did.

Cawing flocks of crows flew overhead, blown by the wind like flakes of soot as they headed toward their nighttime roosts. Below the heedless black birds, the last few zoo visitors, scattered groups of two or three, hurried toward the parking lots near the Bronx River Parkway and Fordham Road.

But the hunter had someplace else he needed to be.

Moving faster, staying in the lengthening shadows, he kept to his course.

West.

Toward the African Plains.

* * *

"We all decide who wins," Smithfield said.

Everyone nodded. It was the only fair way.

Wilson said, "We get together afterwards and vote."

More nods.

"And fill each other in." Smithfield's lips turned upward. "Every last detail."

Their favorite part from the beginning.

"We decide where yet?" Kushner asked.

"Great Western Gun Show," Akeley said.

"Salt Lake City, that is?" Kushner asked.

Akeley nodded.

"Listen, though," Wilson said. "If we can't, like, agree, who gets the tie-breaking vote?"

Everyone looked at him, but no one spoke. They all knew the answer to that one.

There.

The prey. As unaware, as self-deluding as the monkey had been, and the bear. Another degraded animal that had convinced itself it was wild, free, unfettered.

The hunter felt himself relax. He was in time.

Just.

It was standing half-hidden behind a screen of bare forsythia. Leaning forward, head hunched low, fierce dark eyes focused on something the hunter couldn't see. Then, almost imperceptibly, it shifted its weight, muscles tensing as it assumed a predator's classic pre-attack posture.

Time to put an end to this.

Moving as fast and silently as a shadow, the hunter came up behind it. "Don't do that," he said.

His prey jumped, swung its head around, and stared at him.

"What the fuck are *you* doing here?" it asked.

They drew lots. Each got a different zoo, a different part of the country. Minnesota, Miami, San Diego, Washington, the Bronx. The targets: the zoos' biggest and fiercest animals, or their rarest, or their most difficult to approach.

"I think they've got the whole Big Five at my zoo," said Crede, who'd drawn San Diego.

"Yeah, but I've got pandas," said Smithfield, who was headed to Washington.

Only Wilson seemed to have some reservations, now that their plan was becoming a reality. "Yeah, but—" he said. "I mean, aren't all these things going to be, like, too easy to kill?"

His words drawing scornful looks from the rest, as if they'd all long since considered that possibility, and discarded it.

Akeley said, "Sure. But who said it was about the kill?"

"Well—" Wilson fumbled for words. "Then . . . then what is it about?"

Akeley stared at him. "It's about the hunt*," he said. "The plan. The approach. The wait. The moment—the one moment. And the aftermath."*

Just like it used to be.

He looked into Kushner's sickly yellow eyes.

The neurosurgeon. Back in the Executive Suite he'd worn some fancy cologne, but now he smelled like powder and heated steel and sweat.

And something more. Something . . . undone. Unfulfilled.

The hunter let his gaze follow the direction that Kushner had been pointing his Browning autoloader. There, walking along the path that bordered the gray and barren African Plains—nothing like the golden expanse of the real thing—

were the surgeon's final targets.

The little blond girl and her mother. Heading obliviously toward the Asia Gate, walking fast in the gathering darkness, but not faster than a .338 cartridge could fly.

Kushner looked down at the girl, then back at Akeley. The lust for the kill was still strong in him.

"Please," he said. "Please . . . let me finish."

Kushner hesitated in the hallway outside the suite as the others took the elevator down to the exhibition floor. Then he stepped back inside the room. His deeply tanned face was underlain by a reddish flush.

"I have a question," he said. Akeley waited.

"The kills—" The words were cautious, but the surgeon's eyes gleamed.

Akeley guessed what was coming next. "What about them?"

"Do they have to be—" A deep breath. The gleam brighter. "To be—animals?"

Yes: what he'd expected.

The word had gotten around about Kushner over the years. How he'd accidentally shot and killed a porter on safari in Namibia, and then another in northern Kenya. Garbled rumors of yet another death, maybe in the Peruvian Amazon, maybe in Thailand.

Or maybe both. The world was full of potential victims, places where a rich American could get away with murder.

"Well," Akeley said, "aren't we all animals?"

Kushner blinked, then grinned. His lips were wet. "And will it—will it help me win?"

The hunter merely shrugged.

Knowing that the surgeon would take that as a yes.

"What else did you kill?"

The girl and her mother had moved out of sight.

"What?"

The hunter thought about the time he'd lost in the World of Darkness. "I saw the bear and the tamarin. What else?"

"Snow leopard. Bengal tiger." Kushner squared his shoulders. "I don't understand," he said. "You aren't supposed to be here. You aren't supposed to be *anywhere*. This is *my* zoo. You're just the money man."

"Oh?" The hunter unzipped his bag. "And who do you think I am?"

"Akeley—" the neurosurgeon said, then stopped.

The hunter reached into his duffel for the first time all day. "Do you even know who Carl Akeley was?" he asked.

Kushner, looking at the bag, gave a little shake of his head.

"A hundred years ago, a little less, Carl Akeley was one of the world's great sportsmen. He loved to shoot."

Out of the duffel came his Winchester. His elephant gun. There was already a .458 Magnum in its chamber.

"And then he saw that the hunt was becoming a farce, a slaughter. And so he gave it up."

The hunter hefted the rifle in his hands. It was a good old gun. Like him, it was almost ready to retire, but he thought they both had one more shot in them.

"Akeley saw the day coming when the great herds would be nearly all gone, and the honorable hunters of past years would be replaced by amateurs, men who cared only for the kill, not for the contest. So he decided to fight to save what was left."

The surgeon, his tan turned the yellow of rotting cheese, was staring at the gun. He didn't appear to be listening.

The hunter sighed. It was useless trying to explain. He raised the gun to his shoulder.

The surgeon followed the movement with red-rimmed eyes. "What about the others?"

The hunter permitted himself a little smile. "The others," he said, "are behind bars."

The surgeon put his hand to his mouth. His gun bag lay forgotten at his feet. "And me?" he asked.

"You I wanted for myself."

The hunter wrapped his finger around the cold steel of the trigger. With a sudden, smooth movement, he swiveled so the rifle was aimed directly at the surgeon's head.

"Know what?" he said. "I think you should run."

They'd all gone at last, taking their Scotch, their memories, and their anticipation with them.

The hunter sighed. His legs ached as he walked over to the refrigerator and took out a Tusker. Not a great lager, he had to admit, but still. It reminded him of the smell of the savanna, the safari of white clouds marching across the enormous Kenyan sky, the nasal bleats of the migrating wildebeest herds, and, further off, the grunting cough of a lion proclaiming its territory.

All a vanished world in a bottle of beer.

He sat down, unsnapped his cell phone from its clip on his belt, and did what he'd always done at the end of a long day's hunt, just before he pulled the trigger.

He checked to make sure his escape route was rock-solid.

Kushner was shivering uncontrollably.

How cold is it?

"Run where?" he said.

"Wherever you like." The hunter leaned forward, touching the barrel of the Winchester gently against the surgeon's quivering temple. "But start now."

With a sick, despairing look, Kushner turned and stumbled away. He nearly tripped, then regained his footing and ran, legs pumping, arms flailing, northward up the path. The hunter could hear him gasping out the word "Help" again and again as he ran, but he had no air in his lungs to shout, and anyway, there was no one around to hear him. The zoo was closed.

Fifty yards away he got, a hundred, before he came to a break in the wall of bushes. There he hesitated, looking back over his shoulder, as if he might spot Akeley in the gloom. As if there was any chance of ever seeing the hunter, if the hunter didn't want to be seen.

For a moment more Kushner jittered on his feet. Then he reached a decision and turned, intending to go cross-country toward the road that bordered the zoo.

Akeley, having known he'd do that, waited.

For three seconds, four, the surgeon was out of sight. Then he reappeared in a clearing, a tiny gap where a vine-ridden maple tree had come down in a storm. He paused, looking around, listening for any signs of pursuit. But it was nearly dark now, and his pulse was pounding, so his eyes and ears told him nothing.

That's how it usually went. The wildebeest about to be swatted to the ground by the lion, the Thomson's gazelle the moment before it faces the cheetah's rush. Victims so rarely recognize mortal danger until they feel its jaws around their throats.

Kushner straightened and took the first of four steps—just four—that would have carried him to the road and safety. At that moment, when escape suddenly seemed so close, so *possible*, the hunter's index finger tightened.

The Winchester kicked hard against his shoulder. But he

was used to it, and knew how to keep his head still, his eyes focused.

So he got to watch the .458 perform its own brand of surgery on the neurosurgeon's brain.

The doors of the 5 train rattled open before him. He stepped into the nearly empty car, beginning the first leg of a journey that would land him in Panama late that night. There he would collect the money the Big Five had planned to dole out to the "winner" of the zoo slaughter.

And after Panama, where?

Africa, of course. Poor, besieged Africa, just a shadow of what it had once been, but still the only real place on earth. Sitting in this capsule of plastic and steel, he gazed at the continent's limitless skies, tasted the wind-borne dust sweeping across its vast savannas.

The train's doors half shut, then squealed and opened again. Two people entered.

The little blond girl and her mother.

They sat down opposite him. The woman, looking cold and worn, closed her eyes and leaned her head back against the plastic seat. For a minute or so, the girl played with a stuffed monkey on her lap. Then, as if sensing the hunter's presence, she lifted her head and looked directly at him.

Her eyes widened and spots of color rose to her cheeks. He saw her lips move. *You*, she said silently.

He gave a little nod.

The girl stared, as if willing him not to disappear once more. Then she dug her elbow into her mother's side.

"Honey!" The woman didn't move. "Let me rest."

"But *Mom*," the girl insisted, "it's him! The man from the zoo."

The woman sat up. Now her eyes were open.

"*See?*"

The woman saw. The corners of her mouth turned down.

Having savored her moment of vindication, the girl went back to her toy. But her mother scowled at the hunter all the way to East 86th Street, as if she knew—just *knew*—that he'd been stalking them all afternoon, and even now was planning to leap across the aisle and finish the job.

PART V

PART V

ALL SHOOK UP

ERNIE K.'S GELDING

BY ED DEE

Van Cortlandt Park

All three of us turned sixteen halfway through the first summer of JFK's presidency, when all things seemed possible. Lefty Trainor, Brendan O'Leary, and I had spent that summer caddying, drinking beer, and unsuccessfully trying to lure BICs, otherwise known as Bronx Irish Catholic girls, into Van Cortlandt Park. Okay, so maybe not *all* things seemed possible.

It was 9 p.m. on a hot Friday night in August and we were in our usual spot on the curb outside the White Castle under the el station at Broadway and 242nd Street. We were checking out the skirts and wolfing down belly bombs. Local street wisdom had it that the little cheeseburgers were the best way to soak up the quarts of Rupert Knickerbocker beer we'd imbibed across the street, in the park. Three quarts of warm beer for $1.19 on a park bench had loosened our vocal chords for a doo-wop session under a streetlight we'd smashed to make it harder for the cops to zero in on us. Cops didn't like doo-wop or guys our age. But in the dark and without the element of surprise, they were no match for us in Vanny. As my mother said, "You ran through that park like a bunch of savages."

"Here comes God's gift to women," Lefty said.

"Kronek or the horse?" I said.

Patrolman Ernie Kronek was the worst human being in the Bronx. Kronek was a NYPD mounted cop assigned to patrol the 1,100 acres of Van Cortlandt Park. He'd made it his personal mission to torture us. If he'd caught us in the park drinking beer and singing he would have charged at us, swinging his nightstick like he was the King of England on his polo pony. He loved to whack us, then smash the beer. We all had bruises from Ernie K. at one time or another. He truly hated us, but he loved the girls. Every night, about this time, he'd ride across the parade ground to the southwest corner of the park. He'd sit there atop his horse and stare at the girls coming down the steps of the el station. Treating them to a gaze at his manly physique. Asshole. Everybody knew it. Even the other cops.

On the opposite side of Broadway, the local men were gathering in Hagan's Bar to wait for the early edition of tomorrow's *Daily News*. It was a Bronx ritual. Every night around this time they'd leave their apartments and walk to Hagan's to have a cold brew and listen for the bundles to be tossed from the truck. Then they'd have one more while Irv from the candy store cut the bindings and stacked the papers on the outside racks. On Saturday nights the three of us helped Irv put the Sunday paper together. We lugged the early edition off the sidewalk and stuffed each paper with the Sunday magazine, the comics, the sale ads, and the classifieds, which had come earlier in the week. Our hands and faces would be black with printer's ink, but we had two bucks each burning holes in our pockets. Irv always tossed in a free paper, usually a torn one, but we only read the sports section on the back five pages. Between Irv's deuce and the money we made caddying at Van Cortlandt, the nation's oldest public golf course, we didn't need anyone's free newspaper.

"It's gotta be the horse," Lefty Trainor said, as a tall redhead in pale blue shorts giggled and pet the big Tennessee Walker. The horse was named Con Ed for the electric company who donated him. Ernie K. called him "Connie," but it wasn't a female. Poor Connie had the worst of it, having to lug Ernie K.'s fat ass around. We held no grudge against the horse, who after all was just an innocent animal. The cop was another matter; we watched in disgust as he flashed his Ipana smile down on the thirtyish redhead, his square jaw jutting outward.

"Who does the woman remind you of?" Lefty said.

"Maureen O'Hara," I said.

"No, c'mon," Lefty said. "B.O., who do you think she looks like? Seriously."

We'd called Brendan O'Leary "B.O." since kindergarten. B.O. was having a lousy summer, ever since he got dumped by his girlfriend. Lefty and I had been going through every joke known to man and Milton Berle, trying to cheer him up. He'd been a real sad sack, especially when the beer buzz began to wear off. Getting him back to his happy old self was the main reason we started our vendetta against Ernie K. The nuns had taught us that the pursuit of a worthy goal can help take your mind off your own problems.

"Marilyn Monroe," B.O. said, but Marilyn was a blonde. He wasn't even trying. He did, however, smile and wave to his dad, as he pushed through Hagan's door. B.O.'s dad was a detective in Bronx Homicide; that's how we knew the other cops considered Ernie Kronek an asshole. As every Friday night, my dad was already in Hagan's, in his corner near the window.

"I got a buck says he bags this one," Lefty said. "She looks half shit-faced to me."

I'd never bet against Ernie K.; his act was a smooth one.

He had a nose for a certain type of woman. The type my father called "free spirits" and my mother called "hoors." He'd quietly offer these girls a special ride. It was against the police department's rules, but he'd make an exception in their case, winking as if they were coconspirators in some rebellious adventure. He had a soft spot for beautiful women, he'd say. Then he'd have them walk into the park, to a bench behind the trees, near the old stone house, the family mansion, now a museum. Ernie would wait a few minutes, looking around to see if anybody was watching him, then slowly amble toward the meeting spot. He'd have the woman stand on a bench, then he'd pull her up onto poor Connie, letting the woman feel his powerful arms. He had a whole routine; a slow romantic tour of the park's historical highlights, all the while moving deeper into the dark recesses of the park, to his "special spot." We had Ernie K.'s act down pat.

The screech of metal on metal drowned out conversation as the Broadway train clattered to a stop above us. Red sparks floated in the night air. With the exception of creeps like Ernie Kronek and a few others, this was the best neighborhood in the city. We had everything, because 242nd and Broadway was the end of the line, the last subway stop in the Bronx. The place was always crowded, day and night. We had five bars, two candy stores, and Manhattan College just up the hill. Commuters going to or returning from school or work or partying in Midtown got off and caught a bus for Riverdale or Yonkers. Husbands, wives, or mothers, whatever, parked on the Van Cortlandt side of Broadway and waited for their loved ones. Guys bought flowers, others stopped in one of the bars for a quick pop before going home to the bride. An endless supply of skirts floated down from the subway platform above. But most of all, that park across the street. Thank you, Van

Cortlandt family, for the biggest backyard in the universe.

Back to this Ernie K. thing. Looking at it now I can understand that one of the reasons we hated him was that he *was* successful with women. All the girls we knew acted like he was a movie star, or something. Even my sainted mother would say, "He's a fine figure of a man." I won't repeat what my father said, but most of the male population of the neighborhood agreed with him. And on top of that, he was a mean bastard.

"There she goes," Lefty said. "I told you she was a live one."

The redhead slung her big droopy purse over her shoulder and headed off into the park. Not many woman ventured into the park alone at this time of night, so I felt pretty sure Lefty was right.

"I got a buck says he goes in less than ninety seconds," Lefty said, holding his birthday watch up to the light. "He knows this one's a hot number."

"I'm not up for the hunt tonight," B.O. said.

"Come on," Lefty and I whined simultaneously.

We'd been tracking Ernie K. all summer. The idea was to make a record of his on-duty romantic trysts and somehow use it against him. Our plan was to send an anonymous but very specific letter to NYPD Internal Affairs and get him transferred to the ass end of Staten Island, or further, if anything was further than that. But B.O. got cold feet, afraid that somehow it would get back that he was involved and indirectly hurt his dad. He said his dad always talked about how the department hated rats. Cops didn't turn in cops.

"We'll turn his ass in," I said. "Your name won't even come up."

"Naw, I don't mean that," he said. "It's just that my stomach isn't good tonight. We must have gotten some bad beer."

"Beer is never bad," Lefty said. "Food sometimes, beer never."

The sweet smell of anisette cookies wafted up from the Stella D'Oro bakery. When I looked up to breathe it all in, Ernie K. was gone.

"It's Howdy Doody time," Lefty said.

It took a few minutes for our eyes to adjust to the dark. B.O. continued to express doubts, but Lefty and I kept moving. We knew Ernie took his prizes on an L-shaped route: east behind the mansion to the nature trail, then north past the lake and along Tibbetts Brook. Very romantic on a moonlit night, especially if you can ignore the sounds of the train and the roar of cars on the Major Deegan Expressway. Eventually he'd get to the black and silent heart of the park, where we were headed.

Since we knew where they'd wind up we took a diagonal route. Straight across the parade ground, the soccer and rugby fields, to the cross-country course. We all ran high school cross-country and knew the world class course by heart. Across the flat to the cow path, then a sharp left and up through the woods, up along old Mohegan Indian hunting trails. It was a steep, rocky incline to the the top of Cemetery Hill, 150 feet above sea level. B.O. stopped twice to throw up. Not that unusual. Even sober runners do it on Cemetery Hill.

The guidebooks call it Vault Hill, because Stephanus Van Cortlandt, the first native born mayor of New York, built a vault there in 1776 to hide the city's records from the British. Later it became the family burial grounds. Everybody around here calls it Cemetery Hill.

We ducked through a hole in the fence, then weaved between the old tombstones, all of us sweating and gasping. My pulse was thumping in my neck and I was close to tossing some belly bombs myself. We crawled the last ten yards, the wet grass cooling us down. At the edge, we overlooked a small circular clearing against the hill, hidden by trees. We figured it was once an Indian camp that the guidebooks missed. Now it was Ernie K.'s love nook. We weren't there ten minutes when we heard a woman laughing.

"I told you he'd be in a hurry tonight," Lefty said, as he checked his Timex with the glowing green hands and recorded the exact time for the accurate records of our planned indictment of a bastard cop. *Shhh!* B.O. reminded. We were above them, but only about thirty yards away. Our chins against the turf, we all clasped our hands in front of our faces, to block the sound of our breathing. Only our eyes showed over our clasped hands.

We were far enough from roads and highways to hear the sound of crickets. The moon was close to full, so the place was lit like a stage play. We'd be able to see them better, but if we weren't careful, they could definitely see us. Then we heard twigs and brush breaking, and Connie snorting. We spotted the yellow calvary stripe on Ernie K.'s uniform pants. At least the stripe was cool. Only mounted cops were allowed to wear it. Connie stopped in the middle of the clearing. Ernie K. twisted around, lifted the woman off the horse, and slowly let her down. The guy was powerful, I had to admit that.

"It's her," Lefty whispered in my ear.

"Who?" I said.

"But don't say anything to . . ." he said, pointing in B.O.'s direction.

What the hell is that about? I wondered.

The redhead stumbled around, more bombed than I originally thought. She put her shoes in her floppy purse and began

dancing like a gypsy in the movies. Arms waving, hips swaying. Ernie K. tied Connie to a tree, as the dancing redhead
began unbuttoning her blouse. I didn't know a woman like
this, how could Lefty?

"Dance with me, Ernie," she said, reaching around to un-
snap her bra. Then she danced and danced, and stripped and
stripped. Tossing her clothes onto her floppy purse. Until she
was bare ass. Totally bare ass.

I wish I could say we left around this point, because this
part is a little embarrassing for good Catholic boys like ourselves. But no one would believe me. We never left. We always
stayed to the bitter end. Give us a break; we were sixteen
years old and this was the most skin we'd seen outside of *National Geographic*. Besides, most of the sex in Ernie K.'s nook
was hidden by tree branches or blankets. Really. Well, usually.
But not this night; this was Loew's big-screen big, plus Tech-
nicolor and Cinemascope. All we needed was popcorn.

"Bridget Fahey," Lefty whispered.

"No shit?" I said, way too loud, but the redhead's louder
singing drowned it out. I'd heard about Crazy Bridget, but
couldn't remember ever seeing her before. She'd left for California years ago, leaving only her reputation for wildness
behind. The Fahey's lived in Lefty's building, so I believed
him. And I figured if I didn't remember her, then B.O. probably didn't either. B.O. was the problem. The part I didn't
know how to handle. How could I tell him that this bare ass
redhead was the older sister of Margaret Mary, the love of
his life? But Bridget was already naked and dancing in the
moonlight. The damage was done. I figured any notification
could wait. Besides, the nuns always told us that some things
are better left unsaid.

Leather creaked as Ernie K. removed his gun belt and hooked it over Connie. He sat on a stump and began removing the high boots. This was special. Sometimes he didn't bother taking his boots off, but crazy Bridget was singing in Spanish and shoving her ass in his face as she pulled off his boots, like some drunken scullery maid in an Errol Flynn picture.

B.O. and Lefty were silent, and eerily still. I think we all sensed this was going to be a memorable night. For Crazy Bridget it could have been just an average night. Who knows? She bumped and grinded in the Bronx moonlight, imploring Ernie K. to hurry. The older guys in our neighborhood always smiled when they talked about Bridget. After she left, her younger sisters were kept close to the house, rarely straying from the sight of Mrs. Fahey, ever-present in her third-floor window. Lefty said that cloistered nuns had more freedom than Margaret Mary Fahey. But he never said it in front of B.O.

Naked himself, Ernie K. stepped away from the tree stump and began an awkward, limping dance. It was obvious his bare feet were too tender for God's pebbled earth. He moved in a slow yet palsied twist. Chubby Checker would have died of embarrassment. Finally Bridget put him out of his misery and moved toward him, arms spread wide, shaking her alabaster breasts. Moving right up against him. The slap of skin on skin. Ernie K. stopped dancing and wrapped her in his arms. B.O. pulled his hands down from his mouth, to keep his glasses from fogging up.

"Over there, over there," Bridget cried, and pointed to a grassy spot right below us. She pulled Ernie K. by his arm. To right below us. We could have spit on them. With Bridget's insistence the cop carefully laid himself down on the small patch of grass. But no sooner had he gotten down . . . she sprung up.

"Wait right there, sugar," she said. "I need something."

She ran back across the dirt floor of Kronek's love nook toward her floppy purse. I figured she needed some woman thing, but I was more worried about Ernie K. If he leaned back to gaze at the stars glittering over the Bronx he would have been looking right into our faces. Instead, Bridget reclaimed all his attention.

Because she came back waving Ernie K.'s gun.

For the first time in my life I understood how certain moments play out in slow motion. It seemed unreal, half dream, half hallucination. Ernie K. had his hand in the air as if it would stop a bullet. Bridget came within a few feet of him and stopped.

"Give me the gun," he said.

"You don't know who I am, do you?"

"This isn't funny, Bridget."

"What's my last name, you self-centered bastard?"

"You don't want to be doing this. Put the gun down, we'll both walk away. No repercussions."

"No repercussions," she said. "You don't know the first thing about repercussions."

"I'll never mention this to anyone," he said.

"I know that for sure," she said. "You'll *never* mention this to anyone."

I felt B.O. start to fidget next to me. He didn't like stress of any kind. And this was big-time stress.

"What is my name?" she said again.

The cop, on his knees, had been slowly working his way up, but when he started to stand she fired the gun over his head. The muzzle flash lit Ernie K.'s face, showing it a sudden pale gray. But the sound, the shocking blast and its echo, caused the three of us to come off the ground. They had to hear it in downtown Yonkers. Ernie K. went to his knees, then lay flat out. We could see him trembling.

"What is my last name?" she screamed.

It was then that B.O. decided to be a hero. He stood up, yelling, "He's a cop! You can't shoot a cop!"

They both looked up.

"Witness, they're witnesses," the naked mounted cop said.

"I'll goddamn shoot anyone I please," Bridget said.

"But not a cop," B.O. insisted.

"Run for help," Ernie K. said. "Say it's a ten-thirteen."

B.O. turned to run. He knew the location of all the police call boxes in the park.

"Fahey," Lefty said. "Her name is Bridget Fahey."

And there it was, out there for all to know. B.O. stopped cold.

"Mr. Trainor is right," Bridget said. "And this conceited, arrogant police officer knows the Fahey name all too well, do you not? All too well."

Bridget circled Ernie K. Dust rose from her feet as she shuffled to put her back to us. Out of modesty, or a better shooting angle. I didn't know which.

"You shoot me and these kids will tell," he said. "Every cop in this country will hunt you down."

"You exaggerate your popularity," she said.

"You can't shoot a cop," B.O. said.

"Even one who had sex with a sixteen-year-old?" Bridget said. She said it to us. "A sixteen-year-old who happens to be my sister."

Bridget Fahey only had one sixteen-year-old sister: Margaret Mary. The same Margaret Mary who wore the pin of the Blessed Virgin on her school uniform. The same Margaret

Mary who B.O. claimed as the love of his life. I felt my mouth go dry.

"Shoot him," Lefty said. "She has to shoot him, B.O."

"No," B.O. moaned, and then he babbled something and stumbled backward, banging off Van Cortlandt tombstones. He started to run, with his hands over his face. His knee cracked into a rock and he went down. Lefty and I went after him. I picked up his glasses and yelled for him to wait, but he was gone, moving fast. Lefty and I were faster, but we couldn't catch him. The second shot brought us off the ground again, and probably on record pace. Then we saw B.O. make a right on the cowpath and we sprinted hard. Lefty finally brought him down with an open-field tackle.

B.O. was gasping, and crying, and trying to say something about hating us. I handed him his glasses and he smacked them away. But he should have put them on to see the naked redhead galloping toward us across the open field. Bridget came right at us, her hair flying in the wind. She brought Connie to a halt, then she tossed her purse to the ground. The bag was no longer floppy, but full and round. It hit with a thud.

"She cut his head off," B.O. said.

"Oh, stop it, all of you," she said, as she dismounted. She hadn't had time to dress.

Lefty pulled B.O. to his feet. We were only about fifty yards from the traffic moving on Broadway. Bridget stood in front of us, and we all stared at the ground. I focused on her painted toenails. Either dark green or black.

"I didn't shoot him," she said. "God knows I wanted to. But it would only make things worse."

"If Ernie ain't dead," Lefty said, "he's going to make us pay for this."

"He'll do nothing of the kind," she said. "He doesn't want

anyone to know a thing about this. He'll make up some story. Like he went in the lake to save someone, and someone stole his horse."

"We'll tell them the truth," B.O. said.

"He'll say we're the ones who stole his horse," Lefty said, "and we're lying to protect ourselves."

"My dad will believe me."

"Your dad will never know, Brendan," she said. "This has to remain our secret."

"How do you know my name?" B.O. said.

"I know all of you. I know Mr. Trainor, and you, quiet man," she said, nodding to me. "But I know you best, Brendan. For all you might think ill of me now, I'm close to my sisters. And I will do all that is necessary to protect them. Understand me?"

"He should be arrested," B.O. said. "It's rape. It's statutory rape. Ask my father."

Bridget sighed heavily. I heard the old Yonkers bus, the Bernacchia line, chugging home. I wondered if they could see us out in the open field. Or would they even believe their eyes.

"Look at me," she said. "All of you. Look at my face."

That wasn't going to be easy. I knew that if I looked up my eyes would be uncontrollable, caroming around in their sockets like loose pinballs. It hurt, but I looked up, and I'd never seen so many freckles in my life. Freckles everywhere. Everywhere.

"I want you to listen carefully to me," she said. "Especially you, Brendan."

"He should pay for what he did," B.O. said.

"We *cannot* have him arrested," she said. "And after I leave here, none of us will ever speak of this again." She took B.O.s hand. "I truly hate to tell you this, but Margaret Mary didn't want to leave you this summer. She *had* to go away."

In that moment I think we all realized we had just acquired the first deep secret of adulthood. We understood it was a test of what kind of men we would become.

"You know how this neighborhood is," she said. "They'll destroy Margaret Mary. That's why she needs your loyalty and your unconditional love. And in a few weeks, when she returns, I want you to act like nothing happened."

"You got it," Lefty said. "What do we do now?"

She kept her eyes on B.O., as she handed Lefty Ernie K.'s gun belt. His revolver was back in the holster.

"Wipe this clean and reload the two bullets," she said. "Get rid of the empty cartridges. Then deliver this horse to Hagan's bar. Say you found him wandering in the park. I want this man humiliated."

"We'll do it for Margaret Mary," B.O. said. He wiped his eyes with his shirt and put his glasses on. Then he took the gun from Lefty and reloaded. "I'll toss the cartridges down the sewer," he said. "Then I'll tell my dad I found the horse in the park."

Bridget smiled and put her finger to her lips in a gesture of silence.

"You okay, B.O.?" Lefty said.

"Fine," he said.

"Take one last look," Bridget said, and whirled around, a blur of red hair and freckles upon alabaster.

We helped B.O. fold Ernie K.'s uniform and tie it to Connie's saddle. She'd even kept his underwear. Bridget dug in her purse for her clothes.

"We'll take care of the humiliation part, Bridget," Lefty said, but she'd already dressed and was running toward the subway.

The nuns were right: Pursuit of a worthy goal takes your

mind off your problems. I felt oddly relieved, as Lefty and I walked to the phone booth near the White Castle. I grabbed the phone book and began looking up numbers. Lefty, using an accent that sounded like no ethic group I'd ever heard, called the police to report a crazy naked man threatening people near the lake in Van Cortlandt Park. We called the Fire Department, the Parks Department, the Yonkers PD, the FBI, and every newspaper we could think of. We had to go get more dimes.

In less than five minutes, a dozen emergency vehicles were searching the park. Their sirens were almost drowned out by the blare of car horns. Traffic backed up at least three blocks on Broadway. They were all in a line behind Brendan O'Leary, who led Connie right square down the middle of Broadway. He actually looked even better than his happy old self. A man on a mission.

THE PRINCE OF ARTHUR AVENUE

BY PATRICK W. PICCIARELLI

Arthur Avenue

Frank Bernardo stood ramrod straight in front of the full-length mirror in his bedroom for his daily self-inspection. It was a ritual before he left his apartment that he had not missed for as long as he could remember. The black silk suit draped perfectly on his six-foot frame; his alligator loafers shined to a deep gloss, his white-on-white shirt starched stiff as a pizza crust. He smoothed a red-and-black patterned seven-fold silk tie and pinched a perfect dimple under its Windsor knot. A silk pocket square picked up the red in his tie, and his diamond pinky ring shone like a thousand suns.

He ran his hands lightly over his full head of silver hair, careful not to muss what took him nearly ten minutes to style into place. He was fifty-eight, and any man thirty years younger would have killed to have his thick mane. His eyes still sparkled despite what they had seen during his lifetime of service to the Genovese crime family. His had been a life of discipline, honor, and loyalty; a devotion made all the more important since his wife had passed away from the ravages of cigarette smoking. They hadn't had any children, not for lack of trying, and medical tests pinned the cause on a childhood infection of Marie's. It mattered little, *La Cosa Nostra* was his family. It was all he had these days, and he liked that just fine.

Frank Bernardo was a traditionalist. Despite his wealth, he had remained in the Pelham Parkway apartment over whose threshold he had carried his wife upon returning from their honeymoon thirty-five years ago. He still shopped in the same grocery store, still traded stories about the old neighborhood with the same barber who had been cutting his hair since before it went gray. Lose tradition and you lose your humility, your sense of place. Tradition creates order, and order was what *la famiglia* was all about; order was what put the word "organized" in organized crime.

These days tradition was going to hell. The younger generation of hoodlums were little more than wind-up dolls. No moxy, no balls. Half the new breed would flip on the family if they got a traffic ticket. The last ten years had seen scores of made men running to the feds for deals rather than serve one day in jail. Pussies.

He'd never aspired to be anything higher than a captain, knowing how difficult it would be to control over a thousand soldiers as a boss. He was smart enough years ago to realize that this thing of theirs was soon going to get out of control with the passage of draconian federal laws designed to dump their ranks in jail with hundred-year sentences.

Frank Bernardo ruled with an iron hand. No one in his crew ever so much as walked down the same side of the street as a fed, let alone ratted against the family. To even mention a cop show on television brought a barrage of cursing from Frank that would make even the toughest soldier wince. Anyone caught discussing business on a telephone would be severely disciplined.

It was because of the no-phone-for-business rule that Frank found himself preparing for a face-to-face with one of his most trusted lieutenants, Sonny Pescatore. An infraction had been committed and they would meet at Frank's restaurant on Arthur Avenue to discuss what to do about it, or more simply put, Frank would be issuing an edict and Sonny would be carrying it out.

Frank Bernardo walked to his restaurant, the Roman Cave, every day. It was a hike, a little more than a mile, but he wouldn't give in to old age and worse, show his crew that he was getting soft. He'd been making the trek since he bought the joint years ago. Another benefit of the stroll was being able to meet and greet "citizens," as people in his world referred to those who were not "friends" of theirs. Another tradition—and not bad for the ego.

He eschewed a top coat on this brisk spring morning, took the stairs from his sixth-floor apartment to the spotless lobby, and headed west along sun-drenched Pelham Parkway. This was a pleasant residential neighborhood of modest homes and apartment buildings on treelined streets. In recent years most of the Italians were bailing for the suburbs. Those who remained were entrenched, mostly around his age or older, the type of person who was born, married, raised kids, and died in the same house. These were the people who waved, offered condolences for his recently departed wife, and sought counsel. Frank was a man who could bestow favors, solve problems, and put the occasional wayward husband back on the straight and narrow.

Today was no different than any other day. By the time he was approaching Arthur Avenue, he had spoken with over a dozen people, some whom he knew, others who dropped names. One elderly man actually kissed his pinky ring, a symbol of respect befitting a man of Frank's stature. He kept a notepad with him so he could write reminders of phone numbers, people he promised to call, dates he intended to keep, as he strolled and counseled those who needed his help and advice.

Frank entered Arthur Avenue from 189th Street. The avenue was jammed as usual. Tourists looking for a great meal in one of the area's fine restaurants mingled with neighborhood wiseguys, mommies pushing strollers, and the occasional meter maid out to spoil everyone's day.

Whereas he garnered deference and admiration among the older inhabitants of Pelham Parkway, here he felt the emotion go toward fear. Frank was recognized immediately by a group of young men who sported what he liked to call ninety-mile-an-hour haircuts and Mr. T starter sets of gold chains, barely hidden behind a uniform of billowing silk shirts jammed into tight jeans. They averted their eyes as he passed by them, some muttering, "How ya doing, Mr. B.?"

Without losing a step and not making eye contact, Frank shot back, "Don't you fucking guys have jobs?" He got no reply, but hadn't expected any.

Others in the know gave Frank a wide berth, the occasional tourist following suit and wondering just who the hell this guy was. Less than two blocks from the Roman Cave, Frank eyed the competition. Good restaurants the lot of them, but what the tourists didn't know was that many of the established Italian eateries were now owned by Albanians who were passing themselves off as Italians. A lot of the local wiseguys had relocated a few years back because of an overzealous federal prosecutor named Rudy Giuliani who made it difficult for them to run their illegal gambling establishments. This left room for the Albanians to come in and take up the slack, their illegal profits funding new restaurants. But Frank hadn't been scared off because he didn't fear Giuliani or anyone else.

People feared *him*, and from that fear came respect, even from a hotshot federal prosecutor with a bad comb-over. No one fucked with Frank Bernardo.

What the hell, Frank thought, more than enough for everybody, and lamented the passing of the old days. But there were still a few of the multi-generational joints left. Ameci's, where the actor Joe Pesci once worked as a waiter until being discovered by Robert DeNiro, was still going strong. Fucking Pesci, Frank thought; guy makes it big and never comes back to the old neighborhood except to shoot a movie and leave in a limo. Another pussy.

A little further down the street Frank waved to the owner of the Full Moon, where Paul Newman ate while filming *Fort Apache, the Bronx*. It used to be called the Half Moon before they expanded. Frank figured maybe in a couple of more years when the Roman Cave was doing even better than it was now he'd buy the place next door (whether the owner was selling or not) and change the name to the Roman Coliseum.

He crossed the street by Mario's Restaurant, thereby avoiding a bunch of Scarsdale *mamalooks* who wanted to chow down on some meatballs and spaghetti in the same place where Michael Corleone blew away two guys in a scene from *The Godfather*, and walked past the storefront where a lot of the action took place in *A Bronx Tale*. Yeah, Frank mused, the world's a friggin' stage.

The Roman Cave was gearing up for the lunch rush when Frank walked in. Two waiters were folding napkins and a porter was waxing the wooden floor with a power buffer. The restaurant was long and narrow, with two rooms, lighting dimmed to an intimate duskiness. The bartender, a neighborhood fixture named Cheech, was preparing his bank behind the mahogany, black leather—railed bar in the first room. He was wearing the prescribed uniform for the service staff: white shirt, solid red tie, both under a black vest that matched his pants. He smiled and waved with a fistful of cash.

"In early today, Mr. Bernardo."

The restaurant's staff were all men, mostly older neighborhood guys who had honed their skills in the finer restaurants in Manhattan, and were working toward their golden years in a joint closer to home. Frank nixed waitresses early on because he thought they detracted from the upscale theme of the place.

"Hey, Cheech. Got a meeting with Sonny. He in the back yet?" Frank stole a glance at himself in the gold-flecked mirror behind the bar. Looking sharp.

"Yeah, he got here about twenty minutes ago."

Frank nodded. Next to a rat in the ranks he hated to be kept waiting the most, and his soldiers knew it. Sonny, a good kid, was always early. He breezed past the handful of tables in the barroom and through an alcove that led to the dining room.

Sonny Pescatore was seated at Frank's personal table, which was situated in the rear of the dining room and far enough away from the other tables to avoid conversation being overheard. The walls were covered with red and silver wallpaper that Frank had imported from Italy, and each of the twenty-two tables was covered with a crisp linen tablecloth, folded linen napkins, sparkling glasses and utensils, and a foot-long candle supported by a gleaming silver candlestick.

Sonny waved and Frank smiled. Sonny Pescatore, at forty years old, was Frank's personal choice to replace him should the time ever come, though Frank was not entertaining thoughts of retirement, and Sonny knew it.

Sonny stood as Frank approached.

"Frank, how are you? You're looking very fit." He pulled a chair out for his captain and waited for Frank to sit down before he followed suit. There was no handshaking, a custom which didn't fall into Mafia tradition.

Frank patted his stomach. "You watch what you eat, Sonny, get good exercise, and you keep a flat belly. You don't see too many fat old people, you know?"

Sonny smiled, nodding. For ten minutes they made small talk, Sonny knowing that when Frank was good and ready he'd tell him why he had been summoned.

Finally Frank said, "Something's gotta be done about Augie."

Sonny looked confused. "Augie? Which Augie, Frank?"

Frank stared at his lieutenant. The kid was sharply dressed in a dark gray pinstriped suit and a floral tie, and he imagined his shoes were brushed to a high shine. One thing Frank demanded was that his crew dress well anytime business was being conducted; this meant suits, not sport coats, and the first person to grow a mustache would have each hair gouged out with a dull knife. Men in *La Cosa Nostra* were clean-shaven as a matter of tradition.

But as sharp as Sonny was, sometimes he didn't think.

"Augie Pisano," Frank said. "We got only one Augie."

"Hey, sorry, Frank. Coupla new guys we got working the terminal, thought we had another Augie in there somewhere."

"Well, we don't," Frank said. "Keep up, kid. This is your crew."

"Okay, okay. So what's the beef?"

"The beef is, Sonny, that I called Augie last week for a sit-down and he didn't show. No fucking phone call, no nothing.

He had me down here playing with myself for over an hour." Frank's hands were white-knuckled on the tablecloth, which wasn't missed by Sonny. "So this is why he's gotta go. I called him and he didn't come. He's a dead man."

"Frank," Sonny said, leaning closer conspiratorially, "no disrespect, but maybe we should give Augie a pass. He's a good guy, good earner."

Frank waved a hand. "Fuck him. I hear he's also talking subversive about me. You hear anything about him talking subversive?"

Sonny shook his head. "No, Frank. It'd be my job to know that. My ear's to the ground, always is. I don't hear nothing about Augie talking subversive."

"Kid, listen to me. Remember Joey DiChicco? Remember I said a few years back that I thought he was talking to the feds? Remember that? Was I right or was I right?"

"Yeah, Frank, you were right."

"You're goddamn straight I was right. If you hadn'ta clipped him we'd be having this conversation in friggin' jail."

Sonny held up his hands. "Hey, when you're right you're right, boss."

A waiter passed through the dining room and breezed into the kitchen. They waited less than a minute until he came back out carrying a case of Scotch, disappearing toward the bar before they resumed their conversation.

"Okay, so maybe he ain't talking to the feds, but he's sayin' things behind my back, about the way I'm runnin' this crew. That's talkin' subversive. I want you to take care of the problem. Do the Bronx Park thing like we did with that asshole Petey. Bury the prick next to Petey; they can bullshit together about how fuckin' stupid they are." Frank chuckled. "That fuckin' Petey. He knew he was gonna die and all he wanted was that we didn't plant him without his shoes. What an asshole." Frank sat silent for a moment. "I granted him his last wish. If they ever find him, he'll be wearing a pair of alligators."

Sonny swallowed. "You're all heart, boss."

Frank leaned across the table, his eyes cold and piercing. "Listen, kid, watch your mouth. I brought you into this crew and I can have you taken out. You know what I mean?" Disrespect. He hated it.

Sonny let out the breath he'd been holding for what seemed like an hour. "Sorry, Frank. It won't happen again."

Frank examined a well-manicured hand. "Ah, it's okay. Let's eat."

They ate a leisurely lunch of sautéed eggplant, washed down by a twenty-year-old bottle of Chianti Classico. Frank reminisced about his crew's greatest hits ("and I ain't talkin' about the friggin' Top Forty here"), while Sonny nodded in deference to his boss. Shortly after they had finished several cups of espresso and an equal number of cannoli, the Roman Cave opened for business and the lunch crowd surged in. As a handful of tourists mingled with neighborhood people and waited to be seated, Frank dismissed his lieutenant.

"Too many ears here now," he said as he gripped Sonny's shoulder. "Do what you gotta do and call me when it's done. You should be callin' me sooner than later, you know what I'm sayin'?"

Sonny stood up. "Understood." He nodded and turned, leaving Frank to savor the dregs of his espresso.

Sonny Pescatore stood on the sidewalk, a hand reaching into his pocket for a pack of cigarettes. He lit one, dragged deeply, and surveyed the street. Halfway down the block, parked in a bus stop, a shiny black Chrysler 300 with tinted windows flashed its headlights. Sonny smiled, took another pull on his cigarette before flipping it into the gutter, and walked toward the car.

The front passenger door cracked an inch and Sonny grabbed the handle and slid onto the front leather seat. The driver looked at Sonny through tinted glasses.

"How'd it go?"

Sonny shrugged. "Like we expected. Fucking shame."

The man nodded. "Who does he want whacked this time?"

Sonny smirked. "You're not gonna believe this. Augie Pisano."

The man's eyes widened noticeably under the shades. "You gotta be shittin' me. Doesn't he know Augie's been dead since what . . . 1988?"

"Eighty-seven," Sonny corrected. "And Frank oughta know, he clipped him."

"Jesus," the man said, "is he that far gone?"

"I'll tell you how far gone he is. We sat in that friggin' shithole for an hour and he was convinced he was at his old table in the Cave."

The man turned away from Sonny and stared across the street at the McDonald's from which Sonny had emerged. He shook his head. "I heard about people who have this shit, but never knew nobody who actually had it."

Two women in their twenties sashayed by, short skirts clinging tightly to their rock-hard asses. Sonny followed them with his eyes until they turned the corner.

"Your Aunt Connie gets it," Sonny said, "my Uncle Bennie, no problem; they can't hurt us. But Frankie was shootin' off his mouth about guys we had whacked for the last twenty years. He can hurt us."

"That shit he remembers; that he wears the same friggin' dirty sweatsuit every day, *that* he forgets."

"Go figure," Sonny said. Frank Bernardo had been a powerful captain, an old-school mafia boss who believed in *omerta*, the rule of silence, like kids believed in Santa Claus. But after his wife died fifteen years ago and the Roman Cave was burned to the ground by a bunch of Albanians out to thin the competition, Frank began to lose his grip. Maybe old age had something to do with his decline, Sonny thought. He was, after all, pushing eighty, but the reasons for Frank's condition weren't the family's concern. The damage Frank could inflict on the family was.

Frank had become an embarrassment. Demoted to soldier and given virtually no responsibilities, he'd been carried by the family for the last several years despite the fact that he was becoming a Class A pain in the ass. Unshaven and slovenly, he always wore that same moldy sweat suit of indeterminate color, bathed only occasionally, and harassed everyone on the street with whom he came in contact. It'd gotten so bad lately that when people from the neighborhood saw him coming, they'd duck into the first available storefront.

And forget about the young punks. Sonny had bitch-slapped two of them for spitting on Frank just a few weeks ago. But loyalty only went so far; honor and fearlessness were for the young and able. And then there was that bullshit about loose lips sinking ships. *Too many ships with valuable cargo floating around Arthur Avenue to be scuttled.*

"When?" the man asked.

Sonny pulled an untraceable prepaid cell phone from his coat pocket.

With a tangible sadness in his voice he said, almost inaudibly, "No time like the present," and punched buttons on the throw-away phone. He waited a few seconds and said, "Okay," when a male voice answered. He gestured to the driver. "Head slowly down the street when I give you the word."

They waited in silence for a few minutes until two young men dressed in black leather jackets walked briskly up the street toward the fast-food joint.

Sonny poked the driver in the side. "Now."

With the car in gear and slowly rolling up the block, Sonny gazed with a look of melancholy through the plate-glass window at the old man hunched over a cup of tepid coffee, muttering to himself and running his fingers over a bald pate. There were a few patrons in the place, but they all gave Frank Bernardo a wide berth, not out of the respect he once enjoyed, but because he was a slovenly old man who didn't smell right.

The two young punks breezed through the door, now with ski masks securely in place. The Chrysler was almost adjacent to the storefront, and Sonny stared transfixed as the two men extended their arms, black automatic pistols at the ready in gloved hands.

Sonny had to crane his neck as the car cruised past the restaurant. He saw Frank stand, throw back his shoulders, and shake a fist at approaching death.

Sonny grabbed the driver's shoulder. "Stop the car."

"Here?" The driver was incredulous.

Anger flared in Sonny's eyes. "Stop the fucking car!"

The Chrysler came to rest in the middle of Arthur Avenue, engine idling while Sonny watched an old soldier muster up a final bit of pride and face what he knew was his assassination. In those few seconds clarity returned; Frank was once again strong and would face death like a man.

Words that Sonny couldn't hear were exchanged as the gunmen fired a barrage of rounds into Frank Bernardo. Patrons tossed Big Macs and shakes and planted themselves firmly on the greasy floor facedown. Sonny saw Frank mouth a torrent of words, though they were muffled by the thick glass and ringing shots. But Sonny knew what those word were.

Assassinato, assassinato.

As the bullets found their target, the old man got stronger. He pushed the table aside and lunged for the shooters, who retreated as they continued to fire.

"Jesus Christ," Sonny said softly, "he's gotta have ten slugs in him."

Finally, Frank fell to his knees. One shooter stepped deftly around the old man, put the muzzle of the gun to the victim's bald head, and fired one final round. Frank Bernardo toppled over like he was pulled down by a ship's anchor. The two men spit on their motionless victim, dropped their guns, and ran to the door, flinging it open and slowing to a walk as they calmly made their way up the street to where Sonny's car still idled. As they walked they high-fived each other like two adolescents congratulating themselves after winning a soccer game.

The driver threw the car in gear.

"Wait," Sonny said, and clamped a hand on the driver's arm. In the distance the muted sound of sirens pulsated.

The driver was visibly agitated. "Jesus Christ, Sonny! We gotta get outta here."

"In a minute," Sonny said, and stepped out of the car. He walked across the street and waited.

The two gunmen were laughing now and rapidly approaching Sonny. They smiled, seeing their boss and knowing that if this didn't get them their buttons, nothing would.

Sonny let them get to within twenty feet before he pulled

a nine-millimeter pistol and cut the two shooters down with one shot each to their torsos. Surprise and pain swept across the faces of the killers as they dropped to the ground and began crawling away. One made it under a parked car, but left no room for his partner.

Sonny, in a controlled anger, straddled the exposed shooter and put two rounds in his back. Blood pooled on the sidewalk as Sonny carefully stepped over the dead man, leaned under the car, and emptied his magazine into the remaining whimpering wounded hit man.

A crowd had gathered, and when Sonny stood up they turned their backs in unison and began scattering. Sonny jammed the gun in his waistband, walked quickly to the car, and got in. The sirens were louder now, easily within two blocks of the scene.

"What the fuck?" the driver said, as he forced himself not to leave twenty feet of rubber getting off the block.

"The old man deserved better than that. He was a *caporegime*, for Christ sake! Spit on a made man? Laugh? I don't fucking think so." Disrespect, Sonny hated it; he had learned all about respect from the late Frank Bernardo.

Sonny lit a cigarette and inhaled deeply as the car drove onto the Major Deegan Expressway. If the cops could find anyone to admit being at the scene of the killings, they wouldn't be able to remember a face, let alone an age or the race of the shooter.

This was, after all, Arthur Avenue.

YOU WANT I SHOULD WHACK MONKEY BOY?

BY THOMAS ADCOCK

Courthouse

The young guy sitting next to me at the bar looks like an escapee from one of those rectangular states where blond people live who wind up in Los Angeles where my own kid went to escape from me.

He's wearing a cashmere turtleneck and matching tobacco-colored corduroys and a green suede jacket that would be a couple of months' pay if my secretary had to buy it. He's blond, of course, with California teeth and a hundred-dollar haircut.

Two minutes ago he walked in and looks around the place like he knows everybody. Which he doesn't. Then he walked over my way and took a load off.

How this guy found his way to a dive like the Palomino Club, let alone the Bronx, I am about to find out.

So who am I, sitting next to this Jack Armstrong type and doing my bit to be one-half of an odd couple? And what's this bar about?

The Palomino Club is neutral territory for a bunch of us who depend on one another to keep the criminal justice system of the Bronx a going concern. Meaning the cops and the crooks and guys like me, since all roads lead to lawyers.

Over the bar right where I'm sitting, there's a creased photograph of a curly-haired squirt with his ears folded under a cowboy hat and he's sitting up on a big cream-colored horse with a flowing white mane. At the bottom of the picture it says, *Camp Hiawatha 1953.*

That's me in the saddle, by the way. I always sit near the picture of my youth.

I am now a grown-up man of five-foot-six, if you can call that grown. I am sort of round and practically bald-headed. I have lived on the Concourse since my days in short pants. The fact I now get my suits made by a tailor with liver spots over on Grant Avenue who claims he sewed for Tony Curtis after he stopped being Bernie Schwartz from Hunts Point doesn't fool anybody. So says my kid.

My kid says I'm so Bronx haimish there's no way my name could be anything besides Stanley, which it is.

So imagine how curious I am about this tall, sun-kissed, golden-haired guy—goy—who took stool next to me when he could have sat down in a lot of other spots.

The guy orders a cosmopolitan. Nate the bartender cuts me a look that says, *Nu?*

Naturally, I am wondering myself. So I start chatting up Jack Armstrong.

"Look at these," I tell him, holding up both hands so he can see my pink palms. "Soft, hey? Nice?"

"For crying out loud, Stanley—"

This is from Nate, who is rolling his eyeballs like Jerry Colonna used to do on *The Ed Sullivan Show.* I am not currently speaking to Nate on account of he encouraged my kid to break up the firm of Katz & Katz.

Yeah, I get your point, he says to my kid. *You got to be your own person,* he says to her. *You have to find your own space.* Feh! Since when is Nathan Blum talking hippie?

"—Not with the schtick already, Stanley."

I think about telling Nate, *Life is schtick, numb nuts.* But instead I keep him on my list of people to ice, which I hope irritates him like a nail in the neck. He picks up another Hamilton from the little pile of cash on the wet mahogany in front of me and pads off, knowing to bring back another Grey Goose marty, the hump.

I get back to business.

"No kidding, Jack," I tell the golden boy. "Look at these hands."

"It's Blake, actually." He smiles, which blinds me. "Blake Lewis. I'm in from the coast."

Who says this?

Well, what did I tell my kid about Hollywood guys with the teeth she thinks are so freaking fabulous? Phony-baloneys, all of them. No parents in the history of the world ever gave the name of Blake to their innocent little boy, not even to Jack Armstrong here.

"So, Blake, feel the hands."

He touches one palm, then the other one.

"Soft," he says. "Nice."

"Smooth like a baby's pilkes."

"You must be terribly proud of those hands," says Blake Lewis with the suede and cashmere. He sounds *terribly* like somebody who doesn't want you to know he grew up in a split-level eating casserole and Jell-O. "You didn't have to work hard—like your father did."

This golden boy, he knows?

"My old man painted houses," I tell him, playing it casual, like maybe Lewis here hit on a lucky guess. "He had hands rough as shingles. Me, I don't paint."

"I heard that. I heard you're an attorney."

"Not an attorney. I'm a lawyer."

Lewis smiles and swivels on his barstool to scope out the place again. The usual suspects I mentioned are here.

Three fat capos by the names of Peter "the Pipe" Guasta-faro and Charlie the Pencil Man and Nutsy Nunzio are eating bloody steaks in a corner booth. The steaks are so big they're going to have meat breath for the next couple of days.

Down the middle of back dining room is a long table full of potato-faced Irish detectives in shiny suits. They're drink-ing champagne to celebrate a take-down that's going to earn everybody commendations, and making eyes at the bling-bling brown-skinned girls the latest gold-toothed hip-hop prince on his way to bankruptcy court brought along with him.

The local Chamber of Commerce boys are here, with long-legged women they're not married to. One of them de-cides to showboat. He hands over an intriguing wad of cash to a crewcut desk sergeant from the 44th Precinct and says, "Take care of the other guys too." He has not yet learned that send-ing money by cop is like sending lettuce by rabbit.

Hanging around the bar to either side of me are solid-built guys keeping a quiet eye on one another, along with some tab-loid guys, including Slattery from the *Post*.

Slattery came with the detectives from his tribe, but now feels the need to drink something that's not bubbly. He's got buck teeth and a mustache from the '70s he ought to get rid of.

The solid-built guys are nursing seltzer. Their fingers on the glasses are as thick as rolled quarters. They've got enough firepower concealed under polyester suit jackets to hold off an invasion.

Down at the end of the bar, the D.A. himself is getting a bang out of showing a gaggle of Wall Street attorneys the other side of the tracks. And working the room, of course, are my comrades of the Bronx criminal defense bar. They're handing out business cards.

Lewis turns back to me and says, "I hear you're a lawyer who knows how to motivate certain types of people."

He says this with no sense of irony or amusement. I notice I'm still sitting here with my pink palms up in the air, like I'm about to get mugged by a guy who's prettier than anything I ever saw walk out of a Jerome Avenue beauty salon.

This good-looking mugger, he glances up at the memento from Camp Hiawatha a long time ago and says, "You're Stanley Katz, aren't you?"

Then he sticks out a hand that's smoother than mine and I shake it because what else am I supposed to do.

It takes me a long minute, but I am now recovered. Because now I figure what's with the golden boy.

"You know my kid out in Los Angeles." I don't say this like it's a question.

"I do indeed. Wendy said I'd find you here. She says your office is nearby." Lewis nods his expensive haircut in the right direction while he's saying this. Then he says, "According to Wendy, they call you *Consigliere*."

"Nobody named Stanley was ever a consigliere. Except for me," I tell him. "But that's mostly for laughs."

"But not strictly."

He's got me there.

"Counselor, I could use your help," says Lewis.

"For what?"

He tells me.

"You want I should whack Monkey Boy?"

"In a manner of speaking."

Later, when I'm home after listening to this disturbing proposition, which I admit has got a certain appeal, I get Wendy on the horn. It's around midnight in the Bronx, which I know is only 9 o'clock in California.

"Your boy Lewis, he clocked me at the Palomino."

I inform her of this right in the middle of when she's answering "Hello" into the phone.

Even though Wendy is my flesh and blood, I can't help being impatient with her since she's out there with the phony-baloneys now. Which I know all about from reading the unpleasant memoir of a New York writer who went to Hollywood once. The title of this memoir, it's *Hello, He Lied*.

Six months ago—before she started up with her my-own-person business—I gave Wendy the loan of this book, figuring it would disgust her enough to keep her home where she belongs, namely in the Bronx with me. I figured wrong.

We had the knock-down-drag-out.

"How can you bust up Katz & Katz?" I asked her, again in my impatient way. "We got a nice long-standing clientele of decent New York criminals."

"It's not like it's fatal," she said. "Partners split up all the time." She was cool, like she had the questions and answers doped out ahead of time. Like I taught her.

"Right here in New York, kiddo, you got a big future."

"As what? Daughter of the great Stanley Katz who doesn't paint houses? The consigliere? I'm already Stanley Katz's kid. It's not a skill. I have to be my own person, find my own space."

Oy vey.

"In Los Angeles? What's out there for a lawyer?"

"Entertainment law. Like I told you a hundred times."

"A hundred times I still don't get it. What do they know from murder in Hollywood?"

This could have been the stupidest thing I ever said. So I tried to brighten up the moment with a blast from the past.

"Say, kiddo, what's the best thing about a murder trial?"

Wendy didn't give me the setup like years ago when she was a little girl all excited about the game of Papa's punch line.

So I answered me: "One less witness."

"That is so ancient, Daddy."

"You're breaking my heart. Don't leave me. I'm lonely."

"It's a lonely world, Daddy."

"Which makes it a shame to be lonely all alone. You look like your mother. I miss your mother."

"Me too, Daddy. But she's gone. You know."

Then Wendy and the blue suitcases her mother and I bought her for college walked out of my life.

"California is not out of your life," she tells me whenever I call these days and start up with the you-walked-out-of-my-life business. Wendy informs me, "They've got airplanes now."

Okay, I should fly out and visit.

But right now, I need to talk.

"You hear me? Your boy found his way to the Palomino Club."

"Oh—hi, Daddy."

"This guy, Lewis, he's for real?"

What am I saying?

"You can bank on Blake Lewis," says Wendy. "He's a legitimate television producer. He's big-time."

"For me, all he'll produce is a visit from the feds."

"Like they've never been to your office." Wendy says this with a sigh, like when she was a teenager complaining how I embarrassed her in front of her friends. Then she laughs and says, "Don't you want to be on TV, Daddy?"

Is my own kid in on this proposition I got last night?

"Why me?"

"Blake's looking for consultants. It's what he does for his kind of shows."

"What's he calling this one?"

"Unofficially, it's called *The Assassination Show*. Keep it hush-hush, okay? Blake only told me because he had to ask about—well, technical advisors, let's say."

I'm thinking over a number of things I don't want to say to Wendy until I think them over. This seems to make her nervous.

"Well, so, naturally, I sent Blake to you." Naturally.

"Ideas get stolen in the television business, Daddy. So hush-hush."

"Television's for cabbage-heads."

"Speaking of cabbage, did you talk money?"

"Money I don't care about."

"I do. I'm only just getting off the ground here. I did a couple of five-percent series contracts, but you know how that goes."

"Yeah, you sent me copies of your work, kiddo."

"It's mostly boilerplate according to the unions and the producers' association. About a hundred *ifs* in there between a lousy ten grand, which doesn't even pay the rent, and the sky."

"But when you get up there, it's dizzy time. When are you coming home?"

"I kind of want to, Daddy, but what I need right now is a real show-runner client like Blake Lewis. A big fish who can pay me a big commission. I need you to help me reel him in."

"You should have called me, Wendy."

"Where would that have got me? You would have blown me off, right?"

"Not necessarily."

As soon as I say this, I know she's got her foot in the door. And I know she knows that I know.

"Listen, Daddy, this is a good piece of business. It gets me in solid with the biggest thing going out here."

"What's that?"

"Reality TV."

"There's an oxymoron for you."

I have got many things on my mind this morning in the November drizzle that's making my shoes squeak. Not only that, I accidentally step on a liverwurst sandwich somebody dropped on the sidewalk. So this is not a good omen.

I am on the way from my place on the Concourse over to the office on 161st Street around the corner from the marble glory of the Bronx State Supreme Court. This is where it's my calling to help little people through the meat grinder of their lives and take from the big people what the market will bear.

When it looks to me like they can hack the payments, the working stiffs pay me with their little credit cards. Or else I take IOUs, which I almost never collect on. The big people— your old-fashioned wiseguys, your rap music moguls, your disgraced politicians—they pay cash, and lots of it.

In case you hadn't noticed about the times we are living through, weirdness and rudeness is rampant. And it's not just up there at the top, either, it's now trickled down to the bottom of the food chain. Never mind, for me business is brisk.

So here I am running a healthy enterprise for which I could use the help of somebody I can trust, namely my kid. I wrongly thought she was happy being molded into the person who would take over everything her mother and I built up in the Bronx. Which is not a bad little empire.

For instance, I own the building on the Concourse where I have lived since pulling up to the curb in a yellow Cirker's moving van back when Ike was the president. I'll never forget that Saturday afternoon.

My old man was delirious with joy about leaving the Lower East Side behind us for a new life in the North End, which is what you called the South Bronx back then.

"Can you believe it, Stanny-boy, I got us a big apartment with sun in the windows where rich people used to live," he said to me that Saturday. He'd gone to the library to read about the new neighborhood. "Right on the Grand Concourse, copied off the Champs-Élysées in France and built in 1909 in the Bronx—by an immigrant. Imagine that. An immigrant just like me. You know, I was in Paris after the war, Stanny, and I painted. And I don't mean houses."

Right across the hallway from our sunny apartment I met a chubby girl my age with blue eyes and red cheeks and frizzy black hair.

Her name was Miriam Smart, which was perfect for her. Some people get named like that. Like Billy Strayhorn just had to be a jazz musician, and Johnny Stompanato had to be a wiseguy.

Anyhow, I called her Mimi. We were married on her nineteenth birthday.

Mimi and I were the first ones in our families to go through all twelve grades. After Morris High School, we graduated City College together in the days before tuition. I went on to law school and wound with a job in the domestic violence bureau at the Bronx D.A.'s office, where mostly I sent up slobs who fell in love with a dimple but couldn't handle the fact that a whole girl came with it.

Mimi, she was the brains of the Katz family operation. She

went to work in the real estate business on account of being sadly inspired by her grandfather, who had a little farm stolen out from under him back in Romania.

"You should never leave your place," Mimi would say, repeating her grandfather's stern counsel, "no matter how they try to run you out, which they will try to do over and over in different ways."

Sometime in '78 or '79, when a Hollywood movie actor was running for president—such a gag, everybody thought—he brought a gang of reporters along with him to the South Bronx on a campaign tour. Which didn't make sense to people in the neighborhood because we don't vote for actors.

Up until then, I appreciated Hollywood for the movie memories I own, like the first time I held Mimi's hand in the mezzanine of Loew's Paradise up at 188th Street. But this mutt running for president, he said right in front of the cameras on the evening news that my own neighborhood was the worst place you could ever be in the United States of America.

Okay, we had problems. In those years, who didn't? But scaring people so they'll vote for you?

I was angry at this actor. Being the brains of the operation, Mimi figured something besides an insult was going on. "Aha! Now they send in the scary clowns to run us out," she said. So we did not leave our place.

But just about everybody we knew did.

As the neighbors on our floor left, Mimi took over their leases one by one—at quite favorable terms, thanks to a landlord dumb enough to be scared by an actor who played second banana in a picture about a chimpanzee.

On our dime, Mimi kept our floor beautifully maintained and sublet to nice people who were just like the old neighbors except their skin was darker. She never worried how the dumb landlord let the other floors go to hell and generally ignored everything for years, including his unpaid property tax bill. By which time we could afford to buy him out at a distress sale.

Then Mimi put up the apartment house as collateral on a loan to acquire a few likewise distressed commercial spaces surrounding the courthouse, which we rented out to lawyers and bail bondsmen in order to pay our mortgage notes.

Plus, we had plenty left over for Wendy's education, a proper storefront for Mimi's real estate business, and a nice house on a few acres in the Catskills for summer weekends. Mimi loved the country place because of her grandfather's stories about his farm in the old country. I thought about maybe buying a cream-colored horse but I never got around to it.

Also, we had money from not being scared so that I could switch teams and hang out a shingle as defense counsel. This was in one of Mimi's buildings near the courthouse, so I have never had to pay rent. God bless America, as she used to say.

When you have somebody like Mimi Smart behind you, you don't need to be too smart yourself. Or as she used to say, *If law school is so hard, how come there are so many lawyers?*

Mimi taught me to pick my clients right so I wouldn't have to worry about revenues and so I could have a little fun besides—such as when I represented a guy with carnal knowledge of chickens, which is another story. Mimi taught me something every day, until she got sick.

One Sunday morning after a long bad night, I was holding hands with Mimi again. This was in our bedroom in the country. She'd been resting up there for months, lying mostly on her side in order to see her flower garden through the window, and the pond. She was so thin. She said to me, for the last time she said anything, "We did all right, Stanley, you and me."

Now every morning, no matter what I have going, I think about Mimi while I'm walking to the office. In my line of work, it's good to have a pleasant thought to begin the day—as opposed to what I had to think about next.

It should impress the hell out of my Rosary Maldonado, my secretary, that Blake Lewis, big-time television producer, is supposed to drop by. Rosary watches television like most people breathe.

"Don't say a word," Lewis said to me last night, before he'd take an answer on his proposition. "Sleep on it. We'll talk in the morning. I'll be around."

I didn't sleep so good.

Just thinking about this guy in my office, I get itchy like I'm coming down with hives on my back. Never do I have such a feeling before talking to some wiseguy who I know from previous experience is hinky as Halloween, and if I displease him he could jump across my desk and bust my face; or some mook with one eyebrow who goes off his nut and picks up a tire iron when he finds out Sweetie-pie's been playing hide-the-salami with his best friend.

Which is not to mention the celebrity trade of pea-brained rappers and politicians who think with their little heads.

But now here with Lewis, the territory is unfamiliar to me. The pols and the rappers are forever paying the stupid tax. The mook and the wiseguy do what they do for honor, even if their sense of what's honorable is a little cracked. But Hollywood's about money, so you never know what's coming at you.

Speaking of which, half a block away my secretary is flying out the door of Katz & Katz and running up the street at me like a Puerto Rican banshee, waving her hands and hollering in Spanish. Lucky for her she gets to me, because she breaks a heel and almost goes ass-over-teakettle, but I break the fall.

"What's—?"

"Mr. Katz," Rosary interrupts, using the name she reserves for important occasions. Otherwise she calls me Poppy. "J'you know who come to see you?"

I take a wild guess. "Blake Lewis?"

Rosary has newfound admiration for me. She says, "J'you know hing?"

I lay a steadying arm around her shoulder and she hobbles back to the office with me.

It's not just Lewis who's there. It's the steak-eaters and a contingent of polyester suits. Also Slattery.

"Consigliere!" Lewis says as I walk in. Slattery writes this down in his notebook.

I cock my head and say, "Let's go," and the steak-eaters and Slattery follow me into my private office. Rosary, who is flush in the face, stays outside with the polyester.

"What the—?"

Nutsy Nunzio cuts me off from dropping the f-bomb. "Jeez, Stanley," he says. Clear from the other side of my desk I smell the breath. Like a doggy bag you bring home in a taxi. "You think it's okay we do this TV job?"

Nutsy is wide-eyed like an innocent kid. Though knowing of his problems with anger management, it is hard for me to imagine Nutsy ever being a squirt. The Orphan Annie expression also goes for Pete the Pipe and Charlie the Pencil Man.

Lewis is sitting there like the cat that ate the canary. Today he's in one of those outfits like the TV hair helmets wear in war zones: blue denim shirt, safari jacket, starched dungarees.

I ask him, "What did you tell my clients?"

He shrugs. "I hung around the Palomino after you left. I met some people. I gave them the elevator pitch." He turns to Slattery and explains, "That's when you have to put across your big idea to a studio exec before the elevator gets to where he's going."

Nutsy and Charlie nod as the Pipe passes judgment: "Sounds like a plan to me."

Pete does not get his moniker from smoking a meerschaum. It's from rumors when he started off his career and was seen around leaky gas valves that caused industrial accidents around the city. Nowadays he considers himself a good citizen for being involved in the political life of his country. Meaning he takes bets on elections, sometimes doing things to improve the odds in his favor.

"The putz we got in the White House," says the Pipe, "we should do everybody a favor and put Charlie on him."

Which prompts the Pencil Man, alleged to have erased people, to chime in with, "How about I explode his freakin' mountain bike?"

Everybody enjoys a nice wet laugh, including Slattery, who is no doubt dreaming up a streamer for the cover of tomorrow's paper, something cute like, CAN A KILLER TV SHOW CANCEL BUSH?

"You're getting a little ahead of yourself, aren't you?" I ask Lewis. "For instance, what's Slattery doing here?"

"He's my whole advertising budget—zero down for an exclusive on *The Assassination Show*," says Lewis. "One story in one New York paper and—*whammo!*—everybody and his brother are providing us free publicity."

Nutsy gets excited.

"The dough he don't spend for ads, it's that much more for us," he says. "Jeez, I'd like to see the frat boy meet up with some permanent violence. Know what I'm sayin'?"

"I'm not going there," I tell Nutsy, who now has a pair

of blue veins throbbing on his temples. "And I'm surprised you're all speaking to me like you are. In the past, you've been circumspect. Which I appreciate."

"If I catch your drift," says the Pipe, "you shouldn't worry, because Blake here says free speech is legal under the First Amendment to the Constitution."

Charlie says, "We come here this early in the a.m. out of respect for you, Mr. Katz. We don't want to do nothing without your blessing. Besides which, we're cutting you in."

Blake makes like the canary again. With all that's going for him, he doesn't need my blessing and he doesn't need to make an elevator pitch. Hollywood's going to be showering him with money for the honor of underwriting the minimal costs of *The Assassination Show.*

I put my head in my hands.

The deal that's making my scalp hurt is this: Starting with George W. Bush, a couple of hand-held cameras record the pungent conversations of three alleged hoodlums from the Bronx who are plotting to assassinate the president of the U.S. of A., maybe with advice and counsel from their consigliere, which I haven't decided yet.

Such a gag, everybody out there in TV Land is going to think. Which it is: a great circular joke starting with the mis-nomer "reality TV" and winding up right back to the truth of the phrase, which is a lie.

But since we don't pay attention to the criminal whoppers that Monkey Boy and his crew tell us every day, why get our national panties in a twist over television fibs? Maybe you've noticed that from coast to coast, every TV news anchorman and giggly lady has the same sign-off nowadays: "We'll see you here tomorrow night." Really?

Some newspaper critic is bound to call Blake Lewis a hip, groundbreaking genius. I suppose he is. A smart person knows what smart people want. A genius knows what stupid people want.

Let's say my clients don't advance the plot anywhere near Monkey Boy during the ten weeks Lewis has got by way of network commitment to his groundbreaker. Tension will mount just the same. The Secret Service will go ballistic. The Christers will go as bonkers as Nutsy Nunzio. And you can rely on the members of Congress for their usual discernment and maturity in dealing with public controversy that gets them air time.

And at the end of an unsuccessful ten weeks' hunt for Monkey Boy, Lewis simply recruits another pack of "technical advisors" to see about snuffing some other annoying potentate someplace else in the world. The tension mounts all over again. Pure genius.

As I mentioned, I have seen the series contracts Wendy has drafted. Five-percent commission on the tens of millions that Lewis stands to accrue for the worldwide premiere, followed by hundreds of millions more on the succeeding ten-week collections, followed by millions more for repeat performances and millions more for spin-off rights . . .

. . . Well, doing the math, even on Wendy's small-fry projects, I just about fainted.

No wonder the kid wants in on the racket. I'm thinking Mimi would be proud. But when she's got all the dough anybody would ever need, will Wendy come home?

It's now late afternoon and it's a matter of hours before the bulldog edition of the *Post* is on the streets and the s-bomb hits the fan.

Lewis and his advisors and polyesters have gone to lunch at the Palomino and come back, to where Rosary is entertaining them with the story of chicken man that I mentioned.

"Sometimes I think there's a very big neon sign floating over this office," she says, flirting shamelessly with Lewis. "It reads, *Strange people—welcome*."

Anyhow, she relates the referred case of a cash-paying client from Westchester who was nabbed in a naughty motel by the Bronx vice squad. The cops found him bare naked under the covers and happy about it. There were no girls in the cheap room with him, or boys. But there were maybe a dozen chickens from La Marquéta under the Queensboro Bridge.

"The live birds are there to boil and pluck," says Rosary, blushing in Lewis's gaze. "It's against the sanitary laws of the city, but there you are."

"Is your name actually Rosemary?" Lewis asks her.

"Oh, it used to be. I go to mass every day, so I changed to Rosary. J'you like it?"

"It's charming."

Rosary continued with the story of the suburban geek, a CEO called Bill Cunningham. What Cunningham did to violate his secret aviary caused the sheets and walls and carpeting to become sticky with chicken blood, tomato-red turning to rust-brown. Little chicken heads were in a heap by the bathroom doorway, where Cunningham's pinstripes were carefully hung on the knob.

The birds had put up a spirited fight, especially the roosters. There were feathers everywhere.

The D.A. indicted Cunningham for animal cruelty. The geek was sorely embarrassed in front of his golf club buddies, but they rallied around him in support of a sick man. Cunningham kept his mouth shut like I told him.

"Ladies and gentlemen of the jury," I said at the concluding day of trial. Then I said what I always say: "I'll be short. No—I'm already short, I'll be brief."

A laughing jury is not a hanging jury.

I had earlier produced the sole defense witness—Juan Baltasar, proprietor of a chicken stand at La Marquéta. Baltasar testified that Cunningham had been particular about his purchase, insisting that the chicken heads be severed before paying.

"Thus, ladies and gentlemen, Mr. Cunningham had his way with dead chickens—not live chickens. Therefore, he violated no law, because a man cannot commit cruelty against a fowl corpse." I spun around on my heels to address the assistant D.A. at the prosecution table, a sallow-faced guy with the likeability factor of an IRS auditor. "Case closed," I said.

Then I addressed the good jurors and the judge.

"I would only add my personal promise, ladies and gentlemen. Mr. Cunningham—with not so much as a speeding ticket heretofore and who is, as you have heard, innocent before the law—will nevertheless enroll in psycho-sexual counseling at a mental hospital in White Plains. He is a deeply disturbed man, my friends. Yet who among us would care to stand before the scales of justice to hear of our own sins of thought—and actions for which we were never ourselves apprehended. For what it is worth, Mr. Cunningham will dwell among his own disturbed kind as he seeks redemption, beyond the reach of the dear hearts and gentle people of the Bronx. This I promise, on the grave of my own sweet wife." I turn to the bench. "How's that, judge?"

He raps down his gavel and Cunningham scrams out of court, never to be seen in the Bronx again, right as the judge says, "Whatever."

Hearing Rosary tell the story again gives me an idea for the limited counsel I suddenly decide to give Nutsy and the Pipe and Pencil Man. I hand one of their polyesters a couple of hundred bucks and tell him, "Buy some groceries, then hit the mattresses. *Capice?*" Then I give a nod to Lewis to come with me. And before the polyester leaves my office, I tell him, "Send me another button and I'll return him with Blake here—blindfolded, so he can't spill the location where he can film. Same goes for me if I decide to show up. I don't want to know from the mattresses."

Lewis and I walk around the corner to the Palomino, which is mentioned as the genesis of Slattery's story that is now all over town. He's very proud of himself, this Hollywood producer. My friends buy him drinks.

I tell Lewis I need a minute to make a discreet phone call. So I slip out into the street with my cell. But I don't call right away.

I wait for the cars I know are going to show up. The dark blue, unmarked Chryslers with the no-nonsense guys inside. They get out of the cars with their hands firmly inside of their coats, where they're wearing shoulder holsters and federal badges.

I dial my kid's number out in Los Angeles.

She's on the line right when Lewis is bum-rushed out of the Palomino Club.

"You should come home, kiddo."

"We've been all over that—"

"Your big client, Blake Lewis, he's been arrested."

"Where are they taking him?"

"Search me. Maybe Guantánamo."

I walk back to my building on the Concourse and I slip into bed and sleep like a dead person.

ABOUT THE CONTRIBUTORS

Kim Sykes

THOMAS ADCOCK, an Edgar Award–winning novelist, was born in Detroit, raised in the Inwood section of upper Manhattan, and schooled just across the Harlem River in Fordham, the Bronx. A staff writer for the *New York Law Journal*, he has also worked on television drama projects in Los Angeles for Aaron Spelling Productions and NBC. He is coeditor with Tim McLoughlin of *Brooklyn Noir 3* (forthcoming).

Ellen Abrams

KEVIN BAKER is a novelist and historian. His latest book, *Strivers Row*, is set in Harlem in 1943. His father was born on Fordham Road, and many of his father's people lived (and died) in the Bronx.

THOMAS BENTIL works as a case manager on Rikers Island for Fresh Start, a vocational training and re-entry program. He was first bitten by the writing bug while "doin' time" in that *very* place and as a participant in that *very* program. While incarcerated, he wrote and was the managing editor for a jail-based literary magazine known as the *Rikers Review*. In a previous life, Thomas was a mildly successful scam artist as well as a full-time methamphetamine addict.

Athena Gassoumis

LAWRENCE BLOCK is an MWA Grand Master and a recipient of the Diamond Dagger life achievement award of the UK Crime Writers Association. He lives and writes in Manhattan.

Mathieu Motta

JEROME CHARYN'S most recent novel, *The Green Lantern*, was a finalist for the PEN/Faulkner Award for Fiction. A former Guggenheim Fellow, he lives in New York and Paris, where he is Distinguished Professor of Film Studies at the American University of Paris. He was born and raised in the Bronx.

Michael Ortiz

SUZANNE CHAZIN is the author of the Georgia Skeehan mystery series, including the novels *The Fourth Angel, Flashover,* and *Fireplay.* In 2003, she received the Washington Irving Book Award for both *The Fourth Angel* and *Flashover.* A New York native, Ms. Chazin has taught fiction writing at New York University and Sarah Lawrence College. She is married to Thomas Dunne, a senior chief in the FDNY who oversees fires in the Bronx.

P.F. Bentley

TERRENCE CHENG is the author of two novels, *Sons of Heaven* and *Deep in the Mountains.* He earned his MFA at the University of Miami, where he was a James Michener Fellow, and in 2005 he received a literature fellowship from the National Endowment for the Arts. He teaches creative writing at Lehman College, part of the City University of New York. For more information, visit www.tcheng.net.

Keith Mosher

ED DEE was born and raised in Yonkers on the northern border of the Bronx. He spent ten years of his NYPD career as a street cop in the South Bronx. Today these same streets can make him laugh and cry, but mostly wish he could do it all again. He loved this opportunity to write about the old neighborhood, the old songs, the gang, the redhead . . . da Bronx. Ed's latest novel is *The Con Man's Daughter.*

Rebecca Dobson Cosgrove

JOANNE DOBSON, author of the Professor Karen Pelletier mysteries, spent her formative years on Sedgwick Avenue in the Bronx—as far away culturally as one could possibly get from New England's elite Enfield College where Pelletier solves crimes—and occasionally teaches a class. She has spent the large part of her teaching career as an English professor at the Bronx's Fordham University.

Joan Marcus

ROBERT J. HUGHES' novel *Late and Soon* was published in late 2005, and his next, *Seven Sisters,* will be out soon. He is a reporter for the *Wall Street Journal,* where he writes on the arts, philanthropy, and publishing. He lives in Manhattan now, but spent many merry hours as a youth raising a perfectly law-abiding ruckus with friends in the parish of St. Nicholas of Tolentine.

Simon Levy

MARLON JAMES was born in Kingston, Jamaica in 1970. He graduated from the University of the West Indies in 1991 with a degree in literature. His debut novel, *John Crow's Devil*, a *New York Times* Editors' Choice, was a finalist for the *Los Angeles Times* Book Prize and the Commonwealth Writers Prize. James teaches creative writing and literature at Macalester College, St. Paul. He lives in Kingston, Jamaica.

Glamour Shots

SANDRA KITT'S novel *The Color of Love*, released in 1995, was optioned by HBO and Lifetime. She has been nominated for an NAACP Image Award in Fiction. A native of New York, her artwork is displayed in the African American Museum of Art in Los Angeles. She lives in Riverdale, the Bronx.

Lelie Lakin

RITA LAKIN grew up in the East Bronx on Elder Avenue. She attended Hunter College on the Bronx campus and then worked in Los Angeles as a writer/producer in television for twenty-five years. Now she is happily writing mysteries about a group of geriatric lady P.I.'s, including *Getting Old Is Murder*, *Getting Old Is the Best Revenge*, and *Getting Old Is Criminal*.

Christine Herelle-Lewis

MILES MARSHALL LEWIS moved northeast to Co-op City from Highbridge at the age of four. In the 1990s he worked as an editor at *Vibe* and *XXL* magazines, interviewing Afrika Bambaataa, Nas, Rakim, and many others. Author of *Scars of the Soul Are Why Kids Wear Bandages When They Don't Have Bruises* and *There's a Riot Goin' On*, Lewis is also founder of *Bronx Biannual* literary journal. He lives in Paris, France.

Alex Picciarelli

PATRICK W. PICCIARELLI, a former lieutenant with the NYPD, is the author of *Mala Femina: A Woman's Life as the Daughter of a Don*, among other crime-related books. His affection for the Bronx goes way back, and he fondly recalls his uncles telling him that there is no Mafia as they sipped red wine in Dominic's on Arthur Avenue, smoked Italian stinkers, and lamented the passing of Fat Tony Boombatz, who accidentally suffocated in the trunk of a Cadillac.

ABRAHAM RODRIGUEZ, JR. was born and raised in the South Bronx. His first book, *The Boy without a Flag*, was a 1993 *New York Times* Notable Book of the Year. His novel *Spidertown* won a 1995 American Book Award and was optioned by Columbia Pictures. His latest novel, *The Buddha Book*, was published by Picador in 2001. He currently lives in Berlin, Germany, where he is immersed in the local music scene.

S.J. ROZAN was born and raised in the Bronx. She is the author of eight books in the Lydia Chin/Bill Smith series and the standalones *Absent Friends* and *In This Rain*. Her work has won the Edgar, Shamus, Anthony, Nero, and Macavity awards. An architect by training, she worked on the new 41st Precinct, which replaces Fort Apache. Her upcoming novel is *The Shanghai Moon*.

STEVEN TORRES was born and raised in the Bronx. A graduate of Stuyvesant High School, Hunter College, and the City University of New York Graduate Center, he is also the author of the Precinct Puerto Rico series of novels for St. Martin's Press. *The Concrete Maze* is his fifth novel and the first he has set in New York City. For more information, visit www.steventorres.com.

JOSEPH WALLACE was born in Brooklyn, but his favorite place in New York City was the Bronx Zoo, especially on cold winter days when the grounds were deserted, the animals were alert and hungry, and something unexpected always seemed about to happen. He is the author of many nonfiction books and magazine articles (including several about the zoo), and is a contributor to the crime anthologies *Hard-Boiled Brooklyn* and *Baltimore Noir*.

Also available from the Akashic Books Noir Series

MANHATTAN NOIR
edited by Lawrence Block
257 pages, trade paperback original, $14.95
*Two stories selected as finalists for EDGAR AWARDS

Brand new stories by: S.J. Rozan, Jeffery Deaver, Lawrence Block, Charles Ardai, Carol Lea Benjamin, Thomas H. Cook, Jim Fusilli, John Lutz, Liz Martínez, Maan Meyers, Martin Meyers, and others.

"A pleasing variety of Manhattan neighborhoods come to life in Block's solid anthology . . . the writing is of a high order and a nice mix of styles."
—*Publishers Weekly*

BROOKLYN NOIR
edited by Tim McLoughlin
350 pages, trade paperback original, $15.95
*Winner of SHAMUS AWARD, ANTHONY AWARD, ROBERT L. FISH MEMORIAL AWARD; finalist for EDGAR AWARD, PUSHCART PRIZE

Brand new stories by: Pete Hamill, Arthur Nersesian, Maggie Estep, Nelson George, Neal Pollack, Sidney Offit, Ken Bruen, and others.

"*Brooklyn Noir* is such a stunningly perfect combination that you can't believe you haven't read an anthology like this before. But trust me—you haven't. Story after story is a revelation, filled with the requisite sense of place, but also the perfect twists that crime stories demand. The writing is flat-out superb, filled with lines that will sing in your head for a long time to come."
—Laura Lippman, winner of the Edgar, Agatha, and Shamus awards

D.C. NOIR
edited by George Pelecanos
384 pages, trade paperback original, $14.95

Brand new stories by: George Pelecanos, Laura Lippman, James Grady, Kenji Jasper, Jim Beane, Ruben Castaneda, Robert Wisdom, James Patton, Norman Kelley, Jennifer Howard, Jim Fusilli, and others.

"[T]he tome offers a startling glimpse into the cityscape's darkest corners . . . fans of the genre will find solid writing, palpable tension, and surprise endings."
—*Washington Post*

LOS ANGELES NOIR
edited by Denise Hamilton
360 pages, trade paperback original, $15.95
*A *Los Angeles Times* Best-seller

Brand new stories by: Michael Connelly, Janet Fitch, Susan Straight, Héctor Tobar, Patt Morrison, Robert Ferrigno, Neal Pollack, Gary Phillips, Christopher Rice, Naomi Hirahara, Jim Pascoe, and others.

"Akashic is making an argument about the universality of noir; it's sort of flattering, really, and *Los Angeles Noir*, arriving at last, is a kaleidoscopic collection filled with the ethos of noir pioneers Raymond Chandler and James M. Cain."
—*Los Angeles Times Book Review*

NEW ORLEANS NOIR
edited by Julie Smith
298 pages, trade paperback original, $14.95

Brand new stories by: Ace Atkins, Laura Lippman, Patty Friedmann, Barbara Hambly, Tim McLoughlin, Olympia Vernon, Kalamu ya Salaam, Thomas Adcock, Christine Wiltz, Greg Herren, and others.

"The excellent twelfth entry in Akashic's noir series illustrates the diversity of the chosen locale with eighteen previously unpublished short stories from authors both well known and emerging."
—*Publishers Weekly*

BALTIMORE NOIR
edited by Laura Lippman
294 pages, trade paperback original, $14.95

Brand new stories by: David Simon, Laura Lippman, Tim Cockey, Rob Hiaasen, Robert Ward, Sujata Massey, Jack Bludis, Dan Fesperman, Marcia Talley, Ben Neihart, Jim Fusilli, Rafael Alvarez, and others.

"Baltimore is a diverse city, and the stories reflect everything from its old row houses and suburban mansions to its beloved Orioles and harbor areas...Mystery fans should relish this taste of Baltimore's seamier side."
—*Publishers Weekly*